BUILT
TO FAIL

A NOVEL BY
DAVID SPARKS

ISBN 9781973196990

Acknowledgements

I needed lots of fire fighting advice for this book. Adam Fraley spent hours telling me about the life of a young volunteer firefighter and he'd like you to know that despite some similarities, he was not the model for Chavez Simons. Other firefighting advice, particularly on equipment, came from Lt. Paul Salway of the South Portland, Maine Fire Department. Thanks to both.

On the writing side, my editor, Mason McCann Smith deserves mountains of credit for sticking with a first-time author through many drafts which, he assured me, are common for rookies like me. He's a good man.

My dad, Donald Sparks, was my most faithful "beta reader," eagerly reading each chapter as it was written and offering advice. I'm sorry he died before he could see the book in its published form. Other thanks go to my brother Andy who read several drafts and offered legal advice, as well as my daughter Grace and my wife Julie who read along and commented as well. Thanks also goes to Julie for giving me the time and resources to write. I also owe a debt of gratitude to Steve Crosby and Helen Strieder, my oldest friends, for reading a tattered early draft and encouraging me to keep at it.

Cover art by Brendan Coudal, Ballyhoo Designs.
www.BrendanCoudal.com

Dedicated to my dad,
Donald H. Sparks

BUILT TO FAIL

Fitchburg, Massachusetts
1989

It was the picture that went out across the country that Thanksgiving
weekend: a Seagrave aerial ladder fire truck under an impossibly huge pile of
granite building blocks. Twisted red metal was visible in places. The ladder,
the truck's most visible feature, was spiraled in and out of the blocks like a
strand of mutated DNA. The steam rising from the crushed radiator was
backlit by a massive fire. A lone firefighter's helmet lay on the glistening street.

BUILT TO FAIL

Chapter 1

"Engine 34, the Chief needs you at the corner of Water and Fox. Take a position on the southwest corner of Building Two. Report your location." The female dispatcher's voice was faint as it crackled over the radio. Their wailing siren echoed off the squat three-story brick and granite buildings lining the streets in the river section of town.

Tony Francis grinned at Terry Jokkinen, reaching for the mic. He shouted to make himself heard over the siren. "Want me to tell her you're still trying to find a place to park?"

Jokkinen could only shake his head as he manhandled the truck. He was frustrated and embarrassed he couldn't get any closer to the fire. He'd grown up down here in the river section of Fitchburg. Now, every street was blocked with parked cars, dumpsters and apparatus arriving from other towns. The Fitchburg Mill might be the biggest fire in Fitchburg's history, but the department's aerial ladder truck would be late getting there. Jokkinen couldn't get the big truck within three blocks of the flames shooting hundreds of feet into the sky.

He nosed into a cross street, then swore, slammed on the brakes and ground the gearshift into reverse. It was the third street they'd tried. The guys on the back of the fire truck loudly voiced their complaints. Jokkinen looked in his side view mirror and saw Bobby Musello give him the finger. It wasn't an easy ride back there tonight.

Sitting beside him in the passenger seat, 22-year-old Francis laughed. Jokkinen shook his head. Francis was a rookie. Jokkinen was seven years older, already a lieutenant. To a rookie, everything was either funny or exciting.

Jokkinen shouted, "I'll try Pritchard. It will bring us out at Building Five. We won't hit the fire with the tower but we can run hose up the street from there." He made the turn and then concentrated on squeezing between a row of parked cars in front of a 24-hour bar and a beer truck. Francis sat up higher in his seat, looked out the front of the truck's wide windshield, and provided commentary. "Don't scratch the paint, or Lamontagne will have our ass." Fitchburg Fire Chief Roland Lamontagne assigned Francis to Jokkinen's crew thinking the stoic, all-business Finn would be a good role model for the mouthy rookie.

There was a loud wrenching scrape as their big bumper pushed the beer truck out of the way. Francis let out a high-pitched cackle heard even above the siren. Jokkinen exploded. "This is a Class-A Clusterfuck." Then both firefighters laughed at the same time. It was a favorite expression of the Engine 34 crew.

Suddenly, there was clear road ahead of them, and they could see Water St. at the end of the block. The fire lit the sky in the distance.

Water St. was completely clogged. There was no way they were getting any closer to the fire. "Let's just set up here." Francis already had his door open.

Terry Jokkinen looked around and made the decision he'd question his whole life. The fire was three blocks away but they had enough hose to run one line. It was all they could do. "Let's do it, but hold on." He pulled the truck into the alley between Building Four and Building Five. "At least we'll be out of the way." And then, "You run the pumps, Musello and Anderson will run the hose down the street." Jokkinen knew Francis needed experience on the pumps. Francis groaned. He wanted to be close to the fire, but he knew better than to question his crew chief's order. He headed for the back of the truck.

Jokkinen picked up the radio mic. "Dispatch, Engine 34 is in position between Mill Buildings Four and Five and the corner of Pritchard and Water. We are running a single hose back to the fire."

The radio crackled. "34 hold please." Jokkinen seethed. He knew what was coming, and on a fucking open mic. "34, Chief Lamontagne needs you further down Water St., closer to the fire."

Jokkinen didn't want to debate this. Lamontagne was a prick, and Jokkinen needed to get out of the truck and make sure Francis didn't burn out the pumps. He set the mic on the seat without responding.

On his way down the length of the truck, he heard a series of explosions inside Building Five. He jerked his head up in surprise. The fire was down the block — no way Five could be engaged. He reached the back of the truck when he heard another, closer and louder explosion. He looked up. The entire granite wall of Five was bowed out. He screamed, "Move it," jumped at Francis and pushed him away. Then he slipped on the street made greasy by the rain. If he hadn't fallen down, he might have made it to safety with Francis. The first granite block that hit the truck bounced off the aerial ladder and crushed Jokkinen's leg. His helmet flew off into the street.

Ethan Pierce sighed. It was Thursday, his poker night, and thanks to Leo Brunson, here Pierce was, all the way out in Fitchburg. While Brunson hosted the poker game, Pierce found himself on a hard plastic chair to hear a report on a fire.

But Pierce couldn't gin up any real annoyance at Brunson. Totally without pretense, outwardly gruff and consummately dedicated to getting the bad guys, Brunson had become a mentor of sorts to Pierce. Brunson was what the folks in Boston called a "Triple Eagle": Boston College High School, BC undergrad, and BC Law. Very different from most people in Pierce's life, Brunson was born with very little, and he applied a powerful mix of smarts and determination to make something of himself: the Boston FBI office's resident arson expert.

Brunson got the word on all fires, big and small, and at their last Thursday night poker game, Brunson brought up the big Fitchburg Mill Fire that happened a couple of weeks before. The word on the street was that the fire was suspicious and it bore striking similarities to the mill fire in Taunton, the year before. But Brunson suggested to Pierce that what was really suspicious was the fact that Brunson's supervisor told him to stay away from it, just as he had with the Taunton fire. In both projects, there was federal funding involved. Why wasn't the Bureau interested?

Nobody really told Leo what to do, except maybe his wife Joan. "Stay away" served no purpose except to get Brunson's attention. Pierce smiled when he remembered how Brunson suggested, with that twinkling smile of his: "Just because I was told to stay away doesn't mean we shouldn't know what's going on. Maybe you should go out to Fitchburg and have a listen."

One of the things Pierce admired about Brunson was his ability to get people to do something by going at it sideways. Sort of like Tom Sawyer and his fence. Now here Pierce was in the Fitchburg High School gymnasium, while Brunson played poker.

In his tenth year as an Assistant U.S. Attorney, Pierce worked a variety of cases, but he especially enjoyed working with Brunson. Arson wasn't really a federal thing, but when it could be used to go after big fish like members of Boston's organized crime network, he and Leo made a good team. Beyond their work, they'd become good friends, sharing their weekly poker games and the occasional fishing trip.

Fire review meetings were customarily chaired by the local fire chief. Pierce could tell right away that public speaking was not Chief Roland

Lamontagne's forte. He suspected that Lamontagne had fortified himself for the big night with several cocktails. But, Pierce thought, Lamontagne had just been through the biggest two weeks of his career. He ought to cut the man a little slack.

Pierce looked around the high school gym. There were maybe a hundred people there, five rows of chairs. It was a huge fire with lots of mutual aid response, so there were uniformed firefighters from maybe 25 communities seated in the gym. The rest of the spectators were local citizens, drawn by a chance to relive the fire, the biggest thing to happen in Fitchburg in years.

As Lamontagne finished up long-winded introductions of every official in the room, Pierce recognized the guy in a navy blue suit who stood up from the front row and gestured for the microphone. He was in his mid-thirties, around Pierce's age, with longish, prematurely gray hair. *Jimmy Kerrigan.*

Jimmy Kerrigan, former Member of Congress and boy wonder of Massachusetts politics, was two years ahead of Pierce at Harvard Law. In those days, Kerrigan was the rebel on campus. If there was a protest, you could be sure Jimmy would be front and center. Pierce remembered Kerrigan was elected to Congress shortly after law school. A man on the move.

"Thank you, Chief Lamontagne, for the opportunity to say a few words," Kerrigan said into the microphone, "albeit on this difficult occasion."

Pierce smiled to himself. It sounded like Kerrigan was pulling out his funeral speech.

"Two years ago," said Kerrigan, "we at Kerrigan Development made a commitment to the people of Fitchburg to transform these grand buildings, once the mainstay of this community's economic livelihood, into an elder-housing complex, a project dedicated to those who made Fitchburg great."

Pierce looked down the row at people's faces. Jimmy was laying it on pretty thick, but it looked like they were eating it up.

"Now we've come to a bump in the road. It's a serious one, I won't pretend it's not, but we won't be stopped. Tonight, I am here to announce that we intend to rebuild. We owe it to Fitchburg's senior citizens to provide them the kind of housing we promised them. The housing they so richly deserve." Jimmy Kerrigan swept his hair back from his forehead, a practiced, dramatic gesture worthy of a president or a movie star, and the audience erupted in cheers and applause.

Kerrigan waved, sat and whispered to the guy next to him: he looked like an engineering student, chubby, short haircut, even a vinyl pocket protector. To Pierce, the man looked out of place in a hushed conversation with slicky-boy Jimmy Kerrigan.

Lamontagne gaveled the meeting back to order. Next to the head table, an easel held a map of the fire. Smaller versions of the map were distributed to the audience. Pierce examined his copy of the handout. According to the map, the fire started in the first two buildings of the mill complex, then jumped to a building far down the street.

Lamontagne allowed a long discussion of the response to the fire, during which more firefighters than necessary offered their thoughts — or so Pierce thought — and then it was time for the findings of the arson investigation.

A state Assistant Attorney General took the microphone. She explained her role: the State Police conducted arson investigations, but there was always an Assistant Attorney General assigned the job of deciding if there was enough evidence to prosecute.

The woman started in on the investigation process, talking on and on in a grating, pedantic tone with an uptick at the end of every sentence as if she were addressing a room full of idiots.

Pierce studied her further: not bad in a skinny, tight-assed kind of way. A fancy gray dress suit, a little too nice and the skirt a little too short for a state bureaucrat at this kind of meeting. Pierce loved a bit of leg, but it didn't seem to work for her.

Then Pierce focused in. There was something familiar about her. She turned slightly to talk to the state trooper seated next to her. From that angle, Pierce saw her blouse bunched up on her shoulder. A hump, Pierce realized. And if that was a hump, the woman was Mary Cronin. He was embarrassed. She'd been at Harvard Law, too, along with Jimmy Kerrigan. She and Pierce hadn't been close, but he should have recognized her before he noticed the hump.

Now it was the turn of the state police investigator, a heavy-set, pink-faced man, to review the arson squad findings. The buildings went up like a bomb, he said, indicative of the use of accelerants. The third building to catch fire was fully three blocks away from the original fire. None of the buildings in between had a scratch on them. Pierce listened. Clearly, the state police guy thought it was arson.

To every point the investigator made, Mary Cronin raised an objection. A look of surprise crept into the investigator's face. It was almost as if he was on trial.

Yes, the buildings burned quickly, Cronin said, but weren't the wooden floors of the old buildings saturated with years of chemicals?

Yes, we could do further tests for accelerants, but wouldn't the soaked-in chemicals render those tests moot? Pierce loved that one, Cronin actually using the words "render" and "moot" in a public meeting in Fitchburg.

And as to the very weird circumstance of the fire miraculously spreading to a building three blocks away? Cronin suggested flying embers. Pierce considered. It was pouring rain. *Do embers fly that far in the rain?*

"Sergeant, am I to understand that it is your opinion that Engine 34 was parked too close to the fire?" From the incident review, Pierce knew that Building Five, three blocks from the fire's origin in Building One, fell on Fitchburg Fire Department's aerial ladder truck. Far worse, a firefighter lost a leg in the building collapse.

The state police investigator considered. His pink face got darker under the irritating pecking of Mary Cronin's questions. He responded with tightness in his voice. "Engine 34 was positioned fully three blocks away from the closest consumed building," he said. "Chief Lamontagne ordered the truck in closer, but it couldn't get past all the traffic down there. As it was, they used all their hose to lay a line back down three blocks to the fire. In my opinion, it was a good decision by Lt. Jokkinen to position the truck there."

Cronin leaned into the microphone to make sure she was heard. "And that decision cost Lt. Jokkinen his leg, did it not?"

The seemingly random veer in Cronin's interrogation took the audience by surprise. Whispered conversations and shuffling ceased, everyone listened intently.

Pierce thought the state police guy was about to pop that big vein in his forehead. "Yes, it did. But, if I may, Lt. Jokkinen's injury has nothing to do with our investigation of the fire."

Cronin returned her notes to a folder and shut it with an emphatic gesture. "That is exactly my point, Sergeant. We are making too much out of this fire. We can't let the questionable judgment of a local fireman cloud our logic."

Pierce shook his head. Cronin's logic, if there was any, escaped him.

"Maybe it's time we move away from the tradition of certain families getting certain jobs in a community. In my opinion, his injury aside, this fire department needs to examine its hiring practices as well as its deployment of equipment on calls. Incompetence isn't arson. There is not the level of evidence here on which I can base a prosecution. Accordingly, the Attorney General's Office recommends a conclusion of 'no finding.' "

The meeting was over. Angry voices rose around the gym, and Pierce heard Jokkinen's name mentioned in urgent whispers. Jokkinen sounded like a popular guy in town.

The state police sergeant shuffled his material together, scooping them into a vinyl briefcase. He shook his head angrily as he walked to the door, doing the snaps on his blue nylon windbreaker.

Pierce watched Jimmy Kerrigan work the room, shaking hands and slapping shoulders. The guy hadn't lost his touch. Pierce recalled a phrase his mother used after a couple of Sherries. "The guy has more shit in him than a Christmas goose."

Pierce noticed Kerrigan's nerdy colleague standing by himself, seeming bored, looking off into the distance. Pierce put his age at 25, but it was hard to tell with that haircut. One thing was clear, he wasn't missing many meals. Pierce worked his way toward him and stuck out his hand. "I'm Ethan Pierce."

The guy shook hands, but he had nothing to say.

Pierce prompted. "And you are?"

The guy looked away. Pierce couldn't tell if he was bored or just didn't want to answer. He finally gave in. "George Fleming."

"Have a pony in this race?" asked Pierce, doing his best to make it sound like a perfectly offhand remark.

Fleming gave Pierce a puzzled look. "Pony race?"

Pierce tried again. "Why are you here?"

"I do stuff for Jimmy." Then Fleming walked away without a glance or another word.

Pierce stood watching. *Weird guy. Wonder what he does for Jimmy Kerrigan?*

Pierce glanced at his watch. He lived down on the coast in South Dartmouth, a 90-minute drive. Briefly, he considered driving the forty-five minutes to Maynard to catch the last hand or two at Leo Brunson's. But he really didn't feel like staying up late going over the Fitchburg fire with Leo.

Yes, it did seem odd that Leo's higher-ups in the Boston FBI office told him to lay off. It made sense that Brunson sent Pierce to hear the review, and he would want to hear all the details. But Pierce just didn't have the energy to get into that stuff tonight.

Firefighters and Fitchburg citizens crowded out the main door of the gym. Pierce headed to the back of the gym, hoping to find another way out. He saw a door in the back wall and decided to try it. As he reached for the handle, he heard a woman's voice from the other side of the door. "I...can't hold on." There was a pained quality to the voice.

And then a man's voice, urgent: "Bertie, you got to, there's nothing I can do."

Swinging the door open, Pierce found a woman clinging hard to the handles of a wheelchair. She'd gotten the chair the first couple steps down a flight of half a dozen steps.

Pierce hurried forward to help, edged past the woman, faced the front of the chair, and grabbed hold of the steel tubing beside the wheelchair passenger's calves.

Calf, Pierce instantly corrected himself.

The wheelchair passenger only had one leg.

Pierce held on tight and lifted, and he felt an added weight, almost more than he could hold, as the woman eased up on her grip.

Now it was Pierce's turn to sound like he was in pain. "You've got to grab it again, I can't hold him alone." He felt the weight ease a bit as she leaned back.

The man cried out, "Fuck, watch the leg."

Pierce looked down. The man's bandaged leg — his stump — was shoving into Pierce's chest. He felt the chair sliding out of his hands. "Bertie, is it? I'll count to three and say 'heave.' Then we both let him down. One step at a time."

Without waiting for a reply, Pierce started. "One, two, three, heave." Together they eased him down one step. Two more steps, and finally the chair's big back wheels rolled onto the landing.

Carefully, Pierce stood up straight. His hands were shaking, the muscles in his forearms spasming.

Behind the chair, Bertie started to cry quietly. "I thought I was about to drop you, Terry."

Pierce felt dampness on his chest.

"Sorry about the salmon," said the man in the wheelchair.

Pierce looked down. His tie, with its images of salmon leaping out of running water, was smeared with blood, as was his shirt.

The man's stump was bleeding, too, blood wicking through the bandage.

The man stuck out his hand. "Thanks for the assist."

Pierce shook the man's hand, big and calloused.

"I'm Terry Jokkinen."

Lucky Lou's was a favorite Fitchburg fire department hangout, Jokkinen was the man of the hour, and Pierce, with his bloody shirt and tie, was the hero of the day as soon as Jokkinen related their adventure on the stairs.

Each time he told the story, he snarled, "Dumb fucking move. Bertie isn't strong enough to roll me up and down stairs, but what do I know about sitting in a wheelchair?"

Jokkinen's wife Bertie left as soon as Pierce promised to get Jokkinen home, and an hour later, three empty beer mugs were lined up in front of each of them.

Jokkinen's eyes were a little glazed over. "First time out of bed since the accident," he told Pierce, "and I'm still loaded on pain meds."

"What the hell were you doing on those back stairs?" asked Pierce. He flexed his neck. He was in good shape, a regular squash player, but he could tell his shoulders were going to ache in the morning.

"It was a dumb fucking move," repeated Jokkinen. "I wanted to hear what'd they say about the investigation, but I didn't want to be a distraction. I got a couple of guys to wheel me in the back, but then they got a call. So poor Bertie was left there to try to get me home."

"I guess that chair takes some practice."

"I'm not going to be in this fucking thing long enough for Bertie to get good at wheeling me around," said Jokkinen.

"I can tell that," said Pierce.

"So Bertie and I found a spot out of the limelight and listened to that bitch from the state. Have you every heard such total bullshit?"

"I'm a lawyer," said Pierce. "All the time."

"There's no fucking way Building Five caught on from those first two buildings down the block. You think I wouldn't have seen embers flying? There weren't any." Jokkinen lifted his bottle in a toast to Pierce. "Thanks again, by the way. I'll pay for a new shirt and tie."

Pierce shook his head. It was second time Jokkinen offered. Pierce wasn't really feeling the effects of the three beers, but Jokkinen was clearly hammered.

Pierce hesitated, but he felt a strong kinship with Jokkinen that made it seem appropriate to ask: "What are you going to do now?"

Jokkinen smiled and clapped Pierce on the shoulder. "Good for you," he said. "Most people just pussyfoot around it." And then he answered. "In a couple of months, I get one of those whattya-call-its. A fake leg. A prosthesis. And after that, I look for the kind of work a peg leg can do. I get a disability from the department, so that helps. I'll be the first Jokkinen in a long time not on the department." Then his smile faded and his face clouded. "Who does that bitch from the state AG's Office think she is? It sure as shit looked like arson to me. Is she on the take or just dumb as a box of rocks? And dragging my family into it? Jokkinens have been firefighters for three generations. That really pisses me off."

Before Jokkinen was too far-gone to answer thoughtfully, Pierce wanted to hear Jokkinen's opinion on something. So, he prompted: "I guess Jimmy Kerrigan will start building again. Doing the mill retrofit from the ground up."

Jokkinen sighed. "I guess."

Pierce waited patiently, and at last Jokkinen continued, this time in a lower, more stealthy voice. "You know this is his second time, don't you?"

"His second mill project?"

"His second fire. The first one was a year ago in Taunton. Just like this one. Weird pattern. No finding of arson there, either."

Pierce wasn't surprised the news traveled. Massachusetts was a small state. "How do you know that?"

Jokkinen smiled. "I got a friend on the department down there. Chelsea Lightning."

Pierce smiled. "Chelsea Lightning" was the Massachusetts expression for arson, named for one of the state's more notorious cities. In New York it was called "Jewish Lightning." Down in Rhode Island, they called it "Providence Lightning." He supposed in Alaska they had "Nome Lightning."

Jokkinen drained his beer and belched. "Pretty fucking fishy, if you ask me. But down in Boston, everyone looks the other way."

Pierce pulled his Jeep Wagoneer up in front of a three-decker house on Mechanic St.

Careful to avoid the bandage on the stump, Pierce eased Jokkinen out of the big back seat and into the wheelchair.

"I never asked you why you were at the meeting," said Jokkinen.

"I work for the U.S. Attorney," Pierce explained. "A buddy of mine suggested I might learn something out here tonight."

The light rain glistened on Jokkinen's baseball cap with its Fitchburg Fire Department logo. "Did you?"

Pierce smiled. "Yeah, I did."

"What'd you learn?"

"To beware of crazy Finns in wheelchairs."

"Fuck you."

"Fuck you, too."

Laughing, they shook hands.

Pierce wheeled Jokkinen to the front door, and Jokkinen fumbled in his pocket for his key. "You're a fisherman?" asked Jokkinen.

"It shows?"

Jokkinen pointed at the bloody salmon on Pierce's tie. "You should come out some time," he said. "I'll take you out for salmon on the Quabbin. I think I can still fish with a peg-leg."

Pierce grinned. "Captain Ahab, out chasing the great white whale."

"The great New England salmon." Jokkinen opened the door, and Pierce pushed him through. Jokkinen turned his head. "Send me the bill for that shirt and tie."

The next morning, Pierce opened his door to check out the day's weather. He'd pulled on his clothes, including the dress shirt that was still damp from his not-too-successful effort the night before to wash the blood out.

He had intended to drive to Boston and stay at the Harvard Club, but within a block of Jokkinen's house he'd decided it would be wiser to stay put. So he'd checked into Cabin 16 at the Lamplighter Inn, a motel on the Fitchburg-Leominster line.

Silhouetted against the still-low morning sun, a couple stood next to a standard-issue vehicle with state plates.

Pierce couldn't quite make out any words, but the woman's voice was low and urgent, and Pierce could tell she was giving her partner a ration of crap.

Pierce stepped back in his room, not wanting to intrude on the argument. But he kept the door open a crack.

The man was now talking, his voice high and defensive.

Then it was the woman's turn, and Pierce heard: "No more, that's it, we're done."

Inside his door, Pierce grinned. *A little horizontal doesy-doe at the no-tell motel, and the little lady has an attack of conscience. This is good.*

There was silence outside, and Pierce took a peek.

The argument was over, or at least momentarily on hold, and now the couple was in a major lip-lock. The man had the woman backed up against the hood of the state car, her skirt had ridden up her leg, and she had a firm grip on one of his ass cheeks.

It was the combination of the gray dress and the voice that rang a bell in Pierce's barely awake, early-morning brain.

Just then the couple broke their clench.

The woman straightened her skirt, opened the door of the car, and got in.

The guy turned, and as he got in the next car, a luxury Mercedes sedan, Pierce could see him clearly. Jimmy Kerrigan.

The woman backed out and drove past Pierce's cabin. He got a good look at the driver. Mary Cronin. *Holy shit.*

Chapter 2

Burfield, Massachusetts
Present Day

Chavez Simons sprawled in the big leather garage sale chair in his bedroom and pulled the magazine from its protective plastic sleeve: The Girls of the Big Ten. The vintage September 1965 *Playboy*, purchased on EBay for $24.95, arrived in that day's mail. He smiled and took a big breath. As usual he was alone in the house. Carefully, he found the middle of the magazine and lifted the centerfold. He loved this part.

Somewhere down below he felt a vibration. Then he heard a muffled mechanical voice. His fire department pager was on his belt, wedged between the seat-cushion and the side of the chair.

Chavez's eyes widened in alarm as he faced a choice between the two favorite things in his 16-year old life. He made a quick decision. His new *Playboy* would be there when he got back. There was a fire to fight.

The fire horn sounded from across the Town Common. He listened for the code.

Chavez Simons was the most dedicated member of the Burfield Volunteer Fire Department. But he took his time as he carefully closed the *Playboy* and replaced it in its plastic sleeve. He'd searched for that issue for a long time.

*

Wendell Albertson watched as the September wind picked up more of the burning sawdust and spread it into the orchard. There, the sawdust ignited the dried milkweed seedpods, and they took off like tiny flaming hang gliders, high up in the silvery sun.

Wendell heaved a big sigh. He tried stamping the fire out with his steel toed Wolverines. He used the big leaf rake to hold it back. Finally, he emptied their pitiful excuse of a fire extinguisher on the blaze. It was all he could do.

Wendell hadn't wanted to call 911 and put up with all that fuss. But worse, he hadn't wanted to have to go out front and tell his brother Stanley.

Even though Wendell was 84 years old, he was still the younger brother. And even though Wendell and Stanley operated Albertsons' Sawmill together for 60 years, Stanley still acted like the older brother. Wendell knew he'd get the blame.

His call to the fire station made, Wendell found his brother hoisting a 10-foot oak beam onto a truck. They both were a little hard of hearing. He tapped Stanley on the shoulder and shouted, "We got a little bit of a blaze out back."

Stanley took a moment and considered. Then he opined that Wendell, as usual, "fucked things up to a fare-thee-well."

Life for the 1,179 people in the small central Massachusetts community of Burfield was simple. The fire horn's blast signaled the beginning of the best entertainment in town. The horn blew a 2-2-3, three times in succession. All over town, people dropped what they were doing and went to check their fire code list, almost always taped or thumbtacked to the wall in the kitchen, then drifted outside to wait for the excitement to begin.

Hurrying down the stairs, Chavez squinted at the digital read-out on his pager. The mechanical voice repeated the message he'd missed the first time.

Message for Burfield Fire Department: Stand by for activation. Reported grass fire, Barre Road between Wheeler Road and Phillips Brook.

Chavez knew every road in town. The only thing between Wheeler Road and Phillips Brook was the Albertsons' sawmill.

As he wheeled down the gravel driveway in his pick-up truck, he reached down to the row of toggle switches he'd installed on the underside of the dash. He was only going 300 yards across the Town Common, but he turned on the red and white flasher mounted behind his grille. And then, he flicked the second toggle. His unapproved siren whooped. Chavez Simons grinned.

On East Barre Road, Mary Perkins was on her favorite drive of the week, her trip to the farmers market in Princeton. The rolling fields of Omar Fernstrom's llama farm stretched out on the right, a patch of forest on her left. Suddenly, a deafening shriek split the air just behind her. Heart pounding, she checked her mirror.

The only thing visible in the rear window was a massive chrome grille. Inside the grille were three horizontal rows of lights, flashing. The siren blasted again. She yanked the wheel to the right and lurched to a halt in Omar's driveway. Driving his big Chevy Yukon, Billy Wheldon, Jr. topped sixty-five passing Mary Perkins' parked Volvo. She gave Billy the finger in his rearview mirror.

Chavez pulled to a stop at the station, jumped out and ran to the bed of his pick-up for his turnout pants, boots, helmet and jacket. From there, he ran to the Brushbuster, the department's Vietnam War era truck. Originally used as a forestry truck and still outfitted with a welded steel brush cage around the hood and cab, the Brushbuster was the department's all-purpose unit, first out of the station on a call. More than once, riding in the noisy caged truck, Chavez fantasized he was Mel Gibson in a Mad Max movie.

Chavez hopped in the driver's seat and started the finicky diesel engine, waited until it idled without stalling and then jumped in the back seat. Kenny Dutton, an electrician and the captain on the Brushbuster, wheeled to a halt out in the side lot, with the bank of red lights across the top of his Ford Econovan flashing. He hoisted himself into the driver's seat of the Brushbuster, jerked the truck into gear, lurched forward and stopped suddenly. Chavez looked out his window. Squeaky Townsend walked up the driveway. It was as fast as Squeaky ever hurried. Chavez sighed. The only bad thing about being on the Brushbuster's crew was working with Squeaky Townsend. Even though Squeaky worked at the Public Works Department garage right next door to the station, he was always late.

Panting, Squeaky pulled himself into the front passenger seat. His shirt was half unbuttoned over his big gut, and he carried his boots. Dutton looked over as he let the clutch out. "Nice you could make it." Dutton was always pissed at Squeaky. Squeaky just shook his head. After his short jaunt from the DPW, he still hadn't caught his breath.

Dutton clicked on the siren and the lights before they hit the street. The truck's old-style siren began its wail with a low note and then went up the scale to a high warble and then back down. Chavez rolled his window down. He loved the sound of that siren. He shifted his weight and held tighter as he prepared for the big bump when the Brushbuster hit the street.

With the siren and diesel engine at full pitch, they blew through the only stoplight in the middle of town. There were a few cars stopped in both directions. Chavez thought it was unprofessional to smile during a fire call, but he couldn't help it. He really enjoyed it when they ran that stoplight.

Out front of almost every house, people stood to watch the parade down Main St. The Brushbuster was now followed by three firefighters in their personal vehicles, lights flashing. Ruth White drove her old VW van with a police car rotating bubble light on the top. Next came an Olds Vista Cruiser with a white-and-red light on the dash driven by Oliver Johnson. In third was Billy Weldon Jr. with all his lights going. Every couple of seconds, an illegal siren whooped. In the rear, the department's other two trucks, Engine 301 and Tanker 302 caught up and joined the procession.

Nothing beat a fire call in the tiny town.

Chavez smelled the smoke just as he saw Chief 1, a white Explorer, on the side of the road with its roof rack lights flashing. Terry Jokkinen, in his white fire chief's jacket, waved them over. As the wail from the Brushbuster's siren wound down, he shouted as he pointed down a gravel road to the right.

"Wind blowing the fire that way, take the Warren's driveway and set up between the orchard and their field." He motioned them in. Then he pointed to the first two vehicles following. "You and you follow them." He pointed to the remaining truck, driven by Billy Weldon. Jr. "You stay here. And turn off all those fucking lights." Sometimes the Chief needed to rein Billy in.

The road between the Warrens' sheep farm and the orchard was already dense with smoke. Dutton pulled the Brushbuster up and jumped out. Chavez jumped out of the back of the truck and shouldered into his jacket. It read, "Burfield VFD" in fluorescent letters across the top and "Simons" along the bottom hem against a silver reflective background. He grabbed the nozzle on one of the hoses and pulled the hose until Squeaky slowly made his way back to help.

"Head down to the end of the road and then into the orchard. I'll go back this way and come in from this direction." Dutton gave orders, then grabbed the nozzle on the other hose and started to pull. Chavez started down the road.

The firefighters in the two trailing cars drove up the road behind them. Both quickly suited up with equipment from their vehicles. Dutton gave them assignments. "Ruth, pull this hose. Oliver, grab a shovel and move up and down the fire line."

Out on Barre Road, Engine 301 and Tanker 302 maneuvered down the short drive to the sawmill, directed in by Jokkinen on the road. Firefighters' cars and trucks lined the street with lights still flashing.

Panting with the exertion of running in boots and the rest of his equipment while pulling the hose, Chavez reached the end of the gravel drive, the stone wall on the edge of the orchard. So far, the fire remained on this side of the wall. There wasn't much underbrush in the orchard; it was mainly a grass fire. He pulled the trigger on the nozzle pistol grip and a good stream of water flowed. He aimed it at the foot-high flames, knocking the fire down as he moved back toward the center. The hot smoke blew in his face, dampened with the mist from the hose. A rainbow circled the flowing nozzle. He reached up, cleared his eyes, and smiled.

Later, back at the station, Chavez sprayed off each of the big rubber lugged wheels on the Brushbuster. After each wheel, he stood and glanced into the open bay of the station where the whiteboard hung on the wall. Usually it was used to keep track of chores and equipment maintenance. It had been a week since the department's annual certification test, and the Chief kept saying the results would be posted any day. Chavez had worn the yellow cadet firefighter windbreaker since he was thirteen. In three months, when he turned seventeen, he'd finally be eligible to wear the red jacket given to Regular Volunteer Firefighters. Just like in school, he didn't have a good feeling about the test. He hadn't eaten very much and his stomach hurt.

The fourth wheel done, he rolled the hose up on the reel outside the station and hoisted himself into the driver's seat. He always breathed in the smell in the cab of the old truck, the combination of diesel oil, rubber and leather. He started the truck up and listened to the clatter of the old engine and the low rumble of the exhaust. He took a quick look out at the street through the cage over the windshield. When he was a Regular Firefighter, the first thing he would do was take the Brushbuster for a drive around town. Instead, he backed the truck into the first bay of the station and switched it off. It chugged a little as it died.

He saw motion in the side mirror and his heart hit his throat. The Chief was at the whiteboard. Feigning nonchalance, Chavez jumped out of the driver's seat and made his way to the back of the station. Suddenly, he had a hard time catching his breath.

The Chief drew a vertical line down the center of the board. Over the left section, he wrote "Pass" and on the other side of the line on the right, "Next Time." There were three names on the left side of the line and one name on the right. Chavez squinted and his heart fell. "Fuck."

Limping up the plywood stairs to the second-level break room, the Chief turned. "Simons, join me upstairs."

Chavez took another look at the whiteboard, then glanced around the station. He thought briefly about erasing his name before anyone saw it. Then he thought that would be a chickenshit move. Sighing, he followed the Chief up the stairs. He stumbled a little on the first step. His feet felt heavy.

They sat at the Chief's desk in the corner. Jokkinen pulled Chavez's exam from a folder and slid it towards him. Even upside down he could read it, and he looked at it with horror. On the top, in the Chief's handwriting, it read "Facts 37/37." Underneath, it read "Essay 1/10."

Chavez felt tears sting his eyes, and he looked away. He felt like he was going to puke.

Chavez had been an almost a daily presence in the fire station for ten years. He spent more time with Jokkinen than he did with his parents. For his part, Terry Jokkinen treated him like he imagined he'd treat a son — or even a daughter — if he ever had kids.

But this was a new moment for both of them. There was a silence. When the Chief realized the teenager wasn't going to say anything, he started in. "Well, you know your stuff, 37 multiple choice questions and you aced every one." Chavez nodded. He knew he'd done well on those. They weren't hard to read, and all you did was circle the right answer.

"But, you had a hard time on the essays. All you needed was two or three sentences for each. You wrote one sentence for the first one and then nothing on the next nine."

Chavez just hung his head. He was miserable. For a week he'd dreaded this conversation. Longer, really. Unlike other sixteen-year-old boys, Chavez Simons didn't embarrass easily. For the most part he went through life insulated in the world he made for himself. He just didn't want to reveal a secret to the one person whose approval he most sought.

He took a big catching breath as he thought of how to explain it. He really wanted the Chief to understand.

"I run out of time on tests. I just.... I just get nervous when I have to read something, think about it and then write something. The words get blurry." He struggled. "I see white behind my eyes."

Jokkinen sat listening. This was all new to him. The Chavez Simons he knew was a cheerful, can-do kid.

He risked a smile to lighten the mood. "White behind your eyes?" It was all he could think to say.

With that, the dam broke. Chavez never really learned to read very well. It started in kindergarten. How he couldn't use his words. The teachers let it slide, encouraging him to learn "at his own pace." His parents bought into this approach. For Chavez, though, the problem with this approach was "at his own pace" meant "never."

Chavez told the Chief how he relied on his best friend Jason to help him with his reading. A few teachers over the years tried to help Chavez with his block, but most just let him slide. Essay tests were torture. How the words swam before his eyes when it was time to fill an empty space on an exam. He could take fill-in-the-blank tests, multiple-choice tests and math tests, but he froze when he saw a space after a question. He was okay sometimes when all he needed was a sentence or maybe two, but asking him for a paragraph was his biggest fear in the world.

Jokkinen couldn't understand how teachers and parents could just not teach a kid to read and write. Hearing Chavez tell the story, it began to piss him off.

He knew sometimes it took Chavez a little longer than usual to process some written instruction and that he read with his lips moving – his wife always said he did this, too – but he didn't know the extent of Chavez's problems with reading, writing or test taking. He particularly didn't know that Chavez lived in terror over the prospect of doing the essay questions on this test.

Terry Jokkinen admired Chavez Simons. He knew how unusual Chavez was, his clothes, his haircut, his size, his perpetually calm and upbeat style. He was mowing yards when other kids were out playing. His parents were never home. He made his own schedule. He had his own truck. He played the stock market. He called people sir and ma'am. Jokkinen knew he didn't have any close friends except for that weirdo Jason. The other kids must give him enormous loads of crap, Jokkinen often thought. The biggest thing in his life was getting that red jacket. Taking the certification test must have been torture.

Chavez stopped and took a big breath. He just told someone the whole story. His parents didn't know the whole story, Jason only knew parts. His teachers only knew what they wanted to know. It felt good to get it off his chest.

Jokkinen was conflicted. He'd seen Chavez perform under pressure on all sorts of tasks. He knew he was a good firefighter; he didn't need a test to prove that point. The kid even got everything right on the multiple choice. He knew his stuff.

He began to think out loud. "Well, the test is the test. I've been giving that test for ten years. I only give it once a year. It weeds out the wannabes and the goofballs..." He let his words drift off. The kid was hardly a wannabe.

Chavez was quiet. He liked rules and structure. Everybody took that test. "I guess I can wait and take it next time. Maybe I'll get better." Saying it made him feel sick. He counted on being a Regular Firefighter when he turned seventeen. And he couldn't imagine how he would get better on the test.

Jokkinen shook his head slightly. Anyone else would be begging for a second chance. Leave it to Chavez to suggest he wait another year. "Let's think about it for a couple of days." Then changing the subject he said, "Interested in some meatloaf? Today's Wednesday. Mrs. Jokkinen's meatloaf day." The Chief knew Chavez's parents were rarely home for dinner.

Chavez managed a small smile. He liked it when the Chief called his wife Mrs. Jokkinen, and Chavez really liked her meatloaf. Then he shook his head. "I think I'll just go home. I'm not very hungry."

"Are you sure?" *Chavez was always hungry.*

Chavez nodded and stood up. As he walked back down the stairs he took a last look at the Brushbuster before he turned to leave the station.

Chapter 3

Washington, DC
Present day

Sitting on the front step of his Capitol Hill apartment building, Dick Law held a running shoe up for inspection. His glasses were foggy. He usually wore contacts, but he'd decided his eyes were too grainy to put them in. In the early-morning light, he could see the rubber on the heel was dried out and beginning to flake away on the sides. He had a stray thought: if this went well, he'd buy a new pair.

Leaning down to tie the shoe, he felt a little queasy and headachy, but why should this morning be any different? Mornings were for getting over hangovers.

As he rose, he squinted to see the time and temperature sign on the bank at the end of the block: 6:30 am, already 82 degrees. *It's May. Who knew it was so fucking hot in DC at this hour?*

Law stood up and did a few tentative stretches on the steps. He had another wave of doubt. He hadn't run in ten years. *Was it even healthy for a 45 year old to take up running after all that time?* Tentatively, he patted his belly. Fifteen pounds more than the last time he tried this…maybe twenty.

The night before, he mapped out his route on a cocktail napkin with his Tune Inn drinking buddies. The bar, a favorite of Capitol Hill staffers, was Law's second — maybe first — home in the ten years he'd been in Washington. There was a lot of good-natured bantering and posturing about whether he would even get out of bed to attempt a run, let alone finish it. If he hadn't had something to prove to his drinking friends, he was sure he would still be asleep.

He planned to loosen up with the two-block jog to the Capitol, pick up a little speed on the five block hill down to the Mall, and then join the hundreds of other runners who pounded up and down the gravel running paths in the morning. Joining the herd was key. Other runners would pull him along.

Getting in shape was a constant in Law's life, but he didn't really want to cut back on anything. Most of all, he didn't want to cut back on his drinking.

Running might be the key. Without cutting back, he would run himself into better condition. When he felt himself slimming down and breathing better, he would probably eat and drink less.

He had a tendency to hatch these plans when he was drunk, hung over, or well on his way to either condition. Not conducive to effective decision-making, he knew.

The run past the Capitol and down to the Mall wasn't easy, more like running in sand than on concrete, but he ran all the way to the Botanical Garden and merged into a stream of other runners.

He saw the Washington Monument and, beyond, the Lincoln Memorial. Both shimmered in the distance. He squinted, wondering if they were out of focus because of the tropical atmosphere or the sweat in his eyes.

Without thinking about it, he stopped to walk. Just for a minute, he told himself.

"Track!" came an annoyed female voice, and a pair of long-legged female intern types split and went on either side of him.

Lurching to the side of the path, Law muttered, "Bite me." Seeking shelter behind a bench, he pretended to check a shoe.

What started out as his daily dull headache was now a throbber. His breath was ragged, and it felt like someone was shoving a thumb under the ribs on his right side. He rubbed the spot and tried to remember where the liver was located.

His route would take him past the line of Smithsonian museums, over to the Potomac River past L'Enfant Plaza, next to the river to I St., and back up Capitol Hill. The whole thing would be a mile, maybe a mile and a half. It hurt to admit it, but maybe the boys at the Tune Inn were right: no way he could run that far on his first try.

Law started running again, this time even slower. Eventually, turning onto L'Enfant Plaza, he spotted the Potomac, and then the more humid river air blew into his face. He caught a breath mid-inhale. There was a pretty bad rotten stink. His left calf tightened.

He slowed to a walk, then stopped, leaned against the railing overlooking the river, and tried to stretch out his calf. Six feet below him, where the river lapped the retaining wall, he saw a mess of urban detritus. He took his glasses off, wiped the sweat from his eyes, and squinted. Dead rats floated with bloated bellies up. A huge fetid carp, eyes pecked out by seagulls, was wedged into a mangled baby stroller.

Like an exhaust fan over a sewer pipe, a new wave of stench hit him.

He pushed himself away from the railing, and his calf muscle flamed hot. He felt his stomach heave, and he swallowed quickly. "You all right, man?" asked a runner, and Law waved the man away. Law was a master of controlling his vomit reflex — one of his personal skills. He just needed to keep swallowing to stay ahead of it.

The slight incline back up Capitol Hill was torture. The pain in his leg didn't get better. He didn't even try to run, he was now walking with his injured leg held stiff. He risked a look around. He was hurt, but he still didn't want to look like a dweeb.

Intent on taking the most direct route possible back to his apartment, he cut through the parking lot in back of the old brick Eastern Market complex. The dumpsters behind the fish restaurant, full of shrimp and crab shells and steeping overnight, were rancid, far worse than the rats and the carp. He felt an unexpected lurch down below; he couldn't catch it. Grabbing the trunk of a gingko tree, he dry-heaved as quietly as he could. The stomach acid burned his throat.

Whose fucking idea was this?
This was really miserable.

With the window air conditioner on high, Law sat at the small table in his kitchen. His breathing returned to normal and the side-stitch was gone, but his leg throbbed and he felt like shit. He couldn't get his stomach to stop heaving. He considered putting Bengay on his calf muscle, but he was afraid the wintergreen smell would make his stomach worse.

He risked a look at the clock on the microwave. It was already 8 a.m., and he needed to shower and get to work. Congressman Joe Sylvester's new chief of staff had only been on the job a week, but she already warned him about his late arrivals. The little bitch thought the press secretary should be the first one in, not the last.

Using the table for leverage, he eased himself to his feet.

His stomach rolled. He knew what would settle his gut. Just a taste in some orange juice. It wouldn't be drinking in the morning. It was medicinal.

Somewhere in the fog of his mind, the angle of the sun on his pillow didn't seem quite right.

He remembered the Screwdriver, sitting down on his bed to take his socks off and lying back to close his eyes, just for a second or two.

He squinted for the time on the clock next to his bed. 11:33 a.m.

Fuck me.

He was seriously late for work.

Chapter 4

Ethan Caleb Pierce III, Attorney General of the Commonwealth of Massachusetts, tilted his face into the deep blue September sky and enjoyed the warm breeze. It was his favorite time of the year. A perfect fall afternoon, if you didn't have to put up with the manic energy of Hollis Kerrigan.

Pierce turned his head a few degrees to the left. A line of five gleaming white wind turbines, each 328 feet tall, stretched across the mountain ridge that dominated the western horizon. The gracefully curved hundred-foot long blades – three per turbine — stood motionless.

Mildly amused, Pierce looked down at the device in front of him on the draped table. It was an oversized electrical switch, the kind they used in old movies to fry somebody in the electric chair. A thick wire led from the switch across the table and dangled over his lap. The switch was visually impressive, but Pierce was pretty well convinced it was just a prop.

Standing at the podium, Hollis Kerrigan smiled triumphantly at her 150 guests seated on the Burfield Town Common. "As you all know," she chirped into the microphone, "we are here on our first anniversary to take the Matchic Ridge Wind Farm fully on-line. After a successful year operating a single turbine, today we complete the project with the launch of four more units."

Pierce saw Hollis look down to the front row in an obvious effort to catch her father's eye, but Jimmy Kerrigan wasn't paying attention to his daughter. He was whispering to George Fleming, president of Plymouth Engineering, the firm that built and operated the wind farm. Fleming divided his attention between Kerrigan and an iPad in his lap.

Smile frozen in place, Hollis gave up and turned to Pierce. In a voice tight with excitement, she said, "Mr. Attorney General, if you please?"

Pierce might not believe in the switch, but he was a fan of good theater. In a loud voice, he said, "Let's fire this baby up." He flipped his switch from one side to the other.

George Fleming touched a square on the screen of his iPad.

Release brake: all turbines.

Fleming glanced at the wind speed indicator on the screen. Involuntarily, he flinched. *No fucking wind. There never was. What makes Hollis think today'll be the exception?*

He looked at the turbines on the ridge, half a mile away. Not a hint of motion.

Fleming shifted uncomfortably in his chair. Turbine #1 was on-line for a year, and the feeble winds up there had barely generated any electricity at all. Most of the time, that was usually a good thing — exactly what Jimmy Kerrigan and Fleming counted on.

But today, with all these dignitaries from Boston sitting in their chairs alongside the Burfield locals, weren't those limp blades just a little too obvious?

Fleming tried to reason with Hollis. He'd known this would happen, but she wouldn't be talked out of this big performance. It made Fleming look stupid in front of Jimmy Kerrigan. Sweat beaded up on his meaty bald head and trickled down his neck.

"Shit, shit, shit," Fleming muttered.

Jimmy Kerrigan leaned over to Fleming until his lips were uncomfortably close to the engineer's ear. Kerrigan's breath was hot, and it reeked of cigars. "Make the fuckers turn."

Fleming hit another square on the iPad.

Clutch release.

Up on the ridge, the main shaft of the turbine disconnected from the gears which produced power. It worked. Without the friction of the gears, the blades began to turn.

Fleming got up from his seat in the front row and hurried away.

Behind the podium, Hollis shifted anxiously from one foot to another.

Pierce examined her more closely. He didn't know women's clothes, but he supposed hers were expensive. She was the type he saw at fundraisers in the Boston suburbs, but a little over-dressed, he thought, out here in the pucker brush.

As he did when the fish weren't biting, he began to whistle softly and tunelessly.

He seemed to remember that the ridge was densely forested, but they'd flattened it to make way for the turbines. The huge trees were cut back to a fringe around the site. If it weren't for the turbines, it would have looked like a landing strip was cut into the top of the mountain.

He concentrated on the blades of the nearest turbine. There was a twitch, then a slight movement. He squinted, staring hard. The blades were beginning to move. Within minutes, all five turbines were spinning. Pierce sensed a collective breath from the audience.

Hollis cleared her throat into the microphone. "I'd like to call your attention to the map up in front here." Pierce could hear relief in her voice. Sitting on an easel, elevated so it was visible to the audience, the map was a panel of plywood cut into the shape of Massachusetts, with hundreds of tiny bulbs mounted in the central part of the state. Right in front of Jimmy Kerrigan, Pierce noted. Hollis seemed desperate to make a good impression on her father.

"This map represents the number of homes the Matchic Ridge Wind Farm will supply with clean, locally generated electricity."

All eyes focused on the map, with the look of children anticipating the first big fire works explosion on the 4th of July.

But the map remained dark.

A look of panic filled Hollis's face.

According to the map, there wasn't a volt of Matchic Ridge electricity flowing anywhere in the state.

Pierce looked to Dr. Francoise Renault-Obey, the president of the University of Massachusetts, seated next to him at the head table. She seemed particularly absorbed. The wind farm was built on land donated by the university. She'd be eager to get back to the office and brag about how the university had a hand in producing alternative energy — and how much the university would be saving in utility costs.

On Pierce's other side, Congressman Joe Sylvester watched intently. Pierce supposed Sylvester helped on the federal funding, but he took a back seat to Jimmy Kerrigan's clout. Still, whoever pulled the strings, it's not bad to crow about a wind farm in your district. *Sylvester must be sweating bullets waiting for this thing to work.*

Pierce glanced back up at the turbines. He wondered why the map wasn't lit up by now. He looked over at Hollis, and saw her emcee-smile was replaced by a flustered frown. Pierce caught her eye, grinned and gave her a thumbs-up. He knew it would throw her off, but dealing with her at this event hadn't been easy. She was prickly and entitled. He'd never liked Jimmy Kerrigan, and he was beginning to share the same feelings for his daughter.

Fleming slipped quietly behind a curtain that hung as a backdrop to the podium. Just to be sure, he checked to see if anyone was watching. No, he was totally on his own, with no witnesses at all.

Hollis wanted her fucking map lit up with power from the turbines.

Fleming explained to her that it just didn't work that way. What little power they generated up there went into the grid. It wasn't possible to separate electricity and say, this watt came from the natural gas plant at Pittsfield, this watt came from the Putts Bridge Dam, and this one came from Hollis's fucking wind farm. But for her big coming-out party that day, Hollis insisted on getting power "from my wind farm."

Just to shut her up, Fleming laid a cable from the map off into the woods. When Hollis did her pre-event inspection walk-around, he'd told her the cable would carry power from the wind farm. He had to admit, that big cable looked realistic. She bought it.

Chavez stood under an arcade of 200-year-old sugar maples, off to side of the Common.

Chief Jokkinen asked members of the department to volunteer at the event. Even though the Chief was pissed at Hollis for not coming through with the new fire truck she'd promised, Jokkinen said it was a community event and volunteer firefighters did more than just fight fires.

Chavez was proud of the straight rows of white folding chairs. He'd been on the Common at seven that morning to set them all up.

Hollis was still at the podium talking about alternative power. Chavez was a little tired of hearing about the wind farm. It was bad enough they bulldozed his favorite camping spot on the top of Matchic Ridge, it was all people around town seemed to talk about. To make matters worse, his father was the lawyer for the wind farm. Chavez heard about it at home, too.

Chavez saw a man stand up from the front row and move around in back of the bandstand behind where Hollis was speaking. He stood there a second and looked around like he didn't want anyone to see him.

Chavez took a step back behind the big maple so he wouldn't be spotted, but he saw what the guy did.

Every bulb on the map switched on suddenly. All of central Massachusetts glowed. At the podium, Hollis was ecstatic. "There we go." And then she delivered a practiced line: "Ladies and gentlemen, the Matchic Ridge Wind Farm is fully on-line, producing power for the people of Massachusetts and beyond." She looked down at her father and smiled triumphantly. The crowd clapped.

Chavez watched everyone start toward the big tent where they were going to have lunch.

He was supposed to help move the chairs to the tables inside.

But a tall red-haired woman in a State Police uniform was coming right toward him. He stood up straighter and pulled his yellow fire cadet's windbreaker down over his waist. She stopped in front of him. She was almost as tall as he was, and she had medals all over her chest. He glanced down at her high black leather boots and then back up to her face. *She's really pretty.* He glanced away to try and stop staring.

"Is this Hollis Kerrigan's house?" The woman state trooper pointed past Chavez's shoulder. At first Chavez could only nod, and then he found his voice. "Yes … ma'am."

"Are you Chavez Simons?"

What did I do? Then he wondered about the protocol. What was he supposed to call a state trooper? A woman state trooper. He glanced at her boots again. He could only nod.

"Wait here," she said, "I'll get the Attorney General."

Chavez watched as she walked back to the crowd and tapped the shoulder of the tall gray-haired man who was at the head table. Chief Jokkinen said Attorney General Ethan Pierce was going to be at the ceremony, and he was "the real deal." Pierce was talking to a woman who was smiling and tilting her head the way girls did at school when they were talking to the popular guys. Chavez watched the state trooper tap his shoulder again. This time she whispered in his ear.

Pierce broke away from the giggly woman and let the state trooper lead him over.

"Hi, Chief, I'm Ethan Pierce." He stuck his hand out for a handshake. A real adult handshake. Chavez was glad he'd learned how to do a real shake at the station.

But then Chavez was confused. *Did this guy think he was the Chief? I thought he knew Chief Jokkinen.* He looked to see if Jokkinen was around. This guy wanted to speak to the Chief.

"I'm not the Chief, sir," he said. "The Chief's the Chief."

"Just a field promotion, Firefighter. You don't mind, do you?"

"I guess not."

"I know Chief Jokkinen. He told me to look you up. Is this Holly's barn?"

Chavez thought a second or two. He must be talking about Hollis. He'd never heard her called Holly before. "Yessir."

Pierce smiled. "I've got a note here that says I can piss in Holly's barn."

Chavez processed this. *Piss. Holly's barn. He wants to use the bathroom in Hollis' house. The nicest house in town, and he calls it a barn. That's funny.* He nodded.

"Lead the way, Chief," said Pierce, "let's go water the horses. We'll leave Sergeant Doherty here to protect our flank. Sergeant, fire a couple of warning shots if the villagers get too close."

The state trooper smiled and stuck out her hand to Chavez. "I'm Maureen Doherty." Chavez shook her hand, too. She had a real strong handshake. He hoped he squeezed hard enough.

Pierce was already walking toward the house. Chavez let go of the handshake and hurried after him.

"Sir, this way." Chavez tried to guide Pierce up the driveway toward the back door, but Pierce kept stomping toward the front porch. Chavez tried again. "Uh, sir, this way."

Barely slowing, Pierce pointed to the slate sidewalk leading to the porch and the big purple front door. "Firefighter Simons, we are on a critical mission here," said Pierce. "I'm 75 years old, and I need a bathroom. We don't have time for the scenic route."

Chavez stepped closer to explain. "Uh, sir, I mow Hollis's yard. When I have to go to the bathroom, she wants me to use the back door. I don't even know if the front door works."

Pierce smiled. "Son, I don't give a rat's ass if Holly has that door reserved for the Second Coming. I need to take a leak, I'm running out of time, and that's the shortest route." Then he lowered his voice. "And if the front door's locked, I'm afraid we'll give the good folks of Burfield something to talk about, because I'm going to piss off her porch."

Chapter 5

Chavez stood in the bathroom and dried his hands.

He saw Pierce already messed up one of the towels on the rack; the other two towels looked like someone ironed them. He knew Hollis would be angry if she even knew he was in that part of the house, let alone using one of her towels. Carefully he took the used towel off the bar, dried his hands and put it back like he found it. Maybe she'd think only Mr. Pierce had been in there.

Pierce was waiting in the hall, examining Hollis's photographs. "Are you somewhere in this photo, Chief?" asked Pierce.

Chavez took a close look at the picture, a framed photo from the local newspaper showing a bunch of people wearing hard hats and holding silver shovels. "No, sir. I was watching from the side. It was the groundbreaking for the wind farm project."

"That Holly sure does like her ceremonies, doesn't she?"

From the back of the house, the kitchen door suddenly slammed. There were angry voices from the kitchen. Chavez looked up at Pierce in alarm, afraid Hollis was going to catch him in the front of the house. "I'm really not supposed to be here," he said, but the Attorney General pressed a finger to his lips and pointed at his ear.

The voice from the kitchen was male, high pitched and loud. "What the fuck happened out there? I felt like a fool. Fucking Ethan Pierce. Smug Yankee prick sitting there enjoying the whole thing. Tell me again how he got invited?"

"Daddy, I tried to explain." Hollis's voice sounder nicer than what Chavez was used to. "I sent you a couple of emails, but you didn't get back to me. Then I heard he was going to be in the area, and...."

"Sitting out there with those fucking windmills stopped cold and that half-assed map dead and dark."

Chavez looked over at Pierce in alarm. But Pierce looked like he was having fun. He made a motion with his hand, the signal teachers used when they wanted the class to calm down.

"Daddy, it all worked out like it was supposed to." Hollis's voice had a whining quality, like a little girl trying to kiss up to her father. "It just took a little longer."

"George, what happened up there?"

Another man answered. "As usual, there was no wind. I disengaged the clutch on the gears so they'd swing free. That's the only way I could get them to turn."

"You disengaged the gears?" Hollis could really be loud when she got worked up. The sound reminded Chavez of one of his mowers when the belt came loose. "Why did you do that, George?"

"I warned you about this big announcement day of yours." Chavez thought the man sounded frustrated, like he was talking to a little kid. "The wind is iffy up there on the ridge."

"Then why did we put the wind farm there?"

"Hollis, we've been over this a thousand times. We got the site free from the university. The location is acceptable to our regulators and our funders. We don't really have to produce a lot of power to be successful."

Chavez listened closely. That didn't make sense to him. What was the point of a wind farm?

"If the gears were disengaged and we weren't putting out power," said Hollis, "then how did my map light up?"

"It doesn't matter how the map got power. Your little light bulbs went on, it's over, and let's just move on."

But Hollis wasn't through. "George, I want to know. I'm the managing partner of the wind farm, I put my —"

"Jesus, Hollis, knock that shit off." Hollis's father broke in. "You're in the big leagues now, grow up and act like it. Stop being such a spoiled little bitch. Let's go back outside. I need to eat."

Chavez flinched. He couldn't believe a dad would talk to his daughter that way.

There was a slam from the kitchen. Chavez knew it was the screen door.

From the front porch, Chavez and Pierce watched the Kerrigans and Fleming head down the driveway and towards the food tent.

"He was really mean to her," said Chavez.

Pierce took a second or two, considering. "Well, they're not the Brady Bunch, that's for sure."

Pierce changed the subject. "So, where'd you get the handle?"

"Handle?"

"Su nombre, mi amigo. 'Chavez.' Are your folks Mexicans?"

Now Chavez understood. It was a question he was always asked, just not in those exact words. He started his usual answer. "My parents named me after Cesar Chavez. He was the leader of the California—"

"Son, I know who Cesar Chavez was. If your folks aren't Latino, were they labor organizers or hippies?"

Chavez paused. People asked about his name, but nobody wanted to know about his parents. He thought about the rock band pictures in his father's office, his ponytail and his earring. "I guess they wanted to be hippies, but now my dad's a lawyer and my mom teaches yoga."

Pierce tilted his head back and laughed. Chavez watched. *He sure likes to laugh.*

"Well, don't worry about it, it could have been worse, they could've tagged you with something like Che or Fidel. We keep it simple in my family, everybody's named Ethan. We just change the Roman numeral." Chavez listened. He didn't understand what Pierce was talking about, but he thought he was being nice.

Pierce switched subjects. "What's with the yellow jacket? I saw a couple of Jokkinen's crew around here wearing red."

"I'm only a cadet. The red ones are for Regular Firefighters."

"When does that happen for you?"

Chavez's face clouded. "You have to be 17 to be a Regular Firefighter. My birthday's in December." That was true enough, but of course it was only part of the truth. He wouldn't have told the rest to just anyone, but there was something about the way Ethan Pierce was looking at him, as if he honestly cared. Chavez found himself opening up. "I flunked the certification test. I have a hard time with reading sometimes." The last words came out in a rush, and he felt a little sting in his eyes.

"Different people have different reading skills," said Pierce. "It's not the end of the world, as long as you work at it."

"Anyway, the Chief is letting me do a project instead of the essays," said Chavez. Jokkinen proposed the idea to Chavez several days after posting the results of the exam. "I'm studying two mill fires, one in Fitchburg and the other in Taunton. They happened a long time ago. I'm supposed to study why the fires burned some buildings but jumped over others."

Pierce smiled. "Terry Jokkinen's always been interested in those fires." He reached in his jacket pocket and handed Chavez a business card. "Give me a call if you need help. I might be able to give you a hand."

Then Pierce changed the subject yet again. Chavez knew he had to scramble to keep up. "Is that true what they said about the ridge?"

Chavez answered. "About the wind?"

Pierce nodded.

"There's no wind on that side of the ridge. The wind comes from the other side."

Chavez could see Pierce thinking about this.

"So why did they put the turbines on that side?"

"Nobody gets that."

"How did it power up Holly's light bulb map?"

Chavez smiled at that. "Can you keep a secret?"

Pierce chuckled. "Yep."

"I was watching. That other guy went around back and plugged the cord into an outlet on the bandstand. He didn't notice me watching, but I saw him."

Pierce slapped his hand on the teenager's shoulder and laughed. "Chavez, you are good man. You really have your shit together."

Sergeant Doherty came towards them up the walk. "We need to be out of here in 45 minutes for your next event," she told Pierce. "You better get your lunch."

Pierce turned to Chavez. "What do you suppose Holly's having to drink out there?"

"Cider," said Chavez. "She'll have apple cider."

Pierce rolled his eyes. "I've got a top secret mission for you. It's not completely above-board."

"Yes, sir."

"You don't think you'll become a danger to society?"

Chavez saw a twinkle in Pierce's eye. He lowered his voice to sound like Morgan Freeman. "I am no longer a danger to society."

Pierce's twinkle turned into a full-blown smile. "*Shawshank Redemption.* Great movie."

Chavez nodded happily. He really liked Ethan Pierce.

Pierce jabbed his thumb back at Hollis's house. "Go get me a beer out of the fridge. Holly strikes me as a wine drinker, so it'll be down low in the back. Put the beer in the kind of cup they're using out there, and then come and find me."

Chavez had never poured a beer, but this was a special day and he had a new hero. "Okay, I'll find you."

"I'm counting on you, Red."

Pierce watched Chavez approach with the camouflaged cup of beer. As Chavez handed it over, Pierce gave him a shared-secret smile. There were two plates heaped with food on the table. "I asked Sergeant Doherty to get you a plate. She said she got you a little of everything." Pierce saw Chavez eye the plate and smile. The kid was as tall as he was and outweighed him by fifty pounds. By the size of the plate, he could see Doherty took that into account. "Park yourself right here." Chavez hesitated, looking down at the place card where he was to sit. It read "Cong. Sylvester." Pierce moved the place card down a place. Then he took another one of his business cards out of his pocket, folded it once, and used an old-fashioned fountain pen to write "Chavez Simons." He set it down in front of Chavez's plate. "Now you're official." Chavez sat down and pulled up the sleeves of his windbreaker.

Pierce felt motion on his right and saw Hollis with a plate of food followed by Jimmy Kerrigan and George Fleming. Pierce smiled to himself and waited until they were seated to begin his poking. "Hollis, I asked Chavez here to join us. I hope that's okay."

"Well, certainly, Ethan, Chavez is always welcome." She paused to find something else to say. "He….he does such a fine job on my yard." She then took a final shot before surrendering, "Although, I wonder if Chavez might be more comfortable eating with his fireman friends."

Pierce thought about a response but decided to move on. It was just his first shot. He had more ground to cover.

Cong. Joe Sylvester moved in next to Chavez to claim his relocated place at the table. Pierce turned to him. "Joe, good to see you. I can see your hand all over this thing. I can tell there's some clout behind this project." Out of the corner of his eye, he tried to catch Jimmy Kerrigan's reaction to his not-so-subtle shot at his political manhood.

Pierce just let that sit there and took a bite of his chicken salad. He kept himself from making a face as he put his fork down. He took a sip of his beer. *Frigging grapes. There were grapes in Hollis's chicken salad. Figures.* Pierce glanced at his watch. He needed to be out of there in twenty minutes. No more time for preliminaries. Kerrigan was watching him, and Pierce remembered what he always thought: not that bright but cagey, maybe even cunning on a good day. He wondered if Kerrigan still had it. "So Jimmy, last I heard, you were getting rich off low income housing in Texas. What brings you back to your old stomping grounds?"

Pierce saw Kerrigan absorb the jibe. "It's good to be back," he said simply. Pierce considered. He'd have to up his game.

Pierce moved to a sideways tact, Chavez's observation about the paltry winds on the ridge in his mind. "So, Hollis, how do your turbines compare to the costs of producing power by other means?" There was a silence. Pierce heard Sylvester stop talking and listen for her answer.

Hollis rose to the occasion. "Good question, Ethan. Of course traditional power is cheaper to produce, but cheaper isn't always better. If cheaper were better, we'd all be buying our clothes at Walmart. With windpower we are making an investment in our future. The people in my community are happy to pay more for their electricity to be part of a global solution. That's why the government is willing to give us incentives."

Pierce sat and took it in. Direct hit. He watched Hollis to see if she realized how condescending she sounded. She didn't. She just sat there smiling.

Jimmy Kerrigan cleared his throat. Pierce could tell he'd been drawn into the fray. "Well, it's a little more complicated than that. There needs to be a mix...."

Hollis interrupted. "No, it isn't more complicated than that, Daddy, it's really quite simple."

Kerrigan's voice was even, but Pierce could tell he was pissed. It sounded like he was speaking with his molars clenched. "No, it's not as simple as that. Energy production and consumption are global issues and...."

Hollis broke in. "Think globally, act locally. The power of good intentions. Who was it, Gandhi, who talked about good men and women standing by and doing nothing?"

Edmund Burke, Pierce thought as he watched Kerrigan.

Now everyone at the table had stopped talking and was surreptitiously listening to the exchange. Pierce considered: The firebrand Jimmy Kerrigan he knew in law school, the Jimmy Kerrigan who was the anti-war scourge of the United States Congress, that Jimmy Kerrigan would have jumped to his feet, thrown something at his provocateur and maybe tipped his table over on his way out, his fist in the air.

But the Jimmy Kerrigan in this phase of his life took a deep breath and casually got up from the table. He carefully folded his napkin and placed it on his chair. Finally he spoke, his voice as calm and silky as a therapist's. "Well, what a wonderful day. I think I'll go for a dessert. This is such a nice gathering." And then he moved away.

Lunch was over. Chavez had two folding chairs in each hand, headed to the caterer's truck. He felt a hand on his bicep and turned to see Sergeant Doherty.

"Mr. Pierce and your chief would like to see you."

Chavez hesitated. He promised to help with the chairs. But then another thought came to him. Maybe he was in trouble. Was the Chief pissed at him for sitting with Mr. Pierce at lunch? He needed to tell him it was Pierce's idea. Doherty's grip on his arm tightened as she spoke. "They're in a hurry."

Behind the library, Chavez saw a black Lincoln MKS with state license plates. Pierce stood next to the car's open trunk talking to Jokkinen. Pierce wore khaki pants with leather panels sewn on the front and a fishing vest.

Pierce's eyes lit up when he saw Chavez approach. "Chief, unless I miss my guess, you, being a red-blooded son of central Massachusetts, have probably been known to drown a worm every now and then."

Chavez was confused. He didn't know what Pierce was talking about, but he smiled gamely. "Drown a worm?"

Pierce's grin widened. "Fishing, son. The art of angling. In this case, attempting to extract a landlocked salmon from the Quabbin Reservoir heavier than 10 lbs. 2 ounces, the current state record, if I am not mistaken. Your chief and I have made this a tradition for 35 years."

Chavez's eyes widened. He really liked fishing. He and Jason used to fish all the time, but Jason was tired of it now. His face fell. "I'm supposed to help with the chairs."

Jokkinen stepped in. "I think we can find someone to take over." He pulled a radio off his belt.

Turning toward the Lincoln, Pierce looked over his shoulder. "We'll stop at your place and you can get your equipment. Bring something for Sergeant Doherty to shoot at, she gets bored fishing."

Chavez looked at Doherty who shook her head and smiled. He looked back at Pierce who grinned and winked.

Fleming brought the big Mercedes to a halt in front of the first bay in

Kerrigan's four-car garage.

The engine stopped purring, and the lack of motion woke Kerrigan. He opened his eyes and buzzed the passenger seat into an upright position.

It took Fleming two hours to drive from Burfield to Cohasset, and Kerrigan slept the entire way. Fucking Mercedes, thought Fleming. He felt like a chauffeur, driving the big German sedan with Kerrigan snoozing beside him. He much preferred his pickup truck.

Fleming started in. "Are you going to be able to keep Hollis in line?" An odd question, he knew, to ask a father of a 42-year-old daughter, but he needed to make the point.

Kerrigan stretched and said, "How so?"

Fleming hoped he wouldn't have to spell it out for Kerrigan. On the one hand, Jimmy Kerrigan must have some paternal loyalty to his daughter. But, on the other hand, Hollis Kerrigan was an idiot and a loose cannon.

"Back at the picnic," Fleming reminded Kerrigan, "that comment about Walmart, and then the way she treated you. I mean, she's the public face of the project."

"Yeah." Kerrigan grunted. "The Walmart thing went a little far, but she had the rest of her lines down."

"You told her that shit?" asked Fleming.

Kerrigan sighed. Fleming could tell he was uncomfortable, but they needed to have this conversation. "I did, but not in that order. I sat her down one night and explained the country is in the early stages of wind power. In this early phase, what's important is getting some turbines up. Start to get consumers on board. The cost-effectiveness will come later. And I told her: sometimes leaders need to offer symbolic solutions."

"That's not the way it came out," said Fleming. "And what about saying the electricity customers in Burfield are more interested in making a statement than they are in lower rates?"

"That was stupid. I never told her that."

"We need you out there more to keep her in line."

"That's not going to happen. Esperanza wants me home. I'm retired." It was Fleming's turn to sigh. Esperanza was the second wife, significantly younger.

"Hollis needs to keep her story straight for another year," said Fleming. "Then we'll be home free. You need to work with her."

"And it can't be done any faster?"

Fleming remembered a much younger Kerrigan. After six years in Congress delivering the pork for his district, Kerrigan decided to use his contacts with the state and the feds to make some money for himself.

If it were just a nick, a little off the edges, everybody would have looked the other way, like they always did. But Jimmy Kerrigan was always pushing. In Taunton and Fitchburg, he'd strayed over into greedy, particularly with the firefighter in Fitchburg who lost his leg. Kerrigan read the writing on the wall, and he headed off for greener pastures in the South.

Kerrigan had come back to Massachusetts a couple years before. Now rich, he wanted to enjoy a quiet retirement, he'd said. But Fleming knew Kerrigan better than that, and before long they'd been batting around ideas. Stupid federal regulations were like a narcotic for Kerrigan. He just couldn't help himself.

Kerrigan was still vigorous, and there were times when Fleming saw that old gleam in his eyes — like a hawk zeroing in on a rabbit — but he was showing his age. In the old days, a two-hour drive from Burfield to Cohasset would have been an opportunity for Kerrigan to talk, think, plot, connive — not to buzz his seat back and take a nap.

Fleming spoke slowly and patiently. They'd been over this many times, but Kerrigan needed to hear it every now and then to keep him in line. "When the Department of Energy doles out its grants to projects like ours, they consider themselves partners in those projects. Now, in our case, you recall, we used some creative engineering to get them to approve the Matchic Ridge site."

Kerrigan smiled and nodded. Fleming knew he loved a good scam. They staged an elaborate charade testing the winds on the ridge and then in the end, Fleming just faked the data. It was easy to convince the feds. The DOE loved the idea of turbines spinning in central Massachusetts. The fact that Jimmy Kerrigan was a well-connected former Member of Congress was icing on their cake.

Fleming continued. "DOE has specific language in their regs we can take advantage of." He looked over and gave Kerrigan a knowing smile. "We know the first one. The hardship factor. DOE lifted the language from HUD. If the project is interrupted by a natural disaster, they pay to build it again." He looked at Kerrigan for understanding and Kerrigan nodded.

"But DOE's added another wrinkle they call a mitigation relocation. If they approve the site and there's not enough wind, they'll pay to relocate the whole place. They'll pay for 75% of a new site, and I think we can get the state to pay the rest, and we get paid to re-build on that new site. Construction begins all over again. That's what we're shooting for on this one. But, you usually have to wait a year for DOE to get an adequate picture of our piss-poor wind." Fleming knew the DOE regs inside and out. That made sense; it was how he made his money. "Our first turbine was a test, and it worked – it was a dog. Now we need another year for the new turbines to suck the same way."

"Why can't we speed the process up?" Kerrigan still wasn't convinced.

"It's cleaner to wait a year. The winds on that hill really do suck. There's no need for us to expose ourselves by doing anything to the turbines. In a year, we pick the whole thing up and move it to a new site. We use as much of the old equipment as we can, we bill them for new equipment. Maybe we even make money on the land. There's an old orchard on the other side of the mountain where the wind really does blow. I've had my eye on that. We just need to be patient, Jimmy."

"There's no way DOE will let us do it earlier?"

Fleming wondered what it was like to turn into an old man. Did you start to doubt whether you had time to get everything done? Did waiting for a year to cash in on a scheme start to seem like an impossibly long time to wait? It got that way in the last couple of years. Kerrigan split up with his first wife ten years before. Now both wives were costing him a bundle. Was that the reason? Faster, faster, faster. And more, more, more.

Fleming shrugged and thought about deflecting him again, but Kerrigan could get this information with a couple of calls. "Yeah," he conceded. "If the data is 'overwhelming' DOE will waive the year."

"Can't we make it 'overwhelming'?" Kerrigan had always been persistent.

"'Overwhelming' is hard to show."

But then Kerrigan shifted his argument. "You never know about Hollis. She's the wild card. I really wish we could speed this up."

You got me. Fleming revised his earlier thinking about Kerrigan slowing down. He just played a powerful trump card. Instead of defending Hollis, he'd turned against her. Fleming thought about Hollis's performance at the picnic and whether she'd be able to learn her lines correctly. It wasn't a good bet. "I'll see what I can do."

Chapter 6

Katie Shimko adjusted the new nameplate on the edge of her desk. Her mother sent it to her from Cherry Hill when she got the big job last month. She checked the angle. "Chief of Staff" faced her visitors. She couldn't help but preen. After six years as a legislative assistant for her hometown Congressman from New Jersey, she had her first big break, the top job in the office of Rep. Joe Sylvester of Massachusetts. Finally, she was in charge. Now, she needed to crack the whip. She checked her phone, it was 12:23 p.m. She left orders at the receptionist's desk to send Mr. Law in "as soon as he graces us with his presence."

On his way down the marble hallway, Dick Law tested a couple of gaits, trying for a casual saunter. Maybe no one noticed that he wasn't in all morning. He was late, seriously late, but he needed to look like he was coming back from lunch. Entry into the office was key; insouciant, that's what he'd aim for. He drooped one shoulder a bit.

"Katie would like to see you." *Fuck.* The receptionist's words were like a starter gun for every hangover symptom he'd ever experienced. A panicky feeling. Instant headache. Hot and cold sweats. Dry mouth. Fighting off a sudden urge to flee, he straightened up from his new uncomfortable walking style.

Plan B. Purposeful and businesslike. Yes, he'd been out all morning. He'd been sick. A touch of the flu. But he was in now, ready to do The People's Business. Confidence was what was needed. Only a dedicated employee would come in halfway through a sick day. He was Dick Law. Instinctively, he reached up to straighten his tie — only to realize he'd neglected to put one on in his rush to get to the office. Finding his hand at his collar with nothing to do, he let it continue up his face to his hair. His hand came away drenched. *Fuck.* He reached down to grab a wad of Kleenex from a box on a desk. Sweating wasn't good. He reached the closed door to Katie Shimko's little office, took a breath and knocked.

"Come in." She'd only been in the job a week, but Law already hated that voice: New Jersey, nasally, Valley Girl. She said "like" a lot. Today, he added dread to his loathing. He took another breath, opened the door and stepped into the room.

Shimko was seated behind her desk, centered. Everything on her desk was centered. Her desk reminded Law of a teenage girl's dressing table. She had a collection of crystal tchotchkes lined up on either side of her leather desk blotter. On the blotter was a single sheet of paper.

"Dick, thank you for coming in." Even in his distress, Law noticed her voice was unusually formal. *Thank you for coming in? He worked there, for Christ's sake.*

He started talking as he took the seat in front of her. Better to take the offense. "Katie, hi. Sorry about this morning, had a touch of food poisoning, seafood I think, but I wanted to come in this afternoon and get the newsletter out…." She picked up the paper in front of her, he could see it was filled with graphs and charts.

"Dick, as you know, the Congressman has given me complete autonomy on personnel." Law looked up. This didn't sound good. He tried to think of something to say to interrupt her flow, but his mind went blank. He felt new drips of sweat in his armpits. Instinctively he held his arms to his sides.

"I've taken a look at our metrics, and our online platforms are underperforming," she said.

Law tried to shift gears. He was ready to be in trouble for being late. He ran a hand across his damp forehead and tried to interrupt. He only prepared the one speech, he was too foggy to switch gears. "Look, Katie, if it's a problem, I can make it in on time…"

"Dick, I need a press secretary who is more adept at realizing truly cross platform engagement opportunities. To be effective you need to trend up early in the day and I'm not sure that's the space you play in." She looked up, expecting him to understand.

But Law was flummoxed; he shifted to deciphering her new-age vocabulary. *Cross platform engagement opportunities? The space I play in?* All he could do was shake his head miserably.

"I think it's better that you look elsewhere."

Law was shocked back to reality. He understood that part. *This was more than a reprimand. She's trying to fire me. He'd been fired before, he had a catalogue of getting fired euphemisms in his head.* He struggled for control. *This was so fucking unfair.*

"Katie, why don't we consider this a warning? I wasn't totally clear on how you felt about the," he struggled to find her stupid term, "metrics."

Shimko stood up. Startled, Law followed suit, stumbling out of his chair. His legs felt paralyzed from the run.

He'd grovel. "Look Katie, I can tweet more." *He'd try for humor.* He leaned toward her across the desk. "It's just that I have more to say than 140 characters." He stopped and smiled ingratiatingly. *He'd never worked this hard to keep a job.*

She looked down at her desk, lowered her voice, and said, "I can smell booze on your breath."

He tried to regroup. He knew he was sweating like a pig now. "Katie, it might be cough syrup."

She looked back up at him, with an expression of prim disapproval. "It's not just today. It's been every day since I got here."

"Look, Katie, I've been around a long time." It was the only thing he could think of, but he knew it wouldn't work. Katie Shimko was too young to have known who Dick Law used to be.

Shimko picked up her phone and studied it. Law could see she wasn't even focused on him any more. Absently, she said, "You have two weeks. The Congressman has agreed to give you a good recommendation."

The words sunk in on Law. *The Congressman agreed? Sylvester knows. They had worked it out. It was a done deal.*

"Fine." He turned to make his way to the closed office door. He assumed everybody in the office knew. He stood up straighter and patted his hair. *He'd go out with his head high. These fuckers can see some class.*

Law drank that weekend. Of course he drank. He'd been fired. Not that he needed an excuse.

By Sunday morning he was worrying over where he was supposed to go from here. That Shimko was a bitch, but the working world was full of people like her, and it occurred to Law that he was going to need to get it together for his next job. If Shimko and Sylvester were aware of his drinking, then he knew he needed to...not quit, of course, but cut back a bit.

As he sat in his apartment at three in the afternoon, with the Nationals playing the Phillies on TV and a glass in his hand, he remembered Joe Guthrie.

Among Law and his drinking cronies at the Tune Inn, Guthrie was something of a celebrity. Drunk, he walked in the front door of his house and his wife asked where he'd left his Gucci loafers. He hadn't realized he'd made it all the way from the Tune Inn in just his socks. In those same socks, his wife marched him back to the bar to retrieve his shoes. Apparently the whole experience was the shock he'd needed. Word was that he "took the cure" and never drank again.

If anyone knew the trick to slowing it down, Law decided it must be Guthrie, so at 8:00 on Monday morning, when Guthrie walked into the opulent reception area of the Ways and Means Committee — where he was Staff Director — Law waited for him.

Guthrie sat on one end of an over-stuffed leather couch, waved Law onto the other end, and popped the lid on a cup of take-out coffee. "What's up?" The expression on his face was neutral, friendly, vaguely curious.

Law couldn't help himself. He glanced down at Guthrie's shoes. Gucci loafers. Maybe the story was true.

He searched for an opening line. The silence dragged on.

At last Law said, "I don't know if you heard, but Joe Sylvester and I had a parting of the ways on Friday." *Parting of the ways. Jesus.*

"I did hear something about that."

Dammit, thought Law. Word was already getting around. That bitch.

"You know how it is. The new Chief of Staff wanted to bring in her own person for the press job. It was important to her, she's young."

"Yeah."

"But that's not really what I wanted to talk to you about," said Law.

Guthrie gave a noncommittal murmur.

"I wanted to ask you about..." Law stared down at his clenched hands. He was a communications expert. Why couldn't he find the words?

"You're hoping there's something on the Committee staff?" asked Guthrie.

That set Law back. Maybe there was an out. Take a Committee job. Watch his drinking. Clean up his act a little.

Law looked up at Guthrie, who was looking back at him with a friendly expression. Encouraging. But — was it just Law's imagination — somewhat amused, too? As if he knew something Law didn't.

Fuck it, thought Law. "That's not why I'm here," he said. "I wanted to talk to you about...."

"Yes?"

"I heard you ... eased off on your drinking."

"Nope."

"No?"

"I didn't ease off." Calmly, Guthrie sipped at his coffee. "I stopped. There's a difference."

Law waited, disappointed. He'd wanted a lifeline. More than this. A phone rang in the outer office. A secretary answered it. Otherwise, there was only silence. Law studied Guthrie's face, and he realized Guthrie was going to outlast him. He's done this before, thought Law.

"I guess I need to do something about my drinking."

"You guess?"

"I *know* I need to do something." The words were simple, but even so, it felt to Law like saying them was taking a big step.

"Do something?"

Dammit, help me out here, thought Law. "Yeah. Do something. I need to cut back a bit."

"Most people who want to 'cut back a bit' have a bigger problem."

The statement just hung there. Law was silent.

"Do you think you have a bigger problem?"

Even in his confusion, Law sensed this was a turning point. "Yeah," he said. *There.*

"Meet me at 11:45," said Guthrie.

"Today?"

"At the C Street entrance. We'll walk. Bring your lunch."

"Where are we going?"

"A meeting," said Guthrie.

"You mean … like, AA?"

"Exactly."

This was moving too fast for Law. Last night he'd been drinking. Was he going to be able to drink today? What about tonight? That wasn't reasonable. Not possible. He wouldn't be able to sleep. "Do you really think I should go?" he asked, trying to sound casual.

"It's up to you," said Guthrie. He stood and held his hand out to Law, half helping him from his seat, half shaking his hand. "There are a lot of people like us."

"Us?"

Guthrie leaned in close and used a stage whisper. "Alcoholics." Then he feigned a look at the door and put a finger to his lips.

Alcoholic? He'd just come here to learn how to cut back. But, weirdly, it did feel good to hear it, maybe even say it, get it out there in the open. "And you think this is right for me?" It was one last try.

Guthrie opened the office door. "We've been saving a seat for you. Be outside at 11:45. Wear your good socks."

Law's thoughts were jumbled as he walked down the hall outside the office. He laughed when he finally picked up on Guthrie's last line. He must know they tell that story.

Chapter 7

While some long-time New Englanders claimed their relatives came over on the Mayflower, Ethan Caleb Pierce III joked that his forebears owned the boat. Ethan Pierce was comfortable that he was born with money and he dealt with it like everything else in his life — with no ego and a wickedly irreverent sense of humor.

Thanks to Ethan Caleb Pierce I (banking) and Ethan Caleb Pierce Jr. (investing Ethan the First's money), Ethan Caleb Pierce III had even more career choices than a typical graduate of Harvard Law. Freed from the need (or drive) to make money and intrigued by the challenge of public service, he went to work as an entry-level prosecutor in the office of the United States Attorney in Boston. There, he believed he'd found his life's calling, using his formidable intellect and old-fashioned sense of justice to prosecute federal law-breakers. But after ten years in the job, he stood up from his desk one day at lunch and quit, pushed over the edge by yet another politically motivated decision by his politically appointed boss.

Newly married, he took up a life Pierce I and Pierce Jr. would have approved of: a move to the suburbs, a job in corporate law and making money,

Shortly after the death of his wife, with no children and facing retirement from his law firm, the 72-year old Pierce found himself in the parking lot of Harvard Stadium after a football game. With a group of his former classmates, he was sharing old stories and bitching about almost everything. During his third bourbon, Pierce delivered a pithy commentary: that the current Massachusetts Attorney General's casual attitude toward public corruption made him the "eunuch proprietor of a second-rate whorehouse."

It was a throwaway line in a routine discussion of Massachusetts politics, but one of Pierce's classmates had heard enough.

"Put up or shut up, you asshole."

Later, Pierce wondered if a political campaign was ever launched on the basis of a cruder challenge. Six months later he was a candidate for Attorney General. His best line in his campaign speech was a quote from the Chief Medical Examiner of Massachusetts on the occasion of his retirement: "I come to work every day and act like I don't need the job." And then Pierce would pause before his audience and say, emphasizing each word. "Really, I don't need the job." And then he'd add, "and you shouldn't elect anyone who does."

This challenge worked. The voters loved Pierce's straight talk and breezy style.

On Election Day, he crushed the incumbent 'eunuch' Attorney General by 13 points.

Now, he was three years into his tenure as state Attorney General. He loved the job but he was frustrated he hadn't done better cleaning up public corruption. He had no desire to be the eunuch in the whorehouse.

Chapter 8

Chavez Simons always wanted to be a fireman.

It started when he was a toddler, when the blaring fire horn would bring him rushing out to the front porch to watch the giant fire trucks, sirens blasting and colored lights flashing.

From there, he moved closer and closer to the fire station to watch the fire calls, first to the Revolutionary War statue in the middle of the Common, and by the time he was five, all the way to the side of Main Street, across from the station. There, he eagerly watched the firefighters arrive in their private vehicles and then he waved to the three whooping, departing trucks.

He was in kindergarten when a firefighter named Kenny Dutton (Chavez remembered), hanging on the back of a fire truck, shouted "Hi, kid!" as the truck made the turn onto Main Street. Chavez stood grinning as the overflow slosh from the truck's water tank washed over his brown Hush Puppies.

It was a year later, after an afternoon brush fire, that Chavez dared to make his way across Main Street and approached the station. Firefighters were out in the drive, unrolling and washing hose, spraying off boots, and re-filling air bottles.

An old white Ford Explorer squeaked rubber as it stopped beside him. Chavez recognized the fire chief's truck, always the first out of the station when there was a call. Gold lettering on the side read: "Chief – Burfield VFD."

The Chief got out of the truck, stretched, and rubbed his lower back. He had an unlit cigar in the side of his mouth. Red suspenders framed his uniform shirt. Chavez was fascinated.

The Chief limped to the back of the truck, pulled his muddy boots out, and tossed them on the grass.

"Grab those boots, kid."

Chavez hesitated. He knew he was the only kid there, but he just couldn't believe a fireman was asking him for help. Besides, this was the Chief. The Chief asked him for help.

Chavez grabbed the rubber loop of each boot and hurried to catch up. Firefighters lined their boots against the outside wall of the station. One firefighter began to work down the line of boots with a hose.

At Chavez's house, everything happened slowly and quietly. Here, there was loud talk, laughing, people actually doing things!

"Put the boots in the line," said the firefighter with the hose. "Unless you want me to wash you down at the same time I wash those boots." He smiled to show he was kidding.

"When you're done there, c'mon and get a donut." The Chief turned and walked into the station.

Chavez put the boots at the end of the line, then hurried to follow the Chief up a flight of stairs, into a room that looked to him like the exciting, magical sort of place where King Arthur and his knights sat around their Round Table.

"Sit here." Jokkinen pulled a metal folding chair up next to a break table. Then he pushed a donut box over to where Chavez could get a look. "Grab one," he said.

Chavez looked at the box with wonder— chocolate, pink sprinkles, bear claws, maple bars — all there for him to choose. He'd never had a donut before.

"I think I'd like a chocolate, please."

"Grab it. It's not going to eat itself." The Chief handed Chavez a napkin.

Chavez smoothed down his cardigan sweater, picked a chocolate donut out of the box and centered it on the napkin.

Smiling, the Chief asked, "What's your name?"

"My name is Chavez Simons." Revealing his name was always an awkward moment for him. Chavez was sure the question — "What kind of name is that?" — was coming next. It always did. But the Chief surprised him.

"Know what my name is?" the Chief asked.

Chavez shook his head.

"Toivo. Can you imagine that?"

Chavez looked at him blankly.

"Toivo's a Finnish name. Do you know what 'Toivo' sounds like?"

Chavez shook his head.

"TOILET!" The Chief blurted the word, but he was smiling. "All the kids in school called me 'Toilet.' 'Toilet bowl.' 'Toilet paper.' So I know what it's like when people make fun of your name."

Chavez smiled shyly. It felt like the Chief understood him.

"As soon as I could," said the Chief, "I told everyone I wanted to be called 'Terry.' Have you ever thought about a nickname?"

"My parents won't let me," said Chavez. "Besides, I'm used to it. I'm the only Chavez in my school."

"I'll bet." The Chief paused. "It's quite a name to give a kid." He changed the subject. "I see you like firefighting," said the Chief. "How would you like a job?"

"A job?" Chavez's eyes widened.

"You're out here for every fire, anyway." The Chief looked around at his firefighters. "You show up faster than some of my regular guys."

Around the table, firefighters laughed and grumbled in a friendly way.

"Instead of just standing and watching," said the Chief, "you could help out. You could start by cleaning boots and keeping the break room tidy. Do you think you could handle that?"

Chavez could only nod.

"If you do a good job, we'll find more stuff for you to do. How does that sound?"

"That sounds … good."

"You need to check with your parents to make sure it's okay."

"It's okay."

The Chief gave Chavez a considering look, then nodded in understanding.

There was a brief silence. Chavez looked around the room and then back at Terry Jokkinen. He lowered his voice; "Do you think I could have another donut?"

Chapter 9

As a student at St. Mary's School in Lynn, a grim blue-collar town north of Boston, Mary Margaret Cronin felt — even from an early age — a *responsibility* to punish sinners. She started with small efforts like telling the nuns on her fellow classmates. The feeling of satisfaction when a wrongdoer — as defined by God and interpreted by Mary — was punished; it was exquisite.

Mary Cronin thought about growing up to be a nun. She envied the allowance for vengefulness in a nun's job. She knew her principal, Sister Margaret, had a paddle in her top drawer. Sitting behind a big desk bossing people around with a paddle at the ready sounded like a fine life. Fun and doing God's work at the same time.

At the College of the Sacred Heart in Newton, she decided that being a nun with a paddle was too limiting. She would be restricted to reprimanding only a certain age set, and maybe only girls. There were far greater sins going on in the world than in the halls of piddling little Catholic schools.

Instead she decided to do God's work as a prosecutor. After law school, she went to work in the state Attorney General's office. Thirty years later, she became the Deputy Attorney General. She was right in assuming it was her life's work. She decided her job would not end in retirement, but death. For most of the people who came in contact with Mary Cronin, that moment couldn't come too soon.

It was early, barely 7:30 a.m., and Pierce and Doherty were the only passengers on the McCormack State Office Building garage elevator. Pierce carried his morning coffee and, as usual, he was whistling, not exactly a tune, just a toneless high-pitched sound. He knew the whistling drove Doherty nuts, but that was part of the fun.

Pierce punched a button, and the elevator stopped at the floor below their destination. "Always good to be neighborly, Sergeant."

Doherty gave him a skeptical look, and he grinned back at her.

Pierce made his way down the nearly empty hallway to the corner of the building directly underneath his own suite of offices. He seemed to remember that's where Mary Cronin had her little palace.

The reception area contained three desks, unoccupied this early in the morning. An American flag and the white Commonwealth of Massachusetts flag flanked the gold seal of the Office of the Attorney General.

On either side of the flags, framed photographs covered nearly every inch of the walls. Mary Cronin with the Speaker of the House. Mary Cronin with the previous Speaker of the House. Mary Cronin with… Pierce looked down the row. Cronin with the past six Speakers of the House.

A series of Governors. U.S. Senators. Members of Congress. Mary Cronin at banquets, at lecterns, receiving awards. Mary Cronin in a State Police jumpsuit at a fire investigation.

"Can you believe this woman?" whispered Doherty, and Pierce whispered back, "It's better than a presidential library."

The wall at the end of the room was different, dedicated to just two photographs, illuminated by a small overhead spotlight. Pierce walked closer, still whispering. "Sergeant, unless I miss my guess. Yes! Right on the very first try."

The first picture showed Mary Cronin with John F. Kennedy at what must have been a school ceremony. Looking about fifteen, Cronin wore a Catholic school uniform.

Then Pierce looked at the picture to the right: Mary Cronin, a lace doily on her head, with Paul VI at the Vatican. Pierce smiled. The sainted president and the sainted pope. And Mary Cronin.

He heard quiet conversation behind the closed door of the corner office. He knocked twice, opened the door, and stuck his head in.

Cronin sat in a rocking chair on the far side of the room. She had a phone to her ear and a cup of tea by her side. She hung up, put the cup on the saucer, and rocked forward out of the chair all in one motion. "General, what … a pleasant surprise." She smoothed her skirt and straightened herself.

"Sorry to drop by unannounced, Mary." Pierce stepped into the room. "I was just on my way up to the office and decided to stop by." Pierce studied her tailored suit. She looked like a stewardess, back when they were called stewardesses.

"Not at all, General, welcome, come in," said Cronin, sounding like she was showing an invited guest to her home.

So much for surprise, thought Pierce.

She pointed to a table in the corner. "Would you like a cup of tea?"

It was her hot tea station: a fancy looking electric pot, bags of tea, milk, sweeteners, even a little bowl of cookies, all sitting on a linen tablecloth.

Pierce showed his coffee. "None for me, thanks. Carrying my own."

"Ah, Dunkin Donuts," said Cronin. "I hope you don't mind if I freshen my Earl Grey," said Cronin.

What a snob, chuckled Pierce, as he watched her walk to the tea corner. *What's she wearing on her legs? Who wears seamed stockings anymore?*

Mentally he kicked himself. He hadn't come there to check out Cronin's legs.

But seriously, who wears them?

Pierce looked around the room. It was decorated like an old-fashioned living room. Persian rugs covered the floor, and some sheer silky fabric replaced the state-issued blinds.

Cronin turned from her tea station and caught Pierce studying her furnishings. "State décor is so drab," she said. "There's really no reason to go slumming, is there?"

Pierce smiled. He brought some old maps from home, and Doherty hung them on his wall. Otherwise, nothing that wasn't pure government issue. Cronin liked her nice things.

"Have a seat, General, let's chat."

Cronin moved around in back of her desk — an expensive antique, Pierce guessed, the top inlaid with several kinds of exotic wood — and Pierce lowered himself into a spindly chair across from her.

Cronin silently waited for Pierce to speak. This was her home turf. Her power position.

Pierce matched her silence and sipped his coffee. He had no intention of being cowed by her.

He noticed a graduation picture on the credenza behind her. The banner reading "Harvard Law School, Class of 1970" couldn't have been more obvious. He pointed. "You were a couple of years ahead of me. May I see?"

With a none-too-pleased expression, Cronin handed Pierce the picture.

Pierce found his reading glasses and examined the photo. "A lot of familiar faces in here," he said. "A couple of judges, politicos, big-time law firm partners. What a collection." He tapped the glass. "That's you in the front row, holding the class banner. You haven't changed a bit." Pierce looked up to assess her reaction, halfway between pride and suspicion.

She's still wondering why the hell I'm sitting here, thought Pierce. *Good.*

"And in the back row here," said Pierce. "Is that Jimmy Kerrigan? I didn't know him all that well, but he was already on his way up, wasn't he? I seem to remember the two of you were friends." Pierce suppressed a smile as he remembered Kerrigan and Cronin in the motel parking lot forty years before.

Cronin's face went rigid, expressionless, intent on revealing nothing.

"I saw him the other day," said Pierce. "Out in the boonies. He and his daughter are developing a wind farm. Going great guns. Small world, isn't it?"

There. Boom. That's why he'd come.

Silently, her face grim, Cronin held her hand out for the picture.

Pierce saw it trembled a bit, but then again, whose hand didn't tremble at 77?

Cronin stared at the photograph as if she hadn't looked at it in a long time. As if she expected to see something new in it. At last she said, "Small world, General." And then she shifted from the gregarious host Mary to the feared Dragon Lady: "A busy day ahead, General. What can I do for you?"

Pierce stood. He'd done what he needed. "Just stopped by to say hello. I'll let you get back to your work."

Standing in front of the desk, Pierce glanced over the rest of the photos on the credenza. There was Cronin on safari in Africa, at Machu Picchu, atop a Mayan pyramid, at the Taj Mahal, on a Caribbean beach.

To the side were several photos of Cronin in front of a sunny pastel beachfront house. It looked immense. No doubt, expensive.

Cronin slid sideways and blocked Pierce's view.

Opening the office door, Pierce found Doherty sitting in the outer office. "Saddle up, Sergeant. Time's a wastin'."

They walked down the still-empty, early-morning hallway toward the elevator.

"Mission accomplished?" asked Doherty.

"Yup."

"And how was the Dragon Lady?"

"The Dragon Lady is a woman of many secrets, Sergeant."

The fact that Doherty despised Mary Cronin was not a secret between the two of them. Seeing the look on Doherty's face — as if she'd just smelled something unpleasant — Pierce grinned and said, "Sergeant, tell me something."

"Sir?"

"Are seamed stockings making a comeback?"

Doherty snorted. "That's disgusting."

Chapter 10

Chavez and Jason sat on Lookout Point, the highest elevation on Matchic Ridge in the University Forest, breathing hard from the climb. The view from the point was spectacular; the whole town in the valley before them. On a clear day, the tall buildings of Boston were visible, 85 miles to the east. The 3500-acre University Forest tract was donated to the state university system in 1878. In the largest old growth forest in the state, the same oaks, conifers and beeches that were young trees in 1878 stood today in the forest. On the other side of the ridge, the Quabbin Reservoir, completed in 1938 to provide water to metropolitan Boston, stretched eighteen miles to the south.

The boys leaned against a huge boulder that balanced improbably on the edge of the cliff, despite the efforts of generations of local troublemakers. The wind farm fence was twenty feet away.

Chavez parked his pickup in the woods near the Albertsons' Sawmill, and they hiked for half an hour up through the back orchard to the only spot on the ridge with a view of the town. The giant blades wobbled, almost motionless, directly overhead.

Jason finally re-gained his breath and pointed. "Check it out."

Chavez looked over and saw there was a washout under the wind farm fence. "Guess they aren't worried about a sneak attack."

The remark got a laugh from Jason. They'd been talking about "sneak attacks" since they were kids.

It was cooler on top of the ridge than in town, and there was a gentle breeze. Jason reached into his backpack and pulled out a small camera attached to a Velcro strap.

"What's that?" asked Chavez.

"GoPro," said Jason.

"New?"

"Yep."

Chavez eyed the camera. Jason was one of his lawncare employees and Chavez knew how much he earned. The tiny video camera in a clear plastic case must have cost Jason half of what he made all summer.

"What are you doing with that?"

Jason split open a bag of Cheetos, shoved a handful into his mouth, and spoke around them. "Dude. It's an action camera. It's what they use in extreme sports." He handed Chavez his cellphone. "Watch."

While Jason moved the camera around, Chavez looked at the phone. Jason set it to function as a monitor for the videocam. On the screen, he saw the wind turbine.

"I just need to practice." Jason pulled out a nylon tube, from which he extracted a rolled kite. Chavez grinned as he watched Jason assemble a glider kite, the kind you flew with two handles connected to strings. That's why he liked Jason. A videocam. A kite. He never knew what Jason would come up with next.

Jason strapped the camera on the kite and handed it and his phone to Chavez. He took the handles and began to walk away, unwinding the strings. "When I say 'Go,' let the kite fly up into the wind."

The small kite flew up out of Chavez's hand and he lifted Jason's phone and watched. The kite was high in the air and he waved to see himself. He had a bird's eye view of the turbines and they were barely moving. He looked away from the camera into the air. The kite was flying just fine. It was curious.

Since they were kids, the boys camped on the ridge almost every summer weekend. But the wind farm changed all that. The big trees were gone now, and huge earthmovers showed up one day to level the ridge (and their campsite). An eight-foot-high chain link fence blocked off the top of the ridge, with two locked gates sealing off two bulldozed access roads. Then, workers and equipment came to build five huge towers, plus a small pre-fab garage to serve as control room for the facility.

After several months of exploring and experimenting, the boys decided on a new campsite, halfway down the mountain on a mossy spot near a stream.

They settled into the feathery moss for the night with stars visible through the towering trees. Their dying campfire wafted a light smoke into the air.

"Coach Black and Miss Maltz." Jason's voice was low and dramatic, tossing the image out there like a fishing lure.

"Black and Maltz," repeated Chavez, picturing it.

Both teachers taught physical education at the high school. Coach

Black wore gold rim glasses and kept his t-shirt tightly tucked into his gym shorts. Miss Maltz was the only woman teacher who still wanted to be called "Miss." She wore a Springfield College sweatshirt over knee-length shorts. She wore plastic aviator glasses that changed colors in the sun.

Neither boy knew the ages of the teachers, only that they were so old that the thought of sex between them was gross.

Jason added, triumphantly: "In the gym, with Miss Maltz hanging from the rings."

It was one of their favorite games: unlikely — and better yet, unthinkable — sex partners. The idea of Coach Black and Miss Maltz screwing was totally gross, but using P.E. equipment gave the imaginary scene an appreciated aura of absurdity.

"Well?" asked Jason. The way the game went, Chavez needed to try to come up with a pairing to top Jason's.

"Sorry, man," said Chavez. "I'm kinda tired tonight."

"You're a real buzzkill."

Chavez rolled over. "'Buzzkill' is so over. I told you to stop saying it.

Jason persisted. "Okay, Homeslice."

"Stop it."

"What's wrong?"

Chavez sighed. "I flunked the certification test."

"Flunked? Didn't you, like, study your ass off?"

"It had an essay section."

"Oh, shit."

Chavez knew that was all the explanation Jason needed. Jason helped Chavez with his reading and writing since kindergarten.

"Is he going to let you try again?" asked Jason.

"He only gives the test once a year."

"A Class-A Clusterfuck, huh?"

That made Chavez laugh. It was one of the Chief's favorite expressions. Chavez told Jason, and the two boys used it all the time.

"Actually, no," said Chavez. "The Chief said I could do a research project instead of the essay."

"What kind of research project?"

"Looking into two big fires a long time ago."

"I suppose you'll need my help."

"Thanks." Chavez did a knuckle-bump with Jason. He could always count on him.

Jason brought up a topic he knew would improve his friend's spirits.

"Do you have Ariel Pinkerton in any of your classes?"

"I really don't remember." Chavez tried to say it casually.

"Right," said Jason.

Ariel Pinkerton: the girl of their dreams. Ariel Pinkerton wore tight tops, and she had *cleavage*. Ariel Pinkerton wore her blond hair tied in a flipping ponytail. Ariel Pinkerton already had her braces off. And, according to Jason's exacting research, Ariel Pinkerton wore a thong. Every single day.

Ariel Pinkerton, Queen Bee of the sophomore class, commanded a swarm of drones and worker bees. She only dated seniors.

And 'date' wasn't all Ariel Pinkerton was rumored to do with. According to Jason's sources, she could be counted on to offer up hand jobs to her lucky suitors. And maybe even more.

Ariel Pinkerton likely didn't even know Jason Morrill or Chavez Simons existed.

"If you were taking Ariel Pinkerton out," said Chavez, warming to the topic, "where would you take her?"

For the sake of the fantasy, the boys agreed not to discuss the infinitesimal chances of that event ever happening to either of them.

"I guess I'd start by taking her to the Old Mill," said Jason. The restaurant was where Jason's mom took him on his birthdays. "Then to a concert in Fitchburg." Although grimy, Fitchburg was the biggest city near to Burfield, and it was always their imagined go-to destination. "And then back home," Jason finished.

There was a minute or so of silence while they digested the fantasy date.

"What about you?" Jason asked.

"Well…" Chavez had a long list of familiar options. "I'd take her to the P-HOP." The Burfield House of Pizza was the only local restaurant open at night.

"And?" Clearly, Jason was bored with P-HOP.

"I'd buy a plain pizza to go." Neither boy knew what kind of pizza Ariel Pinkerton preferred, so plain was a safe bet.

"To go?" Jason asked. To go was new.

"And then we'd get in my truck," said Chavez, working to create an aura of mystery. "I'd have a mattress in the back."

"A mattress?"

Chavez knew by Jason's tone he had him hooked. "We'd drive to Mt. Wachusett and watch the sun set and the full moon come up."

"The Mt. Wachusett road closes at sunset."

Chavez was prepared for Jason trying to ruin his story. "I have a master firefighter's key. Opens any lock."

"What about the pizza?"

"We might eat a piece or two. That is, before we got down to business in the back of the truck."

"In the back of the truck?"

"Yeah. Ariel Pinkerton loves guys with trucks and a full moon turns her on." Chavez looked over at Jason in the light of the campfire. Jason looked back, speechless and wide-eyed. Then he continued. "We'd kiss," said Chavez. "And she'd jump my bones."

It took thirty seconds for Jason's tortured scream to stop reverberating through the forest.

Finally, Chavez said, "Ready for some Steve?" He rolled over and rooted around in his backpack.

Jason yawned. "Hit me. It's your turn."

Next to their on-going study of all things female, reading chapters out loud from a Stephen King book was their favorite camping activity.

Chavez clicked on his headlamp. He knew just the story. He wanted to scare Jason shitless.

Chapter 11

Chavez unloaded the camping gear and hung the sleeping bags on a line in the back yard of the Simons home on the Town Common. He knew if he left Jason to take care of his own bag, it would just stay rolled up in its stuff-sack until their next trip. A moldy, sticky sleeping bag wouldn't bother Jason, but Chavez couldn't stand the thought of it.

In the driveway, he swept out the bed of his pickup, hosed off the mud and dust, and used a chamois to polish the back bumper.

A year older than his fellow Tantasset sophomores, Chavez was the only kid in the class who was old enough to drive. He was also the only kid to own his own wheels.

Chavez was aware – but didn't really care – that his choice of vehicle puzzled his parents.

When he was ten, he'd gotten Peter and Catherine Simons to OK using his $20-a-month allowance for whatever he wanted. He knew they thought he'd be spending it on candy and other stuff like most kids, but he saved it. And he made his own money. And invested it. For sure, his parents didn't think his allowance would lead to a truck.

At the age of ten, one day he'd rung the counter bell in the shop of Tony Delvecchio, the town's florist, decorator, and lawn-care guru. Working for Tony, Chavez learned from the best.

Six years later, Chavez's lawn-care operation included a crew of five kids, seven mowers, and various shears, clippers, and other garden tools, all staged out of a shed in the Simons's backyard. Chavez's Burfield Lawn Care grossed $1,500 a month, and with stock tips from Tony, Chavez multiplied his earnings. By his sixteenth birthday, Chavez was worth a cool $18,153.

He used $5,750 to buy the F-150.

The first day he drove it into the driveway, his father sputtered, "A truck? What are you thinking? And where'd you get the money, anyway?"

His mom tried to give him her old Volvo wagon. "It's nice and safe," she'd told him.

Chavez thought the Volvo was fine, but it was an old lady's car. Firefighters drove pickup trucks.

It didn't take much discussion to get his parents to cave. They responded the way they always did, ever since he could remember: with a collective shrug, a concession that they just didn't understand this child of theirs.

Chavez was just gathering up the wet rags when he heard crunching gravel. His mother's Volvo came up the driveway.

Catherine Simons slid from the driver's side, carrying an aluminum coffee cup and her iPhone. She was dressed in her yoga instructor uniform: calf-length tights, ballet slippers, a turtleneck and one of her many vests. Pulled back in a ponytail, her light brown hair was stuck through the back of a billed hat.

"Hi, Honey," she breezed, and Chavez leaned down to give his mom an air-kiss. She smelled of incense. Their difference in size was stark: at 6' 4" and somewhere over 250 pounds, Chavez towered over Catherine.

"Hi, Mom." Their relationship was friendly — not as warm as some of his friends', not as antagonistic as some others. She'd long ago given up trying to get him to call her "Catherine."

"Whew, what's that smell?" Catherine asked, drawing back, wrinkling her nose under her ball cap and starting up the walk to the house.

"Let's see, wet clothes, campfire smoke and barbeque potato chips," Chavez said to her departing back, his voice dropping when she was far enough away not to hear about the chips. Chavez knew his mother didn't care much about what he did, where he went or who his friends were, but she hated him eating junk food. "Plus Slim Jims, Ring Dings and fried bologna," he said quietly with a smile.

Chavez helped her carry the groceries in to the antique butcher-block island in the kitchen. The kitchen was a riot of asparagus ferns, jade plants, and Swedish ivy. Catherine slipped her phone into the dock on the counter, and some sort of yoga music began to play. Catherine Simons started a kettle boiling, laid out fixings for green tea and retrieved a lopsided mug Chavez made for her in Montessori School.

Their old Labrador, Cassius, sprawled in the corner on a rug. Chavez eyed the dog. He only got up when his dad came in the house.

"Honey, your father is making his risotto tonight."

Chavez's heart sank.

Risotto nights were the worst.

Peter could barely find his way around the kitchen, despite the fact that they'd lived in the house for fifteen years. Though risotto was his only dish, he needed Catherine or Chavez with him as he cooked to find things. This evening, it was Chavez's turn to cook-sit. He found the butter for his father: right in the refrigerator door, where they'd kept it since before baby Chavez learned to say "butter."

They sat at the dining room table. Chavez pushed a blob of risotto around on his plate. As usual, it was cheesy, and his father had added nuts. Chavez hated nuts in his food.

"Jason and I were up in the Albertsons' back orchard yesterday," Chavez began, "and we saw something weird…"

"Don't let your risotto get cold," said Peter. "I spent a lot of time cooking it." He swirled the wine in his glass, sniffed it, and took a sip.

Chavez obliged by tasting a bit. "Really good," he said, though he didn't like risotto all that much. He liked white fluffy rice but couldn't understand the big deal about gooey risotto. "Jason had a kite," he said, "and we were trying out his new video camera. Anyway, when the kite was flying, I looked over and the turbines were hardly moving. That wasn't weird, because there's usually not that much wind on that side of the ridge. But when there was enough wind to fly the kite, the turbines didn't spin."

There was a silence. When Chavez ate at Jason's house, Jason and his mom talked all through dinner, and that was fun. But Chavez's father liked it to be quiet during dinner.

Catherine smiled encouragingly at Chavez, then looked over at Peter.

Chavez looked at his father, who was fiddling in his lap. Chavez knew he had his phone down there, despite Catherine's no-phones-at-the-table rule.

Chavez continued, now talking to his mother. "And there's something else. Remember my science class went on a tour of the wind farm last year? The guy who led the tour had this wind thing, like a model airplane with its wings cut off? It measures wind speed."

Still looking into his lap, Peter said, "An anemometer."

Chavez looked over, surprised his dad was listening. "Yeah, that's what he called it. The guy had it on a tripod, and its tail spun it around so its propellers faced the wind, you know, like a weathervane? Well, anyway, the guy said that's what the turbines are supposed to do — spin around to face the wind."

Peter lifted his head.

He must be interested, thought Chavez. "But here's the thing. When the kite was in the air, we could tell the wind was blowing from the town. But the turbines didn't turn to face that way. Like the turbines weren't paying any attention to the wind. Also, the blades weren't turning. That seems weird."

Peter's eyes narrowed. "What were you doing up on the ridge?"

Chavez felt defensive. He and Jason had been camping since they were little, and his dad never questioned him before. "It's where we go to camp."

"Technically, you're trespassing," said Peter. "You know that, don't you?"

"Dad, we were outside the fence." Chavez was surprised.

"Did you see the No Trespassing signs on the fence?"

"We were outside the fence, and besides, we've always camped on the ridge."

"There might be things — adult things — going on up there. Things that don't involve you."

"I'm just curious."

"Aren't you too old to be playing up there in the woods? Flying kites? Maybe you should find some more lawns to mow."

Chavez looked to his mom for support. He just wanted to share the news about the turbines. It really was kind of weird.

She shrugged and rolled her eyes. No surprise, Chavez thought. His mother never corrected his dad in front of him.

Chapter 12

Richard Lawson, educated at the University of Iowa and the University of Missouri School of Journalism, was not just a talking head – he was a journalist.

He could write, he could report. He'd been the editor of his high school paper and the *Daily Iowan*.

But his good looks pre-destined him for television news.

His first job after grad school was doing live-on-the-street reporting for the third-ranked television news show in Albuquerque, where the new news director changed his name to Dick Law, ditched his glasses for contact lenses, and "brightened" his brown hair to a distinctive blond. With the name change came a personality change: the low-key, serious, purposeful Richard Lawson became Dick Law, flashy and glib.

He was too big for Albuquerque. Within a year, he was recruited by a "news consultant" employed by Boston's Channel 6, WACI. His appearance in Boston could not have been less subtle. Three months before he began, billboards sprang up all over town, with the blurred outline of a head shot superimposed over the station's logo. The caption on the bottom read, "He's coming…"

He was Dick Law, Boston's big new TV news star: blond hair, chiseled jaw, tailored vested suits. At WACI, Dick Law took over what was renamed "Action News," the first newscast in the market to follow the "If it bleeds, it leads" trend in television news. "Dick Law – Action News" was everywhere. If it was burning, Dick Law was singed. If it collapsed, Dick Law dodged the debris. If it was bleeding, Dick Law stepped around the blood.

Ratings for WACI skyrocketed, propelling the station to number one in the market after only two ratings periods. Dick Law, just 25 years old, was the star, and he was expected to play the role all the time. Station advertisers provided his on-air suits and off-air outfits. He drove a black Porsche 911 with over-sized wheels and a huge spoiler. The tinted windows were changed back to clear before the car was delivered; the dealer wanted people to see who was driving his machine.

The station's PR agency guided Dick Law's dating life. Benefit dinners were his mainstay, always with a date arranged to "add value" to the evening. Dick Law didn't go anywhere that the gossip columnists didn't know about beforehand. His "bachelor pad" apartment, all chrome and naked wood, was written up in the "Living" section of the *Globe*.

Restaurant maître d's gushed when Dick Law and friends dropped in for dinner. Accustomed to eating with many eyes on him, Dick Law was careful with his drinking — in public.

But, after the 11 p.m. news, when Dick Law kicked back in his leather Eames chair in his new apartment, that was when he did his drinking. He had a high-pressure job. He was doing important work. He deserved to unwind. He needed no better excuse as he had his first, then second and maybe third gin and tonic.

It was a great schedule. Late-night drinking, a few hours of dead-to-the-world sleep, maybe a beer at lunch to settle his nerves, and then to the station 90 minutes before the 6 p.m. news. Unless, of course, there was a dramatic fire, a politician's indictment, or a lurid murder — the sort of excitement that required Dick Law reporting from the scene.

His on-the-scene reports were where he began his slide.

At first there were the times when he dragged himself out to cover a story in the morning, and he looked ragged: a little disheveled, pale, jittery, bumming aspirin, swilling black coffee.

At 2 a.m. one night, he arrived at a murder scene on the South Boston waterfront. He could have sworn he set the handbrake on the Porsche, but it ended up half in the water. Dick Law and his Porsche was even bigger news than the murder. The car dealer kept the Porsche on his lot an extra two weeks after he dried it out, to show customers the 911 the famous Dick Law dropped in Boston Harbor.

In that era and in that business, over-indulgence was tolerated — even celebrated. But the incidents started to add up. Dick Law shrugged it off. *Live hard, play hard.* They added to his mystique. Boston was filled with those personalities in those days; professional athletes, newscasters, even elected officials.

But then, more and more, he would leave the station for dinner after the 6 p.m. news all combed and ironed and return wrinkled and disheveled, needing an hour to get back in shape.

Finally, one night on the 11, it all came crashing down. Later, when Richard Lawson felt strong enough to engage in career accident reconstruction, he identified this as the first big domino to fall as his career went sour.

Had he been alert enough to read the hard copy before reading it from a teleprompter on air, he might have gotten the word right.

He might have remembered the context.

And, if he wasn't still shaking off the effects of a 10-ounce rib eye, one Martini, and two glasses of Burgundy, he might have been swift enough to realize the Charles River was being tested for *organisms*.

Even in those days before the Internet, the "virulent orgasm" story was a sensation. The tape of the broadcast made its way into every ad agency in the city and then, at Christmas time, to their clients for use at holiday parties.

Dick Law laughed it off. It could happen to anyone. If you work in the kitchen, you're going to get burned. Doing an 11 p.m. show was beneath him, he said. He was "too old for that shit." The 6 o'clock news was what people watched.

But the slide continued.

A month later, WACI announced they were beefing up their noon news with Dick Law as the new co-host.

Two years later, Gabriela Martinez arrived from Miami to join Dick Law as co-anchor on the 6 p.m. broadcast.

A year after that, Dick Law — the same Dick Law who arrived in the Boston market seven years before with mystery billboards and a star's introduction — was taken off the 6. He was no longer an evening newscaster.

Dick Law was given a 10 a.m. news magazine show, with only the noon news to anchor. A year after that, the station announced he was leaving the noon news to concentrate on the magazine.

At age 34, he was no longer a newscaster. No more high-ratings evening news shows, no more Porsche, no more Dick Law – Action News. Dick Law was the host of a daytime interview show.

As his career slid, his drinking accelerated — but that was okay by him, because his job was no longer getting in the way of his drinking.

He would arrive at the station at 9 a.m. and ad-lib the news magazine from 11 to noon. Once or twice a week, he taped a news magazine segment in the afternoon.

He was diligent about getting to work at nine, but he began every morning with a hangover: sick, headachy, with jitters that switching to decaf coffee did nothing to help. Freed from the noon news, he was clear for lunch at 12:30. He couldn't wait for his lunchtime beer.

On Dick Law's thirty-sixth birthday, he interviewed a young, eager Congressional candidate from the central part of the state. The two men hit it off: both around the same age, both with the hypersensitive egomania common to their professions. Two days after the election, Congressman-elect Joe Sylvester called Dick Law and invited him to give up his television career and become Sylvester's press secretary in DC.

Famous television personalities didn't become staffers to freshman Members of Congress, but Sylvester didn't know that.

He also didn't know Dick Law was making a quarter of the money he'd made when he first came to Boston, nor that the writing was on the wall: Dick Law was clearly in his last job at the station.

After a night of extra heavy drinking, Dick Law called Sylvester and took the job.

It took a week for Congressman Joe Sylvester to acknowledge that he'd fired Dick Law, a staffer with him ten years.

Law wasn't surprised. If his time on Capitol Hill taught him anything, it was that most people who were elected to Congress became assholes.

Most of them didn't start out that way. Among the qualities that got them elected in the first place was a certain glad-handing style of empathy. But they all had an innate trait of general assholery, buried just under the surface like an evil recessive gene. When they got elected, it emerged. It was Law's theory that Members of Congress brought it out of each other.

Sylvester's email, when it showed up in Law's in-box, managed to be both smarmy and oblique at the same time. Sylvester said he understood that people had "their own career paths," and he wished Law well.

Law shook his head as he read the message. He knew the style and the impulse. He himself perfected this tone and drafted these notes. Whoever wrote this for the boss was good. Law hoped it wasn't the new press secretary.

The only puzzling thing about the email was the postscript. Law knew Sylvester wrote it himself, because it was all in caps. Most of the time, Sylvester couldn't figure out how to turn the caps button off on his keyboard. "CALL BOBBY GALVIN AT AGS ASSN, HELP W MTG."

Law remembered Bobby Galvin, a Massachusetts political hack working in DC. Galvin specialized in "advance," arranging events. Every now and then, if you studied the photos from some meaningless event, in the background you would find Galvin looking concerned as he spoke into a microphone in his shirt cuff. The couple of times Dick Law had run into him, he thought Galvin was a self-important gas bag.

Just a week ago, Law would have given the Congressman's upper-case message a dismissive delete on his keyboard. Life was too short for Bobby Galvin. But over the last week, Law's life turned upside down. He was fired, but that was only the start. Even more of a shock to his psyche, he quit drinking.

And now, in rooms full of strangers, he was saying, "Hi, I'm Dick, and I'm an alcoholic."

He stared at the email. *What the fuck?* He reached for the phone and called Bobby Galvin.

The call was brief. The meeting of the national association of attorneys general was coming up in six weeks. Galvin was in charge of arrangements, and he needed a press liaison. Law had been recommended and he was available. Within five minutes, he had the job.

His first task was to attend a meeting that afternoon with the staff and the officers of the association.

So Galvin still wasn't going to be his best friend. But maybe he wasn't that bad....

Chapter 13

Hollis Kerrigan stepped to the front of the classroom, leaned down and picked up a gleaming white model of a wind turbine.

Chavez's iPhone vibrated inside his loose-leaf notebook. He lifted the cover and glanced in. It was from Jason.

THONG?

Jason liked to use caps. Chavez quickly looked up to more closely study the situation. *Maybe.* He let his mind wander as he watched Hollis straighten up in her tight pants.

A laser pointer knifed onto the screen in the front of the classroom, slowly moving up and down the main shaft of a wind turbine depicted on an engineering drawing.

"Each turbine, 328-feet high, has three 116-foot blades." The laser pointer moved from the turbine shaft up and down each blade.

A Google map of the area north of Burfield popped up with five animated windmills spinning away.

"Five turbines stretching a half mile along Matchic Ridge."

The slide changed: "1.5 megawatts" materialized on the screen, and then a cartoon turbine appeared next to the number.

"An individual turbine produces 1.5 megawatts of electricity," said Hollis.

A large number "5" popped into view next to the 1.5 megawatts. Then the 5 multiplied the 1.5. A new number appeared, "7.5 megawatts."

"7.5 megawatts," Hollis Kerrigan's voice moved from pedantic to cheerleader.

Up marched row after row of cartoon houses superimposed on a map of central Massachusetts.

"At projected wind flow, the Matchic Ridge Wind Farm will produce enough electricity to power 1,660 homes."

Hollis Kerrigan waited a beat before projecting her final slide. The words "Matchic Ridge Wind Farm" slowly developed. A low mountain lifted itself behind the words, bathed in an ethereal greenish yellow glow. Then one by one, five glistening wind turbines grew up out of the ridge.

"This is the future, ladies and gentlemen, a public/private partnership dedicated to local sustainability." Her voice dropped to the reverential range.

The dim energy-efficient fluorescent bulbs in Room 102 flickered on.

Mr. Summers bounded off his stool. "That was a truly amazing presentation, Ms. Kerrigan. Thank you for coming to our American Studies class. Truly inspiring."

Chavez's phone shook. He glanced down like a poker player checking his hand.

TRULY an asshole!

"Truly" was Mr. Summers' favorite word. Chavez hid a grin.

"Questions?" Hollis asked, her blue eyes sweeping the class, her left hand resting lightly on the model's housing between the main shaft and the blades.

"Let me start," Mr. Summers gushed. "Ms. Kerrigan, let me again thank you for coming here today. It's a honor to meet a person who is making a difference in so many things we care about locally — and I don't think it an exaggeration — *globally* in the areas of sustainability and climate change."

Vibration:

Summers popped a WOODY.

Chavez smiled. He was always amazed at how fast Jason could text.

"First of all, Mr. Summers, please call me Hollis," Hollis Kerrigan said, smiling warmly at the teacher. "All my friends call me Hollis."

Summers's muttonchops quivered. "Certainly, Hollis, and please return the favor. Call me Bill."

Vibration:

GAG.

"Hollis, you've done a marvelous job laying out the operations of the wind farm and how wind-power benefits all of us. Could you step back a minute and tell us how you got involved? How a community volunteer became one of the most important energy executives in the state?"

Hollis Kerrigan flushed. Not with embarrassment, but with irritation.

Hollis Kerrigan maintained a carefully constructed image: a successful entrepreneur, but conscious of her local marketplace. Today she wore lightweight ivory herringbone Talbots slacks, topped with a taupe ribbed Ralph Lauren sweater complemented by a silk Garnet Hill scarf. She wore Lands End cowhide boots with low heels. Her frosted blond hair was held in place by a Tiffany barrette.

Hollis grew up on the Gold Coast south of Boston. She attended an expensive prep school west of Boston and graduated from Wheelock, several rungs down the ladder from her parents' targets of (in descending order) Harvard, Boston College or Boston University.

Her father, James Sean Kerrigan provided well for his family in the first part of his career by installing them as recognized members of the Boston intellectual/political/educational elite caste. In the second part of his career, he provided for them by making them rich.

After meeting, courting, and marrying while students at Boston College, Jimmy and Donna Kerrigan returned to his hometown where he was elected to the state legislature at age twenty-four, while he was still in law school. Hollis and her brother were largely raised by their mother Donna, as Jimmy Kerrigan worked for votes. After only one term in the legislature, he was elected to Congress where he served three terms.

After college graduation, Hollis's now-former Congressman father lined her up as a "constituent relations coordinator" in the Capitol Hill office of a former colleague of his from Tennessee. Life as a young, single Congressional aide in Washington, DC was at times exhilarating, especially when she was able to use Jimmy Kerrigan's still-potent list of contacts to score invitations to parties and Redskins games. Work was less exciting. Answering emails from her boss's Tennessee constituents was a grind. Her first springtime in Washington brought her to a special place in hell, day after day greeting buses of Tennessee school children on their trips to Our Nation's Capital.

It was after one of those kinds of days that she met Joe Rothstein at a softball game on Anacostia Point. Playing for her Congressional office team, they somehow ended up facing a team of graduate students from American University. After dating a succession of slicky-boy Congressional staffers, Hollis was taken by the skinny bearded guy playing first when she lucked into a walk.

A post-game beer led to a date, the date led to a courtship, the courtship led to an engagement, and the engagement led to a South Shore Country Club wedding.

The Kerrigans could more easily have accepted a young lawyer, a congressional aide, or a local politician — but young love was young love, and Jimmy and Donna wondered if Hollis would ever find anyone able to put up with her high maintenance requirements. Joe Rothstein was acceptable to them … just barely. With a Ph.D. in 18th-century literature, he found an instructor's job at Fitchburg State. The Kerrigans' wedding present was the down payment on the historic "Hale House" on Burfield's Town Common.

The marriage lasted five years before fizzling out. It turned out Hollis was more interested in Hollis than in the marital partnership, and Joe, it turned out, was more interested in men.

With a nice trust fund from Jimmy's post-Congress career, Hollis could have moved to just about anywhere. But she enjoyed living in Burfield, and she told her parents that people in town were pleased that a person "of stature" was living in Hale House. She threw herself into her role as the town's volunteer extraordinaire: the annual HarvestFest, the library building committee, the town's recycling committee, the Unitarian food bank, all of which prepared her – in her mind, at least – to be managing partner of a wind farm.

With a wintry smile, Hollis Kerrigan answered the question. "Well, Mr. Summers, you make it all seem so simple. The fact is that I've been a member of the Worcester County Alternative Power Coalition for three years. My background in both the public and private sectors gave me the ideal experience to build this company."

Chavez thought Mr. Summers looked embarrassed. "What I meant to say was—"

"Perfectly fine, Bill." Hollis shut him down with a dismissive wave. "Before I answer questions from the class, let me lay out the background of the Matchic Ridge Wind Farm. As we all know, we don't want to be dependent on foreign energy, and production of fossil fuels in North America is not environmentally acceptable. As consumers we have to learn to rely on alternative sources of energy. And, as good citizens of the world, we all know we have to do our part locally. Three years ago, I began pulling this project together to answer that challenge. Our federal and state governments are doing their part by offering incentives. I know this is getting complicated, but I'm sure you are old enough to appreciate the big picture." She smiled out at 25 blank-faced teenagers.

"Now, finally! Questions? Here, in the front row."

Chavez sighed. The most urgent hand in the air belonged to Barbara Nevers, the smartest girl in the class, also the most obnoxious and the biggest kiss-ass.

"Ms. Kerrigan, thank you so much for coming here today...."

Chavez felt the vibration even before it happened. He didn't even look down. Jason hated Barbara Nevers.

"…and for showing us that you can do well by doing good."

Chavez shook his head. This was going to be even worse than he imagined. Barbara Nevers was a tool.

"Do you consider yourself a role model for young women?"

Chavez risked a glance back at Jason. Jason mouthed the words "role model" and rolled his eyes.

"What a flattering question," Hollis Kerrigan said brightly, locking eyes with Barbara Nevers. "I'm just proud to do my part. Frankly, it's my belief that young men in this community need role models more than the young women. So many boys don't have fathers in their lives. I hope I'm a role model for them as well."

In the third row, Jason looked up from his covert texting and raised his hand.

Uh-oh, thought Chavez. Jason hates Hollis. Jason used to do Hollis' yard as part of Chavez's lawn crew. Hollis caught him using the bathroom in the front hall of the house after she told him not to. She gave him a real ration of shit. She told Chavez she didn't want Jason on her property again. Chavez now did Hollis's yard personally. And now Jason was probably pissed about the no-fathers comment.

"Ms. Kerrigan, I was up on the ridge the other day and noticed the windmills don't turn very much. The wind doesn't blow from that direction. Are you sure they're in the right spot?"

Hollis looked surprised, but then she recovered. "Good question, Jason. Cost effectiveness isn't really our goal. We are in the early stages of alternate energy, and it's just important to have the turbines function. Having public acceptance is key. Sometimes leadership needs to be symbolic."

Chavez didn't understand this, but he had his own question, "Uh, Hollis, why hasn't the fire department gotten a replacement for the Brushbuster?" Right away, he could tell the question pissed Hollis off, he saw it in her face.

"Well, Chavez, that's a question of projected returns and…." Abruptly, she pulled out her cellphone and looked at the screen. "I'm sorry, I have a conference call with investors…." She flipped over the cover on her iPad, grabbed her model turbine and in three short strides reached the door.

"Hollis, we can't thank you enough," Mr. Summers sputtered, "you certainly are an example of local solutions to worldwide…." — the door closed with Hollis Kerrigan on the other side — "challenges."

Chapter 14

In the third-floor conference room just off the huge atrium of the Capitol Hill Marriott, Bobby Galvin arranged a set of poster boards on an easel. Association staffers were playing the chair game, sitting to be noticed but not so close that they'd be held responsible for something. Law arrived fresh from his noon meeting, carrying a can of caffeine-free Diet Coke. Caffeine hadn't been helpful the previous week.

That apparently was not the case in the Potomac Room, where the overly caffeinated group vibrated with pre-meeting expectation. New to the group and not sure of his role, Law shook Galvin's sweaty hand and took a seat in the corner, as far from the action as he could find.

Galvin's poster boards contained a minute-by-minute progress of the day-and-a-half-long meeting of the state attorneys general. "Attorneys general." Law had to get used to that awkward plural, he was going to be using it a lot in the next six weeks. The only time he had ever heard a plural like that was "gins and tonic." He sighed. He missed gins and tonic.

Law watched as Galvin stationed himself next to the easel and arrayed his equipment on the table. Two phones, an expensive-looking pen, and a digital watch he took off his wrist. Law shook his head.

Galvin picked up the pen and whipped it to one side like he was trying to shake something sticky off his hand. A two-foot pointer emerged. He smacked the poster board on the easel to get attention. "All right, everyone, we've just heard from the General's car. He's on his way from Reagan. His ETA is" — he picked up the heavy watch from the table — "nine minutes."

"The General's car?" A week ago, Law would have rolled his eyes and made a snide comment to whoever was seated next to him. "The *General's* car." Now, he took a deep breath. This was a time for serenity. His new world.

Suddenly the door swung open. A tall woman with short red hair in a Massachusetts State Police uniform stepped into the room. Law sucked in his breath. She was stunning. Her uniform shirt was crisply pressed, covered with medals and tucked into — Law glanced down — what did they call those? "Jodhpurs?" Below the jodhpurs were knee-high black boots. Polished. *What was it that people texted? OMG.*

The state trooper looked around the room, a grim and professional survey. Then she stepped aside.

In the doorway stood Ethan Caleb Pierce III, Attorney General of the Commonwealth of Massachusetts. He stood next to the trooper. She was only a few inches shorter than her 6' 5" boss.

Law's eyes widened as he connected the dots. Ethan Pierce. Massachusetts. Bobby Galvin. Massachusetts. Joe Sylvester, Massachusetts. Joe Guthrie, Massachusetts. Law remembered Pierce was elected in-coming president of the national association the previous year. Did Guthrie make a call on his behalf?

Now it was beginning to make sense. He wondered if Ethan Pierce would remember him. *Please don't have him remember me...*

Galvin hastily dropped his phone on the table and stood up. He tried to take control. "Sorry, General, we weren't expecting...."

Wearing a navy blue suit and a pink tie imprinted with jumping trout, Ethan Pierce surveyed the room with an amused grin and sparkling eyes. He studied people's faces for recognition.

He turned to the state trooper. "Stand down, Sergeant Doherty, they look harmless. Just a bunch of Washington bureaucrats." Pierce drew out the last word to emphasize his joke.

The people in the room were startled by the security check. It was a meeting to brag about when someone brought security.

Law sat with his head partially down, not hiding, but not making it easy, either. He did not want to be recognized in his very first meeting.

"*Dick Law*," Pierce boomed. Then, drawing the words out for dramatic effect: "*Action ... News.*"

All eyes in the room followed Pierce's gaze to the corner. In the corner was a guy no one recognized.

Pierce continued. "Dick Law used to be the best TV guy in Boston."

There was an uncomfortable silence in the room. *If the best TV guy in Boston was in the room, why didn't we know him?*

Galvin filled the gap with forced bonhomie. "I was going to do introductions later, but I guess now's a good time to introduce our newest member of the team. Dick Law, until recently Press Secretary for Congressman Joe Sylvester, is going to handle media for the conference. Today's his first day, and I guess he and our chairman already know each other." Law noted these last words did not seem filled with good will.

Pierce moved to the other end of the table from Galvin, took his suit jacket off, hung it on his chair and sat down. It was not his assigned seat. His seat was at the head of the table next to Bobby Galvin, where there was a neatly typed agenda and a bottle of water.

"Okay, who's running this rodeo? Let's get a saddle on this bronco."

The room shifted with a collective air of unease. Accustomed to the orchestrated entries and exits of the most important figure in the meeting and the carefully scripted progress through a printed agenda, Pierce's loose style and cowboy syntax caused some squirming.

Galvin, still thrown off his game, quickly retrieved his pointer and began his run-through of the upcoming meeting. It took an hour and Pierce listened carefully. As Galvin reached his last poster board, Pierce pushed back from the table and stood up. The staffers around the room collectively jerked their heads. There were always a couple of questions pre-arranged by staff to show the boss was listening.

"Sounds like you've got it in hand, Bobby. Just enough time in Our Nation's Capital for the state's chief law enforcement officers to pick out their chairs on the Supreme Court."

Those few in the room who got the joke — Pierce was poking fun at his fellow attorneys general — smiled. Except for Law, who laughed out loud. He stopped when he realized he was the only one laughing but saw that Pierce was grinning at him, sharing the joke.

Pierce moved and Sergeant Doherty opened the door. "I guess that's it. I'll see you all next month." Then stopped. "Bobby, take a look at the afternoon schedule on the first day. You've got the esteemed Attorney General from Michigan chairing two sessions at once in different rooms. I happen to know he walks on water — just ask him, he'll tell you — but I doubt he can run two sessions at once."

The conference room was filled with the sound of agendas being shuffled and the murmured agreement that Attorney General Enslin was double booked. Galvin stood back and was looking at his poster board in disbelief, partly that he could have made such a rookie mistake, but mostly that an elected official paid attention in a meeting and figured it out. That was a first for Galvin.

Pierce wasn't done. "Bobby, do you mind if I borrow Mr. Law for a bit? He and I need to catch up." He turned and walked out, leaving the door open.

Galvin, still flustered over the turn of events concerning the agenda could only nod. The others in the room, aware that the newest guy in the room was just singled out, only stared.

Law got to his feet and headed to the door. As if being called out —

"Dick Law - Action News" — wasn't bad enough.

Pierce waited in the hall as Law caught up. He stuck out his hand. "Ethan Pierce, I don't think we've ever met."

Law took his hand.

"And this is Sergeant Maureen Doherty, one of the Commonwealth's finest. Be careful of her, she's a trained assassin." Law shook hands with the tall state trooper. It was all he could do not to wince under her grip. He studied her face for a reaction to Pierce's "assassin" remark. All he saw was a polite smile.

Pierce turned. "Walk with me. What are you doing in there? What happened with Sylvester?"

Law hesitated a bit, unsure of how to phrase it. It was only a week. His mind was on other things. He hadn't worked up any talking points to describe the abrupt turn in his career.

"I'm consulting now. My first project is this conference." It was all he could manage on the spur of the moment.

"I heard that empty suit Sylvester fired you. True?" Pierce's long strides were taking them down the hall, following Sergeant Doherty's black boots.

Law looked up at the taller man. "I guess word gets around." He tried to re-group, quickly processing how forthcoming he should be. He started again.

"Joe hired a new chief of staff. She wanted her own person."

"And he fired you. You were there for him since the beginning. Joe Sylvester is a bottom feeder." Pierce was an avid fisherman. "Bottom feeder" was a serious epithet.

They were now on the escalator headed down into the humid atrium restaurant. Law knew there was a very pleasant bar laid out under the indoor trees on the right.

The escalator moved down, Doherty on one step, Pierce on the second, Law on the third. Law was now eye-to-eye with Pierce, who turned to look at him.

"Are you going to stay in DC?"

"I haven't decided."

"How about coming back to Boston?"

"I don't know. I need a job."

Doherty reached up, and her hand was on the small of Pierce's back, turning him as they reached the end of the escalator. Like they were a dance team, thought Law.

Pierce stopped and seemed to look off in the distance. Then he looked at his watch. "Sergeant Doherty, okay with you if we miss this shuttle and catch the next one?"

Law knew the DC-Boston shuttle ran every half hour at this time of day. It would be easy to catch the next one. Doherty nodded.

"Sergeant, are you still the designated driver?"

Law sensed that this wasn't the first time the Attorney General and his bodyguard had this conversation.

Again, Doherty nodded, a slight smile on her lips, playing along with the routine. She turned her head slightly toward Law. *Was that a wink? Did she just wink at me?*

Pierce was already headed to a table shielded by a potted palm. "Let's see what kind of beers these people are brewing down here."

Pierce sampled four different local beers, and he made several trips to the men's room. Doherty accompanied him and discreetly stood guard at the door.

Law kept pace with four tonic waters with lime. He kept waiting for a comment from Pierce, but Pierce didn't seem to notice.

During beers two, three and four, Pierce laid out his idea. "I need someone on my staff to collect public safety data, starting with fire information. Right now it's all over the place, the Fire Marshall's Office, various district attorneys, the state police, and local departments. There's not one central source of historic information."

"Why pull the information together?" Law thought the assignment was pretty vague.

Pierce took another sip and Law watched, trying not to let his envy show. Those beers looked good.

"Without a central database, nobody can learn anything. You don't know anything about patterns. How and why do fires start and spread? What works in terms of prevention? What equipment works?"

Law wondered how to ask the question without coming across as ungrateful. So, he just asked it. "Why me? It sounds like you need someone with more research experience."

Pierce leaned his head back and laughed. Really laughed. It was infectious. Doherty smiled and then laughed along, although Law was unsure what was so funny.

"Law, someone in your shoes can't be too choosy. But, just to be nice, I'll tell you why. You're bright and you used to be a go-getter. Hell, you were the editor of the *Daily Iowan*; you beat out a lot of corn-fed Hawkeyes for that job. We don't know each other very well, but I've always been a big fan of yours, despite that "Action News" bullshit. I'm betting, even working in television and in Congress, that you haven't lost that midwestern work ethic. I need this done, I need somebody good. Now, don't make me beg, Sergeant Doherty thinks it's unseemly. You've got the job. Finish up this jerk-off conference and come back to Boston."

Law just sat there. His eyes stung a bit, as he thought about what Pierce had said about him. He hoped Doherty didn't see his tears. How did Pierce know he was editor of the college paper?

"Okay." It was all he could manage.

Pierce nodded, stood up and shrugged his suit jacket on. Doherty checked her watch. She led the way to the escalator.

A week ago, this would have been celebration time. A new job, back to the old town. Now Law's world was turned upside down. On the escalator, he wanted to look back down at the bar. Instead he faced forward and found a rear view of Doherty in her jodhpurs, two steps above. Not the worst alternative.

Chapter 15

Fitchburg might have been something without the Fitchburg Mill, but most residents couldn't imagine what. The gargantuan granite-and-brick building, designed to support the operation of tons of machinery, had walls two feet thick. Its doorways were framed with wide arched granite. Built by Augustus Fitch in 1831, the mill was the community's economic lifeblood. Crouched over the Nashua River in the center of town, the mill sucked in river water to produce hydropower and coolant for its gears, and then returned the favor by dumping leftover paper dye and other waste products into the sluggish water as it flowed out the other side. One glance at the Nashua told the residents of Fitchburg what color paper the mill was making that day.

The Fitches and their fellow Yankees lived in the grand mansions on Belfer Hill on the east side of town, while their workers — mainly hired French and Finnish immigrants — lived on Munroe Hill on the west side of town.

The mill had more than just a physical presence in the center of town; it had an olfactory one, as well. There was no way to disguise it; papermaking created a rancid stink. In an ironic meteorological twist, the prevailing wind blew the smell of the mill directly up the Yankees' Belfer Hill. They gamely called it "the smell of money," but that did little to mitigate the nasal misery of a westerly breeze on a hot, humid day. On those days, lace curtains blew in the open windows of the three-deckers on blue-collar Munroe Hill, while windows slammed shut all over Belfer Hill.

In the mid-1970s, environmental regulators began to crack down on the smell and pollution of New England mills. The Yankee mill owners might have fought back harder, but foreign competition and high energy costs were already putting their operations on slippery economic footing. All across New England, mills – including Fitchburg – began to close. The prospect of tearing them down was daunting. Mill cities struggled to find re-uses for the buildings.

It was a Saturday and, as usual, the boys were free agents. Jason's mom was sleeping in, Chavez's dad was at the office, and Catherine Simons was quilting with friends. Fueled by caffeine and sugar, Jason rode shotgun in Chavez's pickup, talking non-stop all through the 32-mile trip from Burfield to Fitchburg.

He led off with today's unlikely pairing:

"Mr. Sanderson and Ms. Spencer."

Sanderson was the ascetic, vaguely creepy chemistry teacher who ate three cashews and an apple every day for lunch. Ms. Spencer was the teacher of every boy's MILF fantasies.

Chavez swallowed a sip of Mountain Dew. "Disgusting." And then, after thinking about it a moment or two, "She'd kill him."

After several miles of commentary on passing cars and the usual complaints about popular kids, Jason wound down. "So, who's this old fuck we're going to see?" he asked.

Chavez thought again about his decision to invite Jason. Chavez was nervous enough, wondering if he could ask an adult questions and take notes. He'd brought Jason along for moral support, but the idea that Jason might say "old fuck" in front of ninety-year-old Roland Lamontagne, Fitchburg's retired fire chief, made him even more anxious.

It took Chavez three phone calls to Lamontagne to arrange the meeting, though the first call really didn't count, since Lamontagne hung up on him. Chief Jokkinen said Lamontagne might be senile, but in the second and third conversations, Chavez wondered if Lamontagne wasn't drunk.

Following the directions of his GPS, Chavez drove into Fitchburg, right past the massive buildings that were the Fitchburg Mill.

Halfway up Munroe Hill they found a tiny New England Cape Cod with "231" on the fascia board over the front door. The 3 was missing, leaving an outline and two screw holes.

The boys walked up the crumbling cement steps and rang the bell. There was no response. Chavez took a breath and rang the bell again. He had several elderly lawn-care customers, so waiting for an old person to come to the door wasn't new to him.

Chavez wore his usual outfit with his yellow Burfield VFD windbreaker. Jason wore jeans, a black t-shirt, his gray hoodie, and a new cap, with the Michelin Man on skates and holding a hockey stick. Chavez sighed. He asked Jason to dress up.

From inside they eventually heard mumbling, then shuffling. A deadbolt on the door slid open. Then another deadbolt. Then another. Finally the door swung open, and a tiny, bald man blinked at them from the shadowy interior. A massive hearing aid protruded from one ear. He held a second hearing aid in his hand. "What?" he croaked, as if that was his first word of the day.

"Chief Lamontagne, I'm Chavez Simons. This is Jason Morrill."

"Christ on a crutch, kid, stop yelling. I can hear just fine." Lamontagne inserted a hearing aid. "You woke me up. It takes me a while to get my wits about me."

Chavez began again: "My name is—"

"I know who you are," snapped Lamontagne. "I wrote it on my calendar. Did that asshole Terry Jokkinen tell you I'm senile?"

"Well, no, nothing like that...."

"Come on in, I haven't got all day." Lamontagne waved Chavez onto a sofa in the living room, and he sent Jason to a rocking chair. "Go easy on that chair," he said. "That used to be my wife's. And take that fucking hat off in the house. This ain't no hockey game."

Jason grabbed his hat from his head and sat down in an awkward lurch. The chair creaked. His face flushed, Jason looked stunned. He clutched the chair's arms and tried to keep it from rocking.

Chavez looked around. The couch was covered with lumpy paisley cushions, and a Formica coffee table was strewn with newspapers and ashtrays filled with turd-sized cigar butts. On the floor next to the coffee table was a crumbling cardboard box held together with masking tape.

Lamontagne backed up toward a decrepit tweed Barcalounger, the fabric held together with duct tape, and dropped backward into the chair. Lamontagne grunted as if the footrest snapping up surprised him, and he picked up a cigar butt and a Bic fire starter. He flicked the lever on the fire starter, and a five-inch flame erupted. He lit the cigar with a few wheezy gasps, and a cloud of smoke rose around his head. Chavez looked around, but apparently Lamontagne, even through he was a fire chief, had never bothered to install any smoke detectors. Lamontagne coughed and spat into a filthy handkerchief. "All right, which one of you is the Mexican?"

Chavez knew what the old man was asking. "Sir, I'm Chavez," he said, "but I'm not Mexican. My parents named me after Cesar Chavez, a leader of the California migrant labor movement." Sometimes this was enough of an explanation. Chavez hoped it would be.

Lamontagne examined Chavez. At last, he apparently decided he just didn't care enough to pursue the matter. "Whatever you say," he muttered.

"As I told you on the phone, Chief Lamontagne," said Chavez, "I'm researching the 1981 Fitchburg Mill fire."

"And Jokkinen told you to come talk to me." Lamontagne took another puff of his cigar. "I guess that dumb Finn's getting smarter."

Chavez felt the urge to defend Jokkinen, but he stopped himself. He knew it would be pointless. "The Fitchburg Mill fire was one of the biggest fires in the history of Massachusetts," he said, "and you know more about it than anyone." Chavez practiced this line, to use in case Lamontagne proved to be difficult.

The old man focused again, picked up an amber-colored drink — Chavez could smell alcohol — and relaxed back in his chair. "Terry Jokkinen is right about one thing," said Lamontagne. "I know more about that fire than any man alive, and" — pointing to the old cardboard box — "I have the only records."

"Anything you can tell me?"

"I was in my second year as Fitchburg Fire Chief...."

Once Lamontagne got going, he warmed to the task, clearly relishing re-telling the story.

Chavez wrote as fast as he could in his spiral notebook.

The fire took place on the Saturday following Thanksgiving, 1981. Three of the mill buildings went up in a spectacular nighttime fire. Apparatus from 80 fire departments, from as far away as Portland, Maine, and Albany, New York, raced through the night to help fight the fire.

Chavez risked a look over at Jason, who had scooted the cardboard box closer and pulled out a file folder. Bored with Lamontagne's account, it looked like Jason was using the file folder to hide the fact that he was playing some game on his phone.

The story took an hour to tell. The mill buildings were in the process of being renovated into a low-income housing development. While the buildings themselves were granite and brick, the interior structure of the buildings provided plenty of fuel for the fire. The fire spread rapidly, because of papermaking chemicals that leached into the wooden floors. Miraculously, no one was killed, and there was only one injury to a firefighter.

Eventually, Lamontagne's voice got slower and fainter.

In all, he made four trips to the bathroom — and one bathroom trip involved a detour to the kitchen to refill his glass.

Toward the end, there were longer pauses between sentences. Then he stopped. He was tired.

Chavez turned the pages of his notebook back to the beginning, where he compiled a list of questions. He scanned the list, picked one, and looked across at Lamontagne.

The retired chief's eyes were closed. He had his drink in his hand. "Chief?"

Lamontagne opened his eyes, blinked, and re-focused. "What?"

"This fire was huge," said Chavez, "but it jumped right over two of the mill buildings. Why did that happen? Do fires jump around like that?"

Roland Lamontagne shifted in his chair, focusing on the question. "That fire…." He levered his Barcalounger into an upright position, grasped the arms, and began to stand. "Time for a nap," he said, more to himself than to Chavez.

Lamontagne pried a hearing aid out of an ear and slipped it in the breast pocket of his flannel shirt. He was done.

Lamontagne shuffled down the hall toward the back of the house. He was talking softly: "Really weird, the way that fire hopped over two buildings. Didn't make sense. Jokkinen parked his truck in the wrong place. Lost his leg. Poor son of a bitch." He reached the end of the hallway and turned into his bedroom. "Let yourselves out. Lock it."

Just 15 miles from Fitchburg, Jason insisted on Chavez pulling over at the Cumberland Farms next to the Gardner rotary, so he could re-load on snacks and Mountain Dew.

Chavez fretted about his meeting with Lamontagne. "We didn't get what I needed," he complained. "Chief Lamontagne never said why the fire jumped over those buildings. We need to go back and talk to him again."

Jason ripped open a bag of Taco Dippers and with his mouth full, he said, "Dude." He made the word two syllables, to emphasize his point. "Not … gonna … happen. I've had enough of that creepy little gnome."

"After big fires, they do diagrams of where the fire burned and where it didn't," said Chavez. "There's got to be a copy of the Fitchburg Mill fire map in that box. I didn't get to see the box."

Jason fiddled with his phone. "Does this look like what you need?" he asked.

Chavez studied the screen. Behind an array of Jason's greasy fingerprints, he saw a picture of a piece of graph paper with shapes drawn on it. Some shapes were shaded in, while others were only outlined. The shaded shapes were labeled. On the bottom of the page someone wrote "Fitchburg Mill fire."

Chavez looked up at Jason. "How the hell?" he asked.

Jason gave him as cool a look as he could manage with his mouth full of chips. "I had to do something while Chatty Cathy was going on and on. So I took a couple of pictures of some stuff in that file."

"I thought you were playing Angry Birds or texting or something."

Jason smiled. "Well, yeah, I did touch base with some of my homies" — though they both knew the only "homie" either of them had was the other — "but in between, I took shots of some stuff that looked interesting. Not interesting to me, for sure, but to you and your fire buddies."

Chavez stuck out his right hand. Jason took it. Awkwardly, with his left hand, Chavez reached across the front seat for Jason's shoulder. Jason shook his right hand free from their grasp and recoiled. "Dude! Were you just going for a 'bro'?" Chavez looked crushed. His first-ever attempt at a cool handshake was interrupted before consummation.

Jason smiled widely. "Now I know you're grateful. We'll practice the next time. You'll get better before you know it."

Chavez was proud of his room; it was arranged just the way he liked it. His collections — coins, butterflies and stamps — were on bookshelves next to his Stephen King novels. His prize vinyl LPs were in a plastic milk crate next to his desk, and the Beach Boys "Pet Sounds" album played on his refurbished Radio Shack stereo. His saltwater aquarium gurgled in the corner, and a lava lamp bubbled up orange blobs on the table next to his reading chair.

Except for the noises in the room, it was quiet. As usual, he was alone in the house.

Chavez taped Jason's fire map to a large piece of corrugated cardboard in front of his desk. If he mapped out his projects on something he could see, it helped him with his writing troubles. When they were kids, he and Jason spent hours in the woods doing treasure maps and maps to their secret forts. He had maps all over his room.

His printer spewed out hard copies of Jason's pictures. Chavez watched the tray fill up, amazed at the number of shots Jason had taken of the material in Lamontagne's box. No wonder he was so quiet. On the tab of a manila folder, Chavez carefully wrote "Fitchburg Mill Fire." He grabbed the stack of sheets from the printer. The top one was another map. He looked at it curiously and then taped it on the cardboard next to the fire map. At the bottom it said "Fitchburg Mill Elderly Housing." It looked familiar.

Chapter 16

Peter Simons met Jimmy Kerrigan three years before, at a neighborhood New Year's Eve party at Hollis's house.

Passing through the front hall on his way to the dining room, Peter casually checked himself out in the mirror. He thought he looked good in his trademark denim shirt, tan Carhartts pants and hiking boots. Since it was New Years Eve, he wore a calico bandanna tied loosely around his neck. With one eye on his wife in the living room, Peter maneuvered through the other guests toward the buffet. Years ago when Catherine Simons declared herself a vegetarian, of course he'd joined her. Since then, he cheated every time he could get away with it. He looked forward to coming to Hollis Kerrigan's party ever year. The meatballs were primo.

"Peter." Nervous about his plate of contraband, he jumped and then he drew back. It was Hollis. Hollis always talked louder than she needed to, even with all the noise in the room. She took his arm, and he smiled when his elbow made contact with her breast. Then she yelled in his ear. "My father is here. He wants to talk to me about some kind of project. He wants to know if I know anything about the local permitting process. Do you do that?"

Peter paused, taking his time as he considered the question. He also wanted to prolong the breast-elbow linkage. Hollis was always bragging about her father, who used to be a Congressman from south of Boston. He thought about the question. Yes, he practiced law, but in tiny, undeveloped Burfield, there wasn't much call for "permitting." Usually, when someone wanted to build something, they went to a town board and got their okay unless people thought it was crazy. As a lawyer, you couldn't charge for that kind of thing. Then he thought about his anemic annual billings and his wife's pointed suggestion that he contribute more to the family income. "Yeah," he said shortly, "I do that."

Hollis turned and spoke over her shoulder on their way into the other room. "Daddy's got one of his friends with him. He doesn't really fit in. Try not to make him uncomfortable."

Peter saw they were headed towards two men in the corner. The first guy was in his seventies, medium height with long gray hair; he looked like the kind of actor they'd cast as an Irish poet. He wore a navy blue suit with a white dress shirt and fancy silk tie. The second guy was overweight, maybe 60, wearing a too-small open-necked shirt. In his front pocket, he had an assortment of pens and pencils.

"Peter, I'd like to have you meet my father, James Sean Kerrigan." Peter watched Hollis. She was preening. She was certainly proud of her dad.

The guy in the fancy suit stuck out his hand. "Peter, good to meet you. Hollis has many good things to say about you." Immediately, Peter wondered about what Hollis had said about him. They were only neighbors, he didn't know her all that well, did he have a good reputation as a lawyer?

Kerrigan turned. "Say hello to George Fleming from Plymouth Engineering. He and I work on projects together." Peter stuck out his hand. Fleming just nodded. He had a plate of meatballs in one hand and a beer in another.

Kerrigan started right in. "Peter, since I left Congress, I've mainly been doing housing projects, but with all the recent push toward alternative energy, I've had my eye on some other opportunities. George here has the details. I'll let him explain."

Fleming swallowed the meatball he was chewing. He took a sip of beer and put it down on a nearby table. He pulled a crumpled napkin from his pants pocket and wiped his lips. Peter saw Hollis was getting antsy.

"A wind farm," said Fleming. "Five, one-point-five-megawatt turbines. There are a number of federal grants and incentives to the developer. Burfield is in an area the state has designated as a depressed economic zone, which allows tax credits for investors."

Peter listened closely, Fleming was smart and to the point. He sure didn't talk like he looked.

Fleming continued. "We have an agreement from the university system to donate a portion of the University Forest for the project."

Peter interrupted. "On Matchic Ridge? They'll give you that land? The town would never go for it." He had seen videos of huge wind power turbines. Matchic Ridge was the highest point in town. The University Forest was like a shrine. All those old growth trees. People would be up in arms.

Jimmy Kerrigan spoke up, his voice smooth and calm. "Peter, since you're a member of the Bar I don't need to tell you this, but the town doesn't have much say in the matter. It's university property." Peter started to interrupt, but Kerrigan held up his hand. "And certainly with a project of this scope, our community partners would receive ample benefits. And where there are local permitting requirements, we expect to hire local folks who have some sway in town." Peter thought about what he just heard. He didn't know exactly, but it sounded like there was money available to grease the skids.

Hollis spoke up. "Daddy, people out here are so" — she looked around and lowered her voice — "backward. I don't think they'd go for it, I mean you should see what goes on at Town Meeting."

Jimmy Kerrigan's tone was serious and thoughtful: "Hollis, if I've learned one thing in public life, it's that sometimes people need to be educated. Enlightened people need to show the way. Real leaders in the community. Sometimes it's time for a new generation to step forward. That's why it's imperative in these cases to find the right managing partner. Someone who has roots in the community but stands for new ideas."

There was a silence. Peter didn't know what was coming next. *Were they going to ask him to run the wind farm? Was that what this was about? His astrologer told him his life was going to take a turn. Was this it?*

Kerrigan put his arm around his daughter. "Hollis, we had you in mind as managing partner. Of course you'd have to give up most of your volunteer activities, but the pay is pretty good."

Hollis? Peter was confused and hurt. *Kerrigan wanted his daughter to run a wind farm?* But Peter was partly relieved. He didn't think he was up to the job, but Hollis? Hollis could barely handle her booth at the Burfield HarvestFest.

Hollis looked like she'd had a visit from her fairy godmother. For once, she was at a loss for words. Finally she spoke, affecting a serious, businesslike voice. "Daddy, I think it's…I'm…a good choice. I've spent my career addressing local approaches to…."

Kerrigan silenced Hollis with a wave of his hand. "And, Peter, it's going to be Hollis's first big decision, but I can't imagine a better choice than you for our local counsel." He smiled his brilliant smile, a little more conspiratorially than before. "It will take a chunk of your time. Can you spare it?"

Peter took a breath. When he started out, he imagined his legal practice would be dedicated to social justice. What he really did was largely worker's compensation and disability claims, and not too many of them, truth be told. He paused for a second or two to consider. He didn't want to seem too eager. Then he answered. "Yeah. I think I can handle it."

Chapter 17

Hollis's herringbone slacks made a slight wispy sound as they slid off the ass that, earlier in the day, captivated every male in Mr. Spring's American Studies class. As the pants reached her thighs, she reached down and held them in place. Hollis rarely showed much skin during sex. She spread her legs just a little, bent over the arm of the sofa and propped herself up on a throw pillow.

She wiggled her now naked and upturned bottom from side to side. "Let's go, Peter, I'm ready." She was impatient. She wasn't specifically impatient for sex; she was always impatient.

Peter would have liked to savor the view, but he knew the time window between Hollis's "I'm ready" and "I've lost the mood" was razor thin.

With his pants and black bikini Hanes jockeys around his ankles, he took half a step forward and reached down to adjust his aim.

After three years, Hollis Kerrigan and Peter Simons had this drill down. It took less time than putting new paper in the copier, and it involved just about as much passion. There wasn't that much affection. Office sex just seemed to be part of working together.

Hollis reached back under her with her right hand. Peter inched forward. She made a prim squeaky noise. Peter knew there wasn't much time left. It was her signal that it was time for him to be finished. She gave him five seconds, stood up, and turned around.

"Why do I have to go to the goddam Lion's Club?" She pulled her pants up and zipped.

Peter sighed and pulled up his own pants. He didn't think he was done, but it didn't matter. Hollis always had the next thing on her mind.

"It's the one-year anniversary of the project. The Lion's Club is the only game in town. This is our best shot." Peter did his best to be patient as he explained. He and Hollis Kerrigan had this very same conversation maybe — Peter considered — five times before?

Hollis Kerrigan's aversion to Lion's Club meetings was borne at her family's dining room table, listening to her father complain. For most politicians, Lion's Club meetings were like colonoscopies. They were probing, humiliating and sometimes revealed problem issues. Lion's Clubs offered politicians the best and worst of their livelihoods. The best: a collection of concerned, informed and opinionated citizens, nearly all of whom voted. The worst: exactly the same.

The Burfield Lion's Club met monthly in the dining room of the Burfield Country Club, set above the eighteenth green of their award-winning golf course. In the distance, the turbines spun slowly on the ridge.

During the wind farm permitting process three years before, Hollis, George Fleming and Peter dutifully made the rounds to community groups. For the most part, the older and longer-term residents of town weren't impressed. They didn't take kindly when newcomers — or anyone else, for that matter — hatched ideas that would affect the community. And to be sure, the sight of five 300-hundred foot tall wind turbines on a de-nuded ridge above town would forever change the look of their tidy little New England town.

The wind farm team made an effort to address local concerns. Fleming's engineering firm produced studies rebutting each one of the objections: The "whooshing" noise from the turbine blades? The turbine noise was similar to the decibel levels produced by a distant highway. Yes, birds and bats would die, but at "sustainable" levels. And, as to the highly subjective concern about the "view-scape": Fleming produced reams of surveys of residents in the vicinity of wind farms around the country, mostly in the upper Midwest, Texas and California, that showed that people actually liked the sights of whirling vanes.

While the studies had some effect in getting the project approved, community partnerships closed the deal. That was a term Fleming and Kerrigan used. Peter thought it was a nice way of saying, "bribe."

It was a local bonanza. A new fire truck for Chief Jokkinen. A phased-in new source of property taxes. A 25-year reduced-cost power agreement for residents of the Town of Burfield, the state university system and anybody within the "viewscape" of the wind farm. Unbelievable deals for investors.

In the end, the project was approved by all the required state and local boards.

But there were quiet conditions for all this promised largesse. Nothing would be realized until the wind farm was "at capacity." That was a key part of the deal that most people in town missed. Until now.

Peter knew, as Hollis sat at the head table at the monthly meeting of the Burfield Lion's Club, that capacity had not been met. And she sure as shit didn't want to talk about that today.

A sudden bell clanging got everyone's attention. John "Jack" Cunningham, owner of the Cunningham Insurance Agency and president of the club, used a miniature mallet to rap a mounted ship's bell. The room began to quiet, and he stood and moved to the podium.

Feedback squealed from the microphone. "All right, Lions, let's settle down," he began with a big smile. Peter watched Hollis reach down beside her to retrieve her laptop from her Dooney and Bourke briefcase.

Waitresses finished clearing the tables, but the table conversation continued. Cunningham pressed on. "Lions, I'd like your attention." There was more conversation. "Sergeant at Arms, we may use your services?"

The sound of a gunshot filled the room. All eyes jerked to Leland Bird, owner of Bird Automotive, who stood with what appeared to be a German Luger. The barrel was smoking and the smell of gunpowder wafted over the room. Alex McVie bowed over his empty plate with his hands over his ears. He had continued to chat after Cunningham called for quiet. A daylong ear ringing from Leland's cap pistol was his punishment.

Slowly, McVie stood and reached in the back pocket of his suit pants for his wallet. He extracted a dollar bill and handed it over to a grinning Leland Bird.

After an initial stunned silence, the room erupted in appreciative laughter and scattered applause. Somebody got "shot" every meeting. The Lions loved it.

Peter took a deep breath and looked at Hollis. Her face was screwed into her characteristic frown. She hated fun.

"Thank you, Mr. Sergeant at Arms," Cunningham said from the podium.

"We have a guest speaker today who has been perhaps our most prominent citizen in the past couple of years. Hollis Kerrigan is the founder and managing partner of the Matchic Ridge Wind Farm. In three short years, the wind farm has gone from an idea to reality. And as all of us here in Burfield know, at least all of us who have looked up recently" — Cunningham injected what seemed to be a planned chuckle — "a reality it has become."

Peter watched Hollis turn on her laptop and test the power switch on her laser pointer. Her PowerPoint presentation was her security blanket.

"Yesterday, Hollis went 'full power' up on the ridge when she went from one turbine to five. Today she's here to deliver her first annual report. With no further ado, ladies and gentlemen, Hollis Kerrigan."

Hollis stood to polite applause. She wore a navy Armani pantsuit with a discreet pink pinstripe. The fact that the suit cost more than a good used car was lost on everyone in the room except a fashion-conscious waitress.

As Hollis moved to the podium with her laptop and pointer, Leland Bird moved behind the head table and lowered an old-fashioned movie screen from the ceiling. Leland then came to Hollis's side, reached inside the podium and hit the power switch for a projector directed at the screen. The screen was bathed in white light. Hollis handed him the connecting cord from her laptop. It would link her computer to the projector. He shoved the other end into a port on the podium and went off to dim the lights.

Hollis took a sip of water, cleared her throat and adjusted the microphone. After all the presentations and community meetings, she still had butterflies before a speech. She did fine when making a canned presentation, but she wasn't comfortable just talking. She looked to Peter for encouragement. He saw her looking at him just as he glanced up from his phone. He knew he'd hear about this later.

"Ladies and gentlemen," she began with a smile, "it's lovely to be here at the Burfield Lion's Club. It has been a remarkable year, and I am pleased to be able to deliver the first annual report of the Matchic Ridge Wind Farm."

Hollis scrawled the words on her napkin, which she held in her left hand as a cue card. She crumbled the napkin and placed her left index finger on the laptop's touch screen to display her first PowerPoint slide. In her right hand she held her laser pointer.

Peter had the PowerPoint on his phone, and he followed along. The first slide had "Matchic Ridge Annual Report" on the screen. He heard Hollis read the words. The background featured a stylized caricature of five wind turbines, intentionally smaller than reality in relation to their surrounding. Beyond the layout and design of the PowerPoint —which Hollis considered her forte — George Fleming prepared the text of the presentation.

Hollis trained the laser on the screen to emphasize what she just said. The bright red dot hit a totally white screen, glowing in the darkened dining room.

She looked back down at the laptop and Peter looked at his phone. The turbine blades were turning — Hollis loved that part — but there was nothing on the screen.

"Something's not working here." She smiled gamely, glancing over at Peter for assistance.

Leland Bird shuffled up next to the podium and reached down with blackened fingers. He grasped the connecting cord from the laptop and shoved it harder into the accessory port like he was seating a radiator hose.

"Careful," Hollis said, a little too sharply.

Leland shrugged and moved away.

A look at the screen: Nothing.

Hollis reached down and advanced to the second slide: "A Remarkable Success Story: Community-based, economical, sustainable energy."

Peter looked from his phone to the projector screen. Nothing.

Jack Cunningham rose to his feet to take control of his meeting. "Well, Hollis, looks like the a/v equipment is on the fritz. No biggie. Why don't you just give us the speech without the movie?"

Peter knew this would paralyze Hollis. Her presentations were always on slides. That's how she did it. Reading each point and emphasizing with her pointer. She was fucked without her PowerPoint.

Leland Bird turned the house lights back on. The audience blinked and shifted in their chairs.

Hollis retrieved the crumbled napkin cue card and surreptitiously touched her forehead. She was pale.

Peter was frozen. It was like watching a car accident on ice. Slow moving, but with no recourse.

"Well," Hollis began, her voice a half octave higher, "I guess we have some technical difficulties here...." She recovered a bit. "We may be able to produce electricity, but today we have a faux pax with electrical appliances."

She looked brightly at her audience. Blank faces. "Faux pax" was not a word commonly used at the Burfield Lion's Club.

The speech was finished in record time. Looking down at her computer screen, Hollis read off the bullet points as she pushed rapidly through the slides.

"....dependent on foreign energy and fossil fuels.... alternative sources of energy" She looked up to audience, they seemed bored. She looked back down at the laptop.

"...good citizens of the world...do our part locally...socially responsible investors, public/private investment...stakeholder gainsharing...." Look up, look down.

"...federal and state incentives...five operating turbines." Look up, look down.

Finally, she reached Slide 38 and almost gasped as she spit out the words, "MISSION STATEMENT Matchic Ridge Wind Farm, A Local Sustainable Solution to a Worldwide Crisis."

"Questions?" Peter knew Hollis hated the question and answer part of a presentation, but today she threw out the invitation like a lifeline. "Yes," she said brightly, "Chief Jokkinen."

Peter's stomach lurched. *Hollis' improvised speech must have fried her brain to call on Terry Jokkinen. What was she thinking?*

Jokkinen stood, wearing his white chief's uniform shirt. "Hollis," he began slowly, "that all sounded great. You've finally got your five windmills up and going 24/7."

"That's right, Chief."

"Well, Hollis, I'll be blunt, where's our new fire truck?"

It wasn't as though Hollis Kerrigan didn't know this question was coming. She and Peter prepped for the speech, and the subject of the fire truck and other promised community benefits were a hot topic around town.

But the disastrous experience of having to give her big speech without her slides left her shaken. She paused and her mind went blank. It was clear she forgot what they scripted.

The audience began to mutter.

"Chief," Hollis said, with a long pause. In her brainlock, she reverted to her stump speech she used countless times during the permitting process. "Chief, as a public/private partnership, we are well aware of our responsibility to gainshare with our stakeholders. As capacity is reached, the Wind Farm will trigger the base thresholds of the negotiated stakeholders' formulae..."

Jokkinen cleared his throat to interrupt. "Hollis, I didn't understand a lot of what you just said, but let me see if I can interpret. The Fire Department is a stakeholder." He paused.

Hollis nodded, grateful that the Chief was the one talking.

"And as a stakeholder, we are supposed to gainshare."

Hollis nodded again.

"And that gainsharing is somehow related to a base threshold."

Another nod.

"And all that is somehow tied to a negotiated formula. Or formu*lae* as you put it."

With this, Hollis nodded more vigorously, as if the Chief could now understand.

"Well" — the Chief drew the word out — "let me ask you again. Where .... is .... our ... *fire truck?*"

The intensity of the words had the desired effect, as every one of the people in the audience sharpened their attention waiting for the answer.

Hollis took a deep breath and shifted from one suede boot to the other. "Chief, it's important to get these projects up and going, and then focus on returns."

"Excuse me, Hollis?" The question interrupted her answer, but she looked up gratefully. Don Nichols pushed himself to his feet. He wore his usual fishing vest with a row of bright flies and one red and white spoon stuck in a small strip of wool above the left breast pocket.

Nichols was the town gadfly and the head of the Finance Committee. He could be counted on to take the microphone at Town Meeting and drone on about something or another. Everyone in Burfield knew Don; his eccentricity was matched only by his encyclopedic knowledge of the annual budget and the town charter.

"Yes, Don. Nice to see you. How are you today?" Hollis seemed happy to switch away from Jokkinen's interrogation.

"Very well, Hollis," Nichols began in his ponderous, courtly style.

Hollis loosened her shoulders a bit and stretched the fingers on her clenched hands. Nichols could always be relied on for a good filibuster.

"Hollis, if the Chief's truck is delayed, I assume your other commitments, like the property tax phase-in, will be delayed as well?" He then sat down.

Peter Simons was shocked. He had gone to Town Meeting for years. Nichols was never this succinct. At Town Meeting, people finished complete needle pointing projects during his speeches.

Hollis looked startled. "Don, I think it's safe to assume that all our community partners are in the same boat, but I hope you appreciate the symbolism...."

Hollis stopped speaking. In the front row, Stanley Albertson had pushed himself to his feet. He and Wendell never missed a Lions Club meeting. They didn't socialize much and it was their best meal of the month. Stanley was in his traditional outfit, jeans with a denim jacket. In honor of the occasion he was wearing a knit tie on his flannel shirt. After he stood he stretched a bit. He was stiff from loading wood that morning.

Stanley Albertson wasn't used to speaking in public. He cleared his throat.

"Yes?"

"Yes, ma'am. Stanley Albertson. My brother and me run the sawmill on the north slope of Matchic Ridge. We have a pretty good westerly breeze nearly all the time out there."

Heads nodded in the audience. People in a small town knew which way the wind blew.

"We was reminded of that just last week when Wendell nearly set the orchard afire not mindin' the store. Those flames were blowing due east until

Terry and his crew came and stamped 'em out." There was laughter in the audience. There were a good number of firefighters in the Lions Club.

Standing at the podium, Hollis shifted and seemed to relax. At least Stanley Albertson wasn't asking her a question.

"Anyways, we was wonderin', Wendell and me, we been watchin' your one wind mill up on the ridge for the past year. It's been barely spinnin'. Last week you fired up four more. And the new four ain't spinnin' any faster than the first one."

There were nodding heads and smiles. Stanley seemed to warm to the task of speaking in public.

"I didn't think much about it, I figure people know what they're doing. Especially your crew, with all those federal and state experts. But now I hear you ain't making enough electricity. At least not enough to give Terry here a new truck or give us a break on our 'lectric bills or our taxes. And from the looks of it last week at my place, the boys at the station surely do need a new truck."

The smiles around the room turned to chuckles and outright laughter.

"And what I was wonderin' was, with the wind blowing from the west, and with the windmills on the east, didn't you put your goddam windmills on the wrong side of the mountain?"

Leland Bird fired his pistol. Vulgarity wasn't permitted at the Burfield Lions Club. Maybe up in Fitchburg, but that was the city. Jack Cunningham hit the ship's bell with the gavel. The meeting was over. People pushed back from their tables laughing. Time to get back to work. The Lions were still talking about Stanley Albertson as they headed out of the room.

There was an exhausted silence in Peter's Subaru Forrester as he drove down the winding driveway of the Burfield Country Club. The air conditioning was on full-blast, and the windows were down on the warm final day of summer. Hollis took off her expensive jacket and flung it onto the backseat followed by her briefcase. Her laptop with its impotent dangling connecting cord fell to the floor. There were crescent moon-shaped sweat stains under her silk armpits.

Peter waited. He knew the routine. Recriminations first: "Why didn't you check to see if the laptop connected? Do I have to do everything? You weren't even paying attention, you were fucking with your stupid phone."

Then character assassination: "Those fucking hicks. Can you imagine?"

Then an attack on her allies: "George Fleming is useless. Why aren't we making enough money to give that asshole Jokkinen his fucking fire truck?"

Peter hunkered down grimly. He was used to her blaming and complaining when things got tough. But silence only worked for a while. He knew he needed to join Hollis in her little Kabuki dance of blame or else her guns would train on him.

But he was too late. Hollis turned to him. "You guys didn't do a good enough job with the prep session. What am I paying you for, if I have to go through that kind of shit? Maybe you should have to wait to get paid like everyone else."

This last one always got Peter's attention. The wind farm was paying nearly all of Peter's billing at $200 an hour. He was making more than he ever had. He got paid whether they made power or not. So, that's why he took a little crap from Hollis every now and then. She was a client. Clients can be difficult sometimes. And then there was the sex. But that didn't count.

Peter was doing 35 mph as they headed back into town on Orchard Hill Road. The air in the Subaru cooled and smelled of apples from passing orchards. There was a welcome silence. Peter switched on NPR and spoke without thinking.

"I wonder sometimes, if the wind does blow the other way, why did we put the thing in the University Forest and not on the other side of the ridge?"

There was a silence. Peter kicked himself for bringing up something that would stir Hollis up again.

Instead of being angry, Hollis was a study of calm. Her voice was like a mother's talking to an errant child. "George and Daddy say the site passed all the tests. If it wasn't okay with the Department of Energy, we wouldn't have gotten our grants." And then, "Peter, if you can't support the project 100%, you know we can find another lawyer."

Peter sighed. He knew he shouldn't have brought it up. He wondered what came over him.

Chapter 18

"Okay, pull me out."

Chavez grabbed Leland Bird by the ankles and slid him — on his mechanic's creeper — out from under the Brushbuster.

"What's the verdict?" Jokkinen sat in a lawn chair in front of the truck. Leland spent so much time under the Brushbuster that the Chief figured how to be comfortable while he was working.

Leland rolled into a sitting position and wiped his greasy hands with a rag. "Just like my mother-in-law, cranky and unreliable, but what's the alternative?" He laughed at own joke. "She needs a new alternator, and the clutch ain't too good, neither." He looked up at Chavez. "Been double clutching all the time?"

Chavez nodded. He was only allowed to drive the truck in the driveway, so he never got up enough speed to double clutch, but he knew Kenny Dutton always did.

"When's the new truck coming?"

Chavez knew Leland was just saying this to make trouble. He always said it when he came by to work on the Brushbuster.

Jokkinen heaved himself out of his lawn chair and staggered a bit to get balance on his good leg. "Don't get me started on that. Why don't you stop at the auto parts store and get your mother-in-law a new clutch?"

Leland laughed as he walked down the driveway. Chavez smiled. The Chief and Leland had this same conversation every time he came over.

"Let's go for a donut." Jokkinen headed down the driveway.

"How was your visit with Roland Lamontagne? Was he sober?" Jokkinen was smiling as he drove Chief 1. His favorite oldies station was on the radio.

"Maybe." Chavez thought about the glass next to Chief Lamontagne's chair. He didn't have much experience with drinkers. "Mainly, he was old."

Jokkinen grunted. "That he is. Well, what did you learn?"

"He told us about the fire."

"Us?"

"I took Jason."

"Hmph."

Chavez knew Jokkinen had his doubts about Jason. "Jason thinks I should make my project a video."

Jokkinen looked at Chavez, considering. Finally he answered. "Okay with me, as long as you don't cut corners."

Chavez shook his head. He liked the idea of the video, but right away he knew it would be more work dealing with Jason. "No, I'll do it right."

"Back to Lamontagne. You asked him how the fire spread?" the Chief asked.

Chavez hesitated. "He mentioned you parked the truck where you shouldn't have."

"He would mention that, the little prick. He's never let me forget that I lost a truck. He probably didn't even mention the leg."

There was a silence. The word "leg" jarred Chavez's memory. He remembered his scribbled notes from the end of the conversation with Lamontagne. "Weird way … truck parked in wrong place … leg." Leg? Without thinking, he glanced down at Jokkinen's false leg. When he caught himself and raised his eyes, he found Jokkinen looking at him.

"Yup, I was standing next to the truck. At least I was until a granite block fell off Number Five, hit the truck, and barreled into me. That's how I lost my leg. It was amputated that night. That was the end of my time with the department. I went on disability, and we moved up here. Became chief the next year." He smiled grimly, "Thirty-five years ago, Burfield's department consisted of Squeaky Townsend, another guy, and a jeep. They were happy to have me, even with one leg."

Chavez was embarrassed. "I'm real sorry, I didn't mean to—"

Jokkinen cut him off with a wave. "Don't worry about it, water under the bridge, I just don't talk about it much. But I'm surprised Lamontagne mentioned it. Usually, to Roland Lamontagne, I'm 'the fucking Finn who lost the truck.' So, aside from all that, what'd you learn from the old geezer? What else have you learned?"

Chavez began haltingly, slowly picking up steam. "Fire jumping is when…a fire moves from one place to another….jumping over some place it was supposed to…burn."

"With no explanation," Jokkinen added.

Chavez looked up, grateful that the Chief was willing to help and that he seemed to be on the right track.

Suddenly, Chief Terry Jokkinen broke into loud off-key song, his cracked bass voice drowning out the radio. "It's now or never, come hold me tight. Kiss me my darling, be mine tonight...." And then he stopped, looked at Chavez and grinned.

"Elvis, 1960." Chavez replied quickly. He was not an Elvis fan, but he knew his old songs.

Jokkinen grunted. "Actually, you should listen to 'O Sole Mio' some time. See if it sounds familiar. Same tune, different song."

The Chief pulled Chief 1 into Dunkin Donuts. They went inside and sat at a table. "OK, what about the fire?"

"One article I read said Fitchburg Mill was a good example of jumping. I got a map of the fire."

"Where'd you get a map?"

"From Chief Lamontagne's file."

Jokkinen looked surprised. "He let you take his file?"

"Not really," Chavez began.

"What's that mean?

Chavez picked his phone up off the table and called up his email program. He found the string of forwarded pictures from Jason, went to the first one, and clicked the attachment.

Chavez handed Jokkinen the phone. "That's the map. You have to expand it and move it around a little to see the whole thing."

Jokkinen pulled his reading glasses out of his breast pocket. He held the phone in the palm of his right hand and looked at it curiously. He used a six-year-old phone with oversized raised numbers. He had never texted and did his email on the computer at his office.

"You'll have to show me," he said, trying to hand the phone back to Chavez.

Chavez got up from his side of the table and took the chair next to the Chief. "It's time you learned. You hold your fingers together on the screen and expand them to make the image bigger."

Both leaned over the phone. They were a curious sight at Dunkin Donuts, sitting on the same side of the table, hunched over one phone.

Jokkinen focused on the screen as he moved the image back and forth. The buildings burned in the Mill fire were shaded in, three buildings in all. One and Two were shaded in. Three and Four were only outlined, not shaded. Five was shaded. The streets were drawn in. He looked closer. Five was almost two blocks away from the fire.

"That looks like the map we used in the review sessions after the fire," the Chief said. "Yep, this is the map, I see the buildings."

The map made Chavez more confident. It told a story.

The Chief returned to teaching mode. "The fire burned three mill buildings and left two mill buildings standing. It was really suspicious."

"Chief Lamontagne went over that," said Chavez. "They investigated, but with so many chemicals soaked into the floors over the years, the investigation was...." Chavez searched for the word.

"Compromised."

"That's it, compromised."

Jokkinen continued. "With all those chemicals, every bit of combustible material went up in smoke. That hampered the investigation."

"Those investigators — even back then — had all kinds of fancy scientific techniques," said Chavez. "They should have been able to detect arson. And if it was arson, shouldn't someone have done something?"

"Down in Boston, everybody just looks the other way," said Jokkinen. "That's the way it's always been."

"I don't get it."

Jokkinen paused and finally said, "You will when you're older."

Chavez just shook his head. Then he said, "You know something else that's weird?" He scrolled through his phone. "Look at this." He handed the phone over. This time Jokkinen was more adept, expanding the image to see it better. It was the second map that Jason photographed. Jokkinen read from the bottom. "Fitchburg Housing Authority, Elderly Housing. So?"

Chavez pointed to the proposed new buildings. "See anything you recognize?"

Jokkinen looked more carefully and said, "Get me back to the fire map."

When Chavez called it up, Jokkinen took a look, and then he went back to the housing authority map. "I'm sure I've never seen this map. If I had, I would have seen how it was the same as the fire map."

Chavez spoke. "The fire only burned the buildings that were going to be in the housing project."

Jokkinen went back and forth between the maps.

"Chief Lamontagne told me the guy building the project in Fitchburg was Hollis Kerrigan's father. He also was renovating the buildings that burned in Taunton."

Jokkinen smiled tightly. "Small world, isn't it?" He paused. "Speaking of that, when are you going to Taunton?"

The question surprised Chavez and he gave the Chief a look. The visit with Roland Lamontagne and the connection between the two maps was a big deal. He hadn't thought of what was next.

Jokkinen saw the look. "A *professional*" — the Chief emphasized the word — "would already be down in Taunton."

Chavez looked up, horrified that the Chief would think he was doing a bad job. Especially now that he knew about his leg. Then he saw he was smiling. Just busting his balls. Chavez started thinking about the next step. "I wonder where I can find a fire map for Taunton."

Jokkinen was still holding Chavez's phone. He held out the picture of the housing authority brochure. "See if there's something like this hanging around, too."

They got into the Chief's truck, and Jokkinen said, "Looks like you've got a big date."

"Huh?"

"A message came in earlier when I was holding your phone. You better check."

Chavez looked down. It was from Jason:

Ariel Pinkerton wants to give you a blowjob.

"I...never...Jason..."

The Chief smiled as he started the truck. "Want me to use the siren?"

Chapter 19

While other statewide elected officials crammed into scarce space in the State House, the Attorney General's office commanded the top three floors of the McCormack Building across the street.

Seated in the visitor's chair across the desk from Susan Hill, Lawson tried to get his bearings. He desperately wanted to get off on the right foot in this new job. He quickly assessed Susan Hill: a forty-something professional woman who, he decided almost at once, had no sense of humor. She also lacked a wedding ring, and by the looks of her, she didn't eat much. Still, she was chief of staff to his new boss, Ethan Pierce. Did that make her his boss?

He made a quick scan of the walls. No pictures, no diplomas, no knickknacks on the desk. Nothing to comment on to break the ice.

Susan Hill wasn't making his first day easy. "The Attorney General's policy team?" she said in a singsong voice that, Lawson thought, indicated a lack of respect for his new position. She made comical quote signs with her fingers on both hands as she said *policy team*.

Lawson hadn't really felt the urge to drink in the past seven weeks, but his trip from Washington to Boston was a real test. For someone who hadn't driven much in five years, horsing a 24-foot U-Haul truck up the New Jersey Turnpike and over the Cross-Bronx Expressway was torture. He'd found a short-term condo rental in Concord, right near the train station. In the first hour after he'd parked the truck, he would have killed for a gin and tonic. Or several gins and tonic, he'd thought ruefully.

And now, this. First day on the job. Not exactly the welcome wagon. What the fuck have I gotten myself into?

"I'm happy to be here," he said, trying to sound more positive than he felt.

"How much background did he give you?"

"Well, we had a brief conversation about it at the conference."

She sighed.

Lawson wondered: Is she exasperated at Pierce or at me?

"Listen up," she said, "I'm just going through this once. Ethan Pierce has lots of good ideas, but I don't know where he's going on this one. You are supposed to collect fire data, and your main source is going to be notes from the fire review meetings. Your challenge is going to be getting whoever has the information to cooperate. These people don't know this information is valuable, but as soon as they start to figure that out, you can expect they're going to want to hang onto it. They won't give it to you. With me so far?"

Hill looked at him closely. She'd been talking quickly. "I know you were in television. That makes me wonder how much of an attention span you have."

"I'm keeping up." *Bitch.*

"It's going to take a nobody to get it done. You've got to get out and grovel. Make the people you're asking for information think you're not important. That's why nobody around here wants to be on a policy team. They don't want to be a nobody. That's where you come in." Hill sat back and stared at Lawson.

She's waiting for me to be offended, Lawson realized. Instead, he chuckled. "And I'm that nobody."

"Your lips to God's ears. It's a requirement of the job."

"That's fine with me."

Susan Hill picked up the file in front of her.

"You didn't sign the ethics forms."

"I wanted to talk to somebody about that. It asks for bank account information. Why is that?"

Hill sighed and rolled her eyes. Lawson thought that was probably one of her signature moves.

"Everybody who works here gives permission for the ethics office to monitor our bank accounts. Cuts down on bribery, kickbacks, that kind of thing. You aren't into that, are you?"

Lawson looked at her to see if she was serious. He couldn't tell. "No, I…just don't have a bank account right now. You know, the move and all." The fact was, he was out of money. He had never been much of a saver, and the move and new condo sucked up all his cash.

"Well, when you get one, be sure to let them know." She saw his look and softened. "It's something the Boss takes very seriously. Just do it."

She slid a wallet-sized laminated card across the desk. "Here's a list of the staff's after-hours phone numbers."

He picked it up and studied it. Pierce's home number was first, followed by a number for Doherty. Unexpectedly, he felt a sting in his eyes. The card made him feel welcome, somehow symbolic of a new era in his life.

"What's with the name change?" Hill was reading from the file.

"New job, new city, new life."

"Yeah?" She waited, obviously expecting more.

He started in on his prepared speech: "I grew up Richard Lawson. When I went into television, they changed the name to Dick Law. That was never really me."

She looked at him doubtfully. "Whatever."

A door opened, and Pierce looked out. His face lit up when he saw Lawson. "Action. Thought I heard your voice. Glad you're here. Let's get you saddled up. Did you get your marching orders from Commander Hill here?"

Lawson's mind flashed to the main requirement of the job. For a moment, he considered making a joke: *Nobody Lawson, reporting for duty.*

But he was still feeling his way. Instead he said, "Susan's given me a pretty good rundown."

"I've got something for you." Pierce trotted back into his office, then returned with an old-fashioned call message slip. It looked like it was torn from a spiral binder.

Lawson looked at it. "Chavez Simons." It had an area code from the central part of the state.

"Simons is a good hand," said Pierce. "What he has on his mind might sound a little loco, but I suggest you hear him out." Then Pierce offered Lawson a strange grin, and Lawson decided he needed to learn to interpret Pierce's grins and his weird cowboy vocabulary.

Pierce started to close his door, but at the last instant he turned back to Hill. "Had a nice visit with the Dragon Lady this morning," he said. "She asked about you. I told her you'd be down to visit some time."

Lawson glanced back at Hill. A look of fear was on her face. "Are you serious?"

"Might be," said Pierce, with another hard-to-interpret grin, and he closed his door.

Lawson looked at Hill. Gone was the sassy-girl routine.

Lawson couldn't resist. "Who — or what — is the Dragon Lady?"

Hill almost shuddered. She whispered, as if she and Lawson were old, trusted confidants. "Mary Cronin," she said. "Deputy Attorney General in charge of the Criminal Division. She's been here since Christ was a corporal."

Lawson smiled. He'd never heard that one before.

"Stay away from her," warned Hill. "She hates Ethan Pierce. And if you're part of Pierce's team, she hates you, too."

"Sounds sweet."

"Anything but. She's run the office around here for years, but Pierce's the only Attorney General who has ever stood up to her." Hill's voice dropped another decibel. "I think she deep-sixed a couple of our best cases." Then Hill went silent, looked down, and fiddled with papers on her desk. Lawson could picture her, the moment he was gone, making a sign of a cross.

There was a flurry of motion, and Sergeant Maureen Doherty hurried into the room. "Who's he in with?"

Hill looked up, startled. "He's alone."

Lawson watched Doherty's face go from concern to consternation to understanding. "He hit his panic button," she said to Hill. "I'd better check."

Doherty ducked into Pierce's office.

Fifteen seconds later, she came out again, blushing, shaking her head.

"Welcome to our little slice of paradise," Doherty said to Lawson, "where our leader has nothing better to do than to play games." She gave him a slightly embarrassed smile, then walked back down the hall.

"What was that all about?" Lawson asked Hill.

With a sour expression on her face, Hill shook her head. "The Boss fancies himself an expert matchmaker. He thinks the world of Doherty. We all do. Maybe Pierce thinks you'd be a good match for Doherty." She stopped and studied him. "He must see something in you I'm missing."

Lawson rubbed his face, trying to put this all together. *Pierce sees Doherty and me as a couple?* And then, *why is Hill busting my balls?*

Hill switched topics. "By the way, we don't have room for you over here, so we got you a desk over in the State House." She handed Lawson a key.

He read the room number stamped into it. "22-A?" He thought he was familiar with the State House, but he'd thought the rooms started with three-digit numbers on the ground floor.

"I really don't know where it is," said Hill. "Somebody said it's in the basement." She saw his skeptical look. "Maybe you can work your way up." And then she gave him her warmest smile of the morning.

Once, Dick Law was a big deal at the State House.

The State House is the seat of power in Massachusetts, the Promised Land for every aspiring pol across the state — at least, for those who don't have their eye on Washington. Built in 1798 and commanding the highest point on Beacon Hill, the building's gold leaf dome dominates Boston Common. The interior of the building glistens. Inlaid marble floors are highly polished, pictures of former governors adorn the walls, flags and draperies hang in cavernous interior halls. The splendor of the building was only exceeded by the self-importance its occupants.

As the anchor of Boston's top-ranked television news show, Dick Law would swoop in with a camera crew, tails on his trench coat flying. In a building where television coverage was the highest form of currency, he was used to the fawning attentions of its inhabitants.

But those days were long gone, and the basement, a part of the building Dick Law had never set eyes on, was a land that time — or at least the maintenance staff — forgot.

Entering 22-A, Lawson clicked on the lights and shook his head. It was hard not to be discouraged by his new surroundings. The office had a few wobbly cubicle walls, four mismatched desks, one drafty basement window, a frayed carpet and three antique computers. He put his coffee and the small bag containing a bagel on his desk. He dropped the folded *New York Times*, opened to the crossword puzzle, on the one guest chair that fit, along with his desk and chair, inside his cubicle.

It was 8:10 a.m. He had an hour before his office mates — the Doric Dames — arrived. They were a bunch of blue-blooded women who gave historic tours of the State House and they weren't happy about having their space invaded. On his first day, the crones filled him in on the rules of the office. Most of them made sense, but one of them — no watering the plants from the water cooler — gave him a perverse challenge. Now he filled an old coffee cup with state water and carefully watered every plant in the office. He sat back down and smiled. He wondered how long it would take until they figured out their plants were thriving. Small pleasures. In AA meetings, they said to focus on small pleasures.

He settled down behind his desk and pulled out his cellphone. Some mornings, this call to Joe Guthrie was a pain. Some days it was his lifeline. But he never missed it. It grounded him for whatever surprises the day sent his way.

Call completed, Lawson straightened the pile of material on his desk.

Per Pierce's request, he'd called Mr. Chavez Simons several days before. The call was strange. The guy was friendly enough but he had an unusual voice, deep and formal, very precise. Simons said he needed information on the Taunton Mill fire of 1979.

It sounded simple enough, but it took the better part of two days sifting through piles of documents to find some information. None of it was computerized and he stood at the copy machine a couple of irritating hours scanning the stuff he needed to send. He'd emailed it all to Simons yesterday.

Today, he was checking in to see if it was what he needed.

"Mr. Simons?"

"Yes?"

"This is Richard Lawson from the Attorney General's office."

"Hello, Mr. Lawson. How are you today?"

Lawson rolled his eyes. There it was, that formal tone again.

"I just wanted to make sure you received the information I sent you."

There was a pause on Chavez Simons' end. "Yes, Mr. Lawson, I did. I very much appreciate the information."

Lawson got more irritated. The guy was still formal, he said he appreciated it, but he sure as shit didn't hear it in his voice. *Hell, the fire was 35 years old, did this guy think they just had this stuff on their desk?*

Lawson decided he'd probe a bit. Maybe the guy was teaching a class or preparing a big grant application. Maybe he was just too busy to be grateful.

"Mr. Simons, I was wondering how you plan to use the information."

There was a silence, but then Simons spoke. "I'm working on a research project for my certification to be a Regular Volunteer Firefighter."

Lawson's head buzzed. He couldn't think of anything to say. *Volunteer firefighter? What was Pierce doing on stuff like this? Shouldn't Lawson be doing something more important? Is this what the job was all about?*

There was silence on both ends of the call. Finally Chavez Simons spoke. "Are you there?"

The concern in the guy's voice settled Lawson down. *He needed this job. His boss asked him to do something. But a volunteer fireman?*

"Well, I'm glad we could help." It sounded lame but it was all he could think to say.

But then Chavez's tone changed. "That fire map was just what I needed. When I saw it, I was really stoked. Listen, I've got to get back into class, I just stepped out to take the call." And then he hung up.

'Stoked,' wondered Lawson. What idiot used the word "stoked?" Get back into class? Was the guy a teacher?

And what kind of name was "Chavez," anyway? How may Hispanics were there in small-town Massachusetts?

At 11:40, Lawson pushed himself back from his desk to head upstairs. He had it timed exactly to miss the noontime rush at the fourth floor snack bar and still make it to his noon meeting.

The set of three elevators was just across the hall. Curiously, at this time of day, he was the only one waiting. The Legislature must not be in session, he thought idly. *The citizens are safe for one more day.*

An elevator popped open. Lawson stepped in and stood in the front of the elevator, his usual place, facing the button panel. Less eye contact that way. As new people entered the elevator, he would take a half step back, turn slightly away, and let them push their floor button. He had his elevator-dance down to a science.

The elevator was where the visitors to the State House got their game faces on. Lawson entertained himself by watching people use the elevators' polished brass walls to make their "arrangements." They brushed specks off their power suits, straightened their ties and scarves, smoothed their hair. In a building where the business is power, it was important to look the part.

The doors lurched open on the first floor, and out the corner of his eye, Lawson watched an elderly woman bustle in. She wore a coat that was too warm for the day, and she carried a canvas bag in one hand and an accordion file in the other. Lawson knew the type. A citizen-lobbyist. Dedicated to a pet cause, come to make her views heard. She fidgeted, preparing to read the riot act to some bureaucrat or elected official.

The door closed. Lawson looked up. Floor two. Floor three. *Almost there.* Floor four. He sensed the woman watching him. *Shit.*

The doors opened on four, and in wafted the aroma of American Chop Suey.

The woman exited first, and Lawson kept his head down, reaching forward to hold the rubber safety strip on the door to keep it open. The door bucked in his hand. He risked a glance up. The woman was standing in the hall looking back toward him. He hesitated, but he couldn't stay in there all day. The door bucked again. He got out and took two quick steps to his left.

"I know you."

Lawson flinched.

It happened less these days, so it surprised him more.

He was thirty pounds heavier. His former blond-tinted hair was now its natural brown and receding by the day. But the woman was old enough to remember. He could tell: she knew.

"Dick Law - Action News."

Denying it was pointless. That never worked. The best defense was passive acceptance. That, and a quick retreat.

"You got me." Lawson continued to walk. Half the time, this was where it ended. They just wanted confirmation of their recognition skills. They wanted a brush with a public person.

"I used to love you on Channel 6. Dick Law - Action News." She savored the words.

This was the now-or-never moment. He looked directly at the woman and gave her a smile. Sometimes this worked. "A long time ago," he said. "Thanks for remembering."

But the woman hadn't finished. "All the big stories: the fires, the murders, the trials. You were there. Dick Law - Action News. You were some kind of hunk." The woman was pleased with the memory. "Let me ask you something else." *Please, please don't say it....*

"Whatever happened to you, anyway?"

Chapter 20

Glen W. straightened his place setting and carefully arranged his napkin in his lap. He looked up at Lawson. "Okay, how can I be of service?"

Be of service? The phrase puzzled Lawson. It sounded oddly stilted, not the sort of thing two guys meeting for coffee would say. But Glen gave no sign of being embarrassed at saying it.

Lawson remembered the place as a family-style ice cream place, but it was now a yuppie-fancy location called "Felicitations." Their waitress arrived, and they both ordered coffee, Glen a de-caf. Glen asked for a grilled English muffin. Without butter.

Lawson cleared his throat and started his pitch. "I have a problem at work, and I need a sponsor."

For the last few weeks, Joe Guthrie had been telling Lawson he needed a sponsor in Boston, an in-person sponsor instead of relying on Guthrie long-distance. Someone, as Guthrie put it, who could see his face and tell if he was lying.

Lawson was irritated, maybe even a little pissed off, the first time Guthrie told him that. It was as if Guthrie accused Lawson of being deceitful. But Guthrie was never one to mince words, and Lawson had heard the phrase "rigorous honesty" at meetings. Grudgingly, Lawson admitted Guthrie was right. It was time to cut the cord, and he needed someone local. He'd really miss his early morning phone calls to Guthrie.

It was hard, though. Who was available? Who'd be good? Who wouldn't say "no?" He hadn't been that nervous since the first time he asked a girl out on a date.

Finally, Lawson maneuvered around after his Saturday morning meeting, popped the question, and here he and Glen were in this booth at Felicitations.

"First of all, I'm happy to be your sponsor," said Glen. "At least temporarily, until we both see if it's a good fit. I have time right now for one sponsee, but I'm a stickler for a time commitment. We alcoholics aren't known for self-discipline. As I've gotten older, I've become stricter in my requirements. I apologize if I seem impolite."

Lawson couldn't imagine Glen being impolite. A tight-assed Yankee in a sweater than should have been thrown out twenty tears ago, maybe, but not impolite. Lawson nodded, maybe indicating understanding, maybe acceptance. He wasn't sure which.

"Tell me about yourself." said Glen. He sipped his coffee and looked at Lawson over the lip of the cup, obviously waiting for a response.

No wasting time with small talk with this guy, Lawson thought.

Lawson rehearsed this conversation dozens of times, but now he couldn't find the words. "I'm not sure where to begin."

"Sure you do," said Glen. "At the beginning. What's your story?"

"How long should I take?" Lawson felt himself trying to buy a little time. "You must have Saturday chores."

Glen sat back in the booth. "The wife is at choir practice this morning. I'm supposed to do the gutters, a chore I loathe. She'll never know whether I've done them or not. I'll throw some leaves around the yard to throw her off." He tilted his head back with a mischievous smile.

Lawson took a breath and felt himself grinning. Maybe this guy wasn't such a stiff after all. "I've been sober a little more than seven months," he began.

Glen extended his hand for a handshake. "Congratulations," he said simply.

What the fuck? Lawson blinked back tears. Seven measly months, compared to Glen's — what had Glen said a few weeks before, when he'd told the meeting about his latest AA milestone? — 24 years. An almost unbelievable stretch of time not to have a drink.

But Glen shook Lawson's hand and smiled at him as if seven months was an incredible accomplishment.

"Thanks," murmured Lawson. He couldn't believe he was sitting in a booth at a coffee shop, shaking hands with a guy and starting to cry.

"Your story?" prompted Glen, and Lawson launched into his tale. He started with his television career. It was a great place to start, since most people were impressed, but at the mention of "Dick Law," Glen just looked at Lawson blankly. Lawson was mildly put out that Glen didn't know about his television career. And, curiously, he was a little relieved, too.

Lawson told about the decline of his television career, the move to Capitol Hill, drinking more, more, more. The hangovers. The isolation. Finally, getting fired. The self-righteous anger. The realizing that it was his own damn fault.

Through it all, Glen sat and listened, nodding knowingly at times, swirling his coffee cup with a motion that reminded Lawson of a man swirling ice in a cocktail.

At last Lawson arrived at his return to Boston and his new job for Pierce.

"And that, I guess brings me to my problem at work."

Glen nodded.

"Pierce has me collecting old information on fires. He's pretty vague about the reason he needs all this stuff. Something about learning lessons. And, get this, his chief of staff — she's a real piece of work — she says I'm ideally suited for the job because I'm a 'nobody'."

Lawson gained momentum as he talked, his voice rising as he listed the slights. "And then Pierce has me doing a silly project for a guy named Chavez, for God's sake, who wants to be a volunteer firefighter. And I'm in a crappy office in the basement of the State House with three old bats who give tours. And then yesterday, some woman in the hall recognized me. Do you know what she said?"

Glen shook his head, a sliver of a smile on his lips. "What?"

"She said, and I quote, 'What ever happened to you?'" With that, Lawson stopped. In his put-upon mood, that told it all.

Glen was silent, looking into his coffee cup.

"Are you finished?"

Lawson was nonplussed. *Wasn't it enough?*

Instead of expressing that thought, he caught himself. "Yeah," he said simply. And then, defensively, he took a sip of his coffee.

There was a silence between the two men in the booth, and Lawson wondered if he said something wrong. He looked away nervously, wondered if he'd lost Glen, but when he looked back, Glen was sipping at his de-caf and calmly waiting for Lawson to continue.

"I just wonder if I should be doing something else," said Lawson.

Glen signaled for the waitress. Lawson watched with alarm. *Are we done?* But Glen asked her, "Could you replace this unleaded with hi-test? You may just use this cup, no need to dirty another." He shot Lawson a secret smile. "Yet another thing my wife doesn't need to know about my day."

The waitress returned with his coffee, and Glen savored a sip. Glen's tone was a little more clipped, businesslike. "From your story, it's obvious you recognize the sorry state of affairs when you were drinking." Lawson started to object, but Glen held up one bony finger. "And now, the Attorney General of this state — a man I respect and admire, by the way — gives you a job on his staff. Somehow, he sees the good in you. And he asks you to perform certain tasks that he deems part of your responsibilities, specifically, helping a citizen out with a request. And one of your new co-workers says something that you find objectionable, and then a lady in the hall recognizes you. And, I'm trying to remember here, my memory isn't what it used to be, your office in the State House is in the basement and it's 'crappy.' And finally you wonder if this job is beneath you? Does that summarize the situation?"

Lawson nodded, but felt a twinge of shame. He hadn't meant it to sound like that.

There was no mistaking Glen's message. Lawson knew he'd just been given a talking-to — a very AA sort of talking-to.

Glen smiled wryly, and Lawson noticed how one bushy eyebrow went up and the other went down.

"Thanks," said Lawson. "That helps make things clearer."

Glen raised his hand and caught the waitress's eye. "Do you, by chance," Glen asked her, "still serve that wonderful clam chowder which was a staple of your former establishment?"

Lawson wondered if the waitress understood the convoluted Yankee-ese, but she merely smiled and leaned down close to him. "It's about the only good thing left, honey. They put avocados and sprouts in everything else."

Glen gave her a conspiratorial smile. "I wonder if you would be so kind as to bring me two bowls of the chowder to go? And some oyster crackers?"

"Good choice," she said, as if she and Glen just plotted an armed robbery.

Glen's voice softened. "Humility is one of the cornerstones of sobriety, Richard. Some of us think we are humble just because we are in the program, but it takes work to get rid of years of behavior. I have a sense there wasn't much humility in the world of Dick Law - Action News, was there? Or in Washington?"

He did know, Lawson realized. *He saw me on TV. The little bastard was fucking with me.* He tried to focus. *But that wasn't important, was it?*

"You know the slogan, 'Do the next right thing'?" asked Glen.

Lawson nodded. It was one of the clichés he heard almost every meeting.

"It sounds like your new job offers you opportunities to just that. You are lucky in that regard." He paused and looked at Lawson over his coffee cup. "And you have an opportunity to work on your humility. A two-fer, as they say." Glen sat back, looking pleased with his use of slang. "Do you need me to remind you how damn lucky you are to be sitting here today?"

The guy could be harsh. But maybe, Lawson thought, that's exactly what he needed.

The waitress returned with a bag containing the chowders. Glen shifted it to the edge of the table. "Speaking of doing the next right thing, I need to get this chowder home. There's nothing the Mrs. hates more than tepid chowder. And you can't re-heat good chowder. The cream separates and the potatoes get mealy. By the way, I'd be happy to be your sponsor, if you are still interested."

Glen stood up and brushed English muffin crumbs off his nubby sweater. Even after Saturday morning coffee, he looked neat and tidy.

Lawson reached for his wallet, but Glen held up a hand to stop him. "Let me get this." Glen smiled, his blue eyes twinkling with mischief. "I have a feeling you should be saving your money. You never know how long jobs will last in this economy."

On the sidewalk outside, Glen extended his hand. Lawson took it, and Glen held on and leaned a little closer. "Don't be so hard on yourself. You're doing fine."

Chapter 21

"You did pretty well out there." Jokkinen took a sip of cold coffee.

Chavez grimaced and looked around at the emptying room. His voice was low. "I hate heights. I can't even climb trees."

At 9 p.m., Thursday drill night at the station was beginning to quiet down. Jokkinen and Chavez sat in the break room. It was a hot night, and Chavez was drenched in sweat. Eighteen firefighters spent the last two hours climbing ladders to the Town Hall roof.

Jokkinen smiled, switching subjects. "How's the project coming along?"

"I got some information from some guy in Mr. Pierce's office. Richard Lawson."

"Whoa, you contacted Pierce?"

Chavez looked defensive. "He gave me his card and said to call him if I needed help. If he didn't mean it, he shouldn't have given it to me. I called and this is what I got." He pulled up the email on his phone.

Dear Mr. Simons,

Jokkinen shook his head slightly as he read. "*Mr.* Simons. Do you think this guy Lawson knows he is writing to a sixteen year old?"

Chavez shrugged.

In response to your inquiry, here is the incident map from the review meeting for the July 15, 1979 Taunton Mill fire. I'm sorry to report, I don't have a Taunton Housing Authority map in our files.

Jokkinen handed back the phone. "That's one piece of the puzzle, I'll have to thank Ethan the next time he's out here." He stood up. "Time to get home. I need to visit with Mrs. Jokkinen. You probably need to call what's her name...Ariel? How's that working out by the way?"

Message from Chavez Simons: Yr mom work tomorrow?
Message from Jason Morrill: Y. Sup?
Message from Chavez Simons: Skip school. Road trip.
Message from Jason Morrill: K.

Message from Chavez Simons: 7 am
Message from Jason Morrill: NFW

The 90-mile drive from Burfield to Taunton took Chavez a little less than two hours.

To boys raised in rural Massachusetts, one New England mill city looked a lot like any other. With its declining main street, sub shops, nail salons, and dollar stores, Taunton looked a lot like Fitchburg.

There was no missing the Taunton Mill Community Housing complex of massive 19th-century mill buildings in the center of the city.

Entering through glass doors, Chavez and Jason found themselves in a lobby filled with a bustle of residents of all shapes and sizes, ages, and races. This wasn't a place for standing around, but at first they couldn't figure out where to go.

An electronic voice crackled through a blown speaker. "Can I help you?"

They turned and looked through a window at the most exotic, beautiful woman either boy had ever seen. In person, anyway.

The speaker crackled again. "Can I *help* you boys?"

Jason moved closer to the glass. Over Jason's shoulder, Chavez read the placard on the counter: "Conchita Perez." Conchita Perez wore a low-cut top that showed a lot of tan-skinned cleavage.

"Buenos días." Jason said it slowly, sounding the words out. With two years of middle school Spanish, Jason was the Spanish expert — but Chavez didn't think Jason's Spanish sounded quite right.

Conchita Perez had worked the front desk at Bristol Mill Community Housing for only three months, but she ran the front door security system like an air traffic controller. She looked through her glass partition and examined the two teenagers.

The shorter one with the ridiculous Spanish had on drooping jeans, an unzipped hoodie, and a t-shirt with a rock-band's logo on the front. He had bed-head hair and pimples. Lots of pimples.

But the other boy, he was a strange one. Short hair, neatly combed. Dress shirt. Old man's sweater with fake leather buttons, underneath a bright yellow windbreaker with official-looking patches all over it. Khaki pants. And pimples. They all had pimples.

Conchita stood up so she could look over the counter at him. He had on brown shoes like her uncle wore to funerals.

She pulled a flexible microphone closer to her mouth and said, "Step away from the glass. Speak in a normal tone."

The little one backed up and began again. "Buenos días, señorita."

Conchita felt a smile taking over her face. These boys were the most amusing thing to happen to her all day. "If we're going to communicate," she said, "we might be better off sticking to English. Can I help you?"

She knew they weren't residents. She knew all the residents. Maybe they were religious. Jehovah's Witnesses, maybe. She looked at their hands for literature.

The big one — the neat one — stepped forward. "My name is Chavez."

Conchita couldn't hold in a chuckle. "Chavez? Are you messing with me?"

"No, really. Chavez Simons. I'm a volunteer fireman. I'm doing a project for my certification exam, and I was hoping to get some information on a fire that happened here."

"A fire?" asked Conchita, but she took pity on the big kid with the weird clothes, weird name, and weird story. This was a good break in her daily routine. "We haven't had any fire. Not since I've been here."

"It was in 1979. Back when they were renovating these buildings."

"Oh, that's easy. Hold on." Conchita picked up her phone and dialed a number, purposely leaving her microphone on. "Hi, Florida. Yeah, hi. How's your day goin'? Uh-huh, I know. I wonder if I could send some fellows in to see you. No, not residents. Come on out to meet them in the front lobby."

"How will I recognize them?" asked the voice from the speaker.

"Well, first of all," said Conchita, "they're gonna stand out. They're a couple of white boys. One of them looks like he could live here, but the other one" — she gave Chavez another look — "well, did you ever see those Andy Williams Christmas specials on TV?"

They were buzzed through the door, and a tiny African-American woman bustled up. She had thinning wispy gray hair, cut short. In her hand, she carried a toilet plunger.

"What can I do for you boys?"

Chavez read the lettering on her white polo shirt: underneath "Taunton Housing Authority," it said, "Florida Sampson."

"Hi, Ms. Sampson."

She gave him a quick once-over, as if so few people called her "Ms. Sampson" that it took her a few seconds to remember that she was "Ms. Sampson."

"My name is Chavez Simons," said Chavez. "Ms. Perez said—"

"Spit it out, Mr. Simons." Florida lifted the plunger. "As you can see, I've got things on my mind."

Chavez immediately liked her. "I'm doing a project on mill fires," he said. "There was a fire here in 1979. I'm looking for records."

"Conchita sent you to me because I've been here the longest."

"So you must be the expert. You must know all about this place."

Florida's tone softened. "Damn right I do," she said. "I know the pipes, I know the history. What is it you need?"

"A map," said Chavez. "Showing this place when it was built."

Sampson took a couple of seconds to think. "Let's adjourn to my office. Come along with me." She headed down a hall to the right. Jason and Chavez hurried to keep up. Her legs might be short, but they churned along.

Suddenly she stopped dead in the hall, and turned to Jason. "Here's where you pay to play." She nodded her head toward a men's room door. "Take care of that *situation* in there." She drew out the word "situation."

"Why me?" croaked Jason.

Florida gestured to Chavez. "Your friend here cared enough when he came calling to be respectful and wear something nice. You, on the other hand, dressed for this." She shoved the plunger into Jason's hand, grasped his shoulder, turned him around, and pushed him toward the men's room.

"How'll I recognize this situation?"

"Oh, you'll recognize it," said Florida, smiling wickedly. She reached down, grabbed Jason's belt, and yanked his jeans up. "Just because you are doing plumbing work doesn't mean I've got to see that, son."

Jason glanced back at Chavez, but Chavez, grinning, kept his head down.

"Wash that thing off when you're done," said Florida, "and meet us in the maintenance room. Ask anyone where Florida hangs out."

Florida led Chavez down the hall, unlocked a door marked "Maintenance," opened it, and flicked on a light switch.

Her "office" was an equipment room, with rows and rows of metal shelves neatly stacked with all sorts of supplies. At the end of the room was a huge pegboard with the most complete set of tools Chavez had ever seen. He marveled. Even the Chief would have been impressed.

Florida sat behind a small desk with a gooseneck lamp, and she waved Chavez toward a metal folding chair. "Tell me what you're up to," she said.

Chavez told her the high points of the story.

She listened carefully, nodding from time to time, then gave it a couple seconds' thought. "I started with the housing authority just out of high school," she said, "but I'm the only one left from those days. That's why Conchita had you talk to me. The mill went bust, and it was just standing vacant, gathering dust and cobwebs, swarming with rats. Then they started converting those buildings. Everybody thought that was a good idea. But then there was the fire. Oh, what a fire."

There was a tentative knock on the door, and Florida said, "Go let him in."

Chavez knew Jason was going to be pissed, but he couldn't wait to see his face.

Florida spared him Jason's wrath. "Young man, come on in here," she said. "Thank you so much for performing that task for me. I just did not have the strength today to clear another commode. Sit down next to your friend Chavez and me."

With a grumpy look on his face, Jason unfolded a chair and silently took a seat. Chavez noticed he was sweating and his jeans were splashed.

Florida went to a corner of the room, leaned down, and lifted a large hardbound book from the lowest shelf. It reminded Chavez of his *Time Life History of Rock-n-Roll*. "Finally, someone who needs one of these," she said. "On the twentieth anniversary of this housing project, the board of directors, bless their good-for-nothing souls, decided to publish a commemorative history. Can you imagine? The commemoration of a housing project? What the hell did they think they were going to co-*mem*-morate? Pictures of their own saintly selves, doing good for the less fortunate. Have you ever seen a sorrier bunch of fools?" She opened the book to a photo of men and women in business attire. "Nobody wanted the damn books, so now I'm stuck with 'em." She pointed to two shelves filled with identical volumes. "Anyway, if I remember right, it has what you need." She handed the book to Chavez.

He opened the front cover, and it creaked like an expensive new book that had never been opened. Jason read over his shoulder. The first chapter was a history of the mill, including an aerial view of the aftermath of the fire, clearly showing the burned buildings and the buildings that survived.

Chavez turned to the next chapter, which was all about the construction of the housing project. Jason reached over Chavez's shoulder and pointed out an architect's schematic of the housing project. The mill buildings to be converted were shaded in gray.

"This is exactly what I need, Ms. Sampson," said Chavez. "Thank you so much." He reached for his wallet. "How much is the book?"

Florida Sampson threw her head back and laughed. "It's on the house, son, on the house. Let me know if you need twenty more." She escorted Chavez and Jason to the door. "Son, I know someday you'll make a fine fireman," she said to Chavez. "And you" — smiling at Jason — "keep those pants up. Stay in school. If that doesn't work out, there's always...." She gestured to the plunger next to the desk.

Chapter 22

Lawson's train from Concord blew its whistle as it came into the yard behind North Station. He clicked on his phone to check the time; 7:45 a.m. Again. Not a minute more or a minute less. Idly, he clicked over to his email.

FROM: Mary Cronin
TO: Richard Lawson
Meet me in State House Room 356 tomorrow at 8:00 a.m. Please be prompt.

Tomorrow?

Then Lawson checked the date. His heart skipped a beat. The email was sent late last night.

Tomorrow is today. Fuck.

Lawson leaped to his feet, grabbed his suit jacket, and excused himself to the front of the line forming at the train door. Eight minutes later, he bent over to catch his breath at the side entrance to the State House.

Where the fuck is Room 356? Why isn't she over at McCormack?

He hurried to the elevator, re-considered — *too slow!* — and jogged up the broad staircase at the end of the hall.

One flight, two flights, three flights. Room 356.

Two marble columns framed the door, and gold letters spelled out Speaker of the House of Representatives.

Why here? Out of breath, he straightened his jacket and opened the door into an anteroom large enough for a dozen or more people to sit. At this early hour, the chairs were empty. In individual recesses, busts of former speakers lined the wall. A hard, but attractive young woman sat at the receptionist's desk and looked up from her cellphone.

Lawson sucked in a breath, then puffed it out, catching his breath. "Mary Cronin? From the Attorney General's Office? She said to meet her here."

The woman was a gum chewer. She did something inside her mouth before she spoke. "In there." She pointed at a door.

Lawson knocked.

There was no response.

Lawson stood there, waiting, feeling like an ass.

He glanced at the receptionist.

She snapped her gum and shrugged.

Lawson raised his hand to knock again, and finally: "Enter, please."

He expected an office, but beyond the door was a windowless sitting room, furnished with several leather armchairs and a brocaded sofa, lit by brass table lamps.

A woman was seated on the sofa, reading from a file, holding a delicate porcelain teacup.

Lawson knew from Susan Hill that Mary Cronin was over seventy, but in the muted lamplight, she looked younger. Her hair was an odd color combination of gray with bluish streaks. He caught a whiff of some old-fashioned perfume. And then, looking closer, he saw that she seemed to be bent over at an odd angle. *What's that about?*

Cronin looked at her watch. "You're late, Mr. Law."

Lawson started to apologize, maybe even to make an excuse. But he had the sense, somehow, that even if he'd been on time, she would have found some other reason to berate him. As if commenting on his tardiness — *three fucking minutes* — was a little trick to set him back on his heels before they'd even begun their meeting.

"It's Lawson, actually," he said. His voice seemed higher pitched, pretty nervous.

Cronin inclined her head, sending Lawson into one of the leather chairs. The chair surprised him, as it sucked him downward. He tried to sit straighter, but he still found himself at eye-level with Cronin's chest.

Another trick. He gave up and tried to relax.

"I hope you didn't have a hard time finding me," said Cronin. "A good deal of my business is conducted here in the State House. The Speaker has graciously allowed me to use this office. You're just down in the basement, anyway, isn't that correct? Room 22-A?" She said "in the basement" with a bit of a sneer. "It must be quite a change for you."

"I'm still settling in."

She gazed intently at Lawson over her pair of half glasses, studying him, watching for some sign that she was getting to him. "Different from your television days, Mr. Law?"

Lawson knew some response was called for, but she threw so much at him so quickly that he couldn't for the life of him decide what to say. He looked her over. She had on a finely tailored midi-length skirt, a silk blouse, and heavy gold jewelry. A bit out of place at the State House, thought

Lawson. It was a workplace not known for its high fashion.

"And how are you enjoying your time back in Massachusetts?" she asked. "Are you all set up out there in Concord?"

Lawson felt his jaw drop. *How does she know where I live?* He caught a hint of satisfaction in the twitch of her lips. *She's yanking my chain.*

"I understand you are busy collecting fire data," she said.

Lawson felt a cold drop of sweat sliding down his torso — and then there was a drop making its way from his hairline across his forehead. He attempted a casual swipe with his fingers.

"I always find it chilly in here, Mr. Law, but I've heard it said that alcoholics frequently experience unexpected excessive perspiration. How are you feeling, by the way? Grateful to God for another chance?"

Lawson's breath caught in his throat. *How does she know that? Who told her?*

"Forgive me," she said — making it absolutely clear that she had no intention of apologizing. "That may be too personal?"

Who told her?

"You are collecting fire data." It wasn't a question.

Lawson tried to find his voice. Susan Hill's warning came back to him. *Stay away from the Dragon Lady.* He understood Cronin was dangerous and hated Ethan Pierce, but had Hill neglected to tell him Mary Cronin was a little nuts? "The Attorney General asked me to compile some data..."

"The public policy teams," said Cronin, cutting him off. "Those of us who have toiled in the Attorney General's office for many years watch have watched with some amusement as Mr. Pierce attempts to put his own stamp on the office. Sometimes democracy is such a clumsy form of government, isn't it? But the voters have spoken, Mr. Law, for better or for worse, and it's up to all of us to make the best of things."

Lawson could only nod. He couldn't believe this jabbering woman was in a position of authority.

"I've seen a great deal, Mr. Law. If the number of years I've been in the Office of the Attorney General were United States paper currency, we would be looking at our eighteenth president."

What does she mean by that? And why is she being so obtuse? Lawson did a quick calculation. *Let's see, Lincoln was the sixteenth. Then there was Andrew Johnson. So Grant must have been the eighteenth.*

Lawson got it. Back in the day, he and Ulysses S. Grant were best buddies. He'd spent lots of fifties.

He did another quick calculation. If Cronin entered the AG's Office right out of law school, now she was around 75 years old.

"Early in my career," Cronin continued, her voice colder and clipped, "I had the privilege of personally overseeing this department's public safety investigatory efforts, including all the big fires. I assure you Mr. Law, we did things by the book. There might have been errors made, that's old news as they say. And, I want you to know, I find it personally offensive that this Attorney General would use the smoke screen of a 'public policy team' to nitpick years of good, loyal service by hundreds of public servants."

Lawson digested this. Was she serious? Was she trying to start a fight? Did she mean to send a message to Pierce? Or was she just batshit crazy?

"Let me be very clear, Mr. Law." Cronin leaned forward and spoke even faster. "Leave fire investigations alone. Let closed cases remain closed. Let sleeping dogs lie." She peered at him through narrowed eyes. "Do you understand me?"

Then, out of the blue, Mary Cronin smiled. She shifted on the little sofa, touched her hair, re-crossed her legs, and still with the hand on her hair, stretched her back.

Lawson tried not to recoil. Was Mary Cronin being coquettish? It was all so awkward, like an aging actress reprising her best moves. Lawson felt a little lightheaded. This was all so very fucking strange.

As Cronin stretched, Lawson noticed something about Cronin's back. She hadn't been hunched over when he came in; she had a hump on the back of her right shoulder. It took a real effort to look away from it.

Now her voice came lower and slower. "We need to lead the people of Massachusetts, Mr. Lawson."

"Lawson," he thought. She's been calling me Law, but she knew my name the whole time.

"Our future isn't in tired old fire records," she said. "It's in new technologies, medical research, alternative energy development" — she seemed to be searching for the perfect words — "like wind farms. We need to lead, Mr. Lawson." She plucked a lace handkerchief from under a bracelet around her wrist. She folded it into a point and dabbed at her upper lip. Even in the muted light, Lawson could see she had a faint old lady's mustache. "Perhaps it is a little warm in here, after all. I'll have a word with the Speaker." She smiled again, as if confirming that Lawson had not misheard: *When Mary Cronin complained about trivial things, important people leaped to do her bidding.*

"I'm glad we were able to meet, Mr. Lawson," she said. "Glad we understand each other. Please give my regards to the Doric Dames. They do such valuable work." She picked up a file folder, opened it, and began to read. The meeting was over.

Lawson heaved himself out of the cushy leather chair. He'd been sweating, and his moist slacks made an embarrassing ripping sound as they peeled away from the leather.

He backed away from her, like some kind of peon who'd just been dismissed from an audience with the queen. Mary Cronin didn't look up.

In the elevator, feeling vaguely nauseous, he seemed to be hearing Mary Cronin's voice. Had she been telling him she had friends in the Doric Dames? Are those old biddies spying on me? Was she threatening me?

He caught himself picturing a drink: clinking ice cubes, the smell, the taste. That would settle his nerves.

Instead, he took a deep breath, let it out, pushed the thought away, and took the elevator to the fourth floor snack bar. He bought a coffee and a bagel. At a small table in an isolated corner, he fished in his suit coat for the torn-out *Times* crossword puzzle he'd worked on during his train ride.

Forty-five minutes later, Lawson entered 22-A and triumphantly tossed the *Times* puzzle on his desk.

Thursday was the day Will Shortz's evil crossword crew threw nasty tricks at Lawson. Today, they'd pulled the ploy of sticking two letters in one square, six times in the puzzle. What was the word for that? Rebus? Rhombus? Whatever the word, it hadn't been clever enough to defeat the great Lawson.

Lawson was proud of his returning crossword puzzle skills. He wondered if it was true that you regained brainpower when you stopped drinking. At least he was getting better at crosswords.

While Lawson waited for his computer to power up, his mind shifted back to the strange meeting with Mary Cronin. Idly, he slid open the top drawer of his desk, reached into a bag of Reese's Pieces, and drew out one morsel. They talked in meetings about people in early recovery turning to new sources of sugar. It was a guilty pleasure now, but Lawson was trying not to have it become a habit.

He heard a knock at the door and looked up, half in question, half in annoyance. No one ever knocked on the door at 22-A. Besides, it was 9:15 in the morning. Not too many people in the building this early. He turned back to his computer. The knock came again, louder and more insistent.

Lawson sighed. "Come in." He felt stupid yelling it out.

The door opened and a large folded piece of cardboard came through, followed by the arm of someone wearing a bright yellow windbreaker.

Lawson sat at his desk, taking in his visitor, an over-sized teenage boy with a backpack. His first thought was that the kid wandered away from a school group, but it was too early in the day for a field trip.

"May I help you?"

The boy looked at Lawson expectantly, then quickly glanced around the room.

In the boy's disappointment, Lawson saw it for what it was: a crappy office, dim sunlight coming through the one dusty basement window, boxes everywhere, ailing plants, old-lady perfume in the air. He felt a flush of embarrassment.

"I'm looking for Mr. Lawson? Maybe this is the wrong room?" The kid took a step back to check the number on the door. "I'm Chavez Simons," he said, as if he thought that would mean something to Lawson.

Chavez Simons? Lawson was thunderstruck. Pierce's firefighter was an enormous teenager in a nylon windbreaker. How does this kid get to just pick up the phone and call the Attorney General? And — a stray thought: Chavez Simons isn't Hispanic. And then, I've been busting my ass, pulling information together for a kid's school project. That fucking Pierce. Are his parents big political contributors?

But then Lawson's midwestern manners kicked in and he lurched to his feet. "You found me. I'm Richard Lawson."

Chavez Simons took another look around the room, as if he was thinking about leaving. But then he seemed to make a decision. "I have some more questions. I figured they'd be easier to ask in person, instead of on the phone."

Lawson pulled one of the Doric Dames' guest chairs over beside his desk. "Why don't you sit here?"

Chavez squeezed his bulk into the chair. The desk divider behind him canted backwards a bit. "I expected more people to be at work. There aren't as many people as I thought."

"Well, it's early…." That's so feeble, Lawson thought.

The door to 22-A thumped open. One of the Doric Dames bustled in and then looked away, as if it was commonplace for Lawson to be sitting there with an over-sized teenager in a bright yellow windbreaker.

Chavez stood up and looked at Lawson expectantly. *Jesus, the kid thinks I should introduce him. Like this old bat works with me.* He stood up, too. "Bring your stuff," said Lawson. "Let's go upstairs."

In the elevator, Lawson looked Chavez up and down. Pressed khakis, button-down shirt, cardigan sweater under that yellow windbreaker. He looked like one of the old geezers in the front row of the noon meeting. Brown Hush Puppies?

They got out on the fourth floor, and Lawson guided Chavez to a table outside the snack bar, the same table he sat at earlier. "If we sit over here, we'll have a little more privacy than downstairs." What was it about this kid, Lawson wondered. He seems so innocent, he makes me want to apologize for everything.

"Hungry?" asked Lawson. "We can get you some breakfast."

"I've got some stuff with me." Reaching into his backpack, Chavez pulled out a Mountain Dew and a Yodel. He looked around. "Okay if I eat these here? Some places won't let you."

Lawson nodded. "I'm sure it's fine."

Chavez tore the cellophane off the Yodel. "Want some?"

Lawson shook his head and then he wondered why. That Yodel looked good.

"Sure is hot up here," said Chavez, standing and pulling off his windbreaker.

Lawson saw the kid had a tool in a leather case on his belt. On the other side, he had a pager of some kind. Next to the pager was an empty phone case.

"It's easiest if I show you." Chavez pushed the condiment caddy and the napkin dispenser to the edge of the table, and he unfolded his cardboard.

Lawson glanced around. A few people at nearby tables smiled, but they quickly returned to their coffee and conversation. Lots of odd people carried on lots of strange business at the State House. People only homed in on the famous.

"This is a storyboard for my research project," said Chavez. "It's how they do videos."

Lawson started to say, "I know all about storyboards. I used to work in TV." But he stopped himself just in time. *Who are you trying to impress?*

Chavez pointed to some hand lettering on the cardboard: Fitchburg Mill Fire, 1981. "Here's a map of the Fitchburg fire," he said. "The fire torched this first mill building" — he pointed — "and then it burned the one beside it. But then — here's the weird part — the fire leapfrogged right over the next two buildings, didn't touch them at all, and burned the last building at the end of the block."

"There must have been a ferocious wind," Lawson guessed. "Lots of embers flying through the air."

"Not a lot of wind. And it was raining." said Chavez. "And what about the buildings the fire jumped over?"

"I'm no expert," said Lawson, "but that does sound weird."

"Exactly," said Chavez. "And here's something even stranger. There was another mill fire, in Taunton, two years before the Fitchburg fire. It went up the same weird way, burning some buildings and hopping right over others." Chavez pointed out another block of hand lettering: Taunton Mill Fire, 1979. Below the lettering, Lawson recognized the Taunton map that he sent to Chavez.

While Chavez sipped his Mountain Dew, Lawson studied the display. He hadn't really paid much attention to the Taunton material before he sent it, and until this moment he hadn't caught onto the similarities between the two fires. The cardboard looked like a high school science fair project — a messy one — but now Lawson realized that the kid seemed to be onto something.

"You've put a lot of work into this," he said. "And you've explained it very well. You've been practicing your story, haven't you?"

"Oh, yeah," said Chavez, smiling at the praise. "The Chief said, if I was coming to Boston to meet with the state people" — he nodded to Lawson, as if he was still convinced that Lawson was somebody important — "then I better have my shit together." Chavez looked down, embarrassed. "Sorry, that's the way the Chief talks."

"It's okay, I've heard that expression."

"Anyway, in both these fires," said Chavez, "the fire jumped over buildings. What I'm trying to figure out is: Why would some burn and some not?"

"You have an idea, don't you?"

"Yeah."

Lawson nodded, encouraging Chavez to go on.

"In both towns," said Chavez, "the mill buildings were vacant for a long time, but at the time of the fires, they were being renovated."

"Just a coincidence?" asked Lawson.

"Here's a bigger coincidence," said Chavez. "In Fitchburg, the buildings that were being renovated burned, but the other ones didn't."

"And in Taunton?"

"Look at this." Chavez pointed at the Taunton fire map that Lawson sent him, and then he pointed at another map. "A lady at Taunton Community Housing gave me this architect's drawing of the low-income housing they turned the Taunton Mill into. See? Only the buildings that were being renovated burned."

"Same as Fitchburg," muttered Lawson. With a combination of unease and excitement, he studied the diagrams on Chavez's storyboard. It sure looked suspicious, but it couldn't be this obvious.

"Do you understand?" asked Chavez.

Lawson looked up at Chavez to see if he was being sarcastic. But there was such an eager look on Chavez's face, Lawson could only smile. "I get it," he said.

"There's another thing." Chavez pointed to a photo in the Fitchburg Mill section: a row of dignitaries holding silver shovels, standing in front of a white project construction sign.

Federal agencies required signs like that, listing every individual and agency with a hand in a federally funded project. Lawson knew Members of Congress who would trade family members for signs like this in their district.

Chavez pointed to a similar photo in the Taunton Mill section: more dignitaries with shovels, another sign. "The same developer in both," said Chavez. "Kerrigan Associates. And the same project engineer: Plymouth Engineering."

Lawson squinted, examining the photos.

"So?" asked Chavez. He sat back and waited.

Lawson waited, too. He didn't know what the kid wanted.

"It was arson," said Chavez. "You guys should do something about it."

"These fires were 30 years ago." *Another lame excuse.*

"So?"

"Well, things kind of drift away after a while." As soon as he said it, Lawson felt dumb. *Drift away? Jesus.*

Chavez's face filled with disappointment. "You work for Mr. Pierce," said Chavez. "I thought *he'd* do something."

"I'll look into it," said Lawson, and instantly the look on Chavez's face told him he was being brushed off.

"Will you leave your storyboard with me?" said Lawson. "I'd like to show it to some people."

Chavez gave Lawson a suspicious look. "Yeah." He folded the cardboard and shoved it across the table toward Lawson. "Be careful with it," he said.

"I will," said Lawson. "I know it took you a lot of work."

"Lots of work," said Chavez. "And it's important." Then something occurred to him, and he rooted around in his backpack. Out came a photocopy of another photograph, showing yet another federal project sign. He handed it to Lawson. *Matchic Ridge Wind Farm,* the sign read, and among the credits Lawson saw *Kerrigan Development* and *Plymouth Engineering.* "Kerrigan and Plymouth," he said. "They built a wind farm in Burfield. Weird, huh?"

Lawson considered. "Weird." It took him a few seconds to remember the other time someone mentioned a wind farm to him. Then he had it: Mary Cronin. "Definitely weird," he told the kid.

Chapter 23

Be cool, Lawson told himself. *Act like you've been here before.*

But he couldn't help himself. Standing at the floor-to-ceiling windows in Pierce's corner office, he simply gawked.

He looked down on the gold dome of the State House. Beyond was the curve of Beacon Hill going down to the Charles with the Esplanade stretching out along the river. College rowing crews and sailboats dotted the water. Harvard and MIT lay in the distance, with the sun setting behind.

Lawson had been in many of the city's tall buildings, but this was a *spectacular* view.

The door opened, and Pierce strode in. "Ah, Action, there you are. Sorry I'm late. Sergeant Doherty had a hard time with her directions today. That half mile from the Convention Center to the State House is always a challenge."

Doherty followed, rolling her eyes.

"You don't mind if the sergeant joins us?" asked Pierce. "Your note said you wanted to talk about fire investigations. I'm told that in a previous life, Sergeant Doherty had State Police jobs with real purpose instead of her current assignment. She might have something to add."

"Sure, of course, the more the merrier." Lawson tried casual but it came out stupid. He gave his gut a subconscious pat. He'd been doing a lot of walking and he was trying to cut back on the Reese's Pieces. He hoped it showed.

Pierce and Doherty took seats at the conference table. Lawson heard Doherty's equipment belt squeak against the leather of the chair. He found himself sniffing the air around her. *Lawson, stop! That's pathetic.* He brought himself back to the meeting.

"General, you asked me—"

"*Ethan*, Action. You can cool it on the General business in private."

And I wish you'd cool it on the "Action" business, thought Lawson, but before he could decide whether or not to say it, Doherty chuckled. Lawson wondered if the chuckle was aimed at him or at Pierce.

"Ethan, then. You asked me to return Chavez Simons's call." He stopped and addressed Doherty, "Chavez Simons is—"

"Good kid," said Doherty.

"You know him?"

"We've met."

"I guess I'm late to the party." *What else don't I know?*

"Easy, Action. That's what meetings are for," said Pierce. "Left hand talks to the right hand. The Burfield Fire Chief, Terry Jokkinen, is an old friend of mine. Sergeant Doherty and I were out in Burfield to show my face at the launch of a wind farm. Really, for a bit of fishing with Jokkinen. I met this great kid, and he told me about his research project. I knew something about the subject matter, so I told him to call me. And he did and I told him you'd call him."

Lawson listened. He was embarrassed he showed an attitude. He thought about apologizing but instead he set up Chavez's storyboard on an easel next to the table. It was mended in places with duct tape, and the Post-its needed straightening. It looked out of place in this buttoned-down office.

Pierce waved his hand at the cardboard display. "Let me guess. You stayed up all night, putting together this highly professional exhibit."

"No, no, it's Chavez's," blurted Lawson. But then he saw Pierce's smile and realized the Attorney General was teasing him. "Okay, you got me."

He couldn't help it, but he glanced at Doherty to see if she shared the joke. The grin she gave him was more encouraging than teasing.

"So, fill me in," said Pierce. "What have you and Mr. Simons discovered?"

Chavez's maps and pictures made the story easy to tell. Ten minutes later, Lawson was done.

Pierce was silent as he studied the cardboard. Then he spoke. "It took a sixteen-year old to make the connection on those maps. Something that obvious might have been enough to get people to do something back then."

Pierce looked back and forth, from Doherty to Lawson and back again. The corner of his eye crinkled into the bare hint of a smile. "Okay, here's the other chapter," he said. "In 1981, at the time of the Fitchburg fire, I was with the U.S. Attorney's Office in Boston. I went to the Fitchburg fire review meeting, where an Assistant Attorney General named Mary Cronin announced no evidence of arson. It all seemed pretty straightforward, except for a couple things."

"Like what?"

"For one, a friend of mine, an FBI agent named Leo Brunson, told me there'd been a similar fire in Taunton two years before. He wondered if there was a connection."

"What kind of connection?"

"Just too many coincidences. Jimmy Kerrigan, Plymouth Engineering, a mill renovation project, just two years apart. Where there's smoke, there's fire."

Doherty rolled her eyes.

"Sorry, I couldn't help myself," he said. "But the Fitchburg fire review meeting was where I met Terry Jokkinen. He was a lieutenant in the Fitchburg fire department. He was convinced there was something fishy going on. He'd lost a leg and a truck in the Fitchburg fire, so everyone thought, 'Poor Terry, he's just seeing conspiracies where there's nothing.' But put Leo Brunson and Terry Jokkinen together, they are two men who need to be listened to. When it became obvious the state — in the person of Mary Cronin — wasn't going to do anything, I thought there was enough evidence for a federal prosecution. But my boss, the U.S. Attorney, disagreed. I argued long and hard, but no way was he going to let me do anything about it. Everyone's connected in Massachusetts politics. That's when I quit and went to a law firm downtown."

Doherty shifted in her chair. "Tell him," she said to Pierce.

"What Sergeant Doherty wants you to know is this," said Pierce. "The morning after the fire review meeting in Fitchburg, I saw Mary Cronin and Jimmy Kerrigan swapping spit in a motel parking lot."

"Swapping spit?" Lawson laughed at the old-fashioned phrase.

Pierce gave a tight smile, but he didn't laugh.

Lawson sat there, fitting the pieces together. Mary Cronin, squashing the state's arson investigation in the Fitchburg fire. Jimmy Kerrigan, lead developer on the Fitchburg renovation project. "Let me guess," he said, slowly, still trying to make sense of it all. "Mary Cronin made the no-arson call on the Taunton fire, too."

Unexpectedly, Pierce stood up. He smoothed down the sleeves of his nicely pressed shirt. "Follow the money, Action."

"Pardon me?"

"Why burn a building under construction?"

"I don't understand." Lawson didn't want to mess this up. Once upon a time he'd been a skilled newsman, but that'd been before.

Pierce now had his suit jacket on. Doherty was standing, as well. Lawson stayed fixed in his chair, wishing Pierce would provide a bit more direction.

"Federal funding," said Pierce. "Mill fires. Housing and Urban Development projects. You know your way around DC. See what you can dig up."

Lawson's mind raced with questions. Federal departments were worlds unto themselves. He needed Pierce to be more specific.

But Pierce shifted gears. "I understand you had a little session with the Dragon Lady. How'd that go?"

Lawson brought his mind back to the meeting in the Speaker's office. "I think she wanted to intimidate me," he said. "Get me to stop looking at fire data."

Pierce smiled. "Good, that means we're casting our lines in the right pond. And did she?"

The question perplexed Lawson. "Did she what?"

"Intimidate you."

"A little."

Pierce laughed. "Welcome to the club, Action. Hang in there. If you need help, ask Sergeant Doherty here. She's the one person who seems to cow the Dragon Lady."

Lawson looked over at Doherty, who was holding the office door open for Pierce. She smiled and shrugged.

Lawson still had questions. "What does the wind farm have to do with the Fitchburg and Taunton fires?" asked Lawson.

Pierce paused on his way out of the room. "While you're down in DC, sniff around a little on wind farms. I can't believe that thing that Kerrigan's got going out there in Burfield is legit. It's got to be connected."

"You want to understand the federal financing of two 35-year old projects?" The HUD program specialist stared back at Lawson with a decidedly unhelpful expression. He's been practicing that expression his whole career, thought Lawson.

Lawson shifted in the cubicle's cupped plastic guest chair and tried to think up something that might work on this guy. He wasn't used to having to beg. When he was Dick Law, anchorman, he only had to rely on his name to get any information he needed. Having his face on billboards all over town had an immediate effect on people. Then in his last job he'd been able to say, "I'm calling on behalf of a Member of Congress." Career bureaucrats dropped what they were doing to help out — not always cheerfully, but that didn't matter to Lawson. It was the way it worked.

He remembered what Susan Hill told him. "You're a nobody."

Here he was at HUD, a nobody trying to get something from a nobody. *Fuck.*

But, he needed this information. Lawson's calls from Boston to John MacDonald hadn't been helpful. That's why he was here in person.

After the short early morning plane ride, he'd found MacDonald, the HUD analyst, in a low-slung building down the hill from the Capitol. Less than five minutes into their meeting, Lawson wondered if face-to-face was going to be any more useful than on the phone.

John MacDonald wasn't exactly a people person.

Lawson took a breath. "I'm doing a project for the Attorney General of Massachusetts." *Might as well lead off with my best shot.*

"That's good." There was the slightest shift in MacDonald's expression: *As if I care?* MacDonald sighed. "These are the records we have." He opened a tattered binder.

Lawson leafed through the stack of spreadsheets. It looked like something you'd find in the back office at a tire dealership.

Lawson looked up just in time to see MacDonald sneak a glance at the digital clock on his desk. It was approaching noon.

"I'm less important than lunch," thought Lawson. But then he thought he might as well lay it out there. "There were fires during both renovation projects," he said. "The same developer did both of these projects. I'm trying to figure out how the fires could have benefited the developer."

MacDonald looked at his clock again.

"Am I keeping you from something?" asked Lawson.

MacDonald's face clouded.

"At last," thought Lawson. A reaction from the little bastard.

"Noon meeting," said MacDonald. "Just checking the time."

Noon meeting? In Lawson's experience, mid-level bureaucrats like MacDonald didn't have important lunch meetings. What kind of meeting did a little HUD guy go to at noon? "No way," thought Lawson.

"You could leave me here with those." Lawson pointed to the spreadsheets. "I could study them until you get back. I might not get very far, but it's progress not perfection." An AA expression: "progress, not perfection."

MacDonald looked up from his papers with what Lawson took to be a glint of interest.

"Do we have a friend in common?" asked MacDonald.

Lawson gave him a smile. "Maybe."

"Bill?"

Lawson responded. "I'm getting to know Bill pretty well." *Bill Wilson: founder of AA.* It was AA secret code — mention "Bill."

MacDonald smiled for the first time. "Want to go to a meeting?"

"Got him," thought Lawson. "As long as I have time to get to these." He pointed at the papers.

"Those spreadsheets aren't going anywhere." MacDonald was already standing, reaching for a plaid sport coat. "I'll take you through them after we get back."

In the elevator, MacDonald grinned. "This is my two-meeting day. My home group meets tonight."

With a flourish, MacDonald pushed the tape advance button on his old-fashioned desktop calculator and ripped a two-foot length of printer tape off the machine. He stapled it to another length of tape in front of him. "There you go." He handed the tapes to Lawson. "The top one shows what HUD would have paid for a project where nothing went wrong. The bottom one shows what HUD actually paid, after your friend Jimmy Kerrigan applied for the hardship factor."

It was almost five in the afternoon, and Lawson was so tired the numbers on the spreadsheets seemed to swirl before his eyes.

But he had his answer. The "hardship factor."

After the AA meeting and vending machine sandwiches at his desk, MacDonald spent four solid hours explaining exactly how Jimmy Kerrigan probably made a whole shitload of extra money by taking advantage of a process that only the federal government could have invented.

If there was any "natural" disruption in a HUD project — a fire, for instance — HUD would pay the developer to remain on the job, clean up the mess, start over from scratch, and re-build. The fire was the "hardship." The extra pay was the "hardship factor." But the disaster had to be "natural" – basically defined as anything not manmade.

Lawson squinted at the number on the bottom of the first tape, then looked at the bottom of the second tape. *No way.* He looked again. "I must be reading this wrong."

"The original project would have paid Kerrigan Development $7.2 million," said MacDonald, repeating the figure from memory. "The hardship factor made Kerrigan $13.5 million." He sat back in his chair and grinned. "Some guys have all the luck."

Lawson looked across the desk: "Shouldn't somebody down here have done something about this?" Then he had a thought: "I sound like Chavez."

MacDonald looked back and dropped his grin. Then he shrugged. That was his answer. He began to straighten his desk.

Lawson glanced at the clock: five minutes past five. He listened. The last of MacDonald's fellow cube-farm residents already made their escape.

Of course he wants to leave: But Lawson wanted just a little more. "Would you guess it's the same for the other fire?"

"I'd have to do another analysis," said MacDonald, fidgeting in his chair.

Remembering Pierce's challenge to produce, Lawson cleared his throat. "It would really be helpful if I could get the numbers for the Taunton fire, too."

"Today?" MacDonald's voice was strained.

"Anytime in the next day or two?"

MacDonald smiled. His day was over. "How's the end of tomorrow?"

Lawson reached his hand across the desk for a shake. "Thank you for the information. For the meeting, too."

In the elevator, Lawson remembered his conversation with Pierce. "The hardship factor," he asked. "Is that used with wind farms?"

MacDonald looked like Lawson asked him about a long-lost girlfriend. First his forehead crinkled in thought, then his eyes got bright. It was more life than Lawson had seen from the guy all day. "It's so weird you'd ask that. Five or six years ago, I got a call from this woman at the Department of Energy. They were revising their funding formulae for alternative energy projects. I sent her some language. Later I saw their regs. They pretty much borrowed our concept."

"How much is pretty much?"

"They hung some bells and whistles on it, but it was almost word-for-word."

"What do you think she meant by alternative energy projects?"

"Wind farms. She said something about wind farms, that's why I made the connection."

The elevator door opened and they walked through the lobby and onto the sidewalk.

MacDonald looked down the street toward the Metro station. But then, he stopped and reached in his jacket pocket for a business card and a pen. He scrawled on the back of the card. "That's the name of the woman at DOE. And I wrote my cell number, too, in case you need it."

Lawson sat on the edge of his bed at the Capitol Hilton.

He hadn't known where else to go. The hotel had a great bar; it was where he'd met Pierce at the AG's meeting.

After MacDonald trotted off toward the Metro station, Lawson stood on the sidewalk, trying to figure out what to do. He really wanted to head to the airport and go back to Boston. It was a productive day, but he really didn't want to be here. Washington was his old life, and that meant drinking.

The Tune Inn was just down the street.

He hadn't brought a change of clothes. He could head back to Boston and phone the DOE woman tomorrow from the office. But his experience on the phone with MacDonald was useless. You needed to sit across the desk from these people.

He could do this. He could stay the night in DC. What's the big deal?

Entering the hotel lobby, he'd had to push through a crowd of boisterous conventioneers. A sign in the lobby said something about Bituminous Material Contractors. He smelled the booze.

The first thing he saw when he entered his room: the mini-bar. The mini-bar key lay on the desk. He'd heard stories in meetings about situations like this. He should call down to the desk and get them to empty it.

He needed to call his sponsor Glen. That was obvious. No question. *Make that call.* He found his phone and pushed the top number in his "favorites" menu. It ran and he got his voicemail:

"Hello, this is Glen and you've reached my voicemail. This week, I'll be hiking in the White Mountains with no access to telephone service. I look forward to speaking to you when I return. Thanks so much for your call."

Lawson took a deep breath. He thought about calling Joe Guthrie, but then he'd have to explain how it was he was sitting in a DC hotel with the key to the mini bar within reach. *Shit.*

Lawson's shirt was sticky. He unbuttoned it and pulled it off. The corner of MacDonald's business card peeked out of his shirt pocket.

He glanced at the U.S. government logo and official information on the front of the card, then turned it over. On the back, he'd written MacDonald's cell number. As he punched that number into his phone, he wondered when MacDonald's evening meeting started.

Chapter 24

Still in his topcoat, Lawson sat at his desk and checked his email.

FROM: Susan Hill

TO: Richard Lawson

Be in AG office. 9 a.m. Bring your office stuff.

Finally, he thought.

Each day for the past three he sent Susan Hill a request for a meeting with Pierce, and there was no response.

He was frustrated. Pierce told him to go to Washington. He went, he was back. What he had was important.

But: "Bring your office stuff?"

Lawson's heart hit his throat. *Oh, crap. Fired. I knew this wouldn't work.* His mind flashed to his trip to DC. What else could it be?

Had he done something wrong down there? Was he supposed to get permission to stay an extra day? Was it Cronin? Did she pressure Pierce?

It was 8:30. *Better get this over with.*

He looked around for a box. The Dames kept visitor guides in boxes against the wall. He opened a half-empty box, stacked the guides on top, and flipped up the edges of the box to hide the crime.

They'd blame each other. He smiled. He'd miss that excitement, wherever he was going.

By 8:45, he was sitting in the AG's waiting room. With his box of belongings in his lap, Lawson felt like a homeless guy.

The outer door flew open.

Pierce strode in, followed by Doherty, with damp hair plastered to her head. Lawson watched her closely. *God, she's hot. Even with wet hair. Especially with wet hair.*

Then Lawson noticed: Pierce's hair was wet, too.

The drive from South Dartmouth took at least an hour. What the…? All sorts of thoughts ran through his mind.

"Squash is like life, Sergeant Doherty," Pierce was saying.

Lawson was relieved. They'd been playing squash, not…. And then he caught himself. *Jesus, I'm getting weird.*

"The ball doesn't always come to you," Pierce said. "You have to reach, strategize, maneuver." He looked over at Lawson. "Sergeant Doherty's a racquetball player. A game for the hoi polloi, don't you agree, Action?"

"Never really thought about it," said Lawson. He seriously didn't want to take sides between his boss and Maureen Doherty.

"In racquetball, the ball is always where you can get it," said Pierce. "Life just isn't like that."

Doherty walked off down the hall. "15-11 and 15-12, General. I'm getting closer. Second time out."

"Chin up, Sergeant," Pierce called after her. He winked at Lawson. "You'll get the hang of it."

I wonder what she wears when she plays? Lawson's hand crept to his belly. *How hard it was to learn to play racquetball? How long did they say in AA you had to wait to start dating again?*

"You busy today?" Pierce grinned and pointed at Lawson's cardboard box. "Or do you have tours to give?"

"Tours?" Lawson leaned over and checked out the box. In red magic marker, someone had written "Doric Dames."

"Saddle up," said Pierce. "We've got cattle to drive."

The Lincoln was a smooth ride, and. Lawson had never seen anyone so effortlessly aggressive as Sergeant Doherty. He settled back in the satiny leather of the back seat as they headed out Storrow Drive along the Charles.

For the first fifteen minutes, Pierce worked the email on his cellphone.

Finally, he tucked the cellphone in his pocket and turned to Lawson. "Stan Miles. Sheriff of Berkshire County back when I was just starting out in the U.S Attorney's Office. Good guy. Ran the Berkshire County House of Correction in Pittsfield for years. Not a better place to serve your time. Mrs. Miles did all the baking for the inmates. Didn't have any breakfast today on purpose. Looking forward to the cinnamon rolls."

In the rearview mirror, Doherty smiled back at Lawson.

He had no idea what Pierce was talking about, but he was learning this was one of Pierce's shticks. Start talking in the middle of a subject and challenge someone to catch up. "Sir, what about the cinnamon rolls?" Lawson felt stupid asking the question, but he knew that was his line.

"Jeez, Action, have some respect for the dead," said Pierce.

"The dead?"

"Keep up here. Old Stan kicked the bucket last week. We're going to his funeral. We're not just going for the grub."

It was starting to seem a little unlikely that Lawson was going to be fired today. *Unless Pierce's method of dumping an employee is to joke with him before he pulled the trigger.*

They flashed by the Harvard Business School as the Lincoln entered the Mass Pike.

"I know you've been trying to get in to see me. My schedule's been a mess. Sergeant Doherty had the idea to invite you along today."

Lawson saw Doherty's head jerk sideways to look at Pierce.

"First of all, I never had the chance to thank you," said Pierce.

"For what?"

"The information you and Chavez pulled together. The federal funding link. Not bad for a do-nothing job, huh?"

"Pardon me?"

"The policy team. When I first mentioned it to you, you said it sounded like — and I quote — a 'do-nothing job.' "

Lawson couldn't remember saying it, but Pierce was no doubt right. Pierce was famous for his memory, and Lawson's? Things back then were a little hazy. He'd just stopped drinking the week before.

There was silence in the car as Pierce went back to working his phone. As the Lincoln pulled into Pittsfield, there was no mistaking where the funeral was being held. Cars lined up on Main Street, families in dress clothes and officers in the uniforms of a dozen different law enforcement agencies were walking toward the Congregational Church, and a group of huge young men in tight t-shirts and kilts, carrying bagpipes and drums poured out of a State Police SWAT van.

"Friends of yours?" Pierce asked Doherty.

"The State Police bagpipe band, sir." It was Doherty's turn to be Pierce's straight man.

"You might want to think about giving it a try, Sergeant," said Pierce. He winked at Lawson. "What do you think, Action? She'd look pretty good in one of those kilts?"

"Maybe." Lawson knew this was shaky ground.

"Not sure she has the pecs for it, though."

"My pecs are just fine, sir," said Doherty. "Here we are, right in front." To punctuate her point, Doherty hit the brakes a little hard. Pierce grunted as he rocked forward against his seatbelt.

Everyone playing their role just right, Lawson thought. It was the first time in a long time — outside of an AA meeting, anyway – when he'd felt so comfortable. He laughed out loud, and Doherty grinned back at him in the mirror.

Pierce turned in his seat. "Jackson's Barbeque, in the middle of town. While I'm paying my respects, I suggest you and Doherty have lunch. Have the pulled pork."

"Sounds good."

"Bring me one for the ride home, okay?"

"You got it, sir," said Doherty.

"Honey chipotle."

"And a Brown."

"Of course."

Pierce flung open his door and jumped out. He started to walk away, but then, as if an afterthought, he said, "Action, a word or two out here on the sidewalk. Excuse us, Sergeant, man talk." Pierce slammed the door before she could respond.

Lawson scrambled from the back seat and shut his door, and Pierce led him a few strides away from the car. He had a wicked grin and he leaned close, his voice a whisper. "Her first name is Maureen, but don't ever call her Mo. I think she likes you."

Pierce started to move to the church, but Lawson reached out and grabbed his arm. He really needed to know – this was important.

"Why are you doing this?"

Pierce paused, dropped his grin, and pointed at the state police bagpipers. "See those guys? She was married to one of them once, not one of them, exactly, but the type – big, macho, full of himself. Met him at the academy. Didn't last long. Maureen's a smart girl, big Irish family. She's a marathoner, she reads three or four papers every day, books. She finished first in her class at the academy she's going to be better than the life that was laid out for her." He paused, a slight grin returning to his face. "Now, to your question. You're something of a mystery, Action. To her and to me. Not really who you were, people who have been around town for while remember that. But the jury is out on who you're going to become. A different person, less sure of yourself, humble, more interesting, funny. She sees that. God knows how." He smiled to show he was kidding. "Gotta go. Don't want to miss the opening hymn. One more thing." His face returned to serious. "Maureen Doherty has been with me three years, night and day. She's like a daughter to me. She was hurt in her first marriage and she's a good person. Let me put it simply. Don't fuck this up. You're on the way back, but she's already there.

Make sure you've got your shit together if you are serious." Pierce reached over, squeezed Lawson's shoulder, then went into the church. Lawson stood on the sidewalk and rubbed his shoulder. It felt like something his dad used to do. He turned to find Doherty.

While they waited at the counter in Jackson's, Lawson compared his height to Doherty's. She was a couple of inches taller, but maybe, he thought, it was the boots. He stood up straighter and checked again. Then he thought about what Pierce said. "You're on your way back, but she's already there." He considered that.

They took their sandwiches to a corner table in the sunlight under a hanging asparagus fern. Doherty put hers down went back to the counter. She returned with two brown bottles. Lawson looked up in alarm. *Beer? Didn't she remember? Did she even know? How do I tell her?* And then, *can she drink on duty?*

She set the bottles on the table and looked at him. Lawson wondered if she could tell what he was thinking. She turned his bottle so the label faced him. "Berkshire Brown. Root beer. They make it down the street." And then she smiled and took a sip from her bottle. "The Boss loves it."

Lawson struggled to find something to say as he sipped his drink. Trying to sound casual, he asked, "What's with Pierce and all those cowboy expressions?"

Doherty swallowed her first bite and gave a short laugh. "He loves old Westerns. He watches them late at night. Ever since his wife died."

Lawson looked skeptical, and Doherty saw it. "It's kind of cute, actually. Takes the edge off that tight-ass WASP image. It's a small thing, leave it alone."

Lawson knew he hit a nerve. Clearly, Doherty was as protective of Pierce as he was of her.

They ate their sandwiches in silence for a while, and then Doherty changed the subject. "You need to watch out for Mary Cronin."

"How so?" asked Lawson. He didn't need to be told, but he wanted to hear Doherty's take.

"Cronin does anything she can to screw Ethan Pierce," Doherty went on, "and now she has you in her sights. If she was involved in Fitchburg and Taunton, and you and Pierce go after Kerrigan, you better have a strong case."

"Why's that?"

"She'll hide behind the statute of limitations. Crimes can't be prosecuted after a certain period of time. Plus, she fights dirty. She'll fuck both of you over six ways to Sunday."

Lawson knew his eyes had widened at her language.

She gave him an innocent smile. "We wouldn't want that to happen to my two favorite guys, would we?"

Lawson struggled to catch his breath.

Doherty had a root beer mustache on her lip. It was all Lawson could do not to lean forward and wipe it off.

Doherty and Lawson sat in the Lincoln and watched the mourners exit the church. There was a comfortable silence between them since their lunch.

Pierce emerged into the sunlight, walking down the steps from the church with his hand under the elbow of the widow. Shaking hands, giving hugs, saying goodbyes, he made his way to the front passenger door and got in the car.

The bagpipers began to play "Amazing Grace."

"Okay, Sergeant, let's move out of here with dispatch."

"With dispatch, sir."

"But with dignity. Don't burn any rubber."

As Doherty pulled back onto the turnpike, Pierce twisted the top from his root beer and opened the paper wrapper around his sandwich. He turned in his seat. "Where are we with all this?"

Lawson was still considering his newfound intelligence from Maureen Doherty. "How big a deal is Mary Cronin's statute of limitations?" he asked.

Pierce made a scoffing noise. "Mary would have a rare moment of corporal pleasure if she heard you call it 'her' statute of limitations. But legally she's right, these crimes happened thirty years ago. Even with the new information you and your man Chavez are pulling together, there's no going back and charging them."

"Doesn't seem fair if they're guilty."

"Unless they can be linked to new information of a new crime. And that crime is part of what they call an 'on-going pattern.' Then you can allege a 'criminal enterprise.' Has a nice ring, don't you think?"

Doherty entered the Mass Pike and called the State Police op center and let them know they were en route. Then she accelerated up to 85.

Lawson leaned forward a bit. He wanted to make himself heard, but he didn't want to seem too eager. "I have some new information."

Pierce turned his head slightly. "Fire away."

Lawson explained what he'd learned from MacDonald: the funding process, the hardship factor and the exact numbers. "The bottom line," he concluded, "is that Kerrigan's profit on the projects nearly doubled because of the fires."

"Doubled?" said Pierce.

"I did a memo." Lawson handed it over. He felt like a kid turning in a good essay to a favorite teacher.

Pierce flipped through the pages. "What federal blockhead thought that up? A hardship factor? The developer bills twice?" He paused to consider. "But it can't be arson. Leave it to Jimmy Kerrigan to figure that out. So that's what they did."

"There's more," said Lawson. "You asked me to see if there was a wind farm connection?"

Lawson saw Pierce's head jerk up. "And?"

"The Department of Energy's got a hardship factor, too. They lifted the exact language from HUD. Plus they've got another one called a 'mitigation relocation.' If a wind farm doesn't perform because of low wind, they'll pay to move it. Rebuild somewhere else. So, DOE has two regulations to watch out for."

"Unbelievable. First mill fires and now wind farms. Do these federal agencies just sit around and think of ways they can be scammed? A hardship factor and a mitigation relocation." He paused for a minute, thinking. "Now we need to figure out how they're going to do it." Pierce thought some more and looked over the seat. "Are you a fisherman, Action?"

"Can't say I am."

"Anglers will have you believe they are after a wily and elusive quarry. But the fact is fish have a brain the size of a pinhead. You see a bass hit a lure and they must know it's not real, right? There's even one called a Hula Popper. It has a little rubber skirt around the hooks. But, you throw it next to a lily pad and the bass can't help himself even if the lure does look stupid."

"I'm not sure I get the point."

"Stay up on the metaphors, Action. Greed overwhelms smarts. In fish and in criminals."

The Lincoln rolled to a stop to drop Lawson off at his condo in Concord. From there, Doherty and Pierce were heading to South Dartmouth. For the last fifteen miles Lawson considered how to broach the subject, but Pierce was on the phone.

Lawson got out of the car and stood on the sidewalk. He motioned for

Pierce to roll his window down. There was no choice but to ask the question in front of Maureen Doherty.

"Uh, General, could I bring up another subject?"

Pierce put his phone down. "Make it snappy. Sergeant Doherty won't use the siren on the highway. We need to beat the traffic."

Briefly, Lawson was slowed by the image of Doherty handling the black Lincoln, barreling along with its siren wailing. "Uh, Susan Hill sent me a note this morning and told me to bring my stuff over to your office...." He let the sentence die off. At this point he didn't think he was going to be fired, but he needed to understand.

Pierce slapped the dashboard. "I almost forgot, Action. You're getting a promotion."

Lawson struggled with the news. "Sir?" It was all he could say.

"Associate Attorney General for Communications. Job's been vacant. You fit the bill. Don't have to be a lawyer. Are you in? Sorry for the lack of ceremony."

Lawson had a moment of panic and fleetingly thought of asking for time to make the decision. *Sorry Mr. Attorney General, I need to check with my AA sponsor....*

He took a breath. "I'm in."

Pierce reached out the window for a handshake. "Good answer. It's time." He winked. Then addressing Doherty, "Move it out, Sergeant."

Lawson watched the Lincoln pull away. *It's time? For him or for me?* He saw the driver's side window roll down. Maureen Doherty's arm came out. She gave him a thumbs up.

Chapter 25

Fourteen frozen dinners sat in a grocery bag on the counter in George Fleming's kitchen.

Fleming returned from the Quincy Stop and Shop and clicked on the television as he entered the apartment. Immediately he heard the warning buzzer the TV station used for a weather emergency alert. An earnest young weather forecaster looked into the camera.

"It doesn't happen very often, but when it does, watch out. Tonight we have a surprise, a highly potent low-pressure system moving in from the Atlantic and colliding with a ridge of high-pressure Canadian air over the Long Island Sound. Folks in central Connecticut and Massachusetts better batten down the hatches. This maritime air mass will head north right up the Connecticut River valley. Hurricane force winds and torrential rains are headed your way in the next two to three hours."

Fleming stood in the kitchen, thinking. A month ago, he bowed to pressure. Jimmy Kerrigan wanted the DOE to speed up its finding that the wind farm was in a bad location. Even with the paltry wind flow, he set the brakes on the rotor, oriented the yaw drive so the turbine rarely faced the wind, and vectored the blades so radically the only way they'd work would be in a tornado. It had done the trick. For the past month, the turbine blades barely spun. And, everything would continue to work fine unless there was a big wind. And he'd been watching the weather forecasts like a hawk. Now, *fuck!*

Hurriedly he pulled his laptop out of his briefcase, and clicked into the wind farm's remote control system. A banner ran across the top of the screen: *Power Interruption.* Frustrated, he hit the brake control button just to be sure. No response. He flashed back to the planning session three years before when Kerrigan nixed the expensive back-up power system. "The fucking thing won't run long enough for us to need that. We'll put it in the second site and charge the feds."

Then he thought about going out there and rigging up a battery back up in the control room on the ridge. That might work. Thirty seconds later he was in his truck on the way to Burfield.

Don Nichols had been glued to The Weather Channel for the past hour.

He was an avid weather watcher, and a locally born mini-hurricane was something anyone would want on their bucket list. He studied the satellite images over the Long Island Sound as the storm grew in size and started to move northeast. His personal weather station, with outdoor measuring devices connected to the computerized display in his kitchen, was showing 45-mph winds, the barometer falling like a stone, still almost eighty degrees. At ten, he went outside to watch the high winds move the clouds across the nearly full moon.

Nichols looked up to the west. In the bright moonlight, the turbine blades, which normally were almost motionless, were spinning so fast they were almost invisible.

Nearly invisible, except ... *What the hell?*

Narrowing his eyes, he looked closer.

He tilted his head to change the angle.

He rubbed his eyes and looked harder.

From the turbine furthest to the south, closest to the oncoming wind, a thin trail of sparks spun across the nighttime sky.

Jason's mother was having her last smoke of the day on the back step of her doublewide.

The wind was blowing pretty hard, and she cupped the Marlboro to keep it from going out. It was a long day at work. She sighed and sniffed the air. Despite her two-pack-a-day habit, Darcy Morrill swore her sense of smell was better than a bloodhound's. Now, she was sure she could detect that chemical odor she sometimes smelled before a storm. *What was the word? Ozone. Like air fresheners. There was something else in the air, too. An electrical smell? Like burning wires?*

Everyone in town said Leland Bird could tell what was wrong with an engine by listening to it. He well-knew the sounds from the turbines on Matchic Ridge, an undertone drone, with the whoosh, whoosh of the turbine blades on those rare occasions when the winds blew.

Tonight, the sound was off, seriously off. Different than he'd ever heard it. It sounded like a car engine revving way over its limits.

Terry Jokkinen's pager vibrated, and its tone sounded.

He'd been playing gin at the kitchen table with Bertie. As usual, he'd been losing.

Without bothering to check the message on his phone, he laid his cards on the table and looked apologetically at his wife.

She rolled her eyes and gathered the cards. Interruptions were part of her life with a firefighter.

Jokkinen placed his call to the Regional Communications Center in Gardner.

"Chief, we have a call from a Burfield resident," said the dispatcher. "Mr. Nichols. He reports sparks are flying off the blades of a turbine on Matchic Ridge."

"Hold on a second," said Jokkinen, and he stepped onto his back deck. He could see the wind farm from there and he felt something shoot through his chest. Sure enough, that fucking turbine was lit up like a kid's push-button pinwheel. This wasn't going to be some pissant grass fire.

"Sound the General Alarm alert for Burfield," he told the dispatcher. "Sound it twice." He ended the call, reconsidered, and called back. "Send a mutual aid alert. Repeat, send an alert to our primary forest fire responders."

He headed for his truck, thinking. At this very moment, fire chiefs in 25 surrounding towns were being alerted. They would have to mobilize. This was either going to be a hot one or something he was going to get shit for at chiefs' meetings for years to come.

Chavez Simons's pager vibrated and beeped on his bedside table, and the fire horn blew 3-3-3.

He rolled over in bed and opened his eyes, not sure what he was hearing. He read the LED on his pager.

Message for Burfield Fire Department: GENERAL ALARM.

He jumped out of bed. *This is big.*

Peter Simons, on his knees between Hollis' legs in front of his office couch, jerked his head up. The fire horn might have been in the next room, it was so loud.

Hollis Kerrigan, splayed out with her Land's End corduroys down around her ankles, hissed, "For Christ's sake, Peter, I'm not done."

Then the horn blew the general alarm for the second time.

Peter stood up. He was still dressed. It was the way she liked it.

His cellphone rang, and he checked the number. *Shit, it was Catherine. She never called.* He looked at Hollis, put a finger to his lips, and took the call.

He listened and then pressed the call-end button — and pressed it twice more, a little paranoid about Catherine still being on the line and overhearing — and took a breath, trying to figure out the best way to tell Hollis. "One of the turbines is on fire."

She reacted predictively; "Goddammit, what are you people doing to me?"

"Maybe it's just an electrical thing."

"Why are they blowing that fucking horn? Those fucking firemen. Why don't they just go up there and take care of it?"

On the Town Common, a 70-mile-per-hour gust lifted off half the bandstand roof and tossed it into the front yard of the library.

In the Albertsons' Orchard, the last of the remaining Cortlands were blasted from their trees.

And on Matchic Ridge, the five turbines — adjusted by George Fleming to resist the wind — did just that.

In Turbine #1, closest to the oncoming wind, the heat generated by the spinning blades boiled the lubricating oil in the gearbox, which in turn burned through the gearbox gaskets. Eighty gallons of oil spilled into the nacelle, the RV-sized structure housing the guts of the turbine. As the super-heated oil spewed out onto the blades, it flamed brightly, burning red, then blue, tipped with yellow. The blades flung the flaming liquid high into the windy night.

The pines ignited first, then quickly passed their flames to the birches, beeches, sugar maples, and oaks. Burfield's reputation as a premier source of firewood was well deserved. In less than fifteen minutes, it was a full-fledged forest fire.

The Burfield fire call theater had never opened with such urgency. Three horn blasts, three blasts, three blasts. Then again. Then again. Then unbelievably, the horn blew again. Three blasts, three blasts, three blasts, repeated twice more.

Every able Burfield resident was outside in the hot night, drawn by the high winds, the claxoning fire horn, and the sirens on the volunteer firefighters' personal vehicles.

On the ridge above the town, they saw a spinning, burning turbine, and underneath, the first flames of a forest fire.

Above everything was the full moon.

It was a spectacular sight.

The Chief started the Brushbuster and left it to idle, and when he climbed down, Chavez was there in full gear, ready to roll.

Unbelievably, Squeaky Townsend was there, too. "Fell asleep after work," he mumbled, "on the couch in the DPW garage."

Jokkinen's cell phone rang. It was Kenny Dutton. He was in Worcester, 45 minutes away, at a big church meeting with his wife.

"Looks like he'll miss the show," said Jokkinen.

Chavez moved to the driver's door. This was it, he was sure, his chance to drive the Brushbuster, and on a huge call. But the Chief put a hand on Chavez's shoulder and leaned in. "I know you could," he said. "You know the truck better than anyone, but I just can't let a cadet drive a truck on a call." Chavez's face fell.

"Squeaky, you're driving," said Jokkinen. "You two hurry to the top of the south access road. Get water on that turbine and the woods around it. Maybe you can catch it soon enough to knock it down."

"Why me?" muttered Squeaky. "Kenny'll be here pretty soon, and—"

"You're the first alternate driver," said Jokkinen.

"Fine." Squeaky climbed up into the driver's seat and revved the engine. At least one cylinder was missing. The truck vibrated.

Jokkinen stood by the driver's door. "Just take it easy, Squeaky. It's not a fucking snowplow."

Jokkinen chirped the tires on Chief 1 as he backed down the driveway. As he swung the SUV around, Ruth White chugged her van to a stop on the fire station lawn and popped out wearing a turtleneck sweater, sweatpants and fuzzy slippers. She dragged her gear out of the back seat. Jokkinen leaned across and opened the passenger door. "Jump in."

Jokkinen glanced at the clock on the dash. It was 10:23 p.m., 19 minutes after Don Nichols's call to the EOC. *Not bad.* He hit the siren.

It took him nine minutes to reach the north access road to the wind farm. The radio crackled as Engine 301 and Tanker 302 left the station behind him. During the drive, Ruth pulled her gear on over her sweats, and Jokkinen thought about a command plan. The north road was the further of the two roads from the flaming turbine, but he needed to see how fast the fire was spreading. He had to make a quick decision on mutual aid from the other towns.

He skidded to a stop in the Quabbin Museum parking lot, with its replica of an old wooden water wheel and its sluice heading into a pond. Jokkinen knew it was the nearest water source on this side of the forest.

He picked up his radio mic.

"Engine 301, proceed to the museum parking lot. Drop a hose in the pond."

He thought about the antique Tanker 302. He knew the 1100 gallons on the Brushbuster wouldn't last long, so ideally he'd like 302 to follow the Brushbuster up the south access road to deliver water to the fire. But Tanker 302 was in even worse shape than the Brushbuster. He felt a flash of anger about Hollis's promised new fire truck.

The wind was howling down from the ridge, directly towards town. In their drills, they identified points where they would make a stand against a big fire in the forest, if one ever came down the mountain. Albertsons' Orchard was the first stand of open land to with access from the road.

"Tanker 302, proceed to Crooked Road in back of the Albertsons' orchard. Set up there."

Frannie Polansky's voice crackled through the radio: "Will do. 302 out."

Good man, thought Jokkinen. Polansky was the deputy chief in charge of Tanker 302. A "will do" from Frannie was all he needed.

Jokkinen jumped back in Chief 1, and Ruth White, bulky and awkward in full gear, clamored in beside him. Jokkinen yanked the lever to engage the four-wheel drive, and he raced up the winding road so quickly they outran their headlights into turns.

They exited the forest on the far northern end of the wind farm. The operations shed stood to their right.

Jokkinen stared up through the windshield. The wind grabbed hold of flames in the treetops and whipped them higher than the tops of the turbine blades. The forest was burning. Really burning.

Jokkinen was used to low burning brush and grass fires, maybe a structure fire like a barn or, rarely, a house. But this was a spectacular fire. A for-real forest fire, the kind you see on the news, so immense and fierce that even here, at the far end of the wind farm, it assaulted all his senses: he smelled the smoke and the sizzling resin, heard the crackling evergreen needles and explosions in the oaks, felt waves of heat against his face.

Jokkinen jumped out and climbed onto the bumper for a better look. The fire spread half a mile across the ridge to the fourth turbine, and it was making its way down the ridge, too, heading toward town.

The first thing Ruth White noticed when she opened the truck door was the wind. It simply staggered her, lifting her heavy fire jacket and flaring it out behind her like a cape. She'd never been in wind like this.

She tossed her helmet back onto the seat. In this wind, she couldn't hope to keep it on.

She looked up. Flames leaped across the ridge, and heavy storm clouds blew across the moon.

White heard the sound, first the roar of the wind — somewhere in the middle of the musical scale — accompanied by the low "woofing" noise of the turbines. But what she really noticed was a grinding noise. Like her garbage disposal working on a fork, she thought, but higher and louder.

She looked down the line of turbines, all illuminated by the blazing fire. Turbine #1 was totally involved in the fire, and now sparks were coming from Turbine #2.

Then she noticed the heat. It tightened her face and it felt like it was singing her hair. She needed her helmet after all, even if she had to hold it on with her hand. She looked over at Chief Jokkinen, wondering how long they were going to stay up there.

Jokkinen now had a sense of the size of the fire and the direction it was moving. He needed to get back down the ridge. "Let's go. Get in."

White scrambled for her door.

In the museum parking lot, Engine 301 was in position, its six-inch suction hose in the millpond.

Jokkinen looked at Ruth White. She was an assistant in a veterinary office and had been a firefighter for ten years. She never complained about the overly male atmosphere in the station, in fact most of the guys looked up to her. "After this, I need to drop you back at the station."

White looked up sharply but the Chief continued.

"I'm going to run things out here, but we're going to need a shitload of mutual aid. I need you to coordinate command and control from there. Think you can handle that?" Jokkinen knew what her answer would be.

"Hell, yeah."

"Okay, pay attention now."

The Chief dug around between the front seats and pulled out a folded map of the town. He handed it to White along with a pen. The interior lights of the truck were on. Beads of sweat ran down White's face and into her turtleneck. She reached into her jacket and pulled her sweater away from her body, first one side, then the other.

Jokkinen called the regional communications center on his radio. "Dispatch, stay on the line. Patch me through to all units. And get Chief Winchell at the Burfield Police Department patched in."

He waited, and the dispatcher came back. "All set, Chief."

"All units, I have commands for all units," said Jokkinen. "Matchic Ridge is fully engulfed in a forest fire. The fire is burning from the south to the north and east. Engine 301, stay in position at the millpond. You will have the first engagement, but be prepared to evacuate as soon you need to." Jokkinen knew his whole department was on the line, as well as everybody with a public safety scanner. In a town like Burfield, that meant nearly everyone. He took a breath to steady his voice. He knew his tone would be important. "It will be your call to evacuate. *Do not be heroes.* Do you copy?"

"301, gotcha." The Chief looked up across the parking lot. Stevie Gray commanded Engine 301. Stevie waved from the driver's side of the truck.

Jokkinen reached over and tapped a spot on the map. When White didn't respond, he grabbed her hand holding the pen and guided it to the spot and motioned to mark it. White understood. She drew an *x* in the museum parking lot and wrote *301* next to it.

"Tanker 302, stay in position on Crooked Road. Confirm."

"All set here, Chief."

This time, White didn't have to be told. She drew an *x* on the map and wrote *302*.

"Dispatch, do you copy?"

"Right here, Chief."

Jokkinen retrieved a pair of reading glasses from the cup holder where he kept them. He drew a line around the ridge, marking water sources, then marking locations where mutual-aid crews could do the most good. He went back on the radio. "Dispatch, I need mutual-aid apparatus at the following locations." He named them off. "Read those locations back to me."

The woman's voice came back, reading off the list.

"All other responding mutual aid apparatus should report to the Burfield station and will be deployed by Firefighter White. Copy?"

"Copy, Chief."

"Chief Winchell?" Terry Jokkinen didn't relish this conversation with Burfield's weak-sister police chief.

Winchell's voice came over the speaker. "Chief Jokkinen, it's Chief Winchell. I'm monitoring the situation."

Jokkinen purposely slowed his voice. "Chief, we are going to fight this fire with our own equipment on the edge of the forest, on the east and the north. In an outer circle, I've formed a perimeter of mutual aid responders."

"We're in good hands, here, Chief."

Hearing this, Jokkinen rolled his eyes at White before he continued. "This fire is huge. With this wind, it's likely to jump our equipment. If it does, the neighborhoods on the north and east side of the mountain will be in danger. An evacuation is your call, but I'd strongly suggest you start clearing people out of those areas." Jokkinen paused. He knew this would make Artie Winchell shit his pants.

Jokkinen waited. There was a silence from Winchell's end. Jokkinen waited for questions. There were always questions from Artie Winchell.

Finally, the radio crackled. "O…K." The word was drawn out and then there was a silence. "Over and out." Terry Jokkinen had been listening to radio traffic his whole career. Artie Winchell didn't sound too good.

In the tiny police station, Winchell put the mic down on his desk, stood up, and headed for the bathroom — quickly, unbuckling his gun belt as he went.

Winchell started out working for Burfield's parks and recreation department. When that was disbanded, he'd moved into law enforcement. Winchell's stature in town was based more on grudging acceptance than on respect. Artie's police station was always neat as a pin, with nice flowers out front, and Artie always wore a fresh uniform. Somebody needed to be chief.

When Winchell returned from the bathroom, he was alarmed to see a stream of local residents headed up his carefully tended walk. Worst of all, there was Hollis Kerrigan, obviously in full bitch mode, right in front. Peter Simons was with her.

Hollis marched into the station. "Evacuation, Artie?" Hollis's voice was like a knife. "Artie, that's crazy. Jokkinen's gone off the deep end. You don't need to evacuate anything."

Winchell sat behind his desk. Hollis must have heard the conversation about evacuation on a scanner. He fretted: "Jokkinen knows his business, but if I tell the people to evacuate their houses in the middle of the night, and it turns out there really wasn't any danger...." He gestured at a map on his desk. At Jokkinen's instruction on the radio, he scribbled over the areas Jokkinen wanted cleared of residents. It amounted to half the town. "How am I supposed to do *that*?" He stood up and walked to the window as if that would give him the answer. The fire station across the street was empty, with its three big garage doors up, everyone out at the big fire.

"Artie?" True to form, Hollis wasn't letting up. "Just let them do their job and put the stupid fire out."

At the window, Winchell said, "I'm thinking, Hollis. I have Chief Jokkinen's recommendation under consideration."

In the distance, a symphony of emergency vehicle sirens could be heard, getting louder. There were two different sirens, the high-end whoop, whoop of a police cruiser and the European style claxon horn used by newer fire trucks. Then, blue, red, and yellow lights flashed across the walls.

Three state police cars wheeled into the circle in front of the police station.

Then a huge, shiny hook-and-ladder fire truck pulled into the driveway of the fire station. It was easy to read the gold lettering on the door: *City of Gardner Fire Department.* Five firefighters piled out of the Gardner truck. Ruth White came out of the station to greet them.

"What the fuck are *they* doing here?" said Hollis.

Peter Simons scooted his chair back as three Massachusetts State Police officers pushed into the room. A towering African American with sergeant's stripes on his bulging short sleeve shirt, was in the lead. Artie Winchell staggered away from the window and took refuge behind his desk.

"Are you the Chief?" asked the sergeant.

Winchell mumbled, as if he hoped they would leave him alone: "I'm Artie Winchell."

The sergeant paused for a few seconds, carefully studying Winchell. Peter could tell: the sergeant already knew everything he needed to know about Burfield's police chief. "Chief, what's the situation here?"

Winchell gulped, took a breath, cleared his throat, and squinted, reading the sergeant's nametag. "Thank you for your prompt response, Trooper. I'm sure we are all grateful for your … diligence."

"It's Sergeant," the man said. "Sergeant Oscar Weaver. Now, Chief" — he spoke very slowly, as if that would help Winchell understand — "what's … going … on?"

"Uh, we have a fire in our…." Winchell hesitated as he searched for the word. "Wind farm."

"It's a forest fire," said Hollis. "And it's not that big a deal."

Weaver turned to her. "Who are you, ma'am?"

"I'm Hollis Kerrigan, president of the Matchic Ridge Wind Farm."

"So, Ms. Kerrigan, it's your windmills that are burning up there on the hill."

Hollis's lips started to move, but at first no sound came out, and Peter could tell this wasn't going to go well. Peter pictured this state police guy pulling over preppy women like Hollis in their foreign sports cars, speeding, drinking coffee, talking on their phones, and giving him lip.

He tried to intercede. "I'm Ms. Kerrigan's attorney."

Sergeant Weaver said, "Does she need an attorney?"

"That isn't what I meant," stammered Peter. "It's just that—"

"Do you have anything to add which would help the situation here?"

"No," said Peter.

Hollis said, "I just think we are over-reacting."

Weaver was just about done with the bullshit. "Maybe you'd like to explain that to someone who loses their house?"

Hollis puffed her indignation, but Weaver turned away from her. "Chief, what is the status of your evacuation?"

As Winchell turned the map so it faced Weaver, Peter saw that the broad back of Winchell's uniform shirt was drenched with sweat. "I was evaluating the evacuation recommendation. In this area right here." Using a bright yellow highlighter, Winchell drew a circle around the area of town that Jokkinen suggested twenty minutes earlier.

Weaver grabbed the map. "Okay, let's make this happen. Rocco, take this area here." He pulled the highlighter out of Winchell's fingers and drew an oblong shape on the map. "Joey, take this area. I'll take this section. Each of us will take a local as a guide. Use your sirens and lights. Make two passes through with loud speakers. Then go back and go door-to-door. Everybody up and out. Call in if people need rides. Chief you stay here to maintain command and control." He held the map out to Winchell. "And get a picture of this map on the town's website."

The Brushbuster died halfway up the mountain.

The antique truck just couldn't take Squeaky Townsend's clumsy combination of gear grinding and engine racing as they squeezed through the tight turns on the access road. Chavez tried to help out, explaining the truck needed double clutching, but Squeaky was an unwilling and inept student.

The muffler tore off on the first big bump, and the unmuffled roar of the engine, the tortured transmission, and the screech of the tree limbs tearing at the ladders on the side of the truck was deafening.

And then, all that noise was gone, and in the sudden silence, sitting in the darkened cab, Chavez heard the ominous rumble of the wind-whipped fire coming down the mountain.

Above it all, there was the high-pitched screaming of the over-worked turbines as they were blasted by the wind.

Squeaky ground the truck's starter over and over again. Each time, the truck's battery produced less power, until there was just a futile clicking.

Without the battery, the truck's radio went dead. Chavez tried the walkie-talkie. It powered up, but there wasn't any signal. Chavez wondered if the repeater tower on the fire station had come down in the high winds.

He pulled out his phone, called the Chief's cellphone, and got Jokkinen's voicemail. He left a message: "Hi, Chief, this is Chavez. The Brushbuster died halfway up the mountain. It's blocking the road. Squeaky and I are walking down the access road."

"No, we're not," said Squeaky. "We're staying with the truck."

Chavez did a quick assessment of their situation. Stuck on the road. No radio. The fire headed towards them. With fat, unwilling Squeaky Townsend.

This was — to be sure — a Class-A Clusterfuck.

Pierce was just about done for the night. He stood on the back deck of his house on Mishaum Point.

The southerly wind was blasting, blowing right in his face, chasing clouds across the moon. When the moon was out, it illuminated the white sands of Barney's Joy Beach across the bay.

Doherty had dropped him at the main house. He had just about finished his second scotch when he heard knocking at the front door.

It had to be Doherty, he thought. They had an early start in the morning, so she had gone over to the guesthouse. He was the only one who lived out here on the point past September. Pierce opened the door. In white running shorts and a Red Sox t-shirt, Doherty stood on the porch with her phone in her hand.

"I thought you'd be interested in this," she said. "I got a heads-up from our Command Center. The Burfield wind farm is on fire."

Pierce stood there and absorbed the news. Then he gave Doherty a cockeyed grin. "So — they are really going to do it. Unbelievable."

Lawson was on his back in bed, thinking. People in AA talked about the power of prayer but Lawson hadn't gotten that far. Right now, he was content with just reflecting on his day.

His phone buzzed on the bedside table. Since he'd gotten his promotion, he'd started leaving it on at night. He didn't know why, it just seemed the thing to do.

He looked at the screen display. "Maureen Doherty." His eyes widened. Yes, he programmed his phone with her cell number he got from the laminated card, but he never expected...

"Hello." He practiced saying it out loud, once. Then he clicked the call. "Hey, Maureen."

There was no answer. He must have hung up on the call. Panicked, he squinted at the screen to figure out how to call her back. *What did she want? To chat? A date? Don't be stupid, Lawson.*

The phone rang again while he had it close to his face and he almost dropped it. "Uh, hi. Uh, Maureen?" It wasn't the tone he was aiming for.

"Is that you, Action?" Doherty sounded business-like.

Lawson consciously took a breath so he could equal her tone. "Yes, yes it is."

"Did I wake you up?"

"No, not really."

"Because it sounded like some geezer answered his phone and dropped it."

Lawson didn't know what to say. He was having his first call with Maureen Doherty and she was giving him shit. *Just like Pierce. What was it with these two?*

"What's up?" It was the first coherent thing he'd said.

"The wind farm's on fire. Thought you should know."

"Uh, thanks, uh," he struggled to come up with something. "Do you think I should go out there?" It was an automatic response: Dick Law would have gone — drunk, sober, or anyplace in between.

Doherty gave a short laugh. "I don't think so, Action. Not unless you've got some fire fighting experience I don't know about."

Lawson absorbed this. She sounded warmer, more playful.

She switched gears. "OK, gotta hit the sack. Don't let the bed bugs bite."

Lawson smiled. His mom used to say that.

Doherty spoke again. "Tell the Dragon Lady I said hello. Sorry to wake you guys up."

"What?" The call clicked off.

"I think we ought to stay here," said Squeaky. "That's what they say when you're lost. Don't wander around. Makes things worse for the rescuers. Besides, I got asthma."

"Squeak, we're not lost," said Chavez, "and anyway, no one knows we need rescuing." He looked over. Squeaky had been a Regular Firefighter forever, but Chavez knew none of that mattered. "We're stuck on the access road. Our radios don't work. Nobody's coming to rescue us. We need to get down the hill."

As if to prove his point, Squeaky began coughing, a little at first, then long and deep.

Chavez looked out the window of the truck. Smoke swirled through the trees, and when he looked back at Squeaky, he saw the truck cab was smoky from the burned-out engine.

Chavez reached over and slapped Squeaky on his sweaty back. Squeaky finished his fit by resting his forehead on the steering wheel.

"Let's get going," said Chavez.

"I'm the senior officer on the truck," wheezed Squeaky. "What I say goes, and I say we wait here."

Chavez thought quickly. Squeaky was the worst fireman in the department. Probably the worst fireman in New England. And Chavez knew they needed to get back down the road. He needed to call his bluff.

"If you want to stay here," said Chavez, "that's fine. But I'm going down the hill." He reached into the back seat. "I'm taking an air pack. That leaves two for you. I'll try to find some guys to come back for you." He pushed his door open and squeezed out though the brush next to the truck.

Then he heard Squeaky. "Wait." Squeaky tried to push his door open.

On Barre Road, the truck from the Town of Royalston had a suction hose dropped into Fletcher Pond. The four-man crew was wetting down the grass field in front of them.

On Amherst Road, the City of Fitchburg truck parked next to the Swift River. Firefighters unrolled two hoses and began soaking a stand of trees.

Two miles away, the five firemen from the Town of Athol were doing the same thing, pulling water from Stony Creek.

When the mutual-aid firefighters looked up at the ridge, they saw all five turbines on fire, spewing sparks into the wind.

Halfway down the ridge, the forest was ablaze.

Ash and glowing embers carried over their heads.

Squeaky bent over with both hands on his knees. "I gotta stop." His belly hung out of his undershirt over his belt. His back hunched up and down as he tried to catch his breath. Then he dropped to his hands and knees on the gravel road.

It hadn't been smooth, that was sure, but they'd made it halfway down the access road.

Chavez had to give Squeaky credit. The flames and smoke and embers seemed to have energized him — at least for fifteen minutes or so.

Once or twice, Chavez let himself think they might make it down without stopping. But now Squeaky stopped, and getting him going wasn't going to be easy.

The smoke was heavier now, visible, swirling around their chests every time the full moon came out from behind the clouds. Worse, he could hear crackling behind them. How far behind? Chavez wondered. No way to tell, but definitely getting closer.

They'd worked out a system for walking. Squeaky trudged along with one heavy hand on Chavez's shoulder, Chavez carried the air pack on the other shoulder, and every five steps he gave Squeaky a shot of air. Squeaky was quiet, his usual non-stop complaining trumped by his struggle for breath. Little by little, Squeaky's heavy breathing turned into a wet wheezing sucking sound.

And now he was on hands and knees in the middle of the access road.

In first aid class, they said getting the victim to talk was important. Chavez didn't know if Squeaky could be called a victim, but he sure was acting like it. "Squeaky? How are you doing? Talk to me, Squeak."

No response. With the wind roaring around them, Squeaky might not have even heard. But was he acting hurt, or was he really hurting?

Chavez glanced behind him, up the road, toward the fire. The smoke was so thick, he knew he wouldn't see anything, but embers were swirling all around, and everything told him the fire was getting close.

"Squeaky! I need you to talk to me."

Slowly, Squeaky lifted his head. Chavez unhooked his Maglite from his belt and pointed it into Squeaky's face. He was a mess, with tears pouring out of his eyes and leaving ashy tracks down his pudgy cheeks and into his beard. A double stream of snot flowed through his mustache and into his mouth. "What?" His breathing was so heavy, he gasped the word out.

Chavez got down on one knee and looked into Squeaky's face. "We really need to get out of here. Can you walk some more?"

Squeaky shook his head miserably.

A wave of panic washed over Chavez. *What would the Chief want me to do?* He looked back up the mountain. Through the smoke, he saw a yellowish sky. The fire couldn't be moving that fast, could it? He gave himself a shot from the air pack, then gave a long one to Squeaky. He checked the pressure valve. Almost out. Normally an air pack would last 45 minutes, but that was for a regular guy, not Squeaky.

"Okay, Squeak, let's get you up." Chavez stood up, set his feet firmly on the road, grabbed Squeaky's turnout coat, and gave him a tug.

Squeaky hardly budged.

"Squeak, you've gotta help. When I pull, you need to get your legs under you and lift up."

"Just leave me."

"I can't do that."

"Can't breathe. Just leave me."

Chavez squatted in the road, frazzled.

They needed to get back down the hill or the fire would catch them. Sure as shit he didn't want to die because of fucking Squeaky Townsend. *But what would the Chief say if I left him?*

He remembered the times at the station when the Chief said you just had to yell at Squeaky to get him to do stuff. He thought about the swear words the Chief used. He'd never used that kind of language to an adult, but with Jason, yeah.

He leaned down and shouted, urgent, forcing his voice to pierce through the howling wind: "You're being a total fucking asshole."

Chavez saw Squeaky draw back, surprised.

"I don't give a rat's ass if you turn into a crispy critter," Chavez yelled, "but I'd have to explain it to the Chief, and he wouldn't understand. So get your lard-ass up, and let's get going. And, I don't want to hear none of your sorry shit."

Squeaky looked up through bleary, teary eyes. "You can't talk to me that way."

Now Chavez was so frustrated he was close to tears, too. Swearing hadn't worked. "Look Squeaky, I don't want to die up here, and I'm not leaving you. Everybody would miss you around the station. Now c'mon and help me here. Please?"

"Okay." Squeaky moved to get his legs under him.

Amazed, Chavez gave him a hand.

The fast-moving maritime air mass turned tricks when it hit the

Quabbin Reservoir. The Quabbin's geography — ridges on the east and west — funneled the 70-mile-an-hour winds up the valley, which in turn sopped Quabbin lake water up into the air.

At the northeastern end of the reservoir, the low, moisture-laden clouds encountered the higher Matchic Ridge, engulfed in flames. The clouds experienced what meteorologists call an "orographic lift." Slowed down and lifted, they were heated by the fire and spun by the whirling turbines.

The result: the storm dumped its load. Up on Matchic Ridge, three inches of rain fell between midnight and 1 a.m.

Then the wind stopped and another eleven inches fell before dawn.

The Chief careened onto the south access road, the rear of the Explorer slewing on the wet gravel. He listened to Ruth White on the radio back at the station, giving instructions to mutual aid units.

Out the corner of his eye, he saw Kenny Dutton tighten his grip on the crash bar.

Minutes before, when the falling rain signaled a turn for the better in the battle against the fire, Jokkinen thought to check his cellphone. When he got Chavez's message, he was on his way. As Jokkinen drove from the museum parking lot, Dutton finally arrived, out of breath and dressed in a suit and tie. Jokkinen waved Dutton into the shotgun seat of Chief 1, and away they'd gone.

The wipers on the SUV couldn't keep up with the torrents of rain, and the headlights, translucent with age, only made a dim glow.

Under his slipping tires, Jokkinen felt streams of water coming down the rutted tracks on each side of the road. He reached down and shifted into four-wheel drive. The truck lurched forward, and Dutton grunted.

Jokkinen thought about the Brushbuster. What a dumb fucking move. He kicked himself for sending the Brushbuster up the access road. Of course the old truck wouldn't make it up this road. Especially with Squeaky at the wheel.

At each turn, the smoke got heavier. Seeing the road was now almost impossible, so Jokkinen aimed for any space clear of branches, the limbs and underbrush on either side of the narrow road giving him kind of a funnel to aim for.

"What's that?" Dutton had his face pressed against the windshield. "Slow down."

At Dutton's warning, Jokkinen hit the brakes and skidded to a stop.

The yellowish headlight beams picked up something reflective, and Jokkinen's heart leaped. He knew right away it was the luminescent strip on a firefighter's turnout coat.

Two figures emerged from the haze, the wider one leaning on the taller one.

Dutton jumped from the truck, reached Squeaky and handed him the mouthpiece on a fresh air pack. He took it and breathed deeply.

Jokkinen stepped in and put his arm around Chavez, holding on longer than he needed to. "Nice job," he murmured. He was pretty sure there were tears running down his face. He was thankful for the rain.

Then Squeaky pulled the mask off his face. "Chief, Chavez swore at me."

The crews from the Engine 301 and Tanker 302 cheered as the thunderheads came over the ridge, illuminated from below by the fire in the trees, and dumped torrents of rain on them and onto the forest fire.

They were all glad to get soaked.

"Hold your positions," came the voice of command and control officer Ruth White through their radios. "Everyone on ember patrol."

The rain came down so hard, Ruth White called off the 26 pieces of mutual-aid apparatus still en route to Burfield. "Burfield thanks all of you," she told them. "You guys are great."

Despite the order, 20 continued to respond to the call with wipers pushing the drenching rain. What the hell, they were almost there. Nobody wanted to miss this.

The City of Hartford truck turned around after going through the tollbooth entrance to the Mass Pike. With lights flashing and a siren whoop, it ran over the cones separating the east and westbound traffic, did a U-turn, and blasted through the booths back onto Route 84. The tollbooth operators had seen cars do that, but never a 100-foot articulated emergency vehicle.

The mutual aid trucks forming the back-up line on Jokkinen's perimeter stayed in place in the rain.

Alphonse Vitale, deputy chief from Gardner, was conflicted. He desperately wanted to show off his new hook-and-ladder truck to Terry Jokkinen. It was parked in front of his old friend's station, but his crew wanted to get back to Gardner and Jokkinen was nowhere to be seen.

Sergeant Weaver and his two State Police troopers returned to the police station where there were only a few diehard townspeople left. When they learned Artie Winchell had gone home to bed, then they sped off into the night.

Chapter 26

George Fleming sat in his truck in the Hubbardston rest area on Route 2. It was around seven in the morning, and behind him in the east, the sun was just coming up.

The night before, he'd made it out there in record time, but he knew he was too late when he started to run into fire trucks on their way to the fire. Twenty miles away from Burfield, he saw the flames in the distance.

His plan to use a battery back up and release the controls on the turbines might have worked, but he'd never know.

Resigned, he pulled over and watched the drama of the fire unfold. All five turbines were on fire, and the mountain was burning as well. Then, by the light of the full moon, he watched the mass of dark clouds build up, just to the south of the reservoir. And the rain came — pounding, drenching curtains of rain. It must have put the fire out, but he didn't know. The rain clouds covered the moon, and the night went black.

Now, the sun was just hitting Matchic Ridge. Fleming stretched his back. It had been a long night in the truck. He looked, squinted, and looked again. "Fuck," he muttered. He retrieved binoculars from under the seat. "Unbelievable." He heaved a big sigh, picked up his phone, and made the call.

"Can you hear me?"

"Yeah." Kerrigan's voice was a little garbled.

"You heard about the fire?"

"Hollis called me all night long. Crazier than a shithouse rat. It was on all the local news, even CNN. Front page in this morning's *Globe*."

Fleming remembered Kerrigan got up at an ungodly hour, and he still went down to the end of his driveway for the print editions of the *Globe* and the *Herald*.

Fleming didn't know how long he could hold onto the call signal, so he started in. "Four of the turbines are down." He waited, but Kerrigan didn't respond. "Can you hear me?"

"How the fuck did that happen?"

It was never easy to give Jimmy Kerrigan bad news. The guy still thought he was a Member of Congress. "I set them so they wouldn't turn."

"Yeah, that's what you were supposed to do. So?"

"The storm was sudden. Nobody saw it coming. When it hit the turbines, there was no give. They burned out. I couldn't re-set the controls."

Fleming hurried ahead, hoping to avoid a tantrum from Kerrigan. "I've thought about this all night. The feds won't relocate a wind farm that was damaged by heavy winds. I mean, it's hard to make the case we have to move because there's no wind when there's been a windstorm. That means there's no chance at a mitigation relocation." Fleming let that sink in, waiting to hear griping from Kerrigan.

Instead, Kerrigan responded with one word, "Yeah."

"We need to go for another hardship factor." Fleming paused. He was sure Kerrigan didn't know they could do this. He might have been a Congressman thirty-five years ago, but Fleming was the one who knew the law. It was always that way.

Fleming continued, "It's in the DOE regs. Same as HUD. Just like we did before. You know the drill." Fleming waited.

"Are you sure?"

"Absolutely. The wind farm was damaged by the storm and the fire. The feds pay us to re-build on the same site. We just need to change strategies." He tried to sound upbeat, but he knew what was coming.

"What the fuck else have you fucked up?" said Kerrigan. "What a total fucking disaster. Do I have to do everything?" Right on cue, Kerrigan's voice went from angry to whiny. "Why is it nobody thinks of me and my reputation?"

Fleming knew the tone; he'd been hearing it in Burfield for three years now. There was a lot of Jimmy Kerrigan in his daughter Hollis. "Why me?" was their response to just about anything.

But he knew when either of them dropped into whiney; it was time for him to take over. You just had to eat some shit to get there.

"Jimmy. Are you done?" Fleming heard silence.

Finally he heard a short "Yeah." But Kerrigan wasn't done. "We would have made more money going the other way." Fleming held the phone away from his ear and looked at it as if that would get Kerrigan off his pity-pot.

"Now are you done?"

"Yeah."

Fleming would have liked to have him calm down more, but he needed to ask the big one. "You need to get to the Dragon Lady."

Kerrigan's response was inarticulate, a cross between a howl and a moan. "NO…….."

"Yes, Jimmy. Same as before. It's considered a natural disaster as long as we can prove there was no human error. We're going to need Cronin and the state arson people to say there was no human error," said Fleming. "And we need the site cordoned off. Now. Right away."

"Why?"

"One of the towers is still standing. I can see it from here."

"So?"

"We can't let anyone up there. The four turbines that are down, they're destroyed by the fire. But the rain must've put out the fire in the one standing. If someone gets up there, they'll see I changed the settings so it would fail."

Fleming knew he was at a key point. He knew what had to be done, but it was Kerrigan who had the clout to do it. You just needed to hang in there with Jimmy until he found his balls.

Fleming could tell Kerrigan was thinking. The connection had improved, the sounds were crystal clear, and he could hear heavy breathing. He waited. Going hat in hand to Mary Cronin was a big ask. Their initial relocation scam hadn't needed her. She was going to be pissed to have been cut out. Better him than me, thought Fleming.

"Jimmy?"

"I'll take care of it."

Fleming knew Kerrigan was licking his wounds. It always happened this way. They'd been through this same drill so many times. "You'll call her?"

The phone went dead. Fleming wondered. He could rely on the young Jimmy Kerrigan. Would the older Jimmy Kerrigan do what needed to be done?

Chapter 27

Lawson couldn't be sure if he was dreaming or there was a buzzing in his room. As he returned to consciousness, his hazy mind focused on the flashing glow on his phone on his bedside table. When he picked it up he saw it was 4:10 a.m. and the caller was Ethan Pierce.

"Yeah," Even though he knew it was Pierce, it was all the greeting he could muster.

"Action, have I caught you at a bad time?"

Lawson tried to focus. Even at four in the morning, Pierce made jokes. "No. I was just…." instinctively, he thought about lying, telling his boss he was up and functioning; then he remembered. There's nothing to apologize for. That was his old life. It's four in the morning, for Christ's sake. "I was asleep. But I can tell you aren't. What's up?"

"That bass hit the Hula Popper."

At first Lawson struggled to understand, then he remembered Doherty's call. The fire. And Pierce comparing Kerrigan to the fish that couldn't keep from biting on the funny lure.

Pierce was moving on. "How far along is Chavez's video?"

Chavez's video, what does that have to do with anything? Lawson tried to come up with an answer. "Uh, he's got that big storyboard I showed you in your office. Beyond that—"

Pierce cut him off. "Did you send him the information on the money Kerrigan made on the mills, the stuff you picked up in DC?"

Lawson felt a flash of anger bring him out of his pre-dawn confusion. "Ah, no, I thought that was for you."

"You need to get him that information. And I need the video right away. When can you get it done?"

Lawson's anger flared brighter. *Why does Mr. Chavez Simons need this information – which I uncovered, thank you very much – right away?* "Okay." Lawson drew the word out. Pierce, who heard everything, picked up on it. His voice was more patient.

"Richard, sorry for the rush job here, I really don't have time to explain. I need the story of the mill fires, and I need it today. I need everything we know in it. The best way to do it is with the information the kid has collected. You're the man to get it done."

Lawson felt better, but now he was embarrassed. He made his new boss, the Attorney General, explain himself. And for the first time, Pierce called him Richard.

"I'll head out there first thing." Lawson felt good saying it.

"He's been up all night putting the fire out. Take him some Mountain Dew, he lives on that squirrel piss, but unless I miss my guess, he'll jump through hoops to get this done."

Lawson thought about this. Maybe the kid was a good example. "Okay. I'll make it happen. Are you going to be available later in the day to talk about it?"

"Afraid not. I'm on my way to Logan and then to DC. If you need me, call Doherty. You have her number?"

Lawson paused, figuring the best way to answer. "Uh, yeah, I think I can find it."

Pierce chuckled and Lawson heard laughter in the background. Only then did Lawson realize Pierce was in the car. Doherty must be driving. "You're a good man, Lawson. Thanks for doing this." And then the line went dead.

Five minutes later, Lawson stood in the shower, thinking about the call. Yeah, Pierce busted his balls in front of the woman he had a crush on. And yeah, he had to put down a flash of his own assholery. But there was something else gnawing at him. Then he came up with it. It was the second time in the last couple of days Pierce had thanked him for something. In the ten years he worked for a Member of Congress he couldn't remember being thanked for anything.

With another Mountain Dew in hand, Jason scooted his desk chair across his bedroom on its casters. He hit a key on a laptop and sat back. "Done." He looked at Lawson and rubbed his eyes. "Dude, what about the music? I'm tired of asking."

Lawson sprawled on a beanbag chair, his assigned seat all day. They'd been at it eleven hours. He wore a pair of jeans and a sweater. When he got dressed at 4:30 that morning, he didn't have the energy to put on anything else.

Chavez was on his back on Jason's bed with his head on his wadded up cardigan. A line of Mountain Dew cans was against the wall. Two pizza boxes were stuffed in a wastebasket. Male body odor battled garlic for dominance in Jason's small bedroom.

They had been at work on the video since seven. Sure enough, Lawson found Chavez at the fire department after most of the other firefighters went home to bed. Lawson wasn't sure how glad Chavez was to see him, but the assignment from Pierce to finish the video that day seemed to energize him.

Lawson and Chavez banged on the door of the house trailer and pried Jason out of bed at 6:30. Chavez needed a short mid-morning nap, but on the whole, he'd been in good spirits all day. The same couldn't be said of Jason. Lawson knew the type, but he didn't expect to find it out in the sticks. Jason was a fucking video diva. Right away Jason was in a great mood, energized by the task ahead. But as the day went on, he grew testier and testier, pretty much keeping pace with the number of times he "suggested" a music background.

The video was four minutes, thirty-two seconds. Lawson hadn't done all that much. If there were credits, he supposed, he would be the executive producer. Jason knew his stuff. He and Chavez wrote and re-wrote the narration and at one point, Chavez went home for a jacket and tie. Jason and Lawson arranged a table at the edge of the room to look like an anchor's desk. They shot Chavez from a little higher angle than usual — Jason's idea — to minimize his double chin.

It was maybe the twentieth time Jason asked. Divas got their way by making the same request over and over. Each time, Lawson said he didn't think it was a good idea, and each time Chavez said he'd think about it. But, Lawson considered, Jason had earned the right to get something he wanted. The production values were news-show quality, and Lawson knew the content was superb. Whoever Pierce was showing this to was going to be impressed. But, Lawson thought, that still wasn't a good enough reason to make a perfectly good news segment into a fucking head-banging rock video. The video was done, he needed to get it to Pierce. But Jason had his fingers on the keyboard. It all could disappear with one keystroke.

Lawson pretended to relax, leaned back in his beanbag chair and sipped his Diet Coke. "We need to think about credits."

Jason looked up. This had his attention. "Credits?"

Lawson pressed on, he wanted to get this out there so Jason could hear the whole thing. "What we've got here is a first-rate independent news documentary." He saw Jason nod. "Presented in a cutting-edge format." Another nod, more vigorous this time. Lawson blanked out. *What to say next?* Suddenly he channeled that evil bitch Katie Shimko: "If you're going to play in documentary space, you're going to need credits at the end so your names are hash-tagged. So when it goes viral and trends…." Jason's eyes narrowed. Lawson wondered if he'd used the right lingo. He decided to add a clincher. "The Attorney General wants it on YouTube."

Chavez stood up. Lawson flinched, even though he was ten feet away. The kid was really ripe. Chavez looked at Jason. "What do you think?"

Jason scribbled on a pad. He put it on the desk for them to read and started in on the laptop. "Here's what I'm putting at the end."

Lawson asked it, just to be sure. "And no music, right?"

Jason mumbled, hunched over his computer.

Lawson looked at Chavez who just shrugged.

"What?" He needed a clear answer from Jason.

"I said okay, Dude. No tunes. On this version."

"Are you sure you got it? Check again to see if it's all there."

"Jesus, Action, I've looked twice. It's there, I can see it attached to the emails. Both of them."

"Hang up, watch it again, tell me what's at the beginning and at the end. Then call me back."

The phone went dead. Doherty called back a minute later. "Action, the last guy who sassed me like this accidentally fell over his Corvette's hood and spent the weekend in hospital." She paused, and whispered as if she didn't want to be overheard. "It opens with a picture of the Fitchburg fire, and it closes on the credits. And it's good, really good."

Lawson felt a burst of pride. "Where are you guys?" He'd been wondering all day.

"Can't tell you." Her voice lowered even further. "Everybody around here calls it by its initials." And then she hung up.

Eagerly, Lawson pondered the clue, then he stopped. *Fucking everything in Washington is known by initials. FBI, DOJ, DOE. Her hint didn't help at all.*

The elevator opened, and Jimmy Kerrigan looked around the penthouse floor of the Prudential Tower. Back in the 60s, it was Boston's first high-rise, the place you moved when you made some money and you didn't want to live in a fancy suburb or on Beacon Hill or in Back Bay. The last time he'd been in the building to see Mary Cronin was in 1981, right after the second fire. She'd been down on the 7th or 8th floor.

He knocked quietly on her door.

After only a moment or two he heard the door unlock from the inside. She always was a light sleeper. The door opened, and Cronin stood there in a robe. She recognized him and touched her hair. He hadn't seen her in thirty years, and he consciously kept from considering how she'd changed. He had a job to do.

He held out an Au bon Pan bag and grinned. "Room service! Are you still drinking Earl Grey?"

Kerrigan evaluated. He always thought he was good at quick reads, and this didn't look good. Cronin was somewhere between surprised and pissed. There wasn't a scintilla of good will in her face or body language. She cinched her robe tighter.

"The security desk?" That was her greeting.

Kerrigan brushed his hair off his forehead. "An old constituent from Braintree. He buzzed me up. Don't blame him when it's time for his Christmas bonus. I got his kid into West Point." He tried his smile again, but he could tell it didn't work.

Kerrigan looked past Cronin into the apartment. "Nice digs." He stepped past her into the foyer. The 50th floor apartment faced the east with a magnificent view of the city leading out to Boston Harbor. The sun was bright on the horizon at 8 a.m. Local news was coming from the television in the corner.

"Feel free to come in, Jimmy. I don't believe you've been to this apartment, have you? I've lived here for ten years. Before that, I was down on the 25th floor for eight years. I don't believe you ever saw the view from that condo, either."

Kerrigan listened to the tone of her voice. She wasn't surprised to see him anymore, but she was still pissed.

Kerrigan put the bag down on the small breakfast table between the kitchen and the living room. He set out the tea and his coffee. "I got brioches. Are they still your favorite?"

"Why are you here, Jimmy?"

Kerrigan slipped out of his sport coat and draped it over a chair. He saw her watching.

"Cashmere, James? It's a long way from the Basement, isn't it?"

Kerrigan remembered it was Cronin who first took him to Filene's Basement. He also remembered she called him "James" when she wanted him to remember she knew him when. He tried to play on that.

"It's been too long, Mary."

She remained standing. "Jimmy, you picked up and moved to the South and I never heard from you again. I saw you divorced your wife. That was a long time coming, wasn't it? Meanwhile, no notes, no calls, not even a Christmas card. I got the message."

Kerrigan watched, as she seemed to straighten up, he never could tell with her hump. "Two years ago, a nice little feature piece in the *Globe*. Jimmy Kerrigan is back after making his fortune on low-income housing. Now he's going to save the world with alternative energy, and he's passing on his 'expertise' to his daughter, whom I remember was never going to be invited to join Mensa." Kerrigan cringed. The shot at Hollis was on target, but she didn't have to bring family into it.

He tried to interrupt, break her flow. "Mary, I—"

She rolled on. "Frankly, I expected a call from you when you were building the wind farm, because you and I know, Jimmy, you've never done anything the right way in your life, from your papers in law school to Congress to your building projects. But, I must say, I was surprised. You didn't call. I wondered about that, it seemed hard to believe you were doing something on the up and up."

"Mary…"

She waved him off. "And I had to put up with news about you from Ethan Pierce, of all people, who just happened to stop by my office one morning to tell me how well you were doing and how good you looked. She gestured toward the television. Now you've had a little fire out there in the woods, and you're here to see me. What do you need?"

Kerrigan thought he detected a change in her tone. Relieved, he thought his mission was going to be easier than he anticipated. Maybe he should lay his cards on the table. Slowly he began drawing her in. First he went through the details of the mitigation relocation scam. She listened and nodded from time to time like a teacher reviewing homework. When he got to the part of the storm destroying the turbines, he confessed urging Fleming to speed up the process. And then the storm. Cronin just shook her head. He told her about the destruction of the four turbines and the one left standing.

"Anyway, here we are. Fleming is on top of the DOE regs and he says we can still go in for a hardship factor. Re-build on the same location. Not as much money as the mitigation relo, but it's not chump change. But we need the site cordoned off, we can't let anyone inspect the standing turbine. And we need the AG's office to rule it was a natural disaster. The fire review meeting will be around a month from now."

Kerrigan sat back, suddenly tired. There were Hollis's calls all night, then the early call from Fleming. Right away, he showered, got dressed, and drove into town.

He tried to seal the deal. "Well, that's it. I'd sure appreciate your help." Subconsciously, his voice fell into the fake southern drawl he used when he passed money across the desk to some redneck politician.

He could tell Cronin was thinking while she fiddled with her tea and pastry. He looked down, her robe had fallen open at the neck. Her chest was wrinkled.

"How much were you making on the first scam?"

He stalled for time, trying to figure out how much she could know. "Well, essentially the project would be built twice. Each turbine was $2.5 million. There were five of them, and then the cost of the land and site prep."

"The land was free from the University, Jimmy." She looked at him hard. "Remember, I'm on their board? You're hat in hand here. Let's not waste time with your little lies."

Kerrigan shrugged. "Around $20 million." Then he looked up, deciding. "Each time. So $40 million total for the two. That's total project cost, so 20% to Kerrigan Development, we would have made $8 million. But listen, that was for the mitigation relo. Our take on the hardship factor will be less."

Cronin stood, went to a counter in the kitchen and returned with a scratch pad, pen and a pair of reading glasses. She sat down and did some figuring on the pad. Finally she put her pen down and looked over her glasses at him. He watched her warily, wondering what was coming.

"$4 million."

Kerrigan felt pressure under his breastbone. It was as if someone grabbed a giant handful of his gut right above his navel and lifted. His breath caught, and his vision got hazy.

He tried to collect himself. *Hold on here, Kerrigan, this is just the start of a negotiation. He'd been through many of these.* He took a deep breath and made his voice breezy. "By $4 million, what do you mean?" He forced himself to look up at her. He couldn't believe she wanted money, he thought she'd help him out for old time's sake. *Greedy bitch.*

"They way I see it, you are asking me to be your partner. I don't want to quibble over percentages or shares, so let's just make it half: $4 million."

Kerrigan stuttered. "But...but, the $8 million figure was for the relocation."

Cronin smiled even wider. Kerrigan saw she was really enjoying herself.

"I should have been your partner from the beginning. If I had been involved, that cretin Fleming would never have caused the turbines to burn.

You've always been one for the easy way, Jimmy. Four million."

"Look, Mary, I understand, conceptually, how you got to that figure.." His voice faded.

She stood up and swayed a little, unbalanced.

"Goodbye, Jimmy."

Kerrigan felt the pressure on his chest get worse. There was acid in his throat. He looked around for a wastebasket in case he had to puke. This wasn't going well, she wasn't even negotiating. Had she always been this... crazy?

"Look, Mary, let's talk about this. I don't have that kind of money."

Suddenly, Cronin darted into the kitchen. Through the door, Kerrigan saw her rip something off a bulletin board next to an old-fashioned wall phone. She lurched back to him and threw it on the table. He saw it was the *Globe* article. There he was in a big picture with Hollis in front of the first turbine. Several sections of the piece were circled.

"There." With a shaking finger, she pointed to the newspaper and read: "Now Kerrigan spends his life with his Texas-beauty wife Esperanza in their sprawling Cohasset home with the sounds of the foghorns in the distance. Lobster boats work their way back and forth in the cove out front." Her finger moved to another circled section. "Kerrigan says he's reached the time in his life when it's time to give back. He and Esperanza have endowed the Kerrigan Center for Public/Private Partnerships at Boston College."

Cronin sat back and folded the paper. She was breathing hard, almost panting. "You're the big shot you always wanted to be, Jimmy. Hotsy-totsy trophy wife on the Gold Coast. Naming buildings for yourself." She jumped up and hurried to a desk at the side of the room, opened a drawer and returned with a dog-eared ledger book. She referred to it while she wrote on a scratch pad. She tore off the sheet, folded it and handed it to Kerrigan. "I want four million dollars wired into this account by this time next week."

She paused to catch her breath. Her voice became lower and slower, menacing. "Here's the deal. I'll have the site secured in the next hour. I'll conduct the arson review personally. If the money isn't there, you can be sure we'll find something you did wrong. Your time to give back starts here, Jimmy."

He decided. "Look, Mary, that kind of cash takes some time to put together, I can get a little at a time..."

"Jimmy, you're in no position to bargain, but I'll be nice for old times' sake. Before the meeting. I'll give until then. All the money, four million, in that account before the fire review meeting."

Kerrigan sat and thought as he looked at the numbers on the scratch pad. A bank account number and a routing number. He knew the drill. He could get the money, but it wasn't going to be easy. He'd hit that fucking George Fleming for a part of it, it was his fault this was happening. But he could do it. It was the cost of doing business. He pushed back from the table and sighed. He needed some sleep.

"Okay," he said. "Deal."

There was movement between him and the broad expanse of windows. The sun was fully up now, and he had a hard time focusing his tired eyes. He squinted. Cronin was walking away from him. Her robe was on the floor. He looked away. It was something he didn't want to see.

She spoke over her shoulder. "Remember how you used to wash my hair? I still use that same shampoo. Make sure the door is locked."

Kerrigan's stomach lurched again. He felt for his wallet. He kept a Viagra in there. He didn't really need them — it was just for emergencies.

Chapter 28

Chavez left his protective gear draped over the bed of the F-150 in his driveway. He'd get to it later. Despite the daylong supply of pizza and Dew while he was working on the video, he was starving. He checked the garage. Two cars, both his mom and dad were home. Good. He wanted to tell them about the fire. As he trudged up the sidewalk to his house, he stretched his back and then his arms. The adrenaline and caffeine wore off. He was really tired.

He walked into the kitchen and sniffed. He'd missed dinner. He could see lights on in the dining room down the hall. He moved toward the stove. Then he heard his father's voice calling out: "There you are, Buddy."

Chavez smiled, puzzled, but pleased. *His dad never called him that. He was waiting for him. He heard about him and Squeaky.*

"Come on in here. I really want to see you."

Chavez headed down the hall, collecting his thoughts, eager to tell his story. He made the turn into the living room.

They were sitting at the dining room table. His father looked up, startled. His mom looked up from her plate. At the end of the table his dad petted Cassius. Chavez stopped walking and looked closer.

Then it dawned on him. His dad was talking to the dog. The "I really want to see you," wasn't for him, it was for the dog.

Chavez hesitated and tried to hide his disappointment. "Hi," he said again.

Catherine was the first to speak. "Hi, Honey. You must be tired. I've got some veggie chili on the stove."

His dad smiled vaguely. "Busy night, huh? Big fire, big storm?" His phone buzzed on the table in front of him. He picked it up and looked at it.

Catherine looked up, irritated at the phone and then back at Chavez, her face softening. "You go take a shower."

Chavez turned away. Unexpectedly, he felt tears sting his eyes. He was so tired.

Half an hour later, at the island in the kitchen, he finished his second helping of chili. Catherine bustled around, cleaning up. Peter drifted in and out.

Chavez waited until they were both in the kitchen to start his account of the fire. He started casually, testing their interest. They usually weren't into fire stuff. He wasn't wasting the effort if they weren't interested. Chavez saw his mom was following along. He couldn't tell about his dad, he was moving in and out of the room, drinking wine, fiddling with his phone.

If this was a typical fire call or day at the station, he wouldn't have made the effort, but Chavez really wanted to tell the whole story. He skimmed quickly over the beginning: his place on the Brushbuster, the ride to the fire, the trip up the access road, the old truck's demise.

"When the Brushbuster died, we knew we had to get out. The fire was going to come at us right down the hill. Squeaky Townsend was in bad shape — he's kinda fat?"

Chavez looked up again to check if they were listening. His mom had her hand under her chin. She was listening, he could tell. His father still moved in and out. Chavez heard Jeopardy on the television in the other room.

Making eye contact with his mom, Chavez continued.

"So, I helped Squeaky down the hill, I carried an air pack, it took a while, but we made it. The Chief came and found us."

He stopped. His own voice made him sleepy. Towards the end he was so tired. He told the story to the Chief, and then to Jason and Mr. Lawson while they made the video. Now he just wanted to go to bed.

His mom reacted. "Chavez, I'm so proud of you. You're a real hero!" Chavez felt tears from in his eyes for the second time that night. He looked down to hide his face. He couldn't say anything. He wiped his forehead with his napkin. "It's hot in here." He really did feel hot. It might be the pepper his mom put in the chili. He took a sip of water and felt better, he could look up now.

Peter came back in the kitchen.

"Sounds to me like Jokkinen needs to do better maintenance on his equipment." He said it almost absently, trying to be part of the conversation. He was still looking down at his phone.

The mention of the Chief woke Chavez up.

"What?"

"That old fire engine, what do you call it? Brushcutter?"

"Brushbuster." Chavez wondered if his dad actually listened to his story.

"Sounds to me like Terry Jokkinen needs to take better care of his trucks."

Chavez looked at his father's back. He was at the refrigerator pouring wine. *Maybe his dad forgot.*

"You know the Brushbuster is our oldest truck?" said Chavez. "That's the one Hollis promised to replace?"

At the mention of Hollis, Peter looked up sharply. Now the conversation had his attention. He tried to re-group.

"Yeah, I know. But that donation was based on shared community benefits and we haven't reached the point...."

Chavez was usually patient with his father, but he was tired and he was still hurt thinking his dad's warm words for the dog were meant for him. And his dad hadn't listened to his story. His mom listened, but he really wanted his dad to hear it.

"That's bullshit."

Except for the vibrating phone in the front pocket of Peter's corduroys, there was silence in the room. The big clock ticked in the front hall.

Chavez swore all the time with Jason, he'd sworn a lot at Squeaky the night before, but he never swore around his parents.

"We did our best with the Brushbuster. I helped with the maintenance."

He paused to take a breath and continued.

"We kept the Brushbuster going as good as we could. But it's an old truck. That's why Hollis promised us a *new* truck. And all we've gotten for the past year is a line of crap."

Chavez was almost in tears. His father looked off into the other room. Chavez wanted him to listen. "It was Hollis's fucking windmills that burned, and we shouldn't have even been in that old truck. We should have been in a new truck, paid for by Hollis."

Finally his father looked up. At least he was listening now. Chavez sniffed; he needed to blow his nose. Black stuff from the smoke had been coming out of it all day. *All that fucking pepper in the chili didn't help.* He stood up and started to leave the room. He was done.

His father spoke as he walked away. "Hey, Buddy, go get some sleep. You'll feel better in the morning."

Chavez didn't turn, he kept walking.

"Don't call me Buddy. Save it for the dog."

Chapter 29

Jokkinen looked around to see if anyone was watching. He opened the trunk of Bertie's Camry, pulled out a recycling bin, and threw the entire contents into the cardboard section of the dumpster. No sorting today. Then he smiled ruefully. At age 63, it had come to this — getting his kicks out of fucking with the recycling ladies. He missed the days when he could pull his truck up to a hole in the ground and shovel his shit out the back. That was when it was the "Burfield Dump." Later, it became the "Landfill." Now it was the "Transfer Station." *La-di-dah. Might as well live in Wellesley.*

He watched as Peter Simons's antique Peugeot approached along the rutted lane. Saturday mornings at the dump — the transfer station — were usually busy, but at the moment Jokkinen and Peter were alone out there.

If he'd been in his department vehicle, Jokkinen was sure Peter would have recognized him, made a U-turn, and avoided meeting up. Dealing with Peter on the wind farm hadn't been easy. They weren't on the best of terms.

The Peugeot backed in, smoke pouring out the exhaust, and backfired as Peter shut off the ignition. Wannabe hippie car, thought Jokkinen. He doesn't know how stupid he looks. Peter got out and opened the trunk.

Jokkinen stood up and slammed the trunk on the Camry. "Morning, Peter."

Recognizing Jokkinen, Peter paused and stammered. "Uh, Chief. Good morning." Feigning nonchalance, Peter lowered the trunk lid so Jokkinen couldn't see in.

"Saturday morning chores?"

Peter reached up and tugged at his little ponytail. Over the past two years, Jokkinen had become familiar with Peter's nervous habits. Whenever the issue of the promised fire truck came up, he played with that ponytail.

"I was at the office and decided to take a break," said Peter.

Jokkinen decided to jab at him a little. "Don't let me stop you." Jokkinen took a step back, folded his arms, and let the silence grow awkward.

Finally, Peter gave in. He lifted the Peugeot's creaking trunk lid. Inside were two bins, one filled with wine bottles, the other with shredded office paper. Peter lifted the bin of bottles and turned to shield himself from

Jokkinen's view.

Jokkinen didn't say anything. He knew where the wine bottles came from. Hollis Kerrigan's Lexus was parked outside Peter's office almost every night. Everybody knew about it.

Both bins emptied, Peter slammed the trunk lid and hurried back to the driver's side and got in. Jokkinen moved in front of the car so Peter couldn't get away and motioned for him to roll down the window.

Jokkinen looked inside the car. It reeked of some kind of men's cologne, and a Rolling Stones eight-track tape was on the passenger seat.

Jokkinen leaned forward with his arms on the open window. "I've been meaning to talk to you."

Peter gave Jokkinen a glance, halfway between suspicious and fearful. "What about?"

"Chavez."

"Chavez?" Peter reached for his ponytail. Obviously, Chavez wasn't what Peter expected.

"I wonder if we could have a man-to-man conversation. Sort of off the record?"

Peter looked away. "Well, I guess so."

"You heard what Chavez did up on the ridge during the fire." Jokkinen watched Peter try to focus.

"He and I don't talk that much about fire stuff."

"Chavez led Squeaky Townsend down the hill. He probably saved his life."

"I think he was talking about it at dinner the other night. Something about the truck crapping out on them?"

Jokkinen paused to take a long breath. He had a short temper, and Bertie always told him a deep breath helped. This time it didn't seem to have much effect. He was still pissed. "Since you brought it up," he said, "I do want to talk to you about the Brushbuster, too. I know we've been around and around on this. It seems to me, you and Hollis made a promise, and you let us down."

"Chief, you know our output isn't what we predicted."

"Can it, Peter. Save it for the one or two people in town who still buy that line of bullshit."

Peter's lip quivered and he reached for his ponytail.

"You and I both know the truth," Jokkinen went on. "We were never getting that truck, were we? That was just an empty promise. But you know what really pisses me off?" Jokkinen knew he was on a roll. The time for deep breaths was over. "You telling Chavez the truck crapped out because it wasn't maintained well enough. Instead of praising your son as a hero, you keep singing your client's bullshit tune."

Peter studied his hands on the steering wheel.

Jokkinen waited, and at last Peter looked up. At least he seemed to be listening, although Jokkinen thought it still wasn't sinking in.

"Chavez and I spend a lot of time together," said Jokkinen. "We talk about all sorts of things — what's on his mind, what's going on in school, things that bother him, all the stuff that goes on in a kid's life. He mentions his mom every now and then." He fixed his gaze on Peter. "But he never mentions you." Jokkinen let that hang in the air. He saw Peter shrink a bit in his seat. "I get the sense you don't have much contact with him."

Peter nodded.

"I guess there are all kinds of father-son relationships," said Jokkinen. "My dad was a drunk, and he died when I was nine, but I remember he was a good guy when he was around. I don't have kids, so I really don't have first-hand experience. I guess Chavez is as close to a son as I'm ever going to get."

Jokkinen needed to say this. He wanted Peter Simons to know how strongly he felt. Peter looked away.

How could this dumbass ever father a kid like Chavez? It amazed Jokkinen, seeing how different Peter was from Chavez, that eager kid who always looked you right in the eye.

"Anyway, Peter, here's the thing. Your son comes home and tells you something he did that was really terrific — heroic, even — and you just blow him off. You ignore him. And you give him some crap about the truck. I think you owe the kid an apology."

Peter shrugged a little then his shoulders sagged.

Good, Jokkinen thought, maybe I'm getting through to the little shit.

"And, truth be told, I think you owe me an apology, too, for saying that kind of crap. About me letting the Brushbuster go to shit. And letting that loose cannon of a client of yours run around town shooting her mouth off. But my reputation isn't the issue here."

Another car pulled up the drive, trailing a plume of dust.

"I can't tell you what kind of father to be," said Jokkinen. "That's not my place, and I guess it's way too late. But you'd better think about what you're doing." Jokkinen took a step back. "It's a small town, Peter."

Chapter 30

Pierce tore a sheet off a paper towel roll, wiped his hands and his mouth, and pulled his tie out of his dress shirt where he'd stuck it before chowing down on — Lawson counted in amazement — eight slices of anchovy-and-mushroom pizza. Washed down with two beers.

Lawson, sipping a Diet Coke and limiting himself to two slices, couldn't help noticing.

Lawson yawned. In the last week, he'd slept only four or five hours a night. He couldn't remember being this tired.

Then he re-considered. The truth was, this was the first time he'd been this tired without a night of heavy drinking to blame. This was a different sort of tired. It felt good.

In the month since the fire, Pierce treated the upcoming Burfield fire review meeting like a NASA launch. Lawson was right there with Pierce, putting in the planning hours, running what amounted to a set of extensive war games.

The difference was, when Pierce called a halt at two in the morning, he just walked down the street to the Harvard Club. Each night, Lawson still had to make it back to Concord. And then take the train back the next morning.

Pierce decreed they would stay in Burfield the night before the meeting. Pierce and Doherty went to Jokkinen's house, and Lawson checked into the Sportsman Motel, Burfield's only lodging. Lawson wondered why they couldn't find another bed at Jokkinen's for him. Was Pierce trying to keep Doherty away from him? Was this forever, or just before the big meeting? Then he tried to put the thoughts out of his mind. God, he was pathetic.

Pierce pushed his paper plate away from his seat at the end of the long table in the fire station break room, which Jokkinen offered for their final meeting.

"We need to catch you up," Pierce said to Chavez, who missed the first part of the meeting on his run to Burfield House of Pizza. "Thanks for the pies. I appreciate the extra anchovies."

Chavez grinned and shrugged.

"The meeting's at ten at Town Hall. It's been a long time since I attended one of these. Thirty-four years, to be exact." He gave Jokkinen a look, and Jokkinen nodded back at him. "But Action here asked around and got the lay of the land."

"I watched videos of these review meetings," said Lawson, "and they pretty much all run the same way. The local fire chief conducts the first part of the meeting: a general discussion of the response to the fire, equipment and manpower issues, lessons learned. Then the Assistant Attorney General in charge of arson investigations takes over. As we all know by now, Mary Cronin has announced that because of the 'high-profile nature of the fire' — as she put it — she plans to conduct the meeting herself."

Lawson had privately asked Pierce why he didn't countermand Cronin, and put someone else in charge of the meeting. As Attorney General, he had the authority to do that. But Pierce was adamant. For some reason, he wanted Cronin.

He continued: "The Assistant AG — in this case, Ms. Cronin — goes through the findings of the state police arson squad. Then there may be questions from the audience."

"Pretty straightforward," said Pierce. Then he asked Jokkinen, "Terry, is the site still off-limits?"

Jokkinen nodded. "The arson squad has armed guards on both gates. There are big signs all over the place: *Fire Investigation, No Trespassing.* Just for fun, a couple of days ago I drove up there, badge and all, and told the guy at the gate I wanted to take a look around. Nothing doing. No one's allowed inside the fence without express permission from Cronin."

"That includes Kerrigan's people?" Pierce asked.

"We've kept a pretty good watch on the place," said Jokkinen. "I don't think anyone's been in or out. No one but the arson investigators."

"Kerrigan and Fleming?"

"Not even them."

"They may not have been inside the fence," said Lawson, "but I'm sure they've been plenty busy. On the way into town, I drove by Hollis's house. Lights on all over the place, cars in the driveway and out front. They must be getting ready, too."

Pierce looked at Chavez again. Lawson thought he seemed unusually focused on making sure the kid knew what was going on. And then he considered; if it weren't for the kid, they wouldn't be here.

"We are operating on the premise," said Pierce, "that Cronin will announce there is no evidence of arson. Now this next part is where it gets tricky. The minute Cronin declares there was no monkey business, no arson, nothing criminal … then at that exact instant, the wind farm goes back into Kerrigan's possession. I have folks standing by to go into Superior Court to get a restraining order to keep him out of there."

Jokkinen broke in. "What's that all about?"

Pierce smiled and nodded to Lawson. "Action here needs to explain."

After all the hours he'd spent with the DOE engineers, Lawson could probably explain this next part better than his boss. "We know there's only one possible scam in play here: the hardship factor. The people at DOE aren't going to allow a mitigation relocation. So, they're back to their favorite, the hardship factor. The key is, there can't be 'human involvement' in the destruction of the turbines." Lawson looked around the room. "Sorry to sound so obtuse, but that's the way they talk down there. In plain English: we need to find out if the turbine controls were monkeyed with to make them fail."

He paused to collect his thoughts. "Anyway…." He caught himself and smiled. "Anyway" was Chavez's favorite word. He must have picked up the speech habit from him. *Thank goodness Chavez doesn't say 'I'm like' three times every sentence, or I might be saying that myself.* "*Anyway*, four turbines collapsed and burned. That leaves the one remaining tower that survived the fire. Damaged, but mostly intact. That's the one we need to look at." Lawson looked up, scanning his listeners. "With me?" There were nods from around the table.

Lawson continued. "In the nacelle … that's the housing around the guts of the turbine on top of the tower. It doesn't look like much from the ground, but it's about the size of a small RV. In this nacelle, there's a circuit box somewhere. It's different in every installation. Believe it or not in this digital age, but there are actual switches in the box you can inspect. I even watched a DOE training video. It's easy if you know what to look for."

Everyone was paying close attention, Lawson noted, but especially Chavez.

"There's a row of three switches. They control the yaw — that's the direction the turbine faces — the pitch of the blades, and the brakes. If the turbine were operating normally, the switches will all be on 'A.' That stands for 'automatic.' If they've had 'human involvement,' the switches will be flipped over to 'M. That stands for 'manual.' The only time the switches are supposed to be set on 'manual' is during maintenance. There is no way they'd be set on manual for normal operation, particularly in a big storm."

Pierce broke in. "As soon as Cronin announces the decision, they're free to do anything they want to that remaining tower. The first thing they'll want to do is to get their hands on those switches and flip them all to 'automatic.' I'm sure they have a crew all ready to climb the turbine, the same way I have a crew of lawyers at Superior Court ready to file paperwork to stop them." Pierce leaned back and crossed his arms. "I'm betting my lawyers are faster than his climbers." There was a satisfied look on his face.

"They have a crane," said Chavez.

Pierce turned on him like an errant witness, his eyes intense. "They have a *what*?"

Chavez looked down at his hands on the table. Almost apologetically, he said, "My dad told me I might want to leave for school early tomorrow, because Packard Road's going to be blocked in the morning. Mr. Fleming has a crane up in Gardner, in that big parking lot off Route 2. In the morning, they're going to be moving it down Packard Road and up the north access road to the wind farm."

Jokkinen spoke up: "Your dad told you how to get to school?"

"It was a little weird," admitted Chavez.

Lawson watched Chavez carefully and considered: Was Peter Simons now passing on information?

Pierce sighed and ran his hand through his hair. He picked up his pen and prepared his write on his legal pad. His hand shook a bit. It was the first time Lawson ever saw him rattled.

"If they have a crane ready..." said Jokkinen.

"Down comes the tower," said Pierce.

"Switches and all."

"So much for the cavalry riding to the rescue."

Lawson glanced up at the wall clock: 11 p.m. "Where does that leave us?"

"I can't speed up the restraining order process," said Pierce. "Until Cronin announces her decision, there's nothing to restrain." He thought a bit. "We'll just see what tomorrow brings."

"We've talked about Kerrigan and Fleming," said Doherty, "but what about Cronin? What do we have on her?"

Lawson waited for Pierce to make a joke about Doherty's enmity for the Dragon Lady. Instead, he took a pass. "We'll see, Sergeant. The Dragon Lady's been around a long time."

Doherty shook her head.

Pierce stood up and slung his suit jacket over his shoulder. His voice brighter, he addressed Jokkinen. "Bertie still making quiche for breakfast?"

"She sure is."

"Remind her that Sergeant Doherty is staying over. Bertie'll need to double her recipe."

Chapter 31

Jason angled the GoPro around the balancing boulder and watched his phone screen. "The guard is like two football fields away," he whispered to Chavez. "Sitting in that lawn chair by the gate, drinking coffee and having a cigarette. He's there to stop grownups in cars, not ninjas squirreling under the fence."

The two boys crouched just outside the chain link fence that surrounded the wind farm. Chavez pulled his supplies out of his pack. He put on an earbud headset. There was a small microphone attached that hung down near his mouth. Then he pulled the elastic strap of a headlamp around his helmet. On the top of the helmet, they attached Jason's camera. Chavez clicked the camera on and put the helmet on his head. The setup was awkward, but he was used to working with a lot of equipment.

"Try the mic. Remember, it stays on the whole time."

Chavez counted off. "Test, one, two."

Jason listened with his headset. "Get a shot of the turbine." He fiddled with his iPhone. "Let's practice that again."

Chavez rolled over and moved his head around. The image of the lone standing turbine appeared on Jason's iPhone.

"Got it." Jason looked at the image. "Last chance. Are you sure you want to do this?"

"Don't make me more nervous than I already am."

"You can still back out," said Jason. "No one will know."

The truth was, Chavez was far from confident. He peered upward. The tower loomed what looked like miles overhead. It was white at the bottom, but the higher it rose, the blacker it got from the fire. The nacelle was canted at a weird angle, and the blades were also black, streaked with a film of red oil.

The prospect of climbing a 200-foot ladder inside the tower terrified him, but it helped that he was fortified by two Mountain Dews and a Red Bull. His fingers were tingling, there was no backing out now, and he was ready to climb.

Chavez looked at his watch: 10 a.m. They were up most of the night planning their "mission," and they slept in Chavez's room before pretending they were off to school.

"Got your wrenches?"

Chavez patted his fanny pack. "Right here."

"Are you sure about the switches?"

"That's what Mr. Lawson said," said Chavez. "He got it from DOE."

"I'm still not so sure," said Jason. He didn't trust adults very much, and he was still skeptical. On the Web, they'd found videos of the inner workings of all sorts of turbines. Some had circuit boxes, some didn't.

"You watch the video on your phone," said Chavez. "Do you remember what you're watching for?"

"Switches pointing at 'M,'" said Jason.

"As soon as you've got those switches on video, what's the signal?"

"'Cujo!'" said Jason. Since they'd been kids, *Cujo* was their favorite Stephen King book — which made it their favorite book in the entire universe — and "Cujo" was their all-purpose code word. Chavez also heard Jason use it to describe certain girls, but not in a very nice way.

Chavez took a deep breath, trying to settle his nerves. "You have Lawson's number?"

Jason rolled his eyes. "How many times do you have to ask?" He called up the contact on his phone and stuck the screen in Chavez's face. "Dude."

"Stop saying that." He forced a grin. "Here I go."

Chavez got down on his belly and wriggled under the fence. Keeping the turbine between himself and the guard at the gate, he jogged to the tower, climbed a short set of steps and opened the tower door with an Allen wrench. Then he was inside. He paused for a few moments to get his bearings. It was cold, still, and silent. He tilted his head back to look up ... and up ... and up. There was sunlight coming in from somewhere above. He was pretty sure that wasn't right.

"You're in." Jason's voice startled him when it came through the headset. "Dude."

"It looks like something happened at the top." Chavez's voice echoed through the cylinder. "There's sunlight coming in. I think the nacelle separated from the tower in the storm."

"Yeah, the nacelle," Jason echoed. Until their video sessions the night before, neither boy knew the various parts of a wind turbine. Now they had at least a working vocabulary.

A steel ladder ran up the center of the tower, supported every ten feet by brackets bolted to the side. He put his boot on the first rung and gripped the rails. It felt solid enough, but he wondered again if this was a stupid idea.

Jason read his thoughts. "Are you okay to do this?"

"I think so." Chavez felt panicky, he hated heights.

"One step at a time," came Jason's voice. "Don't look down."

Chavez put his boot on the first rung, took a breath, and began to climb.

After a few hours' restless sleep in a lumpy bed at the Sportsman Motel, Lawson made his way across the Burfield Town Common, pulling a wheeled cart loaded with electronic gear.

The Town Hall seemed frozen in time. Built in the early 1800s, with its white columns and rooftop belfry, it made Lawson think of a church.

He dragged his cart up the steps, across the porch, and into the big room that occupied the entirety of the first floor. A balcony looked down from above, and a stage stood at the front of the room. A janitor was setting up rows of antique folding wooden chairs.

Lawson looked around. Three folding tables stood in a row between the stage and the rows of chairs. An American flag and a Massachusetts flag flanked the tables, and the wall behind the stage was decorated with the flag of Burfield — ironically featuring an old painting of this very building — and a quilt depicting the history of the town: farming, lumbering, orchards, a preacher in mid-sermon. Dusty sunlight filtered through high windows, weirdly leaching the color from the room, giving it a sepia, old-time-photograph sort of feel. A large bass drum sat in the corner. On it was written Burfield Brass Band.

Lawson unloaded his equipment onto the stage, wired the components together, connected extension cords, and tested his remote.

Long ago and far away, technicians and interns did all this for him. When he arrived on the scene, everything would already be set up and ready to roll.

He shook off the thoughts. *Get over yourself, Lawson.* He helped the janitor set up the last few folding chairs.

The door clattered open, and the morning light framed a lone figure. Lawson felt a jolt of adrenaline. Even by her silhouette — *particularly* by her silhouette — he recognized Mary Cronin. He glanced at the clock on the balcony. She'd arrived an hour early.

Cronin walked to the front of the room and put a briefcase on the center table. "Up early, are we, Mr. Lawson? Good for you. Does your presence mean the Attorney General will be with us today? It's been a long time since he's attended one of our fire review meetings. It will be good for him to be reminded how government works."

She set a travel mug down on the table next to her briefcase. The string from a tea bag hung over the outside.

This was only the second time Lawson was in Cronin's presence, but she seemed slightly off. Maybe hyper-caffeinated. A little screechy, too. Suddenly he was reminded of the Glenn Close character in *Fatal Attraction*. Just about to boil a bunny.

Lawson thought about responding to her shot at Ethan Pierce, but he just gave her a bland smile and said, "Good morning, Mary. Did you sleep well?"

She sat down at the table. "I always sleep well, Mr. Lawson. I have a favorite motel up in Leominster. The Lamplighter. Always comfortable at the Lamplighter."

The Lamplighter sounded familiar. After a second, Lawson remembered: Pierce's story about that morning, years ago, at the Lamplighter. Jimmy Kerrigan and Mary Cronin "swapping spit" in the parking lot.

Lawson almost laughed out loud. *Wait 'til Pierce hears this.*

"Whoa." Out of breath, Chavez held on tight to a supporting bracket. He had climbed the equivalent of nineteen flights of stairs. "Can you see this?"

"I haven't seen anything but the wall since you started the climb," came Jason's voice. "What do you see?"

"I'm almost to the yaw platform, and there's definitely a crack between the tower and the nacelle. It's almost halfway around. It's where the sun's coming in. I can see where the bolts holding the nacelle to the tower have been sheared off."

"Yeah, I see that."

"What's going on down there?"

"*Nada*," said Jason. "The guard's had three cigarettes in the fifteen minutes since you started climbing."

"Fifteen minutes? It seemed like an hour."

"Squeaky Townsend could have done it in half the time. Okay, enough bullshit, get going. I'm out of food. What's next?"

Chavez looked up at the ladder, examining its supports. "This next part's going to be tricky. The ladder's supposed to be connected to the opening into the nacelle, but it's hanging up there by one bolt."

"Just take it one step at a time," said Jason. "No biggie. You can do it."

Chavez heard an unfamiliar nervousness in Jason's oh-so-familiar voice. He looked up and studied the single bolt that held the top of the ladder.

His radio crackled with Jason's voice. "Let's go."

This was different, way different than the ladder below. Five steps up, Chavez heard a metallic groan from above and felt the ladder wobble. He stopped and held on, stomach rolling. He gasped into the microphone, "Remember that rope bridge we strung across the ravine?"

"Yeah."

"This is worse." He took a deep breath. "Okay, here I go."

Seated at the middle of the three tables, Jokkinen arranged his papers.

From his chair in the front row, Lawson saw Jokkinen's legs. His khakis had risen up, revealing the smooth, hairless off-color of his prosthesis. Lawson forgot Jokkinen was missing a leg. Jokkinen limped a little, but so did lots of guys his age.

Then Lawson considered: Kerrigan, Cronin, Pierce, and another fire. Thirty-four years later. Talk about déjà vu. Jokkinen must have a lot on his mind today.

Jokkinen's three deputy chiefs sat with him. One was a woman. Lawson squinted at her nametag: Ruth White. She was wearing a brand new uniform shirt. That made him think of Doherty, sitting beside him. Funny — in all the excitement, it didn't make him nervous to have her that close. It was nice to have her there, like he had a friend.

Lawson swiveled to glance behind him. The room was almost full, buzzing with excitement, the last arrivals searching for empty seats.

There were maybe 100 uniformed fire personnel there. Jokkinen said there'd be one or more from every responding community. This was a big deal to them.

There was a group of bulky guys in orange windbreakers: the State Police arson investigators. He wondered which ones Cronin got to.

Locals filled the rest of the seats and the balcony, and a few late arrivals were even perching in the windowsills.

Lawson counted three reporters and thought he recognized one as a stringer from the *Globe*. Lawson supposed that they didn't expect much when they got up early and drove out here to Burfield. They may be in for a surprise.

Mary Cronin had a table to herself, with her travel mug of tea, a stack of paper, and several folders.

The wind farm team was shoulder-to-shoulder at the third table. After all the talk about Jimmy and Hollis Kerrigan, it was odd for Lawson to see them in person. He remembered seeing pictures of Kerrigan as a young Congressman. The man had aged well, looking younger than his 77 years. He had on an expensive tailored navy suit with a power tie. Lawson watched as Kerrigan adjusted his jacket cuffs. He was wearing cufflinks. Somehow, cufflinks and a Hermes tie looked out of place in this room filed with uniforms, jeans and wool sweaters.

Hollis Kerrigan fidgeted next to her father. She put her bag on the floor, picked it up, put it down again. She patted her hair. Kerrigan squeezed Hollis's arm. She flinched at her father's touch, and she forced her hands to go still on the tabletop.

Next to them was a beefy guy with a confident smile in an open-necked shirt. That must be George Fleming, Lawson thought. Plymouth Engineering.

The fourth person at their table wore a small stud earring with his hair pulled back in a little ponytail. Under the table, Lawson could see he was wearing pressed Carhartts work pants and expensive hiking boots. He must be Chavez's father. Lawson looked more closely. There wasn't a hint of resemblance to Chavez.

Pierce, on the other side of Doherty, wrote on a yellow legal pad with his fountain pen. Lawson saw Pierce was creating some kind of outline. Pierce wasn't his usual carefree self today. When Pierce arrived and took his seat, Lawson leaned forward and started to greet him; but Doherty gave him a warning shake of her head.

Jokkinen rapped his knuckles on the table. The whispering died down. "As most of you know, I'm Terry Jokkinen, Chief of the Burfield Volunteer Fire Department. We are here this morning to review the response to the Matchic Ridge Wind Farm fire and hear the report of the state arson task force. Before we begin, I'd like to introduce an honored guest, the Attorney General, my friend, Ethan Pierce III." There was enthusiastic applause from the audience. It wasn't every day the Attorney General made it to a fire review meeting.

Then Jokkinen, referring to his notes, presented the operations review. The guy really knows his stuff, Lawson decided, as Jokkinen laid out the events of that stormy night in a compelling combination of technical detail and matter of fact storytelling.

Then Jokkinen opened the meeting up to discussion, and the firefighters all pitched in. If there were one fireman from another town who didn't say something during the operations review, Lawson would have been surprised. Everybody had an opinion. Everyone wanted to tell his side of the story.

Jokkinen handled the meeting well, covering all the bases. He was even calm when Artie Winchell stood up and took credit for the "town-wide evacuation."

Finally, Jokkinen smacked the table and announced that portion of the meeting was over. It was time for a bathroom break.

"Yes!" said Pierce, setting down his fountain pen. Through Jokkinen's presentation and the firefighters' discussion, Pierce never stopped writing, filling page after page with notes.

Lawson and Doherty stood up to stretch, while Pierce joined the procession toward the men's room.

Doherty rubbed the back of her neck and looked around. "Where's Chavez?"

"I was wondering the same thing," said Lawson. "I'm surprised he's missing this."

Chavez's feet slipped out from under him and he slammed down on his back. His helmet with its headlamp and camera and his headset twisted off and slid away.

"Hello? Hello?" Jason's voice was distant.

Chavez found himself lying in some sort of oily goo on the floor of the tilted nacelle. On the floor near him he found the headset. "Hold on. Give me a minute."

"What's going on?"

Chavez felt around some more and found his helmet. He made sure the camera was still attached.

"There you are. What happened?"

Chavez raised himself to his hands and knees. He'd had the breath knocked out of him; he worked to get it back. "I made it to the top of the ladder, pulled myself up into the nacelle, but the floor is way tilted and greasy, and I slipped. I kind of ended up on my back down in the corner. There's oily shit all over the floor. It really stinks. There's definitely been a fire up here."

He paused, now fired with a burst of adrenaline — he'd made it!

"Remember when you burned out that mower? It smells like that, only a hundred times worse. I'm standing in fucking three inches of oil."

"That mower wasn't my fault," said Jason. "Somebody forgot to put the oil back in it."

"Yeah. *Somebody.*"

Jason got back to business. "The camera's covered with slime, and the sun's making it rainbow. Wipe it off and tell me what you see."

Chavez took the helmet off and searched for a clean bit of cloth. His greasy finger was the best he could do. "How's this?"

"Not great, but okay."

Despite himself, Chavez smiled. He liked reporting in to Jason. He felt like an astronaut.

"Dude." Jason's voice sounded urgent. "There's a big clanking noise out here."

"From where?"

"Coming from over on the other side. Like, coming up the road."

Chavez listened: no clanking came through the headset, and the wind through the crack between the nacelle and the tower drowned out every other sound.

"It sounds like a tank," said Jason. "And now I see the top of a crane. It's rolling up the hill."

The crane, thought Chavez. His dad said they were sending a crane. *What are they going to do with the crane?*

"Let me know what the crane is up to," he told Jason. "Meanwhile, let's focus. I need you up here with me. Watch the camera and help me find the circuit box."

The wind whipped around the nacelle. Chavez felt the floor under him shift a little. He felt a twinge of panic. He widened his stance on the slippery floor. "Let's get this done and get the fuck out of here."

Chapter 32

A loud rapping silenced everyone in the room. All eyes fell on Mary Cronin. She brought her own over-sized gavel to the meeting.

"Wonder what else she uses that for?" Doherty whispered out of the corner of her mouth.

Lawson shot her a wondering glance. Doherty had a tight smile on her face, but her shoulders moved up and down in a giggle. She was a woman full of surprises.

"Settle down, children," whispered Pierce, though his fountain pen never stopped its swift, steady path across the legal pad.

"Will the meeting please come to attention?" Cronin waited until there was complete silence in the room. "My name is Mary Cronin. I am the Deputy Attorney General of the Commonwealth of Massachusetts. As many of you may know, the Criminal Division in the Attorney General's office has responsibility for reviewing the report of the state arson squad in order to determine whether a prosecution is called for. I have before me the investigation report, and I will read the salient points."

A classier person would have acknowledged her boss sitting in the front row, thought Lawson, but Mary Cronin wasn't the type.

Five minutes into Cronin's reading, Lawson felt his phone vibrate. Slowly he eased it out, hoping Cronin wouldn't notice. If she caught him, he was sure she'd stop and give him crap. She'd probably love that. Stealthily, he glanced at the screen. It was a message, but he didn't recognize the number:

Chavez climbing turbine.

Lawson's eyes widened. *What the fuck does that mean?* As unobtrusively as possible, he got up and walked to the back of the room. He texted:

Jason?

The response came back immediately.

Yes

He texted back:

Where? Why?

Jason responded:

Up tower. Looking for switch.

Lawson thought about telling him to get down, but then he stopped. Instead, he typed:

How long til info?

This time there was a longer pause.

DK

While Lawson considered this, another message arrived from Jason:

Crane coming up hill

Shit, this was getting more complicated. What should he do about the fucking crane? Lawson's mind went blank. Finally he typed:

Hurry

Jason's response came back almost instantly: an emoji of a little devil with a thought bubble coming out of his mouth. It read:

No shit.

Lawson slipped back into his seat and passed a note to Pierce. He'd written it in big letters so Pierce wouldn't have to use his glasses. WE NEED A BREAK NOW!

Without a moment's hesitation, Pierce stood. With his 6'5" height, he towered over the crowd.

Cronin was still droning on about the tests they'd done for accelerants, but she stopped mid-sentence when he saw the Attorney General in front of her. She looked at Pierce with a mixture of surprise and irritation. "Yes, General?"

"A point of very personal privilege?"

"What is it, Mr. Pierce?"

"A plumbing problem, your honor. Could we take a ten-minute break while I visit the facilities?"

"We just had a break, Mr. Pierce."

"Hard to plan for, Your Honor."

Cronin stared hard at Pierce, and her face twitched as if she was going to argue. But how, thought Lawson, can she possibly start a public discussion about the Attorney General's 75-year-old bladder? That was too much, even for Mary Cronin.

"Ten minutes," she said. "Please be expeditious."

"Your lips to God's ears, Mary." Pierce smiled. "The spirit is willing, but the pipes are old."

A ripple of laughter ran though the older, mostly male crowd.

Ten minutes later, Pierce sauntered from the men's room, clearly taking his time.

Lawson and Doherty waited outside.

"What's up?" Pierce asked.

Lawson leaned close and said in a low voice, "Chavez is climbing the turbine tower."

Pierce looked startled but then he smiled. "He's up there now?"

"He and Jason apparently decided to take matters into their own hands. Chavez is climbing, and Jason's monitoring him from the ground."

Pierce's grin widened. "That young man has his shit together. Good for him. Let's give him some time."

"There's something else," said Lawson. "Jason says the crane is coming up the hill."

Pierce's smile disappeared. "Those pricks. I knew it."

Cronin's gavel rapped in the meeting room.

"I'll slow things down in there," said Pierce. "Action, you figure out what's going on with the crane."

Chavez tilted his head, aiming the camera at the machinery inside the nacelle, and Jason spoke: "That's the gear box."

Chavez moved his head so the headlamp beam and the camera aimed to the other side. "That's the main shaft. Now tilt up a little bit." After a few seconds, Jason said, "I'm sure that's where it was in one video, but it's not there. Turn all the way around and face the other wall."

Chavez shifted his feet. It was harder to turn around up here than Jason knew.

"Now look up," said Jason.

"There it is." They both said it together.

But now there was a new tone from Jason. Quieter, more serious. Jason called it his television golf announcer voice when they were fooling around, but Chavez took it as an alert to listen more carefully. "The crane is all the way up on the ridge. They parked it outside the gate."

"What's it doing?"

"They're raising the crane way up in the air. Man, that thing is fucking huge. It's outside the fence, but it's as tall as the tower. And it's got kind of a hook thing on the end of it, like they're getting ready to grab hold of the tower. Maybe you'd better come down."

Chavez's breath quickened and he felt a flutter in his chest. He thought quickly: He could get down a lot faster than he'd gotten up. Then he decided: He could do this. He examined the steel box on the wall. It was just like in the video, but fire-blackened and warped.

Chavez aimed the headlamp beam at the lock hole on the front. It needed a star-head Allen wrench. He pulled the ring of wrenches out of his fanny pack and began to search through them.

A metallic boom echoed through the small, enclosed space.

"Dude, they just dropped the hook thing onto the nacelle. Now they're reeling it back up like they're fishing."

"Hold on." Chavez couldn't think about the crane. Finally he got a wrench to fit in the little hole. It turned, but the door to the box wouldn't open. "Fuck."

"What?"

Chavez was too focused on the box respond. He wiggled the door back and forth with the wrench turned in the hole, but there was something else holding it. He felt around the crack between the door and the box. His heart sank. The metal wasn't just warped — the fire actually welded it shut.

Jason came back. "They pulled the hook back. Now, they're lowering the whattyacallit onto the roof."

Chavez wanted to concentrate on the box, but he needed to know. "The boom?"

"Yeah, that's it. The boom. The tip of it, where, you know, they have that big pulley thing? They're lowering it towards you."

A metal-on-metal noise, like the sound two train cars made when they hitched together, echoed through the nacelle. Instinctively, Chavez ducked. There was a groaning sound, and then a vibration under his feet. *Was the nacelle shifting?*

Chavez's thoughts flashed back to the prep meeting. The bad guys needed to get to that circuit box. It'd be a whole lot easier to get to if the nacelle was on the ground when they got access to the site. *They're going to knock this thing down!*

Cronin gaveled the meeting back to order. "I will now continue. Though what we're doing here is important, I have other things that demand my attention."

Doherty rolled her eyes at Lawson. She mouthed the word: "Bitch."

On the other side of Doherty, Pierce stood up. "Madame Chair."

Cronin couldn't look more irritated. "What is it now, Mr. Attorney General?"

"Will you be entertaining questions during your presentation, or should we wait until you've concluded?"

Cronin grew even more peeved. "The report has been written, Mr. Pierce, approved and signed off by all the necessary authorities." Cronin paused, apparently considering the consequences of refusing to let the Attorney General ask questions at a public meeting. "But certainly, in the interests of transparency and the public good, questions will be entertained."

"Thank, you Madame Chair." Pierce looked down at his legal pad. "I have noticed the room is filled with fire professionals. On behalf of the citizens of the Commonwealth of Massachusetts, I thank you for your ongoing service to our communities, and I thank you for the dedication you demonstrate today by your attendance at this meeting."

There was a shuffling amongst the firefighters and a collective murmur of appreciation.

Cronin glared at Pierce, but she was powerless to stop him.

"I wonder," continued Pierce, referring to his legal pad, "if you can take us through the arson squad's procedures for detecting the presence of ignitable liquids and fire accelerants, and how you distinguish between the two. Then, could you enlighten us as to whether you searched for non-liquid ignitable materials such as propane? Also, I'm sure we'd all be interested in hearing if the arson teams are using the new portable hydrocarbon sniffers and how that approach differs from your previous use of canines?"

Pierce sat down. All around the room, people shifted in their seats. There was a rumble of whispering. The fire personnel perked up. Lawson whispered to Doherty, "How does Pierce know all this shit?" Doherty just shrugged.

Looking like she was passing a kidney stone, Cronin said, "This office is charged with determining whether an arson prosecution is called for. I am not...."

But a fire captain from Pittsfield was on his feet, offering himself as an expert. And a firefighter from Stow had a question, which a female fire lieutenant from Gardner answered. The discussion was off and running.

Questions and answers, discussion and opinions — it roared along for twenty minutes, while Cronin sat at her table, chewing on her lower lip as if she intended to draw blood.

When the discussion began to wind down, Pierce stood up again.

"Thank you, folks. All very interesting. I always enjoy hearing from the troops on the ground. Now, I have some other questions about the training and certification procedures of the arson team."

Cronin brought the gavel down with a bang. Even under her perpetual tan, Lawson could see she was beet red. "I am sorry, Mr. Pierce, but I don't see how this furthers the purpose of this meeting. I have just about finished summarizing the report, and I and others in the criminal division have considered it. It is our job to determine if the evidence warrants a prosecution."

Lawson's phone vibrated silently, and he pulled it out. It was a picture. He studied the photo, taking a few seconds to figure out what he was seeing. It showed the boom of a crane resting on the roof of the turbine. It was surreal, like two giant erector sets doing battle. Lawson turned it sideways to make sure he was seeing it right.

Then, a message:

Crane on roof!!!!!!

He showed it to Doherty and whispered, "We need another break. I've got to do something."

"I'll take care of it," said Doherty, and she scooted her chair back.

"What?"

"Just watch." Doherty got up and moved to the back of the room.

Cronin was still speaking: "Mr. Attorney General, perhaps you should convene a further meeting of fire personnel to discuss these issues. Maybe your new PR person, Mr. Lawson here, could make some effective use of his time by arranging such a meeting."

Suddenly the room was filled with a simultaneous cacophony of buzzers, chimes, and vibrations.

A synthesized voice came from everywhere and nowhere: "Attention, firefighters. This is an emergency report drill. Test begins now."

Every firefighter leaped to his or her feet.

The message came again: "Attention, firefighters...."

By the time the message was repeated the third time, every firefighter had left the room.

Everything suddenly caught up with Chavez.

He'd just climbed the equivalent of thirty flights of stairs, the last half like an obstacle course. He'd fallen in the tilted nacelle. And he was covered with some kind of fucking gunk.

"What's going on?" asked Jason. "You're just standing there."

Chavez didn't want to tell Jason he was thinking of chickening out — but maybe this was too ... fucking ... hard.

Jason's voice came back, breezy and Jasony: "Hurry it up, Dude, get that box open and let's get out of here. The faster you get it down, the sooner I eat."

Chavez was too nervous and tired to laugh, but it was funny that Jason was talking about food. He was just trying to cheer him up. "Okay." It was just a grunt.

He was going to need both hands to work at the box, and he wedged his butt between the turbine gearbox and the wall of the nacelle. He leaned closer so the headlamp beam shone on the crack between the door and the box housing. It looked like there were two places that were melted, with the metal fused together.

BOOM! It felt like someone dropped a metal beam on the roof. Instinctively, he ducked. Now it was obvious — they were trying to knock it down. He felt the nacelle sway even more. He wedged himself in tighter to keep his balance.

"What the fuck is going on? You're all over the place."

"The box is fused shut. I'm going to try to cut it open."

"How long's that going to take?"

Chavez held the wrench in the lock hole with one hand and reached down to his belt. Carefully, he unstrapped his multi-tool and pulled it out of its case. Holding it in front of him, he used his teeth to pull out the saw blade. The multi-tool brochure said it was diamond encrusted and would cut through anything. He tasted blood as he pulled the saw away from his mouth. He still had his doubts about whether the saw would "cut through anything," but he knew it was pretty fucking sharp.

Chavez worked the blade against the first of the two welded spots. He started sawing. Every now and then he stopped to rest and check his progress. His hands and shoulders hurt from the climb, and his legs shook from the pressure it took to maintain his balance on the slanted slippery floor.

Twice more the crane clanged on the roof. Each time Chavez steadied himself and kept sawing.

Sure enough, the diamond blade cut through metal, but it was slow. He couldn't be sure, but he thought he was done with the top metal blob, and he moved to the bottom. Finally he felt the blade slip through. Again, he turned the wrench in the hole. Nothing. The door was still stuck on the edge.

"Fuck," he muttered.

In his ear he heard Jason echo, "Yeah, fuck."

"Okay, one big pull." Chavez grabbed the top of the circuit box door with one hand while turning the wrench in the lock slot with the other. Putting his weight into it, he jerked backward. The door popped open, and again Chavez fell on his butt into the oily muck. He rolled over, got to his knees, and stood up.

"What happened?"

"I fell down again."

"Jesus."

Chavez felt the nacelle shift. He listened for the banging on the roof. For the moment: nothing.

But the floor under his feet was definitely more tilted then when he got up there.

"Clean off the lens again," said Jason. "This is the money shot."

Chavez wiped his hand across his chest, then reached up and carefully rubbed his forefinger on the lens.

"Better?"

"Good enough."

Chavez tilted the headlamp and the camera into the open circuit box. He could see the switches clearly. He lowered his head so the camera could get a good picture. "Got it?"

His earpiece exploded. "*CUJO*! Now get your ass out of there."

Lawson watched Fleming join the mob of firefighters. Following, Lawson found him in the parking lot, smoking a cigarette and talking on his phone. Lawson stood close, waiting until Fleming was done with the call. He thought he heard the word "crane." There was activity all around them, as firefighters talked on radios and phones in their vehicles. Fleming ended the call.

Lawson stepped forward. "I'm Richard Lawson."

"I know who you are." Fleming took a drag of his cigarette and blew it in Lawson's direction. "What?"

Lawson held up his phone so Fleming could see the image of the crane in Jason's latest message. "Couldn't help but overhear your call. Is this what you're doing?"

Fleming took a quick look at the phone. "None of your business."

"You guys don't take possession of the site until there's a ruling."

"Just getting ready." Fleming showed Lawson a mean smile. "The crane's on the other side of the fence. We aren't in violation of anything." Fleming sucked on the cigarette, threw it down on the pavement, ground it out with his shoe.

Lawson flared. "That's bullshit. Look closer. The boom's on the tower. That's not the other side of the fence. Do I have to stand up in there and call you on it?"

Fleming seemed to pay attention to the change of Lawson's tone as he paused and considered. Then he answered. "Do what you have to do. You're a washed-up drunk and your boss is an inbred Yankee dilettante. You don't have a lot of credibility. We're about to win this one. Why don't you take a seat on the bench where you belong?" He turned to go back inside.

Briefly Lawson fixated on the washed-up-drunk comment, but he shrugged it off. He needed to protect Chavez. "There's a kid up there in the tower."

Fleming stopped and turned. "Right. Go have another drink."

"Chavez Simons. He's a volunteer firefighter. The son of Peter Simons, your lawyer."

Lawson watched Fleming process that information. Then, Fleming took a step toward him. Lawson thought he was going to swing on him and he braced himself. He hadn't been in a fistfight since sixth grade, but he got himself ready.

Fleming got uncomfortably close and leaned in to Lawson's face. "For the record, I didn't just hear that." His breath stank of coffee and cigarette smoke. "But if I were you, I'd get him the fuck out of there, 'cause that tower's coming down." He poked Lawson in the chest with a forefinger. "And as for you, you can go fuck yourself."

Fleming turned away and walked back toward the building.

Rubbing his chest, Lawson wished he felt different, but it really did hurt.

Lawson took his seat, shaken from his exchange with Fleming.

Pierce was sitting with someone new, a youngish woman in a business suit. Together, they were going though some papers. Pierce had his reading glasses on and several sections of the top page were circled in the distinctive blue ink of his fountain pen.

Doherty returned and sat beside Lawson. He asked her, "Let me guess.

You had something to do with the fact that the hall just emptied?"

Doherty whispered, "It's an unannounced regional emergency operations test, put on by the State Police Op Center. All volunteers have to contact the Center as fast as possible. All the departments compete for the best ratings. It takes about twenty minutes. To keep people on their toes, it's done by surprise."

"You're incredible." The second the words left his lips, Lawson regretted them. *What a stupid thing to say.* Cautiously he looked over at Doherty.

She was slightly embarrassed but obviously pleased. "I have friends," she said as she reached down and flicked something off her jodhpurs.

Then Lawson saw Fleming return to the wind-farm-team table. Fleming had gone off somewhere from the time he poked him in the chest in the parking lot. Another cigarette? Or a phone call? Fleming sat down next to Kerrigan, leaned close, and whispered in his ear. It was clear he was worked up. After listening a while, Kerrigan held up his hand, silencing Fleming. For a few seconds, Kerrigan looked off, thinking. Then, slowly, he shook his head.

Lawson watched and wondered what that was about. What had Kerrigan said no to?

As long as Chavez was up in the tower, thought Lawson, maybe they would keep the crane away. Fleetingly, he thought about texting Jason to tell Chavez to stay up there. Then he kicked himself. He couldn't do that to the kid. What if Kerrigan just okayed the crane? Lawson wouldn't put it past Kerrigan.

Cronin's gavel came down. She looked different, somehow, calmer, maybe a little bleary-eyed. It was a long morning. Lawson wondered if she was tired. But then a thought occurred to him: Does she keep a little stash in her purse?

"Let's get back to business, people," said Cronin. "We certainly have had an eventful morning. We've heard the report from the arson squad, and an interesting and informative line of questioning from our esteemed Attorney General." She slurred the word "esteemed." Lawson studied her more closely. *She's definitely had something.*

Jason was quiet.

Chavez asked, "Are you there?"

"I thought I could do a screen shot of the video feed and text it to Lawson, but it's not working. We need to take him the camera."

Chavez was quiet for several seconds. "I think we have a problem."

"What now?"

"I can't get down."

Jason started right in. He was ready for this, it happened before when his best friend got up high and panicked. "Take a breath and just start out slow. One foot after another. Look straight ahead. Don't look down."

"That's not it. I can't get down."

"Dude, just baby steps."

"The ladder's gone."

"What do you mean — *gone?*"

"The ladder? Up at the top? It wasn't held up very well when I came up it, but one of those crashes I heard, that must have been the ladder. There's nothing there, and it's too dark down there to see very far. It's just gone."

"Where are you?"

"I'm in the crack between the nacelle and the tower. Nice view from here." Chavez struggled to sound calm. "What happened to the crane?"

"It just lifted up a couple of minutes ago. They lowered the boom. Get it? 'Lowered the boom?'"

"Stop it."

"Just funny, that's all. Anyway, it's let go of the tower and kind of backed off."

Chavez shifted his focus. This was good news, but he still had a major situation. "Back to my problem."

"Remember that video we watched of those crazy wind farm dudes in Oregon?"

Chavez's mind fogged. They'd watched wind farm videos all night. How the fuck was he supposed to remember which one was from Oregon? And, most everyone in the videos was pretty much crazy for doing that shit. Now he was one of them. "No."

"The rescue drill? Remember, the guy in the video pretends he's scared of that lame buzzing noise, so he lowers himself with a rope?"

"Yeah, I think."

"There was a white duffle bag labeled 'Self Rescue' hanging on the wall. Look and see if there's one up there."

Chavez shined his light around the walls. At the other end of the nacelle, he saw what looked like a backpack on the wall. "I see something. I'll get down there." He skated through the oil and looked more closely. The backpack wasn't white, but it did have the words "Self Rescue" stenciled on the side.

"I'm taking it off the wall. Now I'm unzipping it." He felt the floor shift under him. "We need to hurry. This thing doesn't feel good."

Jason's voice came back loud: "Don't open it. Hold tight for a couple of minutes."

"It might fall down any second."

"Calm your titties, Dude. Just sit there, I'll be back to you."

Chavez squatted against the side of the nacelle and closed his eyes. All of a sudden he was very tired. And really hungry, too. He wondered what was going on in the fire meeting.

Lawson felt the vibration in his pocket. He pulled it out and looked at it. By now, he didn't care who saw him looking at his phone. He glanced toward the front tables. Mary Cronin's eyes were on him, and her face wore an expression of curiosity, worry, and fury.

Have video of switches. Need to bring to you.

Lawson handed the phone to Doherty, who studied the image, registered what she was seeing, and passed the phone on to Pierce. He smiled and nodded.

"It's time for a decision," Cronin was saying. "After carefully examining all the evidence, the Criminal Division in the Attorney General's office finds there was no human cause in the fire at the Matchic Ridge Wind Farm. We judge that the fire was caused by natural means, specifically the high winds in the storm on the 15th and 16th of October."

The room erupted in noise, immediate commentary from every firefighter. Hollis jumped up with her fist in the air like she was at a football game. "Yes!" she shouted. Jimmy Kerrigan dragged her back into her chair. Fleming smiled grimly.

Pierce was on his feet. "Madame Chair." His distinctive voice instantly silenced the din.

With exaggerated courtesy, Cronin said, "*Mr.* Attorney General, do you have something else to add?"

"Madame Chair, might I have a minute or two before we conclude?"

Cronin's face clouded. "We've followed well-established protocol," she said. "I believe we're finished here." She raised her gavel.

"Just a minute or two?" asked Pierce.

Cronin wavered. Lawson could feel the intensity of her desire to bang it down on the table and put an end to all this.

But she couldn't possibly refuse the Attorney General — and suddenly, she was calm, even magnanimous. "Please make it brief," she said.

"Since we have such a good complement of firefighters here," said Pierce, "I thought it might be appropriate to screen a video on certain historical aspects of firefighting in Massachusetts. I'd welcome the input of the folks here before we put it up on the Web."

"This isn't at all the purpose of this gathering," objected Cronin.

"Anyone who needs to get on the road is certainly welcome to do so," said Pierce. He smiled around the room. "However, I'm told Chief Jokkinen plans to spring for pizza afterward."

Lawson heard a firefighter say, in a stage whisper that carried through the room: "I'll have pepperoni."

"Fine, Mr. Pierce," said Cronin. Now she was hyper-chipper, almost carefree. But it seemed to Lawson that she was having a hard time speaking. "Mishter Pierce," she said. "Do what you like."

"I'm back," said Jason. "I just watched the rescue video on YouTube again. I know what to do. Unzip the duffle bag. The first thing you come to should be a harness thing."

Chavez pulled the zipper and reached inside. "I've got it. Now what?"

"Hold it. We've got a problem." Jason's voice was filled with alarm. "They're raising the crane again. Wait a second."

"What?" Chavez hated having to rely on Jason for information.

"They're back with the hook. They're trying to snag one of the blades."

"Are they going to pull the tower over?"

"Don't think about that."

Chavez's heart was racing faster than ever, and he had a huge ache in his side. *Don't think about it.* "Oh, fuck."

"Yeah, fuck. Let's get going. Put the whole thing on."

Chavez struggled into the harness. It was like some safety equipment at the station, but when he put equipment on at the station, the Chief told him to take his time. This was a different deal.

"All strapped in?"

Chavez looked down. "I guess so."

"There should be a big metal loop on your chest."

Chavez felt with his hand. "It's there."

"Reach behind you, there should be a nylon bag back there. It'll be under your ass. You can find your ass, can't you?"

"Stop fucking around."

"Zip open the end. The first thing you'll find is a clamp hook on the end of a rope. A carabiner. Pull it out and hook it onto something solid. In the video, there was a big ring on one of the pieces of machinery."

"Got it. It's hooked."

"Run your hand down the rope into the bag and pull out a metal tube thing with a button on it. The rope runs through it. It's called a descender. Do you have that?"

"Got it. Jesus, the fucking floor just moved again. I need to get out of here."

"Focus. The descender has another carabiner on it, click that onto the ring on your chest."

"Got it."

"You're going to slide down the rope. It's called rappelling."

"I know what rappelling is."

"So you've rappelled before?"

Chavez didn't answer, and Jason said, "I didn't think so. So listen to me, Dude. I know all about this stuff."

"From watching a video?"

"The rope in your butt bag goes through the descender. The push button on the descender is the brake. Squeeze if you want to go faster."

"Like that's going to happen. I'm ready," said Chavez, though he wasn't looking forward to what was coming next. He checked his equipment. "Are you sure? There's just this one thin rope? And it slides through this metal thing?"

"That's how this thing's supposed to work. Why would they put it up there in the video if it didn't work?"

The nacelle shifted slightly, and there was a metal groan. Chavez decided. "Let's go."

"Now open the trap door."

"Where's the trap door?"

"In the floor with a little handle. It should be under the rescue duffle. Look around."

Chavez moved his headlamp from side to side. Not there. Quickly he was frustrated. "I can't see through the oil on the floor. Maybe this thing doesn't have a fucking trapdoor."

"Look under your feet."

Chavez took a step back and shone the light straight down at the floor.

Jason's voice crackled in his ear. "There it is. The square opening. There's a handle on that one side. Try it."

Chavez leaned down, grabbed the handle, tugged the trapdoor open, and flipped it back with a clang. Oil flowed out the opening, and daylight flooded in. Cautiously, he looked over the edge. He could see the ground, three hundred feet below.

"Don't look down."

"Too late."

"You ready?"

"I'm ready."

"Well?"

Chavez took a few deep breaths.

"What's going on?"

"Just thinking."

"About what?"

Jason had been his best friend forever, he didn't have to explain.

"The sooner you make it happen," said Jason, "the sooner we eat."

Chavez thought he'd rather throw up than eat.

"Sit on the edge."

"I'm there. I'm sitting in oil."

"Need a Cujo?"

"Yeah, I guess."

"Count of three. Ready?"

"Ready."

"One, two, CUJO!"

Chavez shoved off the side and immediately he felt the rope pull on his chest, and the straps on the harness took the weight. He was floating in air right in the trap door. Gently, he squeezed the descender and began to drop. He looked up and saw the trap door ten feet above him, getting smaller and smaller. He thought about looking down but kept himself from doing it. He thought about trying the brake, but he decided not to do that either. Everything was going just fine. He just needed to reach the fucking ground.

A shadow passed over him. He glanced up and saw the crane with the hook on the turbine blade. Like a giant praying mantis, he thought.

Chavez relaxed. He was going to make it down. He leaned back and checked the view. And he really was hungry now that he wasn't going to barf. Then he remembered Jason's instructions. The rope coming out of the bag. A thought occurred to him. "What happens when all this rope comes out of the bag?"

There was a silence from Jason's end. Finally he came back. "They must have measured it."

"I sincerely fucking hope so."

Lawson felt his phone vibrate. He pulled it out and read:

Back on earth. Coming now!

Letting out a big breath of relief, he handed the phone to Doherty, who read it and handed it back. Lawson felt her hand touch his, and there was a jolt up his arm. *Did she mean to do that?*

He caught Pierce's eye and gave him a thumbs up.

Pierce hit a key on the computer (Doherty had taught him how), and Chavez's video flickered to life on the monitor in the front of the room. First on the screen was the *Time* magazine cover picture of the crushed Fitchburg fire truck. Then, the image shifted to Chavez, in jacket and tie, seated at what looked like a newscaster's desk.

Jimmy Kerrigan muttered, "What the fuck is this?"

"My name is Chavez Simons," began Chavez. "This is my project in fulfillment of my certification exam to be a Regular Volunteer Firefighter in the Town of Burfield."

The firefighters in the audience chuckled, laughed, then settled down as Chavez, on the monitor, began to tell the story of the two mill fires. His voice continued steadily, but the image in the video cut away time after time, to news articles illustrating the overall story of the fires. Then the video shifted to a comparison of the fire maps with the schematics of the housing projects. The camera zoomed in and out on the maps and diagrams; no one could miss the similarities. The video displayed the two silver-shovel photos, with circles around Kerrigan and Fleming's faces. Then, the company logos: "Kerrigan Development" and "Plymouth Engineering."

The video shifted back to Chavez sitting at the anchor desk. "To me, there was a obvious connection between these fires. And they sure were suspicious. What would be someone's motive for arson? And why didn't anyone do anything about it?"

The screen switched to a computer-generated graphic — "Hardship Factor" — and then segued into a PowerPoint presentation with Chavez — using data supplied by Lawson — narrating how a project under construction could pay off in the event of a natural disaster.

Then he delivered his body blows: the money Kerrigan Development made in Fitchburg and Taunton when the hardship factor was applied. Each number materialized on the screen. There were whistles from the audience and whispered commentary.

Lawson shot a glance at the wind farm table. Jimmy Kerrigan looked ready to explode, but Fleming still looked bored. Curiously, both Hollis and Peter sat up straight and paid attention, as if this were all news to them. Hollis even took notes.

Lawson glanced at Cronin. Half-turned in her chair, she watched the monitor, shook her head, and struggled to keep her face expressionless.

Now camera returned to Chavez. "The fires in Fitchburg and Taunton were suspicious. The maps matched, and everyone made more money with the hardship factor. A very expensive truck got crushed." Chavez brought a newscaster's seriousness to his face. "A top-notch firefighter — one of the best firefighters ever in Massachusetts — lost his leg." Chavez looked right into the camera. "Why did everyone look the other way?"

"The End" appeared on the screen, and closing credits rolled:

A ChaJay Production
Chavez Simons, Reporter

A picture of Chavez at the anchor desk flashed on the screen.

Jason R. Morrill, Producer, Director, Videographer

A picture of Jason appeared, looking like a serious filmmaker. He even wore a pair of sunglasses perched on his head.

The monitor went black, and the room burst into conversation. What were quiet whispers now became urgent commentary.

Cronin stood and began packing her folders and papers into a briefcase. Then, looking across the audience, she said, "Mr. Attorney General, this is all highly irregular. Firefighters from Burfield and from more than twenty other communities risked their lives fighting the Matchic Ridge fire, and these professionals have worked long and hard to investigate it. And you have turned these proceedings into some kind of carnival show. It's disgusting." She took a ragged breath. "The Fitchburg and Taunton fires occurred years ago, well outside the statute of limitations." She banged her gavel again. "This meeting is adjourned." She shoved the gavel into her briefcase. "On behalf of the Office of the Attorney General, I want to apologize to those whose reputations were sullied here today."

As Cronin moved away from her table, her shoe caught on a folding chair. She stumbled, then indignantly straightened herself.

Kerrigan nudged Fleming, and they got up to follow Cronin.

"There's the kid," came a firefighter's voice, and all around the room, heads swiveled toward the back of the room.

Chavez stood inside the door, wearing a harness, and he was covered in some sort of reddish greasy stuff. He held his fire helmet in his hand, and electronic equipment hung from his neck. Jason was next him. Chavez gave Lawson a shy smile and a wave.

Beside Chavez and Jason, the door swung open. Doherty came through leading half a dozen men and women in blue FBI windbreakers. The last person in the FBI squad was dressed in a suit instead of a windbreaker. Two Boston television crews capped off the parade through the door. Lawson smiled. *The FBI brings along their own media coverage.*

Two agents shut and blocked the door.

The room fell utterly silent: even for professional firefighters, accustomed to excitement in their day-to-day lives, this was like something from a television show.

People in the balcony leaned over the rail, trying to see what was happening below.

Chavez and Jason made their way through the crowd and Jason handed Lawson the mini-camera and a cord. "Plug this into your USB. It's already cued up."

"If I might have your attention again," Pierce said, "I realize this is unusual, but events are unfolding here this morning. I think it's better to deal with this situation now, if I can ask for the indulgence of those in the hall."

The hall quieted and there were no objections. This was a shitload better than going back to work.

Lawson plugged Jason's camera into the laptop, and a bouncing, poorly lit video appeared on the monitor.

People shuffled, trying for clear angles to the monitor, curious for what surprises were coming next.

The greasy image zeroed in on a scorched steel box.

This was followed by half a minute of the camera wobbling up, down, and sideways.

A hand turned an Allen wrench in a lock hole.

"You better fast forward," whispered Chavez. Lawson sent the video racing ahead. In super-fast-motion, hands sawed at the box.

"That's it," said Chavez, and Lawson set the video to real-time speed.

The box sprang open. Then there was a jumble of images as Chavez fell down and his helmet and the camera fell off. The image righted itself, and a blurry finger cleared the picture. A beam of light played across the mechanism inside the circuit box. There were three switches, each with a clearly labeled

A position and M position.

All three were set on M.

There was a jerking motion, with shadows racing in all directions. Finally, the image coalesced into Chavez's grinning face. He flashed a "V" sign, and he shouted something. There was no audio, but Chavez and Jason provided the sound live for the audience in the room: "Cujo!"

The screen went dark, and after a moment's silence, the room exploded with applause.

Lawson looked around the room.

Fleming whispered urgently in Kerrigan's ear. Lawson knew Kerrigan was getting the bad news about the switches.

Hollis sat at the table and looked around with a puzzled look on her face. Not a clue, thought Lawson. Switch A and Switch M meant nothing to her.

Peter remained in his chair, fiddling frantically with his ponytail, staring down at the table in front of him as if he wished he could be someplace — anyplace — else.

Firefighters and Burfield residents waited for whatever excitement was next.

The television crews ran their cameras, but the reporters stood and watched, as mesmerized as everyone else. Lawson hoped the producers back in the studio were running the feed live. This was real news.

"As you can see," said Pierce — speaking with the voice of a man accustomed to commanding attention — "we have several new guests." He gestured at the FBI man in the suit. "This is Special Agent in Charge of the Boston FBI office, Junior Martinez."

Pierce indicated the agents ringing the room. "And these fine gentlemen and ladies are his associates from the FBI public corruption squad."

"Agent Martinez and I will need to sort this out," continued Pierce, "but here's the general rundown. The video of the switch box you just saw will be evidence in a federal case of conspiracy to commit fraud against the United States government. It clearly shows that there was 'human involvement' — as our friends at the Department of Energy like to call it — in the destruction of the Matchic Ridge turbines during the storm in October."

"As Cadet Simons here showed in his remarkable video, the wind farm scam isn't the first rodeo for these cowpokes." Lawson saw Doherty shake her head and smile at the cowboy lingo. "Mr. Kerrigan and Mr. Fleming will be charged in the Fitchburg and Taunton fires, as well, and I'm sure the fact that a firefighter was injured in one of the fires will be taken into account when the charges are drawn up."

Lawson looked over. Jokkinen looked down at his hands. This was a long time coming.

Jimmy Kerrigan smacked his hand on the table, and stood up. "This is total bullshit! Those fires happened thirty years ago. Any first-year law student knows about the statute of limitations. You can't make that stick. And that video? The wind must have changed those switches." Calmer, he sat back and folded his arms. "You're blowing smoke out your ass, Pierce."

"Mister Attorney General." Mary Cronin half staggered, half lurched to her feet. Lawson assumed she had balance problems because of the hump, but this was more than that. She'd really been dipping into that purse. "The statute of limitations…"

"Can it, Mary." Pierce held up a hand. "Sit down."

Cronin's jaw dropped, and she sank back into her seat.

"Time for a short legal lesson for those non-lawyers in the audience," said Pierce. "Those people who were fortunate enough to find honest careers." There was a round of laughter. A lawyer joke always went over well, especially if a self-deprecating WASP Attorney General told it. "The statute of limitations says that most crimes can't be charged after seven years."

Lawson watched Kerrigan. He sat smugly, smiling.

"That is," Pierce continued, "unless there is evidence of what they call — I love this term — 'an on-going criminal enterprise.' That's why our esteemed Deputy Attorney General gave us a big boost."

Lawson watched Cronin's face freeze, and the tan fade.

Pierce gestured and said, "Ms. Swanson?"

The woman who had been going through documents with Pierce handed Lawson a memory stick and said, "Click on the file called 'wire transfer.' "

Lawson brought it up on the laptop, and a second later it came up on the monitor for everyone in the room to see. It was an official-looking bank document containing a series of numbers.

"I suppose you can define 'criminal enterprise' several different ways," said Pierce, "but in my family, the word 'enterprise' meant money." Pierce smiled at the laughter. "There were generations in my family whose only 'enterprise' was making it to the mailbox once a month, but we'll leave them out of it." More laughter. Pierce's got to know he has them, thought Lawson, or he wouldn't be making all these jokes. And then he had a second thought. Would he?

Pierce pointed to the monitor. "Just this morning, a sum of money was wire-transferred into an account in the Cayman Islands. When they are first hired, employees of the Attorney General's office sign an ethics form. And every year thereafter, they file a document listing all their bank accounts. The form gives our ethics office permission to monitor their accounts — for this very reason, I might add. Ms. Cronin's form only lists an account at a savings bank in Lynn.

"But we found another account Ms. Cronin maintains in the Bahamas. Lo and behold, that account received a $4 million transfer just this morning at the beginning of business, just about" — Pierce checked his watch for effect — "two hours before issuing her favorable decision on the wind farm. There's a fancy legal term for that: *fishy*."

A ripple of laughter ran through the crowd.

Pierce continued. "The $4 million came from a bank in the Caymans. I think we'll figure out who maintains that account."

"You smug prick," snarled Kerrigan. He started to stand, but thought better of it as an agent moved in behind him.

"And when the wire transfer came in this morning, Special Agent in Charge Martinez decided to come on out to the party."

Pierce smiled at Kerrigan. "So, let me sum up. Chavez and his friend Jason, aided by Mr. Lawson, dusted off those old fires and showed how you folks did that scam. Now we have a video of the switches — recorded shortly before you thought you'd destroy the evidence — of the conspiracy involving the wind farm. Now we have the payoff, made just this morning. That fits even the most dubious juror's definition of an on-going criminal enterprise."

Martinez gestured, a casual wave of his hand like a maître d showing guests to a table. The FBI agents motioned for Kerrigan, Fleming and Cronin to stand up. They pulled their hands in front them, snapped on handcuffs and began to lead them out of the room.

Hollis stood with her wrists out in front of her. She even pushed the sleeves of her jacket up to her elbows. But nobody came towards her. She looked around, perplexed, and slowly dropped her arms. Peter Simons eased her back into her seat.

Lawson wondered at the look on her face. Could it actually be disappointment?

Chapter 33

In the mirror on his closet door, Chavez watched himself as he slipped into his red Burfield VFD windbreaker, with "Simons" in block lettering over the department seal on his left breast. The Chief said he could wear it today.

Chavez couldn't remember a bigger birthday. It was Christmas vacation, and he was going ice fishing with the Chief, Mr. Pierce, Mr. Lawson, and Sergeant Doherty. And tonight was his special Regular Firefighter award ceremony.

He reached down and peeled a label off his new khakis, an early birthday gift from his dad. They had a special flannel lining. It was going to be a cold day.

Lawson rolled out of bed, feeling good, and flashed on how he used to feel waking up. *A different life.*

His thoughts turned to Maureen Doherty. They had been turning to Doherty a lot, lately.

Since the fire review meeting, there were a couple of long phone conversations and some playful texting. He was going to see her in Burfield today, and they were going to play racquetball the coming weekend. He stood up, and sucked in his gut. He wondered whether wearing a medium t-shirt to play racquetball would be pushing it.

Last night he'd received a text from Doherty:

Boss wants to go ice fishing tomorrow after press conf. Bring your longies!

The message was curiously erotic to him.

Doherty? Long underwear?

He shook it off. *Jesus, Lawson, get a grip.*

Then he worried. Back in the Midwest, ice fishing meant standing around on a frozen lake, cold and miserable, nipping schnapps from pocket flasks until everyone staggered back to their cars. How was he going to do that? Maybe he could get a hole in the ice near Chavez. The kid would have

Mountain Dew.

He puzzled over what to wear. He had an old pair of boots, but what about a coat? The only warm thing he had was his tweed Brooks Brothers topcoat. It would have to do.

Doherty went for an early morning five-miler and watched the sun come up through the steam of her breath on her return leg.

Now she sat in the Lincoln on East Street in Padanaram, the small village just over the bridge out to Pierce's house, idling the engine to keep warm.

Ethan Pierce was a man of few secrets, but once a week, before Padanaram Beauty opened for the day, Pierce sneaked into the salon for a facial. Doherty smiled. When she asked him about it, Pierce began a story about going to a fancy spa with his wife. Midway through the story, his voice trailed off. Doherty didn't think it was right to push him for details, but Pierce's secret gave her a powerful weapon. In Pierce's world, men his age didn't get facials.

She glanced at the digital clock on the navigation system. They needed to get to Burfield at 10. Lawson was meeting them at the fire station.

She felt a little flutter. It would be the first time they'd seen each other since he'd suggested getting together for racquetball. She didn't want her excitement to show in front of Pierce. The man could read her like a book.

Doherty had her warm clothes in the trunk, including her huge State Police parka and a pair of Nike field boots. It was the closest she had to ice fishing gear. She was a city girl. She'd never been ice fishing before.

At 7:30 a.m., Jokkinen pushed his empty plate across the table. He needed to get to the station a couple of hours before the press conference.

He wondered about warm boots. He had some old insulated Wolverines in the mudroom. Terry Jokkinen hated ice fishing. And then he had an odd thought. "Does a guy with only one foot get half as cold as everybody else?"

When he got to the door, Bertie handed him a birthday card for Chavez. Jokkinen remembered it was Chavez's birthday: the red-jacket day for the kid, nearly as big a deal for Jokkinen as it was for Chavez. But Jokkinen wouldn't have thought about a card. "Thanks, Sweetie." He gave her a kiss on the cheek.

The sun was out, the sky was bright blue, and the temperature was in the mid-twenties. It might even hit thirty by noon. The wind whipped Lawson as he opened his car door, and he buttoned his topcoat over his good suit. He was seriously cold. How was he ever going to spend the day standing out on a frozen lake?

As he drove into town, he saw a "For Sale" sign in front of Hollis's house. He wondered how he felt about that. He supposed it was a small enough price for her to pay.

Two television vans, with satellite dishes on their roofs, were parked in the lot next to the fire station. Camera operators took background footage of the ridge with only one burned-out turbine standing.

Lawson went inside the station, looking for Chavez and Jokkinen. They'd spruced it up for the press conference. The cement bays were washed down, and most of the oil was off the floor. They'd cleared out the center bay and set up one of the long tables from the break room in front of the new Brushbuster, phosphorescent orange with chrome trim circling it like tinsel. It arrived just the day before.

Nearly every firefighter was there, with their red windbreakers over layers of sweaters and parkas.

Lawson found Chavez next to the new truck and extended his hand. "How are the legs? Did you recover from that climb up the turbine?"

Chavez smiled. "A lot better. I could barely walk the next day."

"I see the oil came off."

"I had to use hand cleanser. Really abrasive. My mom wasn't too happy about the bathtub."

"Pretty nice truck, huh?"

Chavez's smile got even bigger. "The best!" He lowered his voice; "I drove it around town this morning."

Lawson laughed and slapped him on the back.

Pierce's black Lincoln cruised to a stop in the driveway. Lawson glanced up at the clock: twenty minutes before they were set to begin. He walked out to the car. Pierce was finishing a phone call, and he held up a finger to say he'd be another minute. Lawson moved toward Doherty's side and opened the door for her. She climbed out through an eddy of warm car smell: leather, coffee, wet wool and something else, some kind of perfume. Was she wearing perfume on duty? Lawson felt something move in his chest.

Doherty got out and stood next to him, but Lawson stood frozen with his hand on the door handle.

"Hands off the state vehicle, sir."

His reverie interrupted, he stepped back, surprised. Doherty looked right at him and smiled, a gorgeous, happy smile.

"I thought you were serious," he said.

"What makes you think I wasn't?" she asked. "Sir?" Her smile told him otherwise.

On the other side of the Lincoln, Pierce finished his call and got out to greet Chavez. "Nice jacket, Chief, and happy birthday!"

"Thanks."

"Probably the hardest earned jacket in the Commonwealth — and the most deserved."

Chavez looked away in embarrassment.

There was a loud crunching from the road out front, as Hollis pulled her Lexus up onto the snow bank on the police station sidewalk.

Hollis and her new lawyer, a solemn-faced man who was one of Boston's top white-collar criminal defense lawyers, approached on the fire station driveway. Her high-heeled leather boots slipped on a patch of ice and she flailed her arms for a couple of seconds until she re-gained her balance.

Hollis's face was set into a fiercely rigid expression that Lawson saw many times during his newsman days — the rictus the accused wore when they faced the music. *She might rather go to jail than go through this.* He shook off the feeling. *No, she wouldn't.* Still, he felt a twinge of sympathy.

She was one damn lucky woman.

Television Klieg lights snapped on, and the reflection off the new truck bathed the inside of the fire station with a pumpkin glow. Pierce led Hollis to the table behind a copse of microphones.

Hollis's lawyer took the seat next to her.

"Good morning," said Pierce, with a smile. Not Pierce's widest smile, Lawson noted, but not his "I have to kiss this baby" smile, either. It was his businesslike, 'Let's get this done smile.'

"We are here this morning" — Pierce adjusted several of the microphones — "to make an announcement concerning the future of the Matchic Ridge Wind Farm. As you know, James Sean Kerrigan, George Harold Fleming, and Mary Margaret Cronin have been charged with a variety of state and federal crimes. Hollis Elaine Kerrigan has been named an un-indicted co-conspirator in the crimes related to the wind farm.

"Further," said Pierce, "we are announcing a settlement concerning the operation of the wind farm, so we may bring this unfortunate chapter to a close.

"It is our policy not to answer questions in an on-going criminal matter. Ms. Kerrigan will now read the terms of the settlement."

Hollis took an obvious, deep breath. Her hands, holding her single sheet of paper, trembled. Her pause made the silence in the fire station more dramatic.

"Thank you, Attorney General Pierce, for those kind words." Hollis faltered. Nothing Pierce said was kind, but she collected herself and continued. "My financing team and I will honor all commitments to our partners, as if the wind farm were functioning at peak capacity for the average life of such an installation: twenty-five years.

"The ruined turbines will be removed from the ridge and the area will be re-forested. As compensation, my company will purchase a similar tract of old-growth forest and donate it to the Women's Conservation League of Massachusetts."

Lawson chuckled when Pierce told him, "I'll be god-damned if the university's going to get another forest to give away."

"The Women's Conservation League?" Lawson asked him, picturing an organization full of blue-haired ladies like the Doric Dames.

"Favorite cause of my mother," Pierce told him.

Hollis continued, her lips were so tight, it amazed Lawson that she could speak at all. "The maximum subsidy on electrical power purchase for the Town of Burfield and the state University System.

"A sum paid to the Town of Burfield equal to property taxes paid as if the project were at full capacity.

"Reduced-rate electric power for customers within view of Matchic Ridge.

"Repayment to the state of tax credits taken by our investors.

"And finally, as you can see behind me, a new truck for the Burfield Volunteer Fire Department."

Every Burfield firefighter cheered.

And then, unexpectedly, Hollis got up from the table. She made her way to the new Brushbuster. She struck a pose with her hand on an axe clipped to the side of the truck, and with her other hand, waved to the cameras. Strobes flashed, and cameras clicked.

Lawson felt the last of his sympathy for her dribble away. The woman was shameless. He wouldn't be surprised if she ran for office someday.

Hollis's lawyer stood and took her elbow and whispered to her. Reluctantly, she allowed him to lead her away from the bright lights and cameras, onto the fire station driveway.

The press conference over, Pierce, Doherty and Lawson made their way outside, as well, where they watched Hollis revel in all the attention.

Her lawyer tried to keep her moving toward her car, but reporters held their microphones out, hoping for one more sound bite, and Hollis simply couldn't help herself. "From the very beginning of the Matchic Ridge Wind Farm project, I've been committed to local solutions for global challenges," she said. "Unfortunately, things didn't work out like I'd planned."

The lawyer whispered to her, but she brushed him aside.

"I take full responsibility for removing all damaged equipment from the ridge," she said. "The wind farm site is safely fenced-off, and the ruined equipment is no threat to public health and safety. Therefore, a strategic decision has been made to wait until spring to disassemble it when the access roads are more passable. At that point, the re-forestation of the ridge will begin...."

A dull thumping in the distance gradually became a roar. A massive Sikorsky cargo-helicopter flew low over the town, heading toward the ridge. Suction from the rotors set drift-snow swirling, stinging Hollis as well as her new friends in the media.

Video cameras caught the astonished look on Hollis's face, then swiveled to follow the Sikorsky. While it hovered, a cable played out from the helicopter's belly, and when the copter rose into the sky, it carried the burned out nacelle and turbine blades. Flying across town, it looked like a dragonfly carrying a struggling beetle.

Lawson was stunned. He'd been in on all the planning for the day, and nobody said anything about a helicopter. He looked to Pierce who shook his head. Lawson could tell he was as surprised as he was.

Together, they looked at Doherty, whose face was barely visible in the fur-lined hood of her State Police parka. Making her even harder to read, her eyes were hidden behind a mirrored pair of sunglasses. But Lawson thought he saw a smile.

She shrugged. "Must be some public safety thing. Let's go fishing."

Chapter 34

Leaning forward from the State Police Suburban's back seat, Chavez sent Doherty, at the wheel, down a series of ever-smaller snowy roads until she reached an unmarked lane into the woods. Doherty shifted into four-wheel drive, and the truck bounced down the last quarter-mile to the frozen lake.

Lawson, in the back seat beside Chavez, looked around anxiously, wondering how far out on the ice they would have to walk. Would they build a fire to keep warm? Why hadn't he brought anything other than his topcoat? When was the drinking going to start? Was Doherty a drinker?

Doherty parked at the end of the road, and everyone piled out.

Lawson looked out over the lake. "The ice is thick enough this time of year?" He had heard of ice fishing in January and February, but this was just December.

Pierce paused, considering. "The winter's off to a cold start, and it's a shallow lake. Besides, if we need rescuing, we have trained professionals with us."

Jokkinen and Chavez nodded solemnly, and then burst into laughter. Lawson could tell there wasn't any turning back.

He eased his way to the back of the Suburban to help Doherty unload their gear. She gave him a smile, and he smiled back.

"Let's roll, Action," called Pierce, "no time for canoodling."

Lawson flinched. Pierce had snuck up behind them. He had already changed into a quilted jumpsuit, and now he zipped a State Police parka up over it. He wore a Cossack-style State Police hat on his head.

"Just looking for the tip-ups and ice auger," said Lawson. They were the only ice fishing terms he knew.

Pierce looked at him strangely and then grinned. "Sweet Jesus, Action, we're not in Minnesota anymore."

Lawson corrected: "Iowa."

"Wherever. America's Heartland. Your healthy tall blond Lutheran girls fish with ice augers and tip-ups. Out here, we're more civilized. That topcoat looks great, by the way. Adds some class to this outfit. Doesn't he, Sergeant?"

Doherty huffed a laugh.

Lawson smiled. It *was* funny.

"Lead the way, Chief," said Pierce, and Chavez dragged an ice chest across the lake. Pierce followed right behind him, keeping to the path that Chavez blazed through the snow. "We can thank Mr. Jokkinen for our accommodations today, it's his friend who loaned us this fine edifice."

Jokkinen, bringing up the rear, nodded and smiled.

Warily, Lawson eyed their destination, an ice fishing shack a couple hundred yards offshore. At least we'll be out of the wind, he thought. Sided in weathered cedar and sitting on wooden runners, it was the size of a one-car garage. There were two windows on each side, and a chimney protruded from the roof.

Chavez opened the padlock on the door, and while Pierce loaded the woodstove, Lawson looked around. The room held a half dozen chairs, with a plastic bucket on the ice in front of each. He looked down into one of the buckets. The bottom of the bucket was cut out, and Lawson could see a thin film of ice, clear as glass.

Pierce called to him. "Hey, Sven, your ice auger is over there in the corner. Start drilling, but be careful. Don't lose the auger. It's a cold swim."

Outside, Chavez started a generator. Lights came on inside: hand-painted fish-themed wall lamps.

Pierce stood up, the fire lit in the stove behind him, and rubbed his hands together for warmth. A pleasant campfire smell filled the shack. Pierce began handing out what looked to Lawson like miniature fishing poles. They even had tiny reels.

Pierce moved from pole to pole, baiting hooks with minnows. Lawson maneuvered so he was sitting next to Doherty. This wasn't going to be so bad, he thought.

With the woodstove warming things up, the group settled in front of their buckets.

"All right, Sergeant," said Pierce, "you had your orders. How'd you do?"

Doherty opened a big backpack. "The Boss assigned me to bring each of you your favorite treat. I did some research. So here goes."

Doherty pulled out a large bag of Cheetos and three economy-sized cans of different flavored Pringles. Then she retrieved an aerosol can of Cheese Whiz. She smiled as she handed them to Chavez.

"How'd you know?"

"Jason."

Next she handed a package of mini-wieners to Pierce. Then she passed over a single metal skewer and a jar of Grey Poupon mustard. "His favorite," she said, "but don't tell anyone about the mustard. He likes his reputation as a man of the people." Pierce winked and gave her a thumbs-up.

Next, she handed a Tupperware container and a plastic fork to Terry Jokkinen. He peeked inside: it was quiche.

"Your friends Ethan and Chavez," she explained.

"In cahoots with Bertie." Jokkinen grinned.

"And now for you, Mr. Lawson." She pulled out a giant bag of Reese's Pieces. Lawson was flabbergasted. "How did you know?"

"I'm a trained interrogator, Lawson. Those Doric Dames sing like canaries under pressure."

Lawson was curious. "What did you bring for yourself?"

She smiled and tore open Lawson's Reese's Pieces, grabbed a handful and popped them into her mouth. As she chewed, she spoke to Lawson and handed him the bag. "I thought we'd share." She smiled again, embarrassed. Then she looked over to Pierce. "It was a big bag." Pierce raised his eyebrows comically, and shook his head.

Around the shack, everyone else dug in. Pierce opened the door to the stove and shoved in a couple of more logs. The fire crackled cheerfully.

Pierce dragged the ice chest nearer. "Who wants a drink?"

Here it comes, thought Lawson.

Pierce opened the chest. He tossed a Mountain Dew to Chavez. His mouth full, Chavez mumbled his thanks.

Next he pulled out four brown bottles. Beers, Lawson thought. Here's when the drinking begins. Then he looked closer. They were Berkshire Brown root beers, the same kind they had in Pittsfield. Pierce handed them around.

Pierce looked at Lawson and smiled a warm conspiratorial grin. "Sergeant Doherty said you enjoyed a good root beer."

Lawson risked a glance at Doherty. She didn't look in his direction, but he could have sworn she scooted her chair a few inches nearer.

Pierce cleared his throat for attention. "Everybody got your drinks? All right, a toast."

All five of them raised their bottles.

"To Regular Burfield Volunteer Firefighter Chavez Simons. Congratulations on your certification, and thanks for reminding everyone not to look the other way."

Jokkinen raised his root beer toward Chavez. "Good job, son."

Chavez beamed and then looked down, embarrassed.

"And happy birthday," said Pierce, and he led them in a ragged, off-key rendition of *Happy Birthday to You.*

"And to second chances" — Pierce raised his bottle toward Lawson — "and the guts to grab 'em."

Lawson's eyes stung. He hoped they thought it was the fire. Briefly, he felt Doherty's hand on his shoulder.

"To Maureen Doherty, a true friend, and one of the smartest, funniest, and most dependable people I've ever known. And to Chief Terry Jokkinen, who waited a long time for vindication, and never, ever gave up."

Jokkinen smiled and lifted his own bottle. "To Ethan Pierce, for being …a good man."

These are some really good people, thought Lawson. This was a new feeling, something he hadn't felt in a long time. He liked Ethan Pierce a lot, he admired Jokkinen, Chavez was a good kid. And he had a serious crush on Maureen Doherty.

Suddenly, Doherty grabbed her tiny pole and jerked it. The pole bent double and she reeled the line in quickly while Pierce coached, "Careful, Sergeant, it's not tug of war, use some finesse."

"Shut up, General."

But Pierce wouldn't be denied. All through Doherty's fight with the fish, he kept up his advice: "Loosen up your drag … careful now … that line's only four-pound test … take it easy…."

After five minutes of playing the fish, Doherty succeeded in winding in enough line to yank the fish up through the ice, through the plastic bucket, and onto the floor of the shack. It flopped between her State Police boots.

"Good first effort, Sergeant," said Pierce. "A fine specimen of *Salvelinus namaycush,* known commonly as a lake trout. The state record for that fish is 24 lbs. Yours, I'm estimating, is approximately three pounds. Quite a bit shy of the record, but it will nonetheless be fine at dinner this evening. I'll be pleased to share my private recipe with you: butter, almonds, and …"

Doherty picked the trout up and gently pulled the hook from its mouth. She dropped the fish through the bucket, through the hole in the ice, and back into the lake.

There was a silence in the shack. There was an unspoken agreement that Pierce would be the next one to speak.

"Sergeant, let me ask you a question." Pierce paused for effect. "You *do* know why we're here, don't you?"

Doherty was quick with her comeback. "It's the journey, not the destination. You fish your way, and I'll fish mine." And then she added, "When you catch your first *Salvelinus namaycush*, you can decide what to do with it. Mine has just re-joined his pals."

With that she reached in the minnow bucket, pulled out a wriggling minnow, baited her hook, and let it down through the ice.

Pierce could only shake his head. It was the first time Lawson ever saw him speechless.

"So, what's going to happen?" asked Chavez.

"If recent history is any guide," said Pierce, "now Sergeant Doherty continues to show all of us up by catching more lake trout."

"You know what I mean."

Pierce nodded. "Yes, Chief, I know what you mean. You have strong feelings about this."

Chavez looked down, embarrassed.

Pierce noticed his reaction. "It's nothing to be ashamed of, we all needed a dose of your moral compass." He shifted in his chair and took a sip of root beer. "Okay, back to your question. Maybe things are more complicated than they should be, but this is the criminal justice system, this is politics and this is Massachusetts. But yes, they're finally going to pay. Kerrigan, Fleming, and Cronin have been indicted on a nice little buffet of charges, including conspiracy to commit fraud, tax evasion, arson and assault." He glanced at Jokkinen as he emphasized the word "assault."

"And so they're in jail?"

"Out on bail," said Pierce, "but that doesn't mean things aren't happening. As the pit gets smaller, the rats get more vicious."

"Since they were arrested, they've turned on each other. Every day, we get more information from one of them. That little speech I gave about a 'criminal enterprise' wasn't just hot air. We can go back to the Fitchburg and Taunton fires and level charges. It's up to a jury, but my bet is all three will serve time. So, yes, Chavez, somebody is finally doing something."

Chavez nodded, but didn't say anything.

Pierce raised his root beer in Jokkinen's direction. "Same scam, same characters. It took thirty-five years, but justice may be served."

Jokkinen raised his bottle to Pierce and joined him in his toast. "Finally." And with a chuckle he said, "Same tune, different song."

"Let me ask you something," said Lawson to Pierce. "I've been wondering. How did you tie Cronin in?"

Pierce took a big gulp of his root beer and belched softly. "It all started the day Sergeant Doherty wanted to stop and visit Mary in her office. Maureen wanted to ask Mary where she got her stockings."

"Oh please." Doherty picked up a chunk of ice from next to her hole and threw it at Pierce. Laughing, he ducked, but the ice still clipped his Cossack hat.

Lawson admired Doherty's aim. *Is there anything this woman can't do?* Then he caught himself. *God, Lawson, you're pathetic.* He smiled and shook his head. He had it bad.

"Any-way," Pierce strung the word out to bring attention back to his story, "I was struck by a couple of things that morning. First, there's a rogue's gallery of politicos on Mary's wall and half of them should be in jail. Second, Mary lives high on the hog; all those trips to exotic locations, the beach house. None this was really a surprise, I mean she's got a year-round tan, right? It's just that nobody ever took her on.

"The key was, Ms. Cronin dutifully signed the new ethics form I set up when I was elected. That gave us an edge. I had some folks check her filings and they figured there was no way she was paying for all that on her salary. So, on the day of the fire, Agent Martinez and I were headed to Washington. We were going to try to convince his higher-ups to go into federal court down there for a search warrant to find Mary's secret bank account."

Another sip of his root beer. "The problem is, you can't just get a federal judge to give you a warrant just because somebody's obviously on the take, they see that all the time." He stopped and smiled at his own smart line. "That's where Chavez's video came in."

Chavez's eyes got bright and he smiled.

"That federal judge was really impressed. It was all laid out, plain as day. That sealed the deal for us. We went back and found Mary's beach house – in Palm Beach, of course – and dug up the bank account she used to pay for it – in the Cayman Islands, of course. Agent Martinez and his people kept watch on that account. I don't mind telling you they were pretty nervous when Kerrigan waited until the last minute to ship her the money."

"Gotta water the horses." Pierce stood up and went outside.

When he came back in, Jokkinen was waiting. "What happens to Hollis?"

"You've got a little grudge against our 'unindicted co-conspirator'?" said Pierce.

"I wouldn't say *little*," said Jokkinen.

Pierce smiled. "Being clueless isn't a crime," he said. "But she's going to pay. The wind farm was built to fail, it was built with funny money, it never would have paid any of their stakeholders a dime — and I'll bet Jimmy Kerrigan planned to leave the scam as his legacy to Hollis. But now Hollis is going to have to come up with ten times what her father stole. In this state, sometimes having to pay up is worse than going to the pen. There's a certain honor among jailbirds in Massachusetts politics."

"What about my dad?" whispered Chavez.

Pierce spoke softly, the fun gone from his voice. "His signature is on quite a few faked documents, Chief," he said. "Nothing quite illegal, but unethical enough that he's probably not going to work as a lawyer anymore."

Chavez looked up, surprised and hurt.

Pierce continued in a brighter tone. "It's not the end of the world. He's got a second chance. It's up to him to take advantage of it." Pierce looked over and caught Lawson's eye before he continued, "I'm sure there's other work around here for a bright guy like him. Maybe he can be the police chief. From what I saw at the fire review meeting, this town could use an upgrade."

Chavez dropped his head and Jokkinen put a hand on his shoulder.

Suddenly the tip of Doherty's tiny rod dipped, and everyone gathered around her bucket as she began to haul in her second lake trout of the day.

As they approached the Suburban, Doherty called to Chavez, "Drive this thing to the top of the hill." She tossed him the keys. "You need to get in practice for that new fire truck. Be careful of the Boss, he's delicate." Pierce got in the front with Chavez, shaking his head and grumbling something inaudible.

Doherty opened the rear door, got in, and pulled Lawson in behind her. Jokkinen got in the other side. As they bumped slowly up the rough road, she said, "It sure is cold in here." She slid closer to Lawson.

Lawson felt movement. Doherty had slid her hand into the pocket of his topcoat. From there, her hand wormed through the slit in the topcoat pocket. He sat dead still. Then he felt it snake into his pants pocket. His breath caught, but the hand stopped on his thigh. He began to relax a little. It felt good there. Plus, it was warm.

Pierce said, "Colder than a penguin's pecker in here, campers. Better huddle together for warmth."

Busted, Lawson thought. *The guy is amazing.*

There was a young trooper waiting in the Attorney General's Lincoln. He jerked awake as the Suburban braked beside him.

Now Doherty was all business, supervising the unloading of the Suburban and distributing the fishing gear, warm clothes, backpacks and coolers.

Chavez stood with Pierce, Lawson, and Jokkinen, sheltered a bit from the wind by the wall of the fire station.

Pierce said, "Sorry to miss your big night tonight, Chief."

"At least you got to see my new jacket," said Chavez. "The Chief will be there, and Jason, and my mom." Chavez thought a second and added almost in surprise: "And my dad, too."

"Chief Jokkinen, do you mind if we leave the Suburban at the station?" asked Doherty. "Someone will be back to pick it up tomorrow."

"What's going on, Sergeant?" asked Pierce.

"Change of plans, General," said Doherty, with unusual formality. "Trooper DeSantis will drive you in the Lincoln back to South Dartmouth. I'm going to ride with Mr. Lawson in his personal vehicle."

Let it go, Ethan, thought Lawson, hoping this would be enough.

The wind whipped around the station. Lawson glanced up at Matchic Ridge. It looked odd in the fading milky winter light, now missing all its towers.

But Pierce started in. "And pray-tell, Sergeant, why does Mr. Lawson need company?"

Lawson saw a faint smile on Doherty's face. "It's been a cold day, and Lawson drives an old Honda with a bad battery. He doesn't know how to use jumper cables. Someone should help him."

"I," Lawson started to defend himself, but a look from Doherty silenced him.

Pierce played along. "Red to positive, black to negative, Sergeant."

Doherty pulled her parka hood up over her ears. "General, I also thought I'd catch a ride with Lawson because he lives nearer to my home. I have the day off tomorrow." She paused. "And, if you must know, I have an appointment tomorrow morning at the beauty shop. For a *facial*." She said the word slow and deliberate.

Pierce looked straight into Doherty's eyes. There was a moment's silence. He smiled and said, "Nicely played, Sergeant."

The freezing cold seats of the small Honda were a shock after the big warm Suburban, and Lawson's battery really was weak; it was the nature of a 15-year old car.

After several tries, the engine caught.

The mercury vapor lights out front of the station threw harsh light into the dark car. Their breath frosted the windshield. With her huge State Police mitten, Doherty reached down and managed to click on the defroster.

She looked into the backseat, filled with clothing and old copies of the *New York Times*. "Christ, Action, do you live in this car?"

"Uh, Maureen..." The name sounded strange. He didn't think he'd ever called her by her name before. "I wonder if you could call me Richard, or even Lawson. That name 'Action' is a joke of Ethan's, and it was long time ago."

Doherty interrupted, "I grew up in Boston, *Richard,* and my mom used to have the news on while she made dinner. Back in the day, she had a serious crush on Dick Law - Action News. So did I." She paused, then added, "I like the Richard Lawson version better."

She took her giant mitten off, reached over, and slipped her hand in his coat pocket and through the slit.

"I'll call you Richard," she said. "But can I have an 'Action' every now and then, just for special occasions?"

That made Lawson smile.

End

Sparks, David
Built to fail

Made in the USA
Columbia, SC
09 May 2018